THE DEVIL
BE DAMNED

Visit us at www.boldstrokesbooks.com

Praise for Ali Vali's Fiction

Carly's Sound

"Vali paints vivid pictures with her words...*Carly's Sound* is a great romance, with some wonderfully hot sex."—*Midwest Book Review*

"It's no surprise that passion is indeed possible a second time around"—*Q Syndicate*

The Devil Inside

"Vali's fluid writing style quickly puts the reader at ease, which makes the story and its characters equally easy to get to know and care about. When you find yourself talking out loud to the characters in a book, you know the work is polished and professional, as well as entertaining."—*Family and Friends*

"Not only is The Devil Inside a ripping mystery, it's also an intimate character study."—*L-Word Literature*

"*The Devil Inside* is the first of what promises to be a very exciting series...While telling an exciting story that grips the reader, Vali has also fully fleshed out her heroes and villains. *The Devil Inside* is that rarity: a fascinating crime novel which includes a tender love story and leaves the reader with a cliffhanger ending."—*MegaScene*

The Devil Unleashed

"Fast-paced action scenes, intriguing character revelations, and a refreshing approach to the romance thriller genre all make for an enjoyable reading experience in the Big Easy...*The Devil Unleashed* is an engrossing reading experience." —*Midwest Book Review*

Deal With the Devil

"Ali Vali has given her fans another thick, rich thriller...*Deal With the Devil* has wonderful love stories, great sex, and an ample supply of humor. It is an exciting, page turning read that leaves her readers eagerly awaiting the next book in the series."—*JustAboutWrite*

Calling Out the Dead

"So many writers set stories in New Orleans, but Ali Vali's mystery novels have the authenticity that only a real Big Easy resident could bring... makes for a classic lesbian murder yarn."—*Curve*

By the Author

Carly's Sound

Second Season

Calling the Dead

Blue Skies

<u>The Cain Casey Saga</u>

The Devil Inside

The Devil Unleashed

Deal with the Devil

The Devil Be Damned

THE **DEVIL** BE **DAMNED**

by

Ali Vali

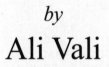

2010

THE DEVIL BE DAMNED

ISBN 10: 1-60282-159-3
ISBN 13: 978-1-60282-159-0

This Trade Paperback Original Is Published By
Bold Strokes Books, Inc.
P.O. Box 249
Valley Falls, NY 12185

First Edition: August 2010

CREDITS
EDITORS: SHELLEY THRASHER AND STACIA SEAMAN
PRODUCTION DESIGN: STACIA SEAMAN
COVER DESIGN BY SHERI (GRAPHICARTIST2020@HOTMAIL.COM)

Acknowledgments

Writing is a solitary exercise that you share only with the characters who tell you their story, but once that's done it takes a team to complete the journey. Bold Strokes Books is my team, and I'm grateful to Radclyffe for her leadership, encouragement, and enthusiasm that have given me the freedom to grow as a storyteller.

Thanks to my editor Shelley Thrasher, a true Southern lady who wields a red pen with authority. Every book is always an adventure, and always a learning experience. Thanks to Sheri for another great cover. Your vision is always spot on. To Connie, Kathi, and Nicole, thanks for taking the journey with me and letting me know when I took any wrong turns. Thanks also to Stacia Seaman for a great job in putting the final book together and for always teaching me something new. Your input is invaluable.

To the readers, thank you for your encouragement and really kind words about these characters. Your kindness is what keeps me at the keyboard.

This last year was tough with the loss of my mom. She was one of a kind, and she taught me what true courage is until she left us. I know she's no longer in pain, but I miss her. Thanks, Mami, for loving me, and for the sacrifices you and Papi made to give us a better life.

Thanks to my partner. You're my best friend, therapist, personal shopper, and safe haven. You've given me over twenty-five wonderful years that make me look forward to every tomorrow. Sharing my life with you is my own happily ever after, and up to now our life together is the foundation from which I draw to write romance. You are a gift and I love you.

Dedication

For C
A lifetime is not enough
&
For Mami
You are missed but not forgotten

CHAPTER ONE

The recent haircut was stylish and made the beautiful face it framed appear as it had the day Cain first saw it. The pink dress was loose but still showed the slight belly that held the future. Obviously the new look was intended to erase the image of what Cain saw as her own mistakes and worst failures.

Emma Casey was perfect. Not because of her appearance, but simply because her partner of fourteen years, Derby Cain Casey, knew she was.

Cain felt in control of the life she'd built because she was. But here before her was the exception to every rule and the person she thought about as she ran her business. Emma was as strong as she was beautiful, and she loved fiercely and devotedly. She'd given Cain happiness, children, loyalty, and love by choice, not out of fear.

"Is it the fish or the company that's got you so down tonight?" Cain asked after watching Emma play with her food. "You push that around any more and someone from the kitchen will probably come take the plate away from you."

"I'm sure it's great, and I love you, but you know what pregnancy does to me. I suppose I ordered fish because I feel like a school of them is swimming around in my stomach." Emma finally moved the dish away and concentrated on her water instead. "I'm not very good company tonight, am I?"

"You don't have to make small talk with me, lass," Cain tapped the side of Emma's head gently, "but if something's swimming around in here as well I'd like to know what it is." When Juan took Emma a little of her spirit had died, and some of Cain's along with it. Failing her wife so completely when she'd needed her most had made Cain lose more than a night's sleep, and no new haircut would erase the image of Emma strapped down like an animal ready for torture.

Emma nodded to the waiter when he came over and removed the dishes, then placed her hand over Cain's. "It isn't what you think."

"What do I think?" Cain asked, and took a sip of her wine.

"That you failed me."

The statement was simple and direct. They had danced around the subject from the day Emma had been released from the hospital, so it was almost a relief to hear Emma finally say it. "We both know I did, and every day I don't find that bastard is one more day I continue to fall short."

"Oh, my love," Emma said, and her eyes filled with tears. "I don't believe that. I only said it because I know that's what's been driving you. We're here, we're whole, and we have so much to look forward to. Despite that, I'm sad that you're focusing so much energy on finding those two that you're missing out on this special time for us."

"I know you want me to forget, but I can't. That's not how I'm wired."

"I know exactly how you're wired, mobster, but right now I need my wife back." Emma smiled. "In case you missed it, I'm going to have your baby, but before that happens I need you to hold my head when I'm puking and rub my feet when I gain the twelve hundred pounds that are coming. Not to mention the two kids we have already."

"Is that your way of telling me I'm losing sight of the big picture?" Cain said, her attention diverted briefly to her main bodyguard, Lou, who was paying the bill.

"You could never ignore me and the kids completely, but even when we're alone, I know you're thinking about that day. When the time comes you'll be ready, so let it go just a little. Trust me, I worry enough for both of us."

"That's not what I want to hear," Cain said as she helped Emma up. Their night out had been the first in a very long month, and Cain had only agreed because they'd reserved a private room at Vincent's restaurant. "I'll try my best, but the hardest person to forgive is myself."

"Juan the idiot has stolen enough from us, so I refuse to give him my fear." Emma kissed the top of Cain's hand. "And I refuse to let him make you doubt yourself, my love. I trust you with my life and, more importantly, the lives of our family. Do you think my love for you blinds me? You can take care of anything he throws at us."

"You might be a little biased, Mrs. Casey, but sometimes that's not a bad thing." Cain waved the waiter away when he approached with the dessert tray. "If Vincent's trout in lemon-butter sauce wasn't the right choice tonight, how about a cup of hot chocolate and a beignet?"

"Only if we can have it at Café Du Monde," Emma said, and shook her head when Cain began to refuse. "Honey, I'm tired of being inside. Besides, you have to relax a little."

Emma put her hand through Cain's elbow as they started out of the restaurant. "Our little adventure robbed Hayden of his birthday party, and I want to make it up to him."

"I'm as relaxed as I'll get for a while. In case you forgot," Cain scanned the area as intently as their guards when they reached the door, "your being pregnant always makes me crazier than it does you."

"But we've got a few months to go." Emma kissed Cain when she got into the car. "I shouldn't tell you this, but I'm looking forward to your hovering. When I was carrying Hannah, I was miserable for a lot of reasons, but I missed being the center of your protective attention the most."

"Remember what you said when I insist on carrying *you* everywhere." Cain laughed softly close to Emma's ear and rested her hand on Emma's middle. Their child as well as their future rested on her shoulders. If something happened to Emma or their family she wouldn't be able to conjure up any more forgiveness for herself. "I love you, lass, and I'm looking forward to adding this little one to our brood."

"That's why I want you to not worry so much." Emma put her hand over Cain's. "We deserve to be happy."

"I've got a couple of things on my to-do list first."

"You're not a slacker, so I'm not concerned."

❖

"The last time you asked for this you did an about-face, so what's different?" asked Annabel Hicks, lead agent of the New Orleans FBI office. She slowly flipped the pages of Shelby Phillips's open file as she spoke.

"I'm in a unique position now, ma'am." Shelby had asked for this meeting but knew better than to set the pace. For the last year and a half she'd forgone a personal life after she'd been assigned to the New Orleans bureau in their organized crime division. But her dedication was about to pay off.

Her first small undercover job as an attendant on Vincent

Carlotti's plane had thrilled her at first, but on a cold night sitting in a field somewhere outside Wisconsin, she'd met the most fascinating but terrifying person she knew.

Cain Casey had held her life in the palm of her hand along with the bugs Shelby had planted that night, and she'd allowed her to walk away. Cain had promised that what had happened would stay between them, but she was also the head of one of the crime families in New Orleans. Along with Vincent and Ramon Jatibon, she ruled the other side of the law Shelby was sworn to uphold.

Just as Cain had surprised her that night by showing mercy, she continued to surprise her every day now that Shelby led the surveillance team that battled Cain. She was as elusive as she was seductive.

"By 'unique position' do you mean Muriel Casey?" Annabel asked. "If that's it, get back to work. We both know Cain is a criminal, but she's not stupid. You going steady with her cousin won't suddenly make you part of the family."

"This isn't high school, ma'am, and Muriel is only part of it. My opening came a month ago and I took it. From what little Muriel has said on the subject, Emma Casey is fine now, but Cain won't forget what happened or the fact that I was there to help. It's now or never if we want to get inside the organization."

"You do this and your team won't be able to get to you if something goes wrong, partly because we'll be the only two in the office who know about it."

"I'm not worried. Cain knows me, but that day in that house with Emma tied to the kitchen table for Juan Luis's sick pleasure, I was on her side, and she knows it. That's the moment I'm planning to capitalize on to build our new relationship."

Annabel fell back in her chair and knocked the tips of her fingers together. "Tell me why you pulled the plug on your first undercover operation and I'll consider it."

The file open in front of her boss held her attention. Had Cain somehow passed along the details of that night, knowing a day like this would be in her future? If so, the lie would cost her. But this was more of her own personal test since she would never even consider this new assignment if she didn't thoroughly believe she knew the woman who was in her sights every day.

"I was afraid I'd been made. Once that happens you can't fight the fear, and nerves will get you killed."

"Are you sure that's all?" Annabel glanced at the open page.

The memory of the night Cain had provided information on Barney Kyle that proved he was dirty came to mind, and Shelby thought of something her father always told her when she asked why he picked law enforcement. *"The devil is tempting not because he's hideous, but because he's beautiful. It's when you're in his grasp and you've gladly sold your soul that he finally shows his true face. Only then it's too late."*

Cain was easy on the eye, but it was time to show the world her true face. "No, ma'am, that's all it was." The decision to lie was easy. Cain wouldn't ruin the chance to play with Shelby.

"Give me a few days and I'll get back to you." Annabel closed the file and smiled.

Now Shelby was certain she'd known nothing. Cain had kept her word. "Thank you, ma'am, you won't be sorry."

"More importantly, make sure you're not sorry you took this chance."

❖

Anthony Curtis could hear the mosquitoes swarming around them as they lay in the tall grass near the Rio Grande in south Texas. Next to him Juan Luis slept, his head propped on the red jacket he'd bought at a gas station the day before, *NASCAR* embroidered across the back in black letters.

Anthony's skin itched too much to sleep, and even if he could ignore that, the air was so heavy with heat it felt like a weight holding him down. As the horde of insects buzzed around Anthony, bile rose in his throat. This shit of a place was as far from Quantico, Virginia, as you could get, and he'd never return to the life he'd built a brick at a time.

He'd fallen from exemplary FBI agent to pariah and target in less time than it would have taken to point his gun at his head and pull the trigger. His former bosses would punish him for all his wrong choices, but that wasn't what fueled his nightmares. He'd tattooed a target on his forehead the moment he taunted Cain Casey into a fight he thought he could win.

He and Juan had left before Cain arrived to find Emma in the same position her sister Marie had died in, but he knew what her reaction would be. His partnership with Juan had started as a farce, but they wholeheartedly agreed that the path to bringing Cain down started and ended with her family, especially Emma.

Their story was well documented in Cain's FBI file, and Anthony knew the power of Emma's reach into Cain's heart. Even though Emma had once betrayed Cain, she was the mother of Cain's children and remained the solid foundation of Cain's life.

"You dumb motherfucker," he whispered to himself.

In his need to show up Annabel and bring Cain down, he'd screwed with the one person who mattered more than anyone to Cain. And not only had he tied Emma on Marie Casey's alleged deathbed, he'd done it on the order of Juan Luis, who'd propositioned Emma more than once.

Cain would kill both of them when she found them, in one of her unusually inventive ways. That's why he was lying in a ditch with Juan now, waiting for Juan's mother to sneak them over the border *into* Mexico.

Juan's uncle Rodolfo would've turned them over to Cain himself, or at least that was the word on the street. There was family loyalty, and then there was getting Cain off your ass for a nephew who'd defied you. Obviously Rodolfo's choice had been easy.

"Nothing yet?" Juan asked without bothering to lift his head.

"Border Patrol went by an hour ago, but I doubt they're looking for anyone running in the opposite direction."

"Don't worry. My mother's *coyote* is the best in the business," Juan said, stretching so hard the bones in his neck cracked loudly. "That's who she had to turn to after my uncle the *pendejo* threw her out."

"What's the story with that?" Anthony asked, if only to forget about the heat. He should've been considering the credentials he still carried and how he could use them to help him, but those were as worthless as his life right now. He had to worry not only about Cain but about Annabel and his old coworkers too. "I thought Rodolfo was like a father to you."

"Rodolfo kill my father before I was born, so he can fuck himself if he thinks of me as his son. The sick *hijo de puta* probably wanted my mother in his bed."

"He told you that?" he asked, surprised Juan was so forthcoming.

"Tío Rodolfo don't have the balls for that. My mother told me what I need to know."

In the distance Anthony heard a vehicle of some kind approaching, but didn't move. It was probably the Border Patrol swinging back around. The engine sounded different, though, and then it stopped, making the insect noises loud again.

"Apurate," someone said to a group of people holding crude luggage over their heads to keep it out of the chest-deep water. Someone harshly whispered "hurry up" numerous times until the fourteen illegals made it to American soil.

"Juan," the man said next.

"Let's go." Juan headed for the water. "It's time to rejoin the land of the living."

For a few more days, anyway, Anthony thought. He lost his shoes halfway across, which made him think about his parents since they'd given him the loafers for his last birthday. Would they even know what happened to him? If Cain found him before Annabel, no. One of his last duties at work was to find Big Gino Bracato and his sons, but wherever Cain had buried them, the graves still held their secrets.

❖

"The script for the next Lady Killer movie is in the final stages, but before we sign, Dallas wants to be considered for the new project the studio is planning on the Ruger book," Angus Christian said to Remi Jatibon. Both Remi and Dallas had chosen the new agent, but they hadn't shared that fact with him because Remi wanted Dallas to completely control every aspect of her career.

Angus was able to negotiate on Dallas's behalf but Dwayne and Steve, Remi's partners, monitored the contracts before anything was signed. With the new system, Dallas's bank account had quickly become a lot healthier.

"I think the director has a few people in mind for that project, but give him a call. The planning meetings I'm involved with are more management driven than anything to do with talent these days," Remi said as she twirled her wineglass by the stem. The restaurant Angus had picked was full, and even with the low lights they could see people discreetly looking at them.

"The role might finally get her to the top of the marquee," Angus said, almost spilling the wine in the glass he held. "She's paid her dues long enough."

"You're preaching to the choir, Angus." Dallas's hand landed on Remi's thigh. "If you're trying to bribe me to just give her the job, Dallas won't stand for that."

"Don't worry. She already gave me the lecture. What she wants is a chance."

"Have you finished talking about me like I'm in the restroom?" Dallas asked.

"I think I have everything I need," Angus said as he and Remi shook hands. "I'll make those calls and get back to you," he told Dallas.

"Thanks," Dallas said. The man was always on edge, but when he dealt with Remi directly his fidgety habits shifted into overdrive. He was still shaking Remi's hand as if he'd forgotten to let go.

"You should smile more, baby," she said to Remi once Angus was far enough away. "I think you make him a little nervous."

"A little? Then I need to bring it up a notch because he needs to stay that way." The waiter cleared away Angus's empty glass and refilled theirs with the wine Remi had ordered. "It's good for him to be afraid of me. I want to keep him from taking advantage of you."

"My protector, huh?" Dallas kissed the side of Remi's neck.

It was hard to let go of the fear that had plagued Dallas's life for years, but Remi had been the model of patience as Dallas dealt with things at her pace. She still hadn't shared a lot of things with Remi yet, not because she thought Remi would judge those choices, but because they belonged more to Katie Lynn Moores than to who she was now.

"For as long as you want."

"Then you'd better cut down on the cigar smoking, because you're in for a long haul."

The waiter approached slowly with pad in hand and hesitated until Remi nodded. Small things like that still surprised Dallas about her lover. For some who knew Remi or knew of her, she was someone to fear, or at least give a wide berth, but the concept was foreign to Dallas.

Remi had set her free. The only worry she had left was losing Remi to the life she chose or to someone else. Remi's loyalty made Dallas believe someone's bullet rather than someone else's heart would be the culprit.

"Did you decide what to do with Kristen yet?" Remi asked after she placed their order.

"I thought for now she can stay with me." She took a sip of wine.

After Remi had dealt with Dallas's old manager Bob Bennett in her unique way, she'd felt comfortable bringing her sister Kristen to live in New Orleans. With Remi and Cain's help, Kristen's identity was as solid as hers and she was now enrolled in Tulane for the summer session. She was due to arrive that weekend.

Dallas wasn't comfortable enough to say yes to Remi's invitation to live together. They spent every night with each other, but having her own place in the French Quarter, she thought, wouldn't make Remi feel hemmed in by a relationship she wasn't ready for, considering Dallas's baggage.

"That way you two will have a chance to get to know each other without us getting in your way." When Remi sighed she rushed on. "I'm not putting you off, baby," she said, and squeezed Remi's fingers. "It hasn't been that long and I want us both to be sure about everything."

"Don't you mean *you* need to be sure?" Remi asked gently. "I know what I want, Dallas, and being apart isn't it. So tell me what I have to do to convince you and I'll do it."

"Remington Jatibon, don't you dare make it sound like you've got to prove yourself to me," she said as her heart sped up. "You need to know everything about me before you commit to anything else. After that you might want to move on, and you should be free to do so without thinking you've got two people to take care of. Believe me, you've done more than anyone else in my life and haven't asked anything in return."

"*Querida*, you're crazy if you think your sins compare to mine," Remi said directly into her ear. No matter how dark the restaurant or how private the space, Dallas had learned someone was always listening in. Like shrimpers with their trawl nets out, they were seeing what they could harvest from every conversation no matter how intimate or mundane. "I hope you choose to trust me with who you are."

"You don't think I do?"

"I didn't say that to hurt you, so don't look at me that way." Remi rubbed her thumb along the skin between her eyebrows as if smoothing down a worry line. "I want you to understand you can move at whatever pace you like and I'll be here waiting no matter how long.

"You can keep whatever secrets you choose not to share because it would be painful to relive them, but I hope you don't. I don't need to hear them because of any trust issues, but because I'll be able to carry some of your load.

"I know that I love you, and time will only strengthen that, not make me lose interest." Remi kissed her lips as she slipped her fingers behind her neck. "The timing is up to you, and I'm sure Kristen will appreciate having you all to herself for a while. Just remember that Emil's still part of the package. I don't want you unprotected."

"I wouldn't dream of trying to argue with you." Dallas initiated their next kiss. She hadn't tried to hide who she was seeing, but so far the tabloids hadn't focused on them. She was sure there were plenty of pictures, but Remi's reputation had a long reach. Enough that the tabloids had left them relatively alone. "I can't wait for you to meet Kristen."

"Just a few more days," Remi said, then moved out of the way as the waiter brought out a dozen raw oysters on the half shell.

"After being away from her for so long, it'll be like a dream, having her in the same house." She accepted the oyster Remi held out to her on a small fork. "You, on the other hand, will be lucky to make it through these before I drag you home to live out a few more of my dreams."

"Check," Remi told the waiter as he brought out the next dish, making Dallas laugh as well as blush.

❖

Breaks in the trees gave a few brief glimpses of the night sky, but Johnny Moores didn't need a flashlight as he made his way along the leaf-littered path. With no moonlight, he used the distant fire as his guide, and even though these trips weren't necessary anymore, he liked to oversee the entire process that was his only livelihood.

His granddad had built this still in the early 1900s and it continued to supply a lot of people in Sparta, Tennessee—including the sheriff of White County—with moonshine so strong it could shave the hair from your chest without a razor. It was time to make a fresh batch to replace the stuff aging in his barn, but that wasn't what was on his mind.

Before he joined the guys helping him, he took the cell phone Bob Bennett had sent him from his pocket and checked it again. Deep in the woods he couldn't pick up a signal, but he glanced at it anyway.

The damn thing still didn't have any messages, and when he punched in the only number in the memory, the prepaid cell it called went straight to voicemail, which in turn said the caller's box was full. The little weasel hadn't checked the phone and had forgotten about their agreement. The only income he had left depended on what was dripping out of the end of the copper pipe here in the backwoods of Sparta.

"You don't know who you fucking with, boy," he said, and snapped the phone closed. "Two more days is all you got before I come looking for you and take what you owe me out your hide." The plastic of the phone felt oily as he squeezed it so hard it creaked.

When Johnny stopped to warm his hands at the fire under the large kettle, Timothy Pritchard said, "Johnny, we got the mash going so you're in time for our first tasting." Timothy and his brother Boone were his partners in the business and the only two men in the county he trusted because he totally controlled them.

He accepted the tin cup from Timothy and sipped the potent brew. His lips went almost numb. "You boys got that shit right," he said, and passed them the cup. "Think you two can handle the rest?"

"What's wrong?" Boone asked. "Something has to be if you're letting us do this on our own. You wouldn't even trust your mama with this still."

"My pa said that bitch died the day after she had me to get out of doing all the work," he said. He spit a mouthful of tobacco juice into the fire, making it hiss. "Can you do it or not?"

"We want a bigger cut if you make us do the whole batch," Timothy said quickly. "What's so freaking important anyway that you'd leave for?"

"Nothing for you to worry about, so drop it." Johnny ran his hand through his thinning blond hair and smiled. Would little Katie Lynn recognize him now that his thick locks were a memory and a lot of white was mixed in along his temples? Her hair was the only thing she'd inherited from him, her eyes and face a perfect copy of her mother's.

He cut his eyes near the still to the overgrown patch that held his late wife's remains. He had killed her during a drunken rage not long after Sue Lee was born, and planting her here was his way of repaying her for her bitching behind his back about how he made his living. He smiled wider as he thought of the useless country girl watching him from hell as he started another season of shine.

"Must be good if it's got you smiling like a hog in knee-deep slop," Timothy said, and laughed. He looked freakish because of the deep scar that started at his hairline and stopped at his top lip. The shocking pink, paper-thin-appearing skin had never faded, and the way he constantly tapped it with his fingers showed that it'd never stopped hurting. Or at least that's what Johnny guessed.

"Don't fret about what's none of your business and concentrate on filling those jars. We got orders and people waiting," he screamed at both men before sitting on the old iron chair someone had dragged out there years before.

He jammed his hand back in his coat pocket where the phone still rested quietly, but he stroked the glossy magazine picture he'd cut out. One of the only pictures of Dallas and Remi together with only their names written at the bottom, it said they were attending a movie opening in a city named Metairie.

The edges of the page were dirty because he'd handled it so much, like all the others he'd found of Dallas Montgomery. The resemblance to the skinny, grubby little fool he'd fed for years was mostly gone, but no new name could fool him or take away what was owed him. Dallas was somebody his Katie Lynn had made up, but it was time to remind her where she came from and who she belonged to.

He got excited thinking about their reunion and what they'd do afterward. Would Katie Lynn be worth more to him as Dallas or in the back room of his cabin? Guys like Timothy and Boone would sell their left nut to bed the rising star once he'd gotten tired of taking his turn.

CHAPTER TWO

"Our numbers are a little off," Katlin said after she glanced at the page in front of her. "But around Lent they usually are. People need to start giving up something else besides liquor and cigarettes for a change."

"Mama would have your ass for saying that about all those good Catholics," Cain said. So far no one had good news during their regular weekly meeting. "Keep an eye on that," she told Katlin. "Sometimes yearly religious sacrifice is to blame, and sometimes someone else is trying to muscle in on us."

"No worries. I've got some guys checking it out. Somebody might be able to undercut us, but they can't provide our level of protection."

"Some people don't care about that. They're only loyal to the dollar, and some of those old shop keeps Da started dealing with are selling out in droves." Cain sat back and put her feet on her desk. "When that happens make sure you check the new guys out before you approach them. The Feds are always trying new tricks to get inside our operations, and we don't need to make their job easy by selling directly to the bastards."

"Muriel's got that part covered," Katlin said.

"Cute," Muriel said. "So far we've been lucky. They've passed the businesses to a family member and they've all checked out."

"Go home," Cain said to Katlin. "You've got physical therapy with Merrick in an hour." The wounds Emma's guard had gotten trying to protect her had healed enough for her to leave the hospital, but she had a lot of hard work ahead of her to get back to where she was, if that was even possible.

"Thanks, boss." Katlin stood and handed her report to Muriel for shredding. "And thanks again for rearranging the pool house for us. Merrick's apartment wouldn't have worked."

"She's family, and I can't pay the debt I owe her in this lifetime, so stop thanking me."

Katlin hadn't lost her place in the organization, but Cain had put her on a lighter schedule until Merrick was able to care for herself. If it had been Emma, that's where she'd want to be, and Katlin and Merrick's relationship deserved the same consideration as hers and Emma's.

"Anything else?" Cain asked.

"Sabana Greco called again," Lou said with a laugh. "She and her mother are ready to come home and she still wants to talk to you." Juan's men had killed Sabana's brother Rick, and while they'd all taken it hard, no one shouldered more guilt than Lou. However, that wouldn't make Cain change her mind about hiring Sabana, even though the young woman had seemed determined not to be held to her promise to finish school.

Lou had been training Rick to look after the Casey family or perhaps guard their daughter Hannah when she started school. Unfortunately Lou had sent Rick to run the most mundane of errands, which had led to his death. Cain knew Lou was still blaming himself and doubted that he remembered she had first asked Rick to drive to the airport to pick up her father-in-law Ross's luggage—nothing to get killed over.

"If everything's working as we planned, our next long conversation shouldn't take place for another two years," Cain said. "Is there a problem?"

"It's *your* plan she wants to talk about," Lou said, holding his hands out like he was a messenger who didn't want to be shot. "She seems to have been studying revenge more than the business classes she's in. Sending her and her mother away gave her the time to ratchet up her anger."

"I sent them away for their own good, but have her come back this weekend and I'll give her the meeting she wants. Only warn her that she might not like my side of the conversation."

"She's angry about Rick, and while she might not like what you're gonna say, you're the right person for her to talk to. Not everyone has walked the walk like you have."

Cain nodded as she looked at the picture her father, Dalton, had first put on the desk when he'd opened the office. It was their family photo and Marie was an infant in their mother's arms, while Billy and she were toddlers. She was the only one of her family not taken out on Big Gino Bracato's order, so Lou was right that she understood Sabana's pain.

"You getting soft on me, Lou?"

"This girl—I think she's going to try something no matter what we say, and if she does, I don't want her to be standing alone." Lou got up and put his hands in his pockets. "I owe that to Rick."

"I still plan to put her off because I can't afford someone with a grudge that'll blind her to everything else."

"Who's the softie, then?" Lou asked with a smile before he left for his chair outside her door.

"You have something on your mind?" Cain asked Muriel when just the two of them were left.

"I talked to Remi and Mano yesterday about our situation. Still nothing."

"The reward goes to the patient hunter, cousin. Wherever our little weasels have hidden, it won't be forever. My memory, unfortunately for them, won't fade with time." She knew she sounded calm, though they were discussing Juan and Anthony, but it was because the new Casey family portrait on her desk held her attention. "If you're concerned I'll let this go, don't be."

"That's a given, but I'll still be concerned about you. After all this you haven't been the same, and that's not a criticism. I love working with you because of how you approach life, and now you seem to do things differently." Muriel pressed her hands on her knees and kept her eyes on the floor as she spoke. "If it's like that here, then it must be like that at home."

"And if I had to guess, I'd say you've been going behind my back and talking to Emma," Cain said, and Muriel's head snapped up. "She told me pretty much the same thing last night, but I know what happens when I relax."

"You do that to yourself and you'll be miserable."

"Are you back with Shelby?"

The way Muriel's forehead scrunched showed how much the question confused her. "What does that have to do with anything?"

Muriel's answer let Cain know what she was gut-sure about. "It has to do with everything. I can't relax until what needs to be done gets done. If this was Shelby, would you appreciate me telling you to relax and forget about a threat?"

"You can't compare my relationship with Shelby to yours."

Cain sighed and dropped her feet to the floor. "On that point you're right because I know nothing of your relationship with her. No," she said when Muriel opened her mouth to interrupt her. "I didn't say that as a reprimand or as an opening for you to tell me something you haven't up till now. You obviously don't feel it's any of my business."

A beat of silence went by as Muriel clearly waited for Cain to finish. "I don't know. That sounded suspiciously like a reprimand."

"My view on this subject hasn't changed, and it won't. Your happiness is important to me, and if this woman gives you that, I'll accept it and wish you the best. But," she raised her finger, "you can't have it both ways, Muriel. Play Russian roulette with your life, but not with mine."

"I'm not sure how this conversation became all about me, and I usually don't get upset with you, but if you can have it all, why not me?" Muriel asked a little louder than she usually spoke to Cain.

"Like you said, you can't compare your relationship with mine. Emma screwed up and we made it through, but you do that with Shelby, and I'll see my family for the rest of my life with a glass partition between us." The phone rang and Cain picked it up and put it back down. "I'll never turn my back on you, you know that, but our business relationship will change if this is the course you choose."

"That's a lot of buts, Cain. Remember, though, this is my family too."

"You're right and you're wrong about that," Jarvis Casey said to Muriel from the door. He made his way inside relying on his cane, weak from a recent bad bout with the flu.

"Da." Muriel stood and took his arm and Cain the other so they could help him into Cain's comfortable seat behind the desk. "What are you doing out?"

"An old man gets tired of looking at the same thing all the time, so no fussing. Besides, after hearing what you just said, I'm glad I made the trip."

Cain kissed him on the forehead. "Muriel doesn't need a lecture, Uncle Jarvis."

"No lectures, but a lesson never hurt anybody," he said and laughed, which caused a round of heavy coughing.

Cain went to the bar and poured him a finger of whiskey. "Don't worry about that either. If I can't argue with Muriel, then who can I go a round with?"

"Thanks," he said after he'd drained the glass. "Muriel." He pointed to the closest visitor's chair. "You're a part of this family, but the family is Cain's. It's our way, and for generations the oldest child of the previous clan chief might have led us. But sometimes someone else emerged as the strongest one. That's the case with Cain on both those criteria. Dalton was my brother, and when he died my loyalties didn't die with him. They went to Cain because they're rightfully hers. If you can't abide by her decisions then you better pick your path and pray she keeps her word that she'll never turn her back on you."

"I can't have an opinion?" Muriel sounded as disturbed with her father as she was with Cain.

"Jesus, Mary, and Joseph," he said, and started coughing again. "I haven't said anything up to now, but you're sleeping with an FBI agent. If you weren't my child and I didn't love you the way I do, I'd say you're insane and I'd ask Cain to banish you myself."

"Women do sometimes drive us to insanity, uncle, but Muriel's choice won't drive her from her place here." Cain tapped over her heart as she looked at Muriel. "Unfortunately, your father's right. Your relationship is what it is, and I don't fault you for your feelings. But you'll have to choose. I won't bend on this—ever."

"I gave her up once, but I don't know if I've got it in me to do it again."

"No one's asking you to," Cain said as she sat next to Muriel. "You were the one who asked me for more responsibility when we were in the thick of this, and even though I didn't think it was right for you, I caved."

"But if I stay with Shelby, you'll cut me out again."

"Not completely, since I'm not a total idiot who depends only on bootlegging," Cain said, and knocked the side of her head with her knuckles. "This thing isn't that thick. You have plenty of choices, from working with the clubs to joining Remi and the guys at the studio. I just want you to be happy and I want to make sure I don't give you any information that you might accidentally share with Shelby. That's for your protection as well as mine."

"I haven't decided yet," Muriel said, sounding like she was speaking more for Jarvis's benefit. "Shelby's different from anyone I know, and it's hard to ignore how I feel with her."

"It's an act," Jarvis said. "You sit there and tell me you believe she's not working when she's with you?"

"We try to leave those things at the door."

Jarvis shook his head and started coughing again. "You said you haven't decided, so let's drop it for now," Cain said, pouring Jarvis a small amount of water. "Let me take you home," she told him, "and we'll let Muriel get back to work."

"I can take him," Muriel said.

"I promised Emma lunch, so it's on my way. Actually, Uncle Jarvis, you can join us if you want."

"I'd love to." Jarvis accepted Muriel's help up and kissed her cheek. "I love you," he told her. "And I'm proud of you. Don't forget that and don't forget what I said."

"With both of you reminding me, how could I?" Muriel answered after she kissed his cheek.

"You can choose the devil himself to love, and I'll still pray for one thing—that you have the kind of happiness I had with your mum. Cain has learned what all the Caseys have at some point—to find the one who completes you is a gift you shouldn't squander." He placed his hand against her cheek and smiled. "My hope for you is that you don't let anything stand in your way when you find that other half you're missing. If that's how you handle it, I'll accept whoever that might be. Do you promise to remember that?"

"Always, Da."

He nodded and smiled so widely he appeared strong again, despite his stooped shoulders and shaky hands. He'd shown Cain what it meant to be a good parent, and she committed the lesson to heart since her children might be in the same situation one day.

CHAPTER THREE

"What now?" Anthony coughed as the dust blew through the windows while they traveled west along what seemed to be a goat path.

Juan sat next to him with his head back and his eyes closed again. "The plan has no changed since the last time you ask me, so stop bitching."

"I realize we're going somewhere. I just want to know where since I'm in a foreign country illegally." They hit another pothole and he wanted to ask the driver to stop before he threw up the Coke they'd given him once they made it across the border.

"Relax, we do that shit all the time and nobody get hurt," Juan said, and finally opened his eyes. "We got to make it to the coast and find the boat my mama gots waiting. Hope you don't get the seasickness."

"Boat to where?"

"Cabo San Lucas," the driver said, as if to put him out of his misery.

"*Sí*, Cabo," Juan said. "My mama's house is there and she help us get back to the U.S. after we take care of a few things."

"Want to share what that is, or do you want to take another nap?" To their right the flat terrain was starting to give way to rock clusters that appeared higher than the truck. Every so often a thatch roof held up by only four posts dotted the desolate area, and Anthony was amazed to see children running close by. The scene was as surreal as he felt.

"I no sleeping, *amigo*, I thinking," Juan said, tapping the side of his head. "You should be trying too, because we in some deep *mierda*. But if you too tired, me and my mama, we take care of you."

"Whatever our plan is, we have to wait before we try to go back. After what happened, Casey isn't the only person we need to worry about. The Feds should be high on your list. I'm sure my old boss and team have warrants out for us right now, and I don't want to spend the rest of my life in a federal prison."

"*Chinga*, the Feds are happy catching the crumbs we give," the driver said. "The real action is like shit under their noses they don't smell."

"Thanks for the big elaborate explanation," Anthony said. The heat was finally breaking even though the sun was now high, and the slightest smell of salt was coming through the windows. "Just remember, Juan—those warrants have my name on them too. You're cracked if you think I don't want some say in whatever we do next."

The truck sounded like it would choke out as it climbed the steepest hill so far, and when they made it to the top they all fell silent as the Sea of Cortez came into view. To Anthony, it seemed out of place butted up against the sparse, harsh landscape, but for some reason he felt a peace that had been nonexistent the prior month.

They stopped at an area with some rickety buildings and a tiny pier that looked ridiculously small with a large vessel tied to it. At the end, a stunning woman stood in a sleeveless white shirt and pants that contrasted well with her dark skin and jet hair. Juan jumped from the vehicle and ran down the long, narrow pier until he was able to wrap his arms around her.

"Take care, *amigo*, and don't fall off," the driver told him, pointing to the boat and laughing.

By the time Anthony made it to the end of the pier the woman was again standing alone, and she looked at him like a lioness with a small animal under her paw. The wide smile he'd seen from the truck was gone and her hands were fists resting on her hips.

"Welcome, Mr. Curtis." She held out her hand to him after a good five minutes of staring. "I'm Gracelia Luis Ortega."

Juan's mother's English was better than his, and from only the brief sentence he could tell she had more polish than her son would ever possess.

"Pleased to meet you, ma'am." It was an inane thing to say, but his mind had gone blank. In fact he couldn't find any trace of her in Juan's features, making him wonder what Mr. Ortega looked like.

"My son took a great chance trusting you," she said, and let go of his hand. "Are you sure you're worthy of that trust?"

The driver's laughing comment suddenly bled away Anthony's calm. He was about to board a boat that would sail over water where gray whales came to give birth, but also swarmed with sharks, the great white being at the top of the food chain. The possibility of being thrown in along the way make him think carefully about his every word.

"I helped him try to take something he wanted and got him out alive when *his* plan didn't work." He shoved his hands in his pockets and tried not to act nervous. "Because I did that, I can never go back to the life I had. That's the sacrifice I made for Juan so, yes, I'm positive I'm worthy of his trust and yours."

"Then you are prepared to do what needs to be done?" she asked, and he nodded. "You're a smart man, so if you ignore the position we're in you won't live past this month, since even my brother is hunting us." Gracelia relaxed one hand and waved him toward the boat. "To board means you admit Juan and I are your only friends."

"I will if you admit I'm not your enemy."

"Done."

He laughed and followed her up the gangplank. "That was easy."

"Don't mistake fast and easy with foolish, Agent Curtis. My son," Gracelia said softly as she got close enough to him that he could feel her warmth, "might act with the inexperience of youth, but I have no such problem. You've been running toward me for the last couple of months, which was smart of you because it gave you time to hide your tracks. That gave me enough time to find out what we're up against. Try to screw us over and I'll present you to whoever will give me the most in return, and believe me, the list is long. Remember that if you do something stupid."

"Done."

❖

The key in Muriel's hand represented a new aspect to her relationship with Shelby, and while it had been easy for Shelby to convince her to accept it, she heard her father's disapproving whisper every time she used it. As she slipped it into the lock she knew she was creating another thin layer in the barrier that would someday separate her from Cain.

"Tough day, baby?" Shelby was wiping her hands on a dish towel.

"Same old stuff." The short conversation was as close as they ever got to talking business, and they'd been careful not to walk any harder on that spread of eggshells. "How about you?"

"Still no sign of Anthony or Juan, and instead of putting more people on it, my boss thinks we need to focus on more important things."

She accepted the drink Shelby held up and the kiss she offered. "Let me guess, the Casey family exploits?"

"For once you aren't my responsibility outside this house." Shelby sipped her drink, wheezing as the aged whiskey glided down. "I asked Annabel for a transfer and she obliged me."

"Let me guess again, you got put on Remi or Ramon's detail so you can still keep an eye on us?"

"Wrong again." Shelby went back into the kitchen and lifted the lid on a large pot.

Muriel looked over her shoulder and smiled at the huge amount of beef stroganoff. "Expecting someone or do I look skinny?"

"Don't freak out, but I invited some people over since I won't see them every day. My team isn't real happy with me for asking for a new assignment, so this is my peace offering."

The whiskey in Muriel's glass was her family's favorite and now a staple in Shelby's house, so it was laced with memories and traditions that made up her life. At least that's what it usually tasted like, but sharing it with Shelby made it taste as if something was missing or different. Her family, especially her father, believed firmly in going with his gut because he'd seen his brother Dalton fly high through life with that as his only weather vane.

Muriel stared at the amber liquid and her gut reaction was to put the glass down and walk out. Then she looked at Shelby. Love pulled harder even though it pulled her away from the familiar and the comfortable.

"I feel special, then," Muriel said, and poured herself a bit more. "You're letting me into the club?"

"Can I be honest with you?"

"Eventually you'll see that I'm probably the only one you can be honest with."

"I'm not happy."

"With?" she asked, and had to place her hand on the counter near the stove to steady herself.

Shelby saw the walls go up immediately and had to play the rest of this talk carefully. "With my job, not you, baby. This next assignment is crap, but I don't want to go back to the old one." She placed her hand on Muriel's face. "If we're always on opposite sides, we won't make it."

"You actually see a solution?"

Shelby took Muriel's drink out of her hand so she could get close enough to lay her head on her chest. "Not yet, but eventually I'll have to because I won't lose you again."

"You sound sure of that, but I'm not."

"Why?" she asked, trying to keep Muriel from emotionally pulling away from her even more.

"Be honest about the problem and what it'll take to fix it. I mean the only thing. I've looked at this from every angle and one of us has to give up what we do."

"I'd never ask you to do that, and I doubt you'll ask me either, so what's the answer?" Shelby looked up and for the first time since they'd met, she clearly saw the amount of sadness in Muriel's eyes.

"Then it isn't a matter of asking but of sacrificing. When the time comes you'll keep your place and I'll change mine," Muriel said.

Shelby suddenly visualized Annabel's expression when she had asked for permission to find a way into Cain's business. Her request was at Muriel's expense, and she had to confess that fact now or lose more than her place within the Bureau. "You'd do that for me?"

"I care for you, Shelby, and I don't think I realized how much until today. If I have to choose, I'll choose you."

"Baby," Shelby put her fingers over Muriel's mouth, "I don't want you to regret a rash decision. You do that and I'll lose you no matter what."

"Stir your stuff and forget about all that tonight. We don't have to think about this right this minute." Muriel smiled and kissed her forehead. The doorbell rang and Shelby didn't move from Muriel's arms. "You want me to get it?" When Shelby nodded, Muriel kissed her again before she moved away.

"Fuck," Shelby whispered as she bent over the counter. She hadn't expected Muriel to say all that, but she couldn't tell Annabel she'd changed her mind. She and Muriel hadn't declared their love, but Muriel seemed at war about it. Shelby loved her and knew what it would cost Muriel with Cain and the rest of the Caseys if she gave in to it and still did what she needed to do. If she was successful, Muriel would never believe Shelby's feelings were genuine, only that she'd used Muriel to ruin her family.

"Shelby," Claire Lansing said, and placed her hand on her back. "You okay?"

"Sublime." Shelby straightened out and moved to the stove.

"Could you get back in there and make sure Lionel and Joe don't have Muriel tied to a chair trying to get information out of her?"

"I was kind of surprised to see her here."

"I'm sure not as surprised as she is that you and the guys are here, and if you're my friend don't start any conversations about what a big mistake I'm making."

"You'll never hear me say that since I understand the allure of someone like Muriel. The Caseys might be why we get paid, but they seem like people who love wholeheartedly when they find the person they give their heart to." Shelby pointed to a bottle and Claire poured herself a glass of wine. "So, my friend, instead of making a mistake I should be congratulating you for taking a chance."

"We'll see," Shelby said, and bit the nail of her index finger. Muriel appeared at the door and Shelby was afraid that at the end of her life she would never be able to look back and say true happiness was something she was familiar with. "Everything okay?"

"I'm sure it will be, so smile and we'll call a truce for tonight," Muriel said, and held her.

❖

"How's he doing?" Emma asked when Cain stepped out of the intensive care unit. They'd had to leave in the middle of lunch when Jarvis got so weak he almost didn't make it out of the restaurant on his feet. Cain had gotten him into the car with Lou's help and had taken him to his doctor when he started having trouble breathing, and from there he'd been transferred to the hospital less than an hour later.

"He's asking for Muriel, but her phone isn't on and the office said she left right after we did." Cain sat next to her and took her hand. "I'm no doctor, but he doesn't look good to me."

"Ms. Casey?" A man in a lab coat stopped in front of them. "I'm Dr. Gamble. How are you related to Mr. Casey?"

"He's my uncle. Is he any better?"

"I asked Mr. Casey if I could share his condition with you and he consented, but I need you to find his daughter. From what he said he's got only one child and she needs to know how serious this is."

Cain nodded. "Tell me what it'll take to get him home and I'll get Muriel here tonight."

"The flu virus has damaged his heart and he's in congestive heart failure. Medication can usually help, but with his weakened condition I don't know how successful that'll be."

"The flu attacked his heart?" It sounded absurd.

"This isn't a joke, Ms. Casey. The virus has weakened his heart muscle and has impaired his pump function. We'll do our best, but the next couple of days are crucial." He glanced at his watch. "I know you just came out but he's asking to talk to you. I'm willing to bend the rules if you use the time to try and calm him down."

Cain stood and held her hand out to Emma. They followed the doctor to the locked doors and waited for him to gain access. Jarvis was lying in bed with his hand over the middle of his chest, as if he were trying to keep his heart in place. Pale and breathing shallowly, he appeared to Cain as if his strength had left his body and what was left was a shell that would soon shatter.

When she bent close he opened his eyes and she smiled at the familiar blue of the Casey clan. "Cain...Muriel," he said softly. He'd lost an amazing amount of ground since they arrived at the hospital.

"I'll get her here tonight, Uncle Jarvis, so save your strength so you can talk to her then."

"No, I need to talk to you first. Promise me...you won't turn her away. I've tried my best..." He reached out for her hand as his chest heaved. "I've tried to keep her safe and to keep her true to who she is, but we both know she's lost. This woman isn't who she seems, and Muriel will be a victim of her ambition. I can't rest knowing Muriel might have to face the world alone because her feelings have dulled her intelligence."

"You need to concentrate on getting stronger. Muriel isn't in any danger of losing her place with me no matter who she picks to spend her life with." Cain came closer and kissed his hand. "I place family above everything else in my life. It sounds like a corny thing to say, but—"

"No," he said, and coughed. "You're so like your father. Dalton spoke like a poet when it came to family and what it meant to him. Do you think he'd be proud of what I've built when it came to mine?"

"As much as I am, uncle, and Muriel is a perfect person to carry on your name. She hasn't forgotten what blood runs through her heart."

"At times I feel like I don't know her. Maybe I'm the one who's forgotten what it means to carry on what my father gave me." His eyes filled with tears and so did hers. It hurt her to see him grasp at what life he had left like a man who'd run out of time before he'd been able to finish setting up his legacy.

"You helped me find my way back to Emma again," Cain said. "Do you remember that day in my office? You stood up to my stubbornness and reminded me what was important." Cain squeezed his hand and laughed. "I wanted to punch you, but you were right, and because you were, I'll need a new picture on my desk soon when we add our little one."

"I have your word you won't tell her about our talk? I can't have her thinking that I doubt her and what she means to me," he said, and squeezed her hand gently.

"Muriel's heart is safe with me, so try and relax." She glanced up at the heart monitor. "You'll feel better if you calm down."

"Find Muriel for me, and hurry," Jarvis said, as if he knew exactly how much time he had left. "Remember what I asked you, and thank you, Cain. You've made me proud, and I'll tell your da and mum what a wonderful spouse and parent you are."

"You can tell them that much later, because you still have a lot of life left to kick around. Close your eyes and rest. I'll be right back with Muriel."

"You'll tell her if I'm too tired, right? Tell her how much I love her," he said, and closed his eyes as if he was too exhausted to keep them focused.

"You have my word she'll know everything she needs to."

"Where do you intend to look?" Emma asked when Cain guided her outside the room.

"The last place I want to, but I don't want to send one of the guys. Muriel needs to hear this from me, and I hope I know her as well as I think I do because we don't have much time." Cain kissed Emma and placed her hand at the bend of her neck. "I hate to do this to you, but could you stay with him?"

"You go, and I'll be fine." She kissed Cain again and sighed when she saw the tears ready to fall from her eyes. "He's a Casey, baby. He's strong enough to fight."

"We can't win all our battles, my love. That's one of the most important lessons I've learned. Sometimes you can fight like the devil, but you're damned to lose it all," Cain said before she turned and headed away with a determined step. A moment later Lou walked in and stood outside Jarvis's room with the other guard who had accompanied them to the hospital.

"She left alone?" Emma asked, unable to keep the panic from her voice.

"Unfortunately I don't get to call the shots," Lou said with no humor, and shrugged.

"Great." She glanced at the exit again before she went back to Jarvis's side.

She hadn't known Jarvis well when she and Cain first met. For a few years Emma had thought Cain and Jarvis were at odds, but one day going through some family photos she found the answer.

Dalton filled the photos he was in with his broad shoulders, thick jet hair, and smile, all of which he'd passed on to his children. In every picture the still frames couldn't dull the obvious mischief and charm Cain had so often spoken of. That afternoon flipping through her lover's history, she'd understood why Cain missed him, and she wished she'd met him.

And in those pictures she'd seen the curse of the Casey genes that had prevailed for generations. Cain's father had been the center of her world for so long. He'd been father, teacher, mentor, and when he died he left a close double behind to remind Cain of her loss. Jarvis had obviously reminded Cain too much of her father and how much it hurt to lose him.

Emma had turned to Jarvis as a way back to Cain, and he'd listened. And in a way because Cain had in turn listened to him, Cain had not only reconciled with her, but become close to Jarvis as well. After her return Cain had spent more time with him, finally seeing past the pain and instead to what a treasure he was.

"Emma," Jarvis said softly.

"Save your strength, Uncle Jarvis."

"I want you." He started coughing and it sounded like he was trying to clear a barrel of water from his chest.

"It's okay. Cain's going for Muriel. I'm sure she'll want to hear whatever you have to say."

"Time's a luxury I don't have," he said, wheezing worse. "I know what the outcome of all this will be, and that's why I left the house today. I've known about this bad pumper for a long time but didn't want to bother you." He held his hand up and she took it. "I've finally lost Muriel. It's like when I saw you with Cain for the first time."

"I hope you know how grateful I am that you helped us get together again," she said, trying to make conversation so he could catch his breath. "You gave me my life back."

"Cain will always belong to you, and that's what I wanted for Muriel. She's lost her heart to this girl, but that will only bring everyone pain," he said slowly, but he seemed desperate. "I want you to promise that you'll talk to Cain so she won't abandon Muriel if she betrays the family."

"You know Cain would never turn Muriel away." She squeezed his hand and sent a silent plea to Cain to hurry. Jarvis's skin was turning ashen, and his eyes were cloudy.

"Promise me, Emma."

"I promise. Whatever happens, I'll be Muriel's advocate. You need to calm down, though, and save your strength for her."

"Thank you, because in times like this it's easy to say the words. But if Cain finds herself boxed in because of something my child has done in the name of love, it'll be just as easy to forget."

"I'll never forget."

"One more thing…" He tried to take a deep breath.

"Ma'am," Dr. Gamble said, "that's enough for now." He turned off an alarm that had started beeping when Jarvis stopped talking.

"Wait." Jarvis reached over with his other hand and winced in pain, but it seemed more important to him to hang on to her. "Tell Muriel all the things you'd tell Hayden or Hannah. You understand me?"

"Yes, perfectly."

"I love her and I'm proud." He was gasping now.

"You have to step out," Dr. Gamble said. "His heart rate is dropping rapidly."

"It's okay, Emma," Jarvis said, then coughed weakly. "Tell her I'll be fine keeping her mother company."

The alarms got much louder after that and it looked like the entire unit's staff came running. Emma stood outside with Lou's hands on her shoulders and watched them try to revive Jarvis, but the heart monitor continued to show a thin green flat line. He was gone, but not before he'd taken care of his child.

Emma placed her hands over her middle, feeling like she had to shield her unborn child from the ugliness and pain that was death. Soon the doctor looked up at the clock and called the time.

"Lou, could you find me a chair?" she asked.

"You'd be more comfortable in the waiting area."

"Do you think Cain would want us to leave him alone?"

They stayed outside the room until the medical staff removed all the equipment Jarvis had been attached to, leaving him at last appearing peaceful. Then the doctor told them to take their time and left them as she sat next to the bed in silence.

"May you go with God, uncle, and be one more soul who looks out for Cain and our children," she thought before she said a more formal prayer for him. As sad as his death was, she prayed that this would be the way death visited Cain—at the end of a very long life after their children were grown and capable of choosing their happiness. It still wouldn't be easy, but it'd be more tolerable than if it occurred in the near future.

"If that happens, my heart will die with her no matter how many years I remain." The thought was morbid but true.

CHAPTER FOUR

Cain drove slowly down the narrow street, hitting more potholes than actual pavement as she headed for the uptown address she'd memorized but had never visited. She'd fought her inclination to drive by it so the act wouldn't be interpreted as aggression against someone she had yet to figure out.

A number of cars were parked in front of the cute, well-maintained house with a front yard full of flowers, so she pulled over a half block down. With each step the dreamer in her wished she wouldn't find Muriel inside, because then she could ignore what that meant. But Muriel's BMW was parked next to the Suburban in the drive.

Before she reached the middle of the walkway to the front door her cell phone rang on the lowest volume. The name on the screen was Emma's and it made her want to sit in case her legs gave out at what was surely bad news.

"Hello." Sweat dampened her upper lip. "When?" she asked. "Thanks, lass, but don't sit there until I get back. Have Lou take you home, then tell him to meet me back at the hospital." The front of Shelby's house blurred through the tears in her eyes, but she took a deep breath to keep them in check. "I love you too, and I'll be fine."

He was gone. So very little of the family who'd been molded by her father was left. Jarvis had been her visible and emotional connection to her father, but he'd been so much more. She wouldn't have been as successful if he hadn't backed her from the moment she'd had to take over. But all those memories and thoughts would have to wait until she was alone.

She knocked and closed her eyes briefly to try to block out the laughter coming from inside, since it only made the pain worse. "If it's the boss, tell her we're off until nine," Shelby said from somewhere in the house when the other female agent Cain hadn't met formally opened the door.

"Agent Lansing, right?" she asked, and Claire nodded.

"I'd like to speak to Muriel." Her hand rested on the door frame involuntarily, covering her shock of finding the agent. She'd expected Shelby, but not this.

"Would you like to come in?" Claire asked, turning around when she noticed Cain staring at Joe.

"My apologies for interrupting your little party," she said, more for Joe's benefit since he was looking at her like he was trying to frighten her. "Have Muriel call me." She'd had enough. This wasn't the night to face one of her greatest fears aside from losing Emma or her children.

Both her father and Jarvis had preached that this would cause her downfall. They said you could build walls thick enough that nothing or no one could break through, but all it would take was someone opening the gates and inviting the enemy in. When she saw Muriel's dinner companions, the warning worked its way into her brain as easily as a hot knife through cold butter.

"Cain," Muriel called to her as she reached the sidewalk. She stood still, unwilling to meet Muriel halfway. "What's wrong?"

Muriel's expression bordered on embarrassment, and Cain swallowed her anger so she could deliver the news that would change her cousin's life forever. At least it had for her the day Jarvis told her about her father. "It's Uncle Jarvis," she said, her attention divided between Muriel and Shelby, who was moving closer.

"Just say it."

"I tried, Muriel, but your cell phone was off and this one was off the hook." She pointed to the house.

"My number's not listed," Shelby said, winding her arm around Muriel's wrist in a blatant act of possession.

"Cain, please."

"I just wanted you to know I tried before it was too late. I'm so very sorry."

Muriel shook Shelby off and grabbed Cain by the shoulders. "What happened to him? Where is he?" The questions came so fast she didn't have a chance to answer.

"We had to take him to the emergency room, where they stabilized him, and to make him more comfortable his doctors moved him to

C.C.U." She didn't break Muriel's painful hold, but she put her hands on the sides of Muriel's neck. "He was sicker than he ever admitted to us, and he's gone."

"Gone?" Muriel asked, looking dazed. "He's gone?"

"I'm sorry and I hate having to tell you like this. I was hoping I'd get you back in time, but I left Emma with him. He wasn't alone." She let her tears fall, unable to control them any longer. "I didn't know he was that sick."

Muriel fell against her and cried, not caring who saw them, and Shelby didn't try to come closer. "I made promises to him, cousin, and only you can break them. You'll never be alone, and I'll always be here for you."

"Shelby," Lionel shouted, seeming to be the most courageous of the bunch.

"See to your guests and I'll see to my family," Cain said to Shelby, and started to lead Muriel toward the car.

"I want to come."

This wasn't the time to argue so she didn't when Muriel held her hand out to Shelby. The ride back to the hospital was quiet except for Muriel's sniffles. Cain locked eyes with Shelby at every traffic light. Had the door to the fortress already been opened and her enemy let in with so little fight?

The answer would come soon, she thought. Shelby and her ilk had been pursuing Cain and her family for so long, anyone would be impatient to finish it. But what was Shelby willing to sacrifice to win?

The possibilities were endless, but for Cain, winning meant keeping those she loved safe and cared for. Did someone work that hard for a job that would only forget you the minute you retired or quit? The answer was simple. What she had or what she did would never compete with who she loved. Nothing was worth having if it caused her to lose the love and respect of those she cherished.

As Shelby looked at her in the mirror, Cain couldn't tell from her expression if Muriel was worth that to her. From her actions, though, her job was everything to her.

❖

"Jarvis died last night," Mano Jatibon said as he began his meeting with his father and sister.

"Cain called me after she took Muriel home from the hospital," Remi said, and accepted a demitasse cup of espresso from her father. "According to her he'd been sick for a while, but it was still a shock to have him go so quickly."

"Jarvis was a good man and was always happy with his place in their family," Ramon said.

"Not all of us are born to lead, Papi," Mano said with a genuine smile. "And some of us would prefer to follow."

"You know better than to think you're not important to me or your sister." Ramon gently slapped him on the back of the neck. "You two just don't remember Dalton like I do. He didn't rule with a hard fist when it came to his family, and Jarvis was content to live in his very long shadow."

"I sent our caterer over there this morning, and I told Cain I'd take over the search until she's done with her obligations," Remi said. The coffee was strong and a bit bitter, which meant her mother had cut back on the heaping spoonfuls of sugar her father loved to add. "So far nothing, and there's no news about Gracelia Luis. I would've bet Juan would run back to his mama."

"Good angle, but let's try something else too," Ramon said. "I asked Rodolfo for a meeting tonight at the club."

"I don't think he'll hand over Juan, Papi, even if you ask nicely," Mano said.

"My brain hasn't gone soft with age, *hijo*." Ramon laughed and play-slapped Remi's hand this time when she wriggled it at him. "It's been weeks since we've talked to him, and I think it's time we remind him about the promises he made to Cain."

"He's got his men on the street, and from the way they're working, they really are looking for Juan and his mother," Remi said, and pulled a sheet from her briefcase with a list of names on it. "This is everyone who's broken away from Rodolfo's crew to join his sister, according to our street contacts. I can't imagine what she promised, but his organization could disappear if he's faced with any serious threat."

"Had to happen eventually," Ramon said. "There's killing to keep the peace and killing for pleasure. One makes you a good protector and the other a psychopath. Rodolfo's been cruel all his life, and while that helped him build his empire, it's also the reason Gracelia could turn Juan against him."

"Why do you think so?" Mano asked.

"Because Rodolfo did a good job raising Juan to be like him, only he never cared for him as much as his mother did. Juan's loyalty lies with her."

Remi nodded. "That's a problem for us because Gracelia Luis has a reputation for being a smart woman who Rodolfo has held back all her life. If she's got something to prove, she'll use Juan and Anthony to make her point."

"The casino's pretty secure now, and the clubs are well protected," Mano said. "Where do you think we're vulnerable?"

"Our partnership with Cain makes us even more secure, but we need to meet with our guys and tell them to be vigilant. I don't want anyone easing up because they think we're untouchable."

"Mano and I'll take care of that," Ramon said. "Before you leave, though, there's something else."

The expression on her father's face was so guarded that she knew it had to concern Dallas. "Don't try to sugar it up because it'll take too long, so just say it."

"Cain and her buddy did an excellent job burying Dallas's past, but while we were examining Bob's system of ripping Dallas off, we fond an irregular but consistent payment," Mano said.

"That's an interesting term—irregular but consistent." Remi knocked on the table loud enough to make her knuckles hurt. "What's that mean?"

"He wired money every month to an account through the Caymans, trying to hide it, I guess, but since it was such a small amount it doesn't make sense."

She knocked on the table again. "Mano, stop talking in circles and spit it out."

"Every month he wired three thousand dollars to a blind Cayman account and stopped when he quit his job," Mano said, and made air quotes. "It's a small amount considering how much Dallas made, especially during the last couple of years."

"Did you call the bank?"

He nodded. "Those banks are open and successful for a reason. They wouldn't even acknowledge the account existed, which is good and bad. Bad because without the access codes we'll never find out, but good that they don't spill their guts when law enforcement calls about us."

"There was nothing in his records?" she asked, already thinking ahead as to how she'd break this to Dallas. It sounded harmless, but

Bob had always done things primarily to keep Dallas manipulated and controlled by fear.

"The night he quit, the guys and I checked everything in his files. This must've been important enough for him to have the transfer codes memorized. At first I thought it was an extra cushion for himself, but if so, it would've been for a hell of a lot more than that."

Remi's brain was moving so fast her head was starting to pound. "He controlled all the money anyway. If their partnership had dissolved any other way than by rolling snake eyes, Dallas would've walked away with nothing."

"Whatever it is, we'll find it," Ramon said. "You've got enough going without worrying about this. Isn't Kristen coming in soon?"

"She moved her flight up to tomorrow."

"Your mother had dinner planned, but it'll have to wait until Jarvis's services are done."

"Anything else for today?"

"Not on my end," Mano said. "I'm going to the casino for a few days to oversee our remodel plan."

"Right now our priority is Cain and Muriel," Ramon said. "Jarvis was a friend and a good man."

"That's true, but our other priority is you, Papi. I admire Cain and Muriel for being so strong despite what must be total heartbreak, but I'm not ready to see if I've got that kind of grit." Remi placed her hand over his.

"Don't think about that." Ramon smiled. "I plan to sit in your mother's garden and enjoy her flowers and my many grandchildren."

"From your lips, Papi," Mano said. "And you," he pointed to Remi, "I've got this covered about the bank, so forget it."

She nodded and stood, wanting to move to burn up the energy building in her gut. When it came to Dallas she would always worry and never forget anything.

❖

The house was beginning to fill with flowers and Cain was waiting for the funeral home to call about the wake arrangements. In New Orleans the Casey brothers hadn't been forced to give up the custom of waking in their own parlor. They didn't like the unfamiliar surroundings of a funeral home.

Many people had abandoned the tradition, but when Cain's father died she had adhered to his wishes and waked him at home. He'd lain in the room where her mother kept her piano covered with family portraits and the windows covered with the finest lace Ireland had to offer. Food and his favorite whiskey served as a tribute to what he loved, but she'd overlooked the biggest comfort at the time because of her pain.

Jarvis had stayed close by from that day on and offered silence when everyone else spoke of how it felt to lose someone so precious. Her uncle knew sorrow because he had lost his wife and brother, but he also knew no words would take away the ache. Now it was her turn to offer that to the person most precious to him.

"Why do people even have formal living rooms anymore?" Muriel asked. Her shirt was perfectly pressed, as were her pants, but her face appeared haggard. "They aren't used except for stuff like this. That's sad, don't you think?"

"Hannah uses ours for tea parties and as a place to set her dolls when they're dressed up for special occasions."

"What events do dressed-up dolls attend?"

The conversation wasn't what she expected, but then her cousin was still in shock from seeing Jarvis's lifeless body the day before. She also remembered expecting that one last piece of advice spoken in that deep voice, but instead she concentrated on trying to remember what he looked like when he smiled at something he found joy in.

"Tea parties, of course," she said, which made Muriel laugh.

"He died angry at me because of Shelby, didn't he?" Muriel asked, but couldn't seem to lift her head to look at her for the answer. "At least he thought I was upset with him for meddling."

"Your father loved you, and he made me promise to protect you always. He asked that *because* he loved you, not because he was disappointed about anything." She sat next to Muriel and nodded to Lou when he pointed to the door. While the funeral home employees rolled in the casket, she put her arm around Muriel and held her as she wept.

Per her instructions they pulled back the Irish flag and opened the casket for this one and only showing. Muriel held his hand while she placed a few things in with Jarvis. A picture of her late mother and one of him with Muriel for company went on one side. On the other was a bottle of aged Jameson to sip when he was reunited with those who'd gone before him or to bribe St. Peter with, as Dalton had joked.

"Why now?" Muriel asked.

"They're ours for only a short time," she reminded her. "You need to think about the years you were blessed with and forget about whatever you think was wrong yesterday. If you don't, I won't have anything to protect because you'll destroy yourself before anyone else gets a shot."

"You were the child he wanted."

"I was the niece he had to put up with." She took Muriel's face in her hands. "Muriel, please don't do this. You need to remember the man he was and honor that memory, Goddamn it. Jarvis Michael Casey married and had one child—one." She stopped to swallow her emotions. "And to hear tell of it all my life, he loved her something fierce." The imitation of the thick Irish brogue made Muriel nod. "Don't tarnish that pride he always had in you by second-guessing it now."

"He didn't say anything else?"

"His final thoughts were of you, your happiness, and assurances for a long life. He was proud of who you are just like I am, and that's it."

Muriel appeared satisfied with the answer, so Cain left her alone to say her good-byes. The time she'd had at the hospital when she'd taken Muriel to see him before the funeral home arrived had given Cain a chance to thank him for being her protector, not physically but of her heart. So she left Muriel in peace to share whatever thoughts and prayers she had with him before the casket was closed for the last time.

"She okay?" Emma asked when Cain joined her in the kitchen. The loose-fitting black dress was new and a good reminder that, as sad as the day would be, the future promised something else.

"Not yet, but time is the only cure." The caterers went about their business under Lou and Katlin's watchful presence, so she took Emma's hand and led her to the back den where Merrick sat in her wheelchair staring outside. "Time and love might not make all of the pain disappear, but it covers a multitude of things, isn't that right?" Cain asked Merrick.

"Yes." Merrick's speech was slow and thick, but vastly improved in a short time with the help of her therapist. "Muriel will miss him."

"Mom," Hayden said, holding Hannah's hand. "Mr. Vincent and Mr. Ramon are here."

"Did you two behave for Dallas and Remi?" Cain asked, lifting Hannah up so she could kiss Emma.

"We plead the Fifth," Hayden said, and tried to smile. "Is Muriel all right?"

"She's sad, but having all of us here will make her feel better,"

Emma said. "Why don't you and Hannah sit with Merrick and watch TV while Mom and I make sure everyone's comfortable."

"I can help," he said.

"I know you can, sweetheart, but I don't want you to have to go through this again. The funeral tomorrow will be bad enough," Emma said as she brushed his hair into place.

When they walked to the front of the house the den was full of people, but the doors to the living room were still closed, with Lou and Katlin standing before them. A few of Vincent's family came up to Cain and talked briefly, as well as some of Ramon's men, including Remi's law partners Dwayne and Steve.

"Sorry as hell, Cain," Vincent said. "Jarvis was old school and there aren't too many of us left."

"Thanks and you're right. He was the last of Da's generation in our family." She accepted a drink from one of the waiters and studied the two people who walked out of the living room holding hands.

"Is that going to be a problem for you?" Vincent asked, pointing discreetly at Muriel and Shelby. "Not the time or place, I know, but it's worrisome."

"It's my problem, Vincent, which means it'll never be yours."

"Pop, lay off," Vinny Carlotti said as he embraced Cain. "We're here for you and Muriel."

"Thanks, and your pop's okay." Cain spoke and heard every word Vinny said, but her main attention was on Shelby, who seemed more interested in their guest list than in Muriel. "Excuse me."

Some of the mourners moved to where the casket was after they stopped and talked with Muriel, who looked like she was swimming underwater against the current. "Muriel, sit and drink this." Cain handed her a weak whiskey and water. "Shelby, why don't you fix her a plate?" She locked eyes with Emma and pointed to Muriel. "I'll help you." Shelby obviously realized it wasn't a request and didn't object when Cain led her away from the buffet table loaded with food and into the kitchen instead.

"If you think you can intimidate me out of her life, you're wrong," Shelby said.

Cain pointed to the door and the kitchen emptied except for the two of them, making Shelby's words laughable. "My cousin loves you, so *you're* wrong. This isn't about scaring you off."

"What's it about, then?" Shelby asked, and accepted the plate Cain held out to her.

"This is your opportunity to tell me that your motives toward Muriel are sincere. Tomorrow, and I speak from experience, will be the worst day of her life because she'll go home to an empty house. Her father won't be here to pick up the pieces if you shatter what's essentially a broken heart." She chose a few things she knew Muriel liked but not enough to overwhelm her and put them on the plate Shelby held.

"Face it. You'll never trust me, so why waste time having this conversation at all?"

"I tell stories about my father all the time, but my mum was just as wise, so I'll give you the advice she gave anyone who wanted to get close to my family." The carrot cake the caterers hadn't touched yet came from Vincent's restaurant, and in Cain's opinion was the best in the city, so she cut a corner piece loaded with cream-cheese icing for Muriel. "If you don't belong and fly too close to the sun you'll get burned, but if you move too far away from it you'll die of the cold."

"What's that mean exactly?" Shelby asked, and swiped up a bit of icing with her thumb.

"If you don't belong, Shelby, I'll burn you so badly you'll be lucky to find work as a rent-a-cop, but if you truly love Muriel, don't walk so far away that'll you'll both suffer for it." When she saw Hayden at the door, she waved him forward. "For both our sakes, I hope your motives are what you say they are."

"That sounds like a threat," Shelby said, and pointed to Hayden, "and with a witness too."

"My life isn't so sinister, Shelby, but that's how you and your buddies define it." She put her arm around Hayden's shoulders and pulled him close. "I told you that because I love my family more than anything in my life, and I don't take it well when someone aims to hurt them. You and I know that you may love her, but you'll never let that interfere with your job, no matter how it affects Muriel. If that's the case, I'll be the one who helps her with those wounds."

"You're that sure of yourself?"

"Sometimes I have to think my next moves out a long way in advance, but in situations like this that's impossible. Some hurts heal but they leave scars so deep that they're never forgotten. If you make and leave them, then you'll have to live with the consequences of your actions."

Hayden nodded in obvious agreement and she led him back to the room where Merrick and Hannah were sitting. Hannah had picked a spot close to Merrick so she could hold her hand while they watched the movie Hannah had chosen. The offered comfort made Cain smile because while Hannah was a little clone of her, her heart was all Emma.

"Why do you think Muriel is blind to all that stuff you said, Mom?"

"Because your heart speaks a different language than your head, and for a lot of reasons Muriel's heart won out this time." She kissed the top of his head. "It seems pretty cut and dried to you and to me, but you'll understand one day."

"I hope I find someone like Mama."

"I hope so too, but not too quick or your mama will blame me if she loses her little boy too fast."

"Cain." Emma came up behind her and put her arms around her waist. "Mr. Hector Delarosa wanted me to tell you he's here to pay his respects."

"Somehow I doubt that," she said, thinking about the Colombian drug-cartel boss. He'd been helpful in their one telephone conversation when he'd given her the information she needed to find out Juan had come back into the country using his dead father's name. A quick flight for a funeral of a man he didn't know meant he wanted something she most probably wasn't willing to give. "Thanks, lass."

"Remember what your mom said," Emma said to Hayden. "You can start dating when you're about thirty." She kissed his cheek and mouthed the word "wait" to Cain while Hayden hugged her.

"Before you ask, I don't know what he wants, and I'm surprised he's here," Cain whispered to her in the hall.

"Don't backslide on me now, mobster. Remember our deal—no more secrets."

"Cain, you do realize who's out there waiting for you," Remi said, quietly joining their conversation. "Not to mention who's out there taking mental notes of your guest list tonight."

"For the record," she said to Emma first, "I don't know what Hector Delarosa is doing here." Then she turned and faced Remi. "And Muriel's too old for me to take her over my knee." Her patience had ended and she couldn't stop the sarcasm from tainting her words.

"I'm on your side, okay?" Remi said, and held up her hands.

"I appreciate that. I need time to give Jarvis the attention and respect he's due. After that I'll take on all this other shit that's popped up." She buttoned her jacket and walked away holding Emma's hand

to greet Hector. The way Shelby looked at her when Hector took her
other hand between both of his made her feel as if someone had started
a stopwatch that was ticking away how much time she had left before
her charmed life ceased to exist.

CHAPTER FIVE

The overcast sky had cleared the beach for the day, but somehow the water of the Pacific seemed even more beautiful to Anthony as he enjoyed the view from Gracelia's terrace. They'd docked a few days earlier and taken a long drive down the coast to the house she owned on a bluff with a panoramic view of the ocean. It was the only place in either direction for at least five miles, but even so usually a few topless sunbathers lay on the beach soaking up the privacy along with the rays.

"Do you like the rain, Agent Curtis?"

Because of where he was and who he was a guest of, he hadn't pushed to find out where Juan was, but he hadn't seen him since their arrival and was fairly sure he wasn't in the large house. Gracelia, though, hadn't let Anthony spend too much time alone.

"Weather isn't my thing so it doesn't really matter one way or the other," he said, watching her as she leaned against the banister, her hair blowing wildly against her shoulders. "You can call me Anthony if you want. Considering everything's that's happened I'm fairly sure I'm not an agent anymore, even if I were working undercover."

"The manhunt your boss has organized seems zealous enough to convince me." She turned and placed her hands on her neck to keep her hair from her face. "But it could be an act, so I'm here to give you a choice."

"If it's a multiple-choice question and the 'b' option is someone flinging me over the side there, I'll go with 'a.'"

Gracelia laughed and her beauty almost made him forget the trouble he was in. "If it's true that you are through with that life, I would like for you to join us." Her English was precise and sounded cultured. "If not, you've recovered from your adventure and are free to go. I'll even arrange transportation to the airport."

"Are you new to negotiation?" he said as she joined him under the large canopy when big rain drops splattered the stone where she'd been standing. "You've made it easy for me to lie to you and tell you anything you want."

"Unless you've got some sort of homing device in your rectum, I doubt anyone knows you're here, so it would be easy for *me* to lie should anyone come looking for you," she said.

The face was beautiful, but for the first time he saw the complete coldness in her eyes and expression. This woman wouldn't need to call anyone to throw him to his death. She'd do it herself and enjoy lunch afterward with no remorse.

"You don't have to worry. No one has any idea where I am. It'd be easy for you and Juan to kill me, and I doubt you'd ever answer for it."

"It took some time but I think you finally understand your position." She smiled at him and sat closer. "You are where I need you, even if it's not what you had planned. And joining my son wasn't in your plans, was it?"

Her hypnotic gaze reminded him of a king cobra's and he felt the allure of telling the truth. But his will to survive was stronger than being that stupid. "My alliance with Juan occurred because we had a common enemy, but you know that already. I thought that after we brought Casey down, my partnership with Juan would end and I'd return to what I do. That's impossible now."

"If you were working undercover I'm sure your boss is willing to forgive pretty much anything." She spoke softly and put her hand on his leg above his knee.

He laughed as he stared at her hand. It was hard to remember the last time someone had touched him except his mother hugging him after a visit. "My job doesn't encourage kidnapping someone and shooting someone else in the head in broad daylight in front of federal agents. We have rules we don't break without losing our freedom, no matter how bad the Bureau wants to catch you."

"Tell me about this woman you took." Gracelia stood and poured him a drink, sitting next to him again after she set it before him. It was the first time since their arrival that she'd bothered to wait on him like she had for Juan.

"I'm sure you know plenty about Juan's great obsession." As he brought the glass to his nose he detected a hint of citrus mixed with a good amount of liquor, and for some reason the odor triggered his desire for a hit of cocaine. "I'm not sure what the attraction is, considering how obsessed she is with Casey."

"My son seldom tells me anything of what he considers failures, so you're wrong. This woman Emma is a mystery to me."

He gulped so much of the drink that a pain shot through the side of his head, making him press his fingers to the spot. "Shit," he said, and flinched when Gracelia caressed his face. "If you and Juan are so close how come he didn't share this with you?"

"Very good, Anthony. You didn't waste too much time at the Academy—you're quite observant," she said, then took her hand away from his face so she could lift her drink.

"I told Juan as much about his father as I could when I raised him. I described what kind of man Armando was and what he did to my heart in the short time I knew him. Those stories gave Juan a sense of himself and what kind of man he in turn wanted to be. It would've been better for Juan to have had both of us guiding him, but for my purposes, what I gave him was enough."

"Your purposes?" He noticed one of the guards moving closer and wanted to yell to keep him away since Gracelia was providing more answers than he had questions. "What's that mean?"

"My brother stole something precious from me, so it's time to return the favor." She kept her eyes on him as the man bent down and whispered in her ear.

"You sound determined."

"Underestimating my determination is a mistake I hope you don't make, Anthony. Remember what I said." She cupped his cheek again and to his amazement he grew hard. "Mistakes that serious will cost you dearly." She glanced down when he squirmed but didn't move away from him. "Be ready to move at six."

"Where?" His pulse pounded in his groin as Gracelia's hand moved down his neck to his chest.

"You look like a man who needs a new beginning, and I'm the woman who can give it to you."

❖

"Mr. Delarosa, sorry to keep you waiting," Cain said, making Hector turn around from staring out the window in Jarvis's study. She'd asked him for a brief private meeting away from curious eyes.

Hector Delarosa was handsome and impeccably dressed, and he immediately took her hand between both of his again. His thick mustache somehow made his smile appear wider, and Cain wondered why he'd made the trip.

"I'd think we are friends by now, so please call me Hector," he said, and bowed his head slightly. "Please accept my condolences on the loss of your uncle."

"Thank you, but is there something else I can do for you?" She knew the question sounded blunt, but she wasn't in a diplomatic mood.

"I see the stories about you are true," Hector said, and laughed. "I wish I had come only because of your uncle, but I was already here and hoping to meet with you."

"So you've brought the DEA to my door as a gift?" She waved to one of the leather visitor's chairs and she took the other. "I've got plenty of admirers without adding to my dance card."

"Your DEA has only suspicion about me, much like the FBI has about you, and I want only to extend my friendship to you. I do that because we have a common problem. A problem best handled among friends."

"I'm sure that's true, but not tonight. My uncle deserves to be laid to rest and I won't take that from him. Once this is over I'll be happy to meet with you. I owe you that for your recent help."

"Discussing history doesn't require payment. It's the future that piles on the debts we must deal with." He put his hands on the chair arms and pushed himself to his feet. "At least that's what my mother always told me. I'll be here meeting with Vinny and his father, and I won't leave until we've had our talk."

"Thanks, and if you need anything while you're here, call the house."

He left and she stayed seated in the chair her father used when he visited his brother's home. They seldom discussed business here but told and retold stories of their childhood until she, Billy, and Muriel knew them by heart. She remembered the last family dinner they'd all shared at Jarvis's before her family had left her one by one.

That night they'd had no premonitions about the future and no sad moments to hint at the pain they'd all endure. It'd been a happy time that stayed stamped in her heart so clearly it made her want to recreate the experience for her own children as much as possible with their own family dinners and outings. That was important because in the end the memories were the treasure she'd inherited.

"I don't think he'd mind you sitting at the desk," Muriel said. She joined her and took Hector's seat.

"I haven't had the chance to tell you how very sorry I am for your loss," Cain said, and took Muriel's hand. "It's just us now, and I'll always be here for you. Don't ever lose sight of that."

"How did you survive this?"

"By remembering the good times, finding Emma, and having you and Uncle Jarvis." She stopped talking when Muriel started to cry. "You'll find your way, cousin, because he raised you to be true to yourself."

"What's that mean?" Muriel asked as she pressed a tissue to her eyes.

"That you're strong in your own unique way. The ache will always be with you, but you'll be able to stand on your own, even if that's hard to imagine now."

"Muriel," Shelby said from the hallway. "The bishop is here to say a prayer for your father."

They stood and embraced until Muriel's emotions were under control. In the parlor Cain's good friend Bishop Andrew Goodman led everyone in prayer before the funeral home removed the casket for the night. The mourners followed soon after, and when Shelby began to comfort Muriel, Cain went in search of her family.

In the den Emma was sitting with her head back and eyes closed holding Hannah's head in her lap, with Hayden pressed against her on the other side. Father Andy's prayers had proved too long for their hyperactive daughter so Emma had taken her back to play with her living jungle gym, since that's how she treated Hayden.

"How can you look at them and take the chances you do?" Shelby asked softly. Cain glanced back at her and saw Muriel wasn't with her.

"Do you remember the night we met?"

Shelby nodded at the innocent-sounding question, but Cain could tell the subject matter frightened her somewhat.

"Don't worry, my bug-extermination crew is the best in the business. At least, for both our sakes I certainly hope so."

"If you really want an answer, it's yes."

"Then you should know better than anyone that even though the surveillance is constant, you still don't have any idea who I am." Emma opened her eyes when Cain picked Hannah up. "And don't take that as a challenge to make you try even harder to figure me out. Turn all that curious nature in Muriel's direction."

"Giving advice now?" Shelby asked.

Emma spoke before Cain could respond. "It beats the hell out of telling you where to get off, Agent Phillips." Emma accepted Hayden's hand to stand up and continued. "I know that sounds rude, but I'm tired and my patience and politeness ran thin about ten minutes ago."

"A couple more months of pregnancy and I'd fear her more than a reincarnated Al Capone," Cain said, and laughed. "Good night, Shelby, and please keep our earlier talk in mind."

"Don't worry, Cain. I keep every one of our talks in mind. So much so that I take notes," Shelby said in what Cain gathered was the most sarcastic tone she could muster.

❖

The traffic along Airline Highway leading out of New Orleans was light at the moment, but Johnny Moores could tell it was a major thoroughfare because it had so many lanes. Now instead of commuters from the suburbs trying to get downtown, a mix of people was either in a hurry to get somewhere or driving slow, talking to the women and men walking in front of the cheap motels.

After he had gone downtown and protested the price of the rooms, one of the employees at the Hilton had suggested the area after Johnny had cursed him. "The little fucker was right. These places are dumps."

The faded red paint of the one he picked appeared almost pink in the glare of his headlights, but he only got a glimpse before a young woman tapped on his window and made a sign for him to roll it down.

"You interested in a good time?"

The memory of a young Katie Lynn popped into his head because the prostitute appeared so innocent and didn't quite look right in her miniskirt and tight Lycra top. His daughter had never dressed like a whore for him, but she never did look quite right when he visited her room at night. That had never slowed him down, though, and this little bitch wouldn't either.

"How much?" he asked as he put his hand on his crotch.

"What are you interested in?" She stepped a little away from the truck door as if to give him a better view of her whole body.

"I'm interested in you not being a cop," he said, swinging the door open and hopping out. "I'm going in and getting a room, and if you're still out here I'll take it *you're* interested in me."

The night clerk accepted a wad of bills for a two-week stay and another twenty for forgetting about the registration form. He grabbed the key from the counter and cursed when the plastic ring with the room number felt sticky.

What didn't surprise him was the little bitch in heat propped against his truck waiting for him. He opened the driver's side and smirked when she jumped in without any other prompting. She would be a good diversion until the morning when he started his search for Katie Lynn and they could have their grand reunion.

❖

"You holding up okay?" Ross Verde, Emma's father, asked Cain when they got back home.

"I'll survive this too, but I'll miss him," Cain said, and poured them both a little brandy. "I hope he knows how special he was to me."

"You're good at getting your feelings across, don't worry about that. I've always known where I stood with you, and we haven't discussed the subject much."

"Thanks, Ross, and thank you for not going back to the farm." The sunroom was quiet, but outside she glimpsed the heightened security Lou had put in place. "You're good for your daughter and I don't need her stressed right now."

"She looked a little upset tonight," Ross said, his eyes on his glass. It was a habit she'd observed whenever he opened a subject that might upset her.

"Your little girl usually only gets upset by one thing, or should I say one person—me." Her admission made him seem to lose interest in the amber liquid. "When she came back here we agreed to two things."

"What's that?"

"That she wouldn't tell anyone that she'd kicked my ass for being a stubborn bastard and dragging my tail when it came to what I wanted—

what we both wanted." They both laughed. "And that I wouldn't keep her in the dark about anything she had a desire to know."

Ross's nod seemed more out of habit than agreement. "What about tonight made her feel otherwise? If you want to talk about it, that is."

"Hector Delarosa's sudden appearance surprised her." Cain's glass was empty, but anymore and sleep would elude her. "He surprised me too, in a way I don't like."

"I'm sorry I thought you'd kept that from me," Emma said as she entered the sunroom. She had traded her dress for the linen robe Cain had brought home the day before as a gift.

"Who's this guy?" Ross asked.

"From what little information I've found on Hector, he's third from the top of the Colombian drug cartel. And with his style and ambition he probably won't have much trouble convincing *himself* that he needs a promotion." Emma sat on the arm of Cain's chair and smiled at the gentle caress to her cheek. "He's the kind of guy that attracts a lot of attention from people I go out of my way to avoid."

"All you big fish attract the Feds," Ross said, and laughed.

"Compared to Hector I'm a minnow in a ditch."

"Not to me, baby," Emma said, and kissed her. "Muriel's girl almost lost an eye, though, when he walked in."

"Shelby isn't our problem because no matter how hard she looks, she'll never find drugs in my business." Cain sat back when Emma decided to join her. "It's idiots like Juan who worry me if they get the impression I'd ever go into business with them."

"I'm here for you if you need my help with anything," Ross said. He kissed Emma good night and placed his hand on Cain's shoulder before he left for his room.

"He really likes you," Emma said. "It makes me sad he missed out on so much when Hayden was born."

"Ross doesn't seem like the type to dwell on the past, so he's building a good relationship with our boy." The temptation to place her hand over Emma's middle was one she never deprived herself of, so she gave in. "Girl, you think?"

"William Cain won't sound too good if it's a girl, so you'll have to trust me, mobster. It's a boy."

"You didn't peek at the doctor's office, did you?"

"When it comes to carrying your baby, I know the difference. It's a boy."

Emma's comment stoked the embers of Cain's ego and her libido. The means for them to conceive might've come from Cain's brother, Billy, but in her heart, Cain felt the children belonged to her alone.

"Mrs. Casey, you do have a way of putting things that makes me want to prove myself to you," she said, and placed her hand inside Emma's robe.

"I'd love nothing better, but don't feel bad if you want to pass because of everything that's going on. You must be tired." Emma ran her fingers along Cain's cheeks and around her lips.

"Do you know what I want?" The silky material of Emma's nightgown made it easier for Cain to move her hand down to the hem.

"I'm getting the general idea," Emma said, and laughed softly.

"The day I get that predictable, lass, is the day I check into a retirement home." She took her time stroking up Emma's legs to the apex of her thighs. The pretty pink panties she'd helped Emma on with after their shower were gone so it was easy to feel how wet Emma was. "After we have Hayden's party I want to have one of our own."

"What's the occasion?" The timbre of Emma's voice hadn't changed but she did open her legs wider.

"A wedding, or at least a ceremony so I can tell everyone we love how much I love you," she said, spreading Emma open and wetting her fingers enough that they glided over the stone-hard clitoris with ease.

"Baby," Emma stopped and leaned farther into her, "we need to go upstairs."

"Not yet." She circled the opening of Emma's sex but didn't push inside. When she laughed at the way Emma's hips tried to chase her hand up, she got a swift pinch to her nipple.

"I thought you weren't interested in a ceremony," Emma said, returning to the topic as punishment, Cain was sure.

"This isn't all about me, and I don't want you to miss out on anything you want. But don't think I'm doing something I'd feel uncomfortable with. I plan to enjoy it as much as you."

"We don't have to plan it right now, do we?" Emma sounded close to desperate.

She didn't want to move, but staying meant Emma would have to keep her clothes on. "I want you so bad I can almost taste you."

And that's what she wanted too—to put her mouth on Emma until she'd drained every bit of want out of her for the night. Years of knowing Emma intimately, though, made her realize her release wouldn't wait that long, so Cain inched her fingers in, letting her wife set their pace.

"Later, I promise," Emma said, raking her hand up into Cain's hair and bringing her head forward, "but right now I need you."

It was fast and she swallowed every one of Emma's moans when Emma pressed her lips to hers.

"If my father had walked in here I'd have died of embarrassment, you know that, right?" Emma asked as she lazily ran the tip of her tongue along Cain's lips.

"He closed the doors and dimmed the lights on his way out," she said, her fingers still inside Emma. "I'd be willing to bet he locked them too. He must be on to the fact that I'm a beast when it comes to you."

"How lucky am I, then?" Emma laughed then kissed her.

"Come on. The next part of our evening requires fewer clothes, and the bed." When she stood up Emma wrapped her hands around her neck and, with a little help, her legs around her waist.

This was Cain's salvation, because while the problems and sadness were always still waiting, with Emma she could bury them at least for the night. That was true even if all they did was hold each other so Cain could feel Emma's breath against her skin.

❖

"What do you think Hector wants?" Emma asked a few hours later.

"Leverage is my best guess. I don't follow the drug trade as closely as I should, but I understand there's a power grab going on in Mexico. That means bloodshed there, in Colombia, and here." Emma's skin felt hot against hers, which made her want to drop the conversation, but Emma wanted to know. "New York, Miami, and LA are much bigger markets, but he needs to make inroads here if he wants to outmaneuver any competition."

When Emma rolled over and landed on top of her it was hard to ignore just how rigid her nipples were as they pressed into her chest. "Why do you think that?" Emma asked, her knee landing between Cain's legs.

"Is this really something you want to cover now?" Carefully she rolled them over again so Emma was under her, but she kept her weight off her as much as possible. She wanted to fix her lips around a hard pink nub and not release it until Emma came. "I've got a better bedtime story than that."

Before Emma could turn her down, she worked her hand between them and squeezed Emma's clit between her fingers, then sucked a nipple into her mouth. Later in the pregnancy she wouldn't dare give Emma's breasts this kind of treatment, but now her wife's desire demanded that she be able to feel her teeth scrape along her nipple as she sucked hard enough to almost bruise her skin.

Emma was wet and uttered a keening moan as she pulled Cain's hair to keep her in place. Her green eyes were closed, and when Cain glanced up at her she came close to opening her mouth and letting go. They were married in her eyes and their relationship was so much more than sex, but with her skin flushed and her head thrown back like this, Emma was hers. This part of her belonged to only Cain and she reveled in the fact as she slid her fingers inside Emma.

"Harder, baby," Emma said as the pad of Cain's thumb hit her clitoris every time her hips rose off the bed. "Harder," she repeated as she pulled her hair again.

It was a gift to watch as Emma became lost in the passion she herself had initiated hours before, and Cain wanted to make it last. But Emma's orgasm started the moment Cain felt the walls of her sex clamp down on her fingers and was over way too fast.

"Oh, God, that felt good," Emma said when she was able to slow her breathing some.

"Have I neglected lately to tell you how beautiful you are?"

"My romantic devil," Emma said, and ran her fingers down Cain's cheek to her neck. "You could never tell me again and I'd still know from the way you look at me." Cain's fingers were still buried deep inside, but Emma ignored the wonderful sensation when she saw the tendrils of sadness in and around Cain's eyes, even though she was smiling. "Are you okay?"

"Uncle Jarvis took me by surprise and I'm still trying to adjust. Nothing to worry about."

"That's my job, love, and even if you'd known how sick he was, would you have done anything differently?"

As if to give her question its due, Cain closed her eyes for a moment, then shook her head. "Not too much, but I wish I could say the same for Muriel."

"Muriel's in for a hard lesson about ambition, and not even you can save her from it." She gasped a little when Cain pulled out, but was able then to snuggle up to her side when Cain lay down. "Shelby seems pleasant enough, but something's off about their relationship."

"Muriel was raised with only a toe in the business, though she understands the big picture of our operation from every aspect no matter if she has the specifics or not. Whatever happens with Shelby, she'll be okay and she'd never betray me." As Cain ran her fingers in a circle on Emma's back, her breathing deepened as if sleep wasn't too far off. "She'll be okay because we'll be here for her no matter what. Everyone lives life differently when they know there'll always be a safety net."

"I understand that, baby," Emma said, but kept the rest of what she thought to herself. Her experiences with Cain had given her the greatest joy of her life, but when betrayed, Cain was sometimes blinded to who you were and what you meant to her. If Muriel somehow helped Shelby try to bring Cain down, Emma wasn't sure how quick the fog of rage would clear so Cain would remember what she'd promised Jarvis.

"Or if I'd beat you to it," she whispered with her cheek pressed to Cain's chest, enjoying the steady, slow heartbeat under her ear. Keeping Cain and her family whole was the only thing Emma would be capable of killing for, and that notion didn't surprise her any more than her acceptance of who and what her lover was. Cain was worth everything to her, and if pressed, she'd prove it to anyone who stood between them.

CHAPTER SIX

"Try and get some sleep," Shelby said to Muriel when they were finally alone in Muriel's room. "Tomorrow'll be hard enough, so don't make it worse by being exhausted."

"Go to bed if you want. I'm not sleepy."

Muriel sounded as if she wanted to pick a fight and Shelby was the nearest target. "It won't work, so why don't you just relax and lie here with me," she said, patting the space next to her.

"What?" Muriel stared at her in confusion.

"You aren't going to push me away," she said, standing and moving to Muriel. The only thing Muriel had removed was her jacket, but when Shelby reached for the buttons of her shirt Muriel stopped her.

"I'm not trying to push you away, but I'm not in the mood for company either," Muriel said, letting go of her wrists. "Why don't you go home and come back tomorrow? If you're worried about security, don't be. I'll leave word to let you in."

"You seem to have forgotten who I am to you in the span of a night." Shelby turned and faced the bed. "I thought we'd worked through the bullshit."

The intercom sounded loud in the suddenly quiet room. "Who?" Muriel asked whoever had interrupted them. "I'll be down in a minute."

"It's late, sweetheart. Can't it wait?"

"Go home, Shelby, and I'll see you tomorrow." Muriel waved her through the open door and walked her down to the front door. The woman sitting in the den was young but beautiful, and Shelby almost tripped over her feet trying to place her. "Have one of the guys drive Ms. Phillips home," Muriel told the guard outside. It wasn't until Shelby was halfway home that she realized who the young woman was, but the visit didn't make any sense.

Muriel was having similar thoughts as she walked toward Sabana Greco. Cain had sent the sister of her late guard Rick away since his murder and every couple of weeks denied her request to return.

"Sabana." Muriel accepted her hand before sitting across from her. "What are you doing here?"

"Returning the favor you and your cousin gave my mom and me after Rick." Sabana was short, but she looked good in her slacks and sleeveless tight shirt. Her brown hair was pulled into a ponytail at her neck and Muriel guessed it would reach slightly past her shoulders if she released it. "I'm sorry to get here so late, but my condolences about your father."

"Thank you, and considering how little time it's been since Rick was killed, you probably understand more than most." During that funeral Muriel had been so consumed by everything else going on that she never really took note of the grieving sister. Sabana might've been short but her body seemed strong, and her face was beautiful even though untouched by makeup.

"The shock's the hardest to forget." Sabana crossed her legs and laced her fingers around her knee. "No matter what you went through with them when they were alive that made you expect that they wouldn't be here for you, you never suspect that your last conversation will really be your last. You know what I mean. I have talks with Rick all the time now about the stuff I should've said when he was only a phone call away."

"Cain told me that, and that time dulls the pain though it never really leaves you." Regardless of Sabana's motives for being there, Muriel was glad for the company. "Can I get you something?"

"A glass of water, thanks."

Sabana followed her to the kitchen and they ended up sitting to share some of Vincent's carrot cake.

"Is it all right if I come tomorrow?" Sabana asked. "It's cool to say no if you want."

"It's fine with me, but I won't be able to keep Cain from voicing an opinion."

"Tonight and tomorrow I'm here for you, Muriel. We might not know each other well, but I do understand all this." Sabana reached across the granite island and placed her hands over Muriel's. "My father and my brother worked for your family, so I understand what your dad meant to you. If you ever need anything, I'll be around."

The gesture was sweet and probably not something Sabana did often, which made it comforting. "I'll remember that."

"That woman who just left," Sabana said, pointing. "She was the one who came to our house from the FBI after Rick, isn't she?"

"Yes, is that a problem?"

"She tried to get me to talk about Cain."

Muriel nodded; despite her protests to Shelby, she was tired. "That's part of her job."

"Her job was to find who killed Rick, and it wasn't Cain." Sabana seemed to be stating a fact rather than disagreeing with her.

"It's Cain's theory of small and big fish. I don't agree with how Shelby does her job, but she's important to me." Muriel guessed Sabana to be twenty-four, at most, but she showed very little emotion for someone so young. Her face had stayed neutral throughout their conversation. "You want to tell me why you're really here? And no bullshit about my feelings. I'm not in the mood for games." Her initial feeling for Sabana was bleeding away as if someone had cut a major artery.

Sabana's confident veneer slipped a bit when Sabana lost eye contact with her, and she waited to see if Sabana would tell her the truth. At least what she surmised the truth to be.

"I do feel for you because of your father, but that's not the only reason I'm here."

"That I know. But I don't know if you'll be honest about the real reason."

"There's no mystery in what happened to your father, and while it's harsh, no one's really at fault." Sabana looked up at her again but the way she spoke made Muriel feel her vulnerability. "That's not true with Rick, and I want my pound."

"I never asked about your brother, and I'm sorry about that, but I'm sure Cain's collected all there was on that score. What else is there for you to prove?"

Sabana stood, took a deep breath, and held it as if that was her technique of trying to calm a sudden rage. "I'll see you tomorrow, and I'm sorry I bothered you tonight."

"No answer for me?"

"If you don't understand by now that it's more than just the guy who pulled the trigger, then I sure as hell don't have a shot at educating you because I'm sure better people have explained it already." Sabana's fists beat a constant rhythm against her thigh as she spoke, her words clipped. "Cain's successful because people like my family are willing to stay loyal to her, but that works both ways."

"Is that a threat?"

"I'm not an idiot, Muriel, so don't insult me." Sabana pointed at her, then dropped her hand quickly. "I'm sorry about your dad, but the rest is between Cain and me."

Muriel watched her go, and once the door slammed a silence she'd never experienced closed in on her and fear grabbed her so hard her chest hurt. She had always known who she was, and that constant had helped fuel her confidence. A lot of that self-assurance had been tied up with her father, and he was gone.

"Da, I wasn't ready. What do I do now?"

❖

The mild weather broke the next morning, with the north wind bringing the temperature down significantly. The cool made the morning feel even more somber as the limos pulled up to Muriel's house.

"Why does life seem like we're in limbo?" Emma asked Cain when the car stopped but Cain made no move to get out. "Or am I crazy for thinking that way?"

The front door opened and Muriel walked out holding Shelby's hand, but she appeared angry instead of sad. Cain fanned the fingers of her left hand out and her nostrils flared slightly. That Muriel and her partner weren't getting along, or at least weren't as close as they should be, would make the day grueling.

"When we get home tonight, I promise we'll have a long talk about what happens now," Cain said, her eyes never leaving the window as she stared at Muriel. "And you aren't crazy, lass. You feel the same way I do, and mine is because my world has narrowed."

"That sounds like a bad thing."

"No, it's only reality, love." Cain squeezed her fingers gently.

They were alone, having left the kids at home over Hayden's objections, and Emma was enjoying having Cain to herself if only for the drive to the cathedral.

"My world has narrowed to only you when it comes to total trust."

"Baby, Muriel would no more betray you than she would take her own life. Don't torture yourself."

The limo door closed, and with the dark-tinted windows, Muriel and Shelby disappeared inside. Only then did Cain look at her. "Do you really want me to take that chance?" Cain's words were as straightforward as they were simple.

Emma knew Cain wasn't disappointed in her but was concealing her feelings so Emma could make up her own mind. She sensed Muriel wouldn't throw away or trade her honor for love, but she wasn't absolutely sure. Love made you view the world differently sometimes in order to keep what was yours. Would Muriel cave on something that would hurt Cain in order to keep what was precious to her?

"No," Emma said without hesitation. "I promise your view might be narrow, as you put it, but it's yours alone."

"Then between you and me, I'm sad. Losing Uncle Jarvis was bad, but he's beyond my reach now. Muriel, though, is here, but because of a simple choice on her part, she's just as out of my grasp."

Emma knew the admission was hard, and she hurt for Cain's dual mourning.

"That's not forever, my love. Wait this one out and you'll see I'm right."

"What makes you so sure?"

"Because you can't leave that much of yourself behind in order to make someone happy. You can pull it off for a while, but then love turns to resentment when the other person doesn't commit fully."

"Muriel is willing but Shelby's not as in love?"

"More like Muriel's lost and in search of her place, but Shelby doesn't have that problem. She knows who she is and what she's after."

"As much crap as we've been through, I wouldn't change a moment of our time together," Cain said, and paused. "You are my idea of perfection and you understand me so well you could be dangerous." She kissed the tip of Emma's nose.

Their car stopped in front of the park and Cain glanced in the direction of the beautiful wrought-iron gate that surrounded Jackson Square. "Funerals, weddings, baptisms—they never rest, do they?" Cain said of the two agents who stood at the gate.

"Not our worry today, mobster." Emma squeezed Cain's hand

between hers and smiled. "All you have to worry about is sending Jarvis home to your family."

Bishop Andrew was standing outside and opened his arms to Emma first. When it was Cain's turn he held her longer and whispered something to her that Emma couldn't make out, but it made Cain smile. Watching them, she knew Cain was partly wrong about who she could totally trust. Father Andy had dinner at their house at least once a month, which the kids enjoyed because of his sharp sense of humor and bucket loads of patience. But Cain enjoyed their after-dinner conversation in her office. Behind that closed door was as close as Cain got to confession, Emma was sure, but she knew whatever was said wouldn't go any further.

"Take this lovely lady inside, Derby Cain," Father Andrew said so Emma could hear him. "Because I think those nice people across the way have stared at you long enough."

"Good idea. I could spend my time praying for lightning," Cain said, and smiled.

❖

Gracelia stopped flipping through her magazine when she reached a page with pictures of who the article's writer thought were the top dealers in the Colombian drug trade. Hector Delarosa was pictured second from the top of a tree illustrated on the page. The top box displayed only a shadow because the real head of the cartel was supposedly unknown. The tree growing on the northern side of the border in Mexico didn't have that problem, and the top picture was of Rodolfo.

"You're still a pig, brother, but you look fit," she said to the page. He'd aged, though, possibly because his family had abandoned him, a choice that rested solely on his shoulders.

She still remembered every detail of the afternoon he came home and told her that her lover Armando wouldn't be coming back. It had taken her over a month to find out exactly what happened to him, and the shock of Rodolfo's cruelty had almost made her lose Juan. She and Armando didn't have any secrets between them, so she'd believed him when he promised he was coming back to her and their child. Granted, she would never tame him completely, but that's what she'd loved about him.

"It's time to prune this family tree, Rodolfo, and my waiting is at an end," she said when she finished the article that contained very few facts.

"Ms. Ortega." The man standing before her pulled off his surgical cap as he addressed her. "It's done and it went fine. We tried to give you everything you wanted, and we came close, but we couldn't do the impossible."

"How long before he's ready?"

"In a few hours. We'll need to see him in two weeks to remove the stitches. He'll still be swollen then, but if you keep him still that shouldn't be too much of a problem."

"Is he awake?" Gracelia stood and dropped the magazine into the trash.

"I made sure before I came out," he said, and swept his arm toward the correct entrance.

She stood next to the bed and stared into the dark brown eyes that, from the moment Anthony stepped before her, had reminded her of Armando's. The doctor had wrapped his face in gauze bandages so there were only slits over his eyes and mouth.

"Don't try to talk," she said, placing her hand on his chest. "You're almost done and I plan to take care of you." Anthony blinked and seemed unfocused. "Now you can stop running and take control again."

She leaned over him and whispered into the vicinity of his ear. "You won't regret this because I will share the world I'm about to take over with you."

"Mama," Juan said from behind her.

Gracelia turned around and had to stare for a minute, still trying to get used to the new face that went with the voice she knew so well. "Juan." She held her hand out to him.

"How is he?"

"Good, and hopefully he'll heal as quickly as you."

Juan had undergone plastic surgery the night after they arrived, and while he still had a lot of swelling, she could already tell how different his appearance was. The doctor had erased much of the roundness of his face and the plumpness of his nose, and with his new dark blond hair, he looked very American.

"Alberto got back an hour ago, and he has news."

Gracelia placed her hand briefly on Anthony's shoulder before she pointed toward the door. The waiting room was still empty, thanks to

Lorenzo's quiet presence at the entrance. Lorenzo Mendoza had worked for Rodolfo for years and had gladly left his job with her brother to go with her when Rodolfo took Juan to the States on business. He was older, but had had good instincts and Gracelia had come to totally trust him, so she didn't hesitate to talk in front of him.

"What did he say?" she asked.

"Rodolfo's still in New Orleans, but his man Santos comes in from Biloxi every few days to give Rodolfo updates. So far both the New Orleans and Mississippi operations have blown up on him and he lays the blame mainly on Cain Casey. Your brother thinks that since he made the mistake of getting greedy and taking over some of Casey's territory, Casey's wiped out a majority of his street dealers, which sucks for him since he wanted to control everything from the fields to the dime bags on the street." The skin around his eyes appeared to be bothering him by the way he gently but methodically rubbed his eyebrows.

"Rodolfo has made some stupid decisions, but that wasn't one of them. Controlling everything at every stage was smart business, and that's how we'll do it. The difference will be which people we use, so what's been lost isn't a problem for us." She looked back at Anthony and knew he was the key to getting what she wanted.

Anthony Curtis, in her opinion, had no more quit the FBI than she had forgotten what Rodolfo had done to the man she loved. He might have done some things without the permission of his superiors, but his ultimate goal was to go back and reclaim what he'd lost. When he could work it out, Anthony would trade Juan and her for his mistakes.

I won't give you the chance, though, because I intend to pull you down so deep I'll be the only one who can keep you alive, Gracelia thought. She knew how she'd accomplish that, and the best way wasn't to challenge the Feds and the other cartels directly, but to hit where no one expected. Some would think that was a clichéd approach, but she planned to destroy her opponents psychologically by destroying something they thought was safe and not an important part of their business. As a bonus she'd get Anthony completely on her side, along with insight on how the FBI and DEA would try to stop her.

"Go home and get some rest. Pretty soon we'll put things in motion, and I need you to see all this through." She took Juan's hands and kissed them. "Whatever feelings about Rodolfo you have inside, it's almost time to let them out, but we have to be smart. Think about what you want and embrace this chance, Gustavo Katsura." She kissed his cheek and let the new name that would complete his new identity hit his ears. Armando's grandfather's name was Gustavo, which was her only bow to sentiment. She had picked the last name from the phone book. Emotions sank most people, and she refused to be beaten before she got a chance to try.

CHAPTER SEVEN

Remi sat two pews back from Cain and held Dallas's hand. They'd gotten up early and driven to the airport to pick up Kristen Montgomery, so her nights with Dallas were over until Dallas accepted her offer to live together. Remi wanted to be upset but it was hard, considering how happy the sisters looked even at a funeral.

Dallas's sister strongly resembled her, but Kristen's hair was a deep brown that reminded her of milk chocolate, which set off eyes the same shade of blue as Dallas's beautifully. If Remi had been expecting Kristen to be standoffish, and she had, Kristen dispelled that fear when she hugged her right after she released Dallas. It was, she'd said, the best way to thank her for finally setting Dallas free.

The mass was almost over and she was sending Dallas and Kristen home to reconnect while she went to the cemetery. "Emil will drive you home after this," she said as the last of those receiving communion went through the line. "If you want, I'll stop by later and drop off dinner so you two won't have to go out."

"Bring your pajamas."

"Not here, baby," she said with a smile. "I've got work tonight and I don't know how long I'll be."

"We'll talk later, then, because this," Dallas lifted her other hand, which Kristen was holding, "doesn't change anything."

Cain stood and walked to the altar after the service ended, placing her hand on the coffin as she passed it. When Cain stepped behind the pulpit Remi wondered what it was like to have lived a life touched by so much loss.

"On behalf of the Casey family, thank you for coming to honor the life and memory of Jarvis Michael Casey. If you know us well, I don't have to elaborate on how important tradition is to our family." Almost everyone, including Remi, laughed. "Traditions are important because they provide a roadmap of the future, but they can also be a heavy burden to carry when it's your turn at the yoke.

"Uncle Jarvis carried the weight of the past with ease and honor, doing our ancestors proud by his contributions—the most important two being Muriel and the way he lived his life. We will miss him, his advice, the gentle way he guided us when we tried to take a shortcut along that proven roadmap, and simply because he loved like he lived. He did that without fear and by giving us more than we deserved sometimes." Cain paused and gripped the old wooden slab that the pulpit was made of. Then she took a deep breath.

"I can recall my grandfather saying what every Casey child hears as a welcome to the world. My da said it to me and mine, just as Jarvis said it to Muriel." She took a flask with a small cup for a top from her coat pocket.

"The Catholics, they get a hold of you soon enough, but the whiskey—that's a Casey baptism." She poured a bit of whatever was in the flask into the cup. "No oil or water a priest pours over you can wash that away, no offense, Father Andy. The whiskey's our business, our heritage, our history, and you did well keeping the traditions alive when it was your responsibility to do so, Jarvis. Our mothers, like you, Father Andy," Cain raised the cup in his direction, then toward Jarvis's casket, "didn't understand that first taste was a welcome to a Casey. A reminder of who we are and where we came from." She drank and capped the flask.

"You were a Casey, and a fine damned good one, Jarvis. You were ours, but for too short a time. Now it's our turn to send you off from this world, but with the certainty that a clan up there is waiting for you where the love and the whiskey never run dry."

"Amen," the Casey family members said in unison when she was done.

The funeral pall was removed from the coffin and Remi took her place with the other pallbearers. After they placed the coffin in the hearse, the cars started to pull up behind it. Muriel and Shelby's was first, followed by Cain and Emma's. Remi saw hers fifth in line and figured Dallas and Kristen could take it and she would ride with her parents.

"Are you trying to get rid of me for a reason?" Dallas asked softly. The question held a tinge of disappointment.

"You know better than that, *querida*. Your sister just got here today and I thought this was the last thing you'd want to be doing."

Emil held the door and stayed quiet as Dallas looked up at Remi. "I'm telling Emil to drive me to the cemetery, so you can either come with us or walk, but we'll end up at the same place."

"You should know better by now," Emil said after Dallas and Kristen got in.

"You'd think," Remi said, and laughed. No one liked getting a lecture, especially Remi, but Dallas's words showed they were making progress.

"I'm glad you made the right choice," Kristen said when she climbed in and sat next to Dallas. "But then my sister keeps going on about how wonderful and smart you are."

"A compliment I don't deserve, I'm sure."

Dallas put her hand on Remi's thigh and patted it gently, as if rewarding her dumb-witted response.

"Were you close to Mr. Casey?" Kristen asked, obviously trying to keep up the conversation.

"I knew him practically my whole life after my family arrived in the States." She glanced though the windshield at the hearse. "It's a shame we wait for days like today to realize or admit that we should've spent more time with people like Jarvis."

"That's what I've always thought about Dallas, but it hasn't been safe up to now for us to have that opportunity." Kristen's voice cracked midway through her statement, and Dallas put an arm around her shoulders and pulled her closer.

"Time is a given now, Kristen, not a luxury," Remi said as her phone rang softly.

"Remi, I just got a call from the building supervisor," Simon Jimenez, Remi's main guard, said from the car behind them.

"Is the bathtub leaking or something?" It had to be more for the usually serious Simon to make the call.

"Something's leaking, all right, but it's not anything at your place."

"Elaboration would be good," she said, and laughed.

"A supposed private delivery service dropped off a large box for you at your apartment, and even though a plastic sheet was duct-taped around it, the damn thing was leaking. The doorman called the super because of the smell, and the super ended up calling the cops."

"What the hell...or should I ask *who* the hell was it?"

"Wendy Bruster, and whoever was stupid enough to do this made the body ID easier by stapling her work badge to her forehead."

Remi pinched the bridge of her nose and closed her eyes, trying to conjure up a face to go with the name Simon had provided. When nothing clicked, a string of curses ran through her mind. "What did Wendy do for us?"

"She was one of the new bartenders at Pescadors, and not even the cops have an accurate tally of who works for us where."

Simon had said Pescadors, not the club. Ramon's main interest was the upstairs portion of the business where the gaming tables were located. He referred to the first floor as "the club," which was merely a necessity that had conveniently made money for them because of its popularity after hours. If Wendy had been cleared to work upstairs, Remi's father had checked out everything about her life.

"Call one of the guys and get over there and see what this is about." This could be aimed at them, but the majority of their business took place after dark and at times it attracted employees who were magnets for trouble. It took a different type to work nights in that environment. Such bartenders needed to enjoy crowded bars and dealing with every kind of personality on the other side of the oak. None of their employees had been killed in years. With time Ramon had acquired power along with money and had protected their staff.

"I'll leave from the cemetery."

"What's wrong?" Dallas asked when she ended the call.

"Someone's idea of a sick joke that I'll tell you about later."

She shook her head when Dallas said, "But—"

"Not now, trust me."

They stopped outside the cemetery, and Emil got out and waited to open the car door. Remi smiled when her parents stopped and hugged Emil, since he was now permanently with Dallas and they saw him more often when they spent time with Dallas. Judging from the set of her father's mouth, Simon had already told him what had happened.

"Honey, I think they're starting," Dallas said, causing her to tap the window for Emil to open the door.

Even though the family cars had already driven in, Cain walked back to the gate and waved her over. "Did you get a gift today?" Cain whispered close to her ear.

"At my house just now, yeah. Simon told me a private courier service that didn't make it past the lobby brought it."

Cain nodded and guided her to the first row of tombs. "Who was it?"

"A new bartender at Pescadors. Her name was Wendy and I wish I could tell you something about her, but I've never met her. Who told you?"

"Same thing at my place, only the boxes were dropped off in the alley behind Emma's."

"Boxes?" She slumped against the tall brick wall that surrounded the cemetery and exhaled deeply. "How many?"

"Five, from what I understand, and hopefully there aren't any at the pub in the Quarter." Lou cleared his throat behind them and Cain nodded again. "Today isn't the day for this shit, but we'll have to deal with it as soon as we're done here."

"You have any ideas?" They didn't really have time for Cain to answer fully, but she was curious about the bizarre message someone was trying to send.

"Not yet, but my best guess is someone thinks we're distracted," Cain said, her eyes pinned to something behind her. When Remi turned, she realized Cain was staring at Dallas and her sister walking in with her parents. "I don't know about you, but Emma is the only person alive who can drive me to distraction."

"When it comes to Dallas, I'd say we have something in common, then."

"Good thing for the women in our lives, but not for the asshole sending gifts. I'm going to feed them a roll of tape until they choke on it."

❖

Shelby stood next to Muriel as the pallbearers removed the casket from the hearse. The mausoleum next to the one that held Cain's side of the Casey family was barely visible through the sea of flowers.

That's not what held her interest, though. In her experience with funerals, which was her grandmother's service when she was twelve, the people who'd attended had told her family good-bye at the church. Only her parents and grandfather had been at the burial site as the preacher said the final prayers.

Jarvis's day had been something foreign to her from the start, and it was ending with a sea of people whose numbers rivaled the blooms blanketing the area. All of them truly seemed to mourn his passing as if they'd lost a big part of their private brethren.

If she had one wish, it would be to know their stories—every detail of their lives, not only for her job, but simply because the way they lived every day on the edge of ruination fascinated her.

Her phone vibrated on her hip and she wanted to ignore it as they set the coffin on a wheeled stand on the path leading to the mausoleum. But she answered when she recognized the number as the secure line Annabel had set up to communicate with her during this assignment. If Cain somehow got the information, it would trace back to her ninety-two-year-old grandfather in California.

"Hey, Granddad," she said for Muriel's benefit, then turned and stepped away. "I'm at a funeral and don't have a lot of time." The reminder was more filler than information. Annabel knew exactly where she was, and Shelby truly didn't have much time. The team's new leader, Joe, was standing with a new guy at the gate. One of the good things about this assignment would be to figure out how to make the surveillance harder to spot.

Annabel quickly told her about the new developments and how she was working on a warrant for Emma's and the security footage she was sure Cain's people had removed from the cameras their people had spotted when they arrived on the scene.

"Don't lose sight of Muriel today, and call me if there's anything new from your end. Maybe the distraction of her father's death will help us finally get somewhere."

"I'll call you later, then." When she turned around Cain was staring at her with a perturbed look. Shelby was sure her lack of respect had caused the reaction.

"I'm sorry," she said to Muriel. "Granddad forgot where I was and he sends his condolences."

Shelby took her place by Muriel's side and wrapped her hand in the bend of Muriel's elbow. As Muriel placed her hand over hers, Shelby had a feeling this would be the first of many funerals to come. Annabel's news implied that Jarvis's death had caused a break in the peace that people like Cain, Ramon, and Vincent had achieved. Not that Jarvis was a major player, but his passing was like the end of an era. What would follow was an unknown.

CHAPTER EIGHT

"Y our honor," Sanders Riggole said from the comfortable leather chair in Federal Judge Winston Lemoine's office. Sanders was an associate in Muriel's office, and his opportunity to impress his boss had finally come. He wasn't about to miss the chance to pay off his lingering student loans. "On behalf of my client I take offense that the government continues to think we're hiding something."

"What we're asking for isn't unreasonable, Judge," the federal attorney said. "Our investigation is beginning, and considering it concerns five Casey employees, Ms. Casey's attorney should be more cooperative. Or are they holding back crucial evidence because it implicates his client?"

"If we'd been in open court I'd have slapped you down for that one," Winston said, pointing to the young prosecutor Annabel had sent for what Sanders imagined she thought was a slam dunk. "What exactly do you believe the management at Emma's is holding back? From your report, they turned over the security tapes and gave you access to the cleaning staff who found the boxes."

"We don't know if they're hiding anything unless you grant us the right to enter the goddamn building, your honor."

Winston stood and slammed his hands down on the spotless desk. "Boy, does this look like a cheap barroom to you?"

"No, sir."

His response sounded contrite enough to Sanders, but the damage was done. Back at the office Muriel kept a meticulous file detailing the likes and dislikes of every judge in their jurisdiction, and at the top of Winston Lemoine's tally of dislikes was using the Lord's name in vain for any reason.

Twice a month, Winston frequented the high priced-call girls who worked Ramon's club to get his dose of submission, which always was at the end of a flog wielded by a beautiful woman in high red spiked heels, but the man had to have some enjoyment in life. And even though the girls whipped hard enough to make Winston cry as he jerked off on those shiny red shoes, he never uttered one curse word.

"Your honor," Sanders said, and placed his right hand over his heart, "I can assure you as a Christian that they have everything we had as far as surveillance footage to investigate what happened. But please remember that our law offices are also in that building, and the hub for the security cameras is located on the same floor. This would be an opportunity for the government to trample Ms. Casey's attorney/client privilege."

"Are you willing to let my investigator in with a strict set of parameters as to what needs to be looked at?" Winston asked.

"Certainly, your honor. We have faith in you to protect Ms. Casey's civil liberties."

"With respect, sir," the prosecutor said.

"The warrant is granted. Only my office will execute it," Winston said.

"Sir, our agents will be seriously impeded if they are not allowed in the building, so I ask you to reconsider."

"Do you have the tapes?" Winston asked.

"Yes, sir."

"Did your lab prove they've been tampered with in any way?"

"No, sir."

"Then I seriously doubt you'll stumble on a group of people covered in blood hiding in the Casey Law Firm. You can accept my compromise or appeal—your choice. I doubt that a higher court will overturn this, especially after I call them."

The speech, Sanders knew from his limited experience, was Winston's warning shot across the bow. Attorneys who habitually appealed his decisions had to come back with clear-cut cases to get him to throw them a bone.

Winston's gavel came down and he stood when the prosecutor was smart enough to keep quiet. It might've been a small victory, but Sanders felt great. He'd kept them out, which not only was a win in court but a test of his loyalty.

And *he* was smart enough to know that his true employer rewarded loyalty above all else. To get what he wanted out of life, he needed to get Cain to notice what he could do for her. If that happened, then he could ask her to do what he couldn't do for himself.

❖

"Who were they?" Cain asked the group gathered in her office. She'd sent a reluctant Emma home with Dallas, Kristen, and Ramon's wife, Marianna.

"Two of the cleaning staff, a bartender, someone we haven't identified," Katlin said, then paused as if she knew Cain would have a real problem with who the last person was.

"You and the cops hovering outside like biting flies said five boxes. So far you've mentioned four," she said, already wanting to hit something or someone for taking six innocent lives to send whatever twisted message they had in mind. "Rip the bandage off already, cousin."

"Bryce was the last of our people and was the one with the most damage to his body. Whoever did this tortured him to try and get something out of him."

Bryce White was a young college dropout with a vast knowledge of the computers who made sure all Cain's phones and electronics were clean. Long ago, when she'd left for Wisconsin after Hayden, Bryce had made all the arrangements with Vincent and had carried out the surveillance on Barney Kyle. By his own admission he was a nerd who'd found in Cain someone who accepted him for who he was, and they'd both benefitted from the relationship.

Whoever had killed him had to have lured him out of the windowless room he'd designed when Muriel bought the building. And if they'd tortured him, they knew what Bryce did for her. If they broke him it wasn't devastating, but they would have to change a lot of their security.

"How hard is it to torture a kid who weighs maybe one-twenty soaking wet?" Cain asked, rolling her head around to crack the bones in her neck. "And there's another possibility, Katlin. They might have done it just for the hell of it."

"They'll get theirs soon enough, then," Katlin said.

"Who was it on your end?" Cain asked Remi.

"New bartender upstairs at the club. If you compare at least three of the ones on your side they're about the same level of employee, making Bryce the odd man out." Remi stood and took her jacket off. "What I haven't figured out is why."

"I'm sure you have a theory."

Ramon sat next to his daughter and flexed his hands but stayed quiet. He wasn't impatient. He was worried. He'd told Cain before the meeting that he hadn't been able to get in touch with his son, Mano, and it was driving him insane.

"If they were trying to prove we aren't untouchable, it wasn't much of a threat," Remi said. "Aside from Bryce not one person on the list was valuable to them, so why piss us both off?"

"What we need to figure out is who. Then we'll know the exact reason for the why. Right now I can only guess that it's a simple game of knocking over castles made of wooden blocks."

"I might need that one translated for me, Cain," Katlin said.

"Hannah's like me," she said as she brought her hand down and slapped her other one with it. "She likes to smash blocks from the top down, but if you start to pull blocks from the foundation, the house will crumble just the same."

"So someone's starting a war by taking out people who really have nothing to do with our big money-making businesses?" Remi asked. "Who's that stupid?"

"You can recite the list better than I can," she said before the intercom buzzed. "Yes?" she asked her secretary.

"I know you don't want any interruptions, but Nelson's on the line," she said, meaning the general manager of Emma's. "He wants to talk to you."

"What's going on?" Cain asked Nelson, figuring the building had to be on fire for her secretary to have put him through.

"The FBI is in here and upstairs looking around."

"Impossible. We won that battle this morning."

"Sanders called and told us what the score was, but the team who showed up said they got consent from Muriel. And since it's her office, they didn't need to follow the judge's ruling."

Cain stood and her chair crashed into the wall behind her. "Why are they in the club?"

"Muriel gave consent for that as well."

"Get Sanders on the phone right after you pull the fire alarm and evacuate the building." She knew she sounded calm, but inside, something cracked away from her heart, leaving a cold, empty hole.

The only thing that would've hurt more would've been if Emma had betrayed her.

"Katlin, find Muriel and tell her I need to speak to her." The phone was still in her hand, but she clenched it in the fist resting on the desktop. "Bring her to the house minus her new shadow, and I'll be there shortly."

"Where are you going?" Katlin asked.

"I didn't think I'd have to repeat myself, cousin. Right now isn't the time to ask questions." The receiver rocked a bit when she slammed it down and she put her fingers on it to make it stop. "Remi and Ramon, if you don't mind, we'll finish this later. I've got to take care of something."

"Cain, please." Katlin tried again when the room cleared. "You know I'd never question you about anything, but think before you do something that you can't take back. Muriel's lost, but she's family."

"Find her and drive her to the fucking house and wait for me. If that's too hard a job then tell me and I'll have Lou do it, but if I get there and see Shelby I'll assume your loyalties have gone off-kilter like Muriel's."

"You know better than that." Katlin put her hands on Cain's shoulders. "I don't have to look for Muriel, so why don't we both go to Emma's and talk to her."

If Muriel was there, then she knew the ruling Sanders had won in court. The gates were locked and yet Cain's enemies had slipped in easily because one of the people she trusted the most had opened them from the inside.

"She's there?" she asked, not wanting to believe that possibility.

"Cain, there's nothing in Emma's that will damage you, and Muriel knows better than to let them search her office."

"You look at me and tell me that six months ago Muriel and I would've had to have the conversation about to happen. Love comes to some of us and it awakens the blood of our family, but in others it brings only blindness."

Katlin nodded. "Not that long ago you thought I was blind."

"You were preoccupied with someone who knows nothing but loyalty, so that wasn't a problem." She glanced at the family photo on her desk and remembered the promise she'd made Emma and her uncle. "I know you think I'll be harsh, but I'm tired of beating my head against a wall trying to change something I can't."

"Can I ask what you plan to do about that?"

Cain opened the door and saw Lou talking to Sabana Greco. "When have you ever heard of me beating my head against anything?" The conversation across from her stopped.

"It's not the best time, but I need to talk to you," Sabana said.

"What's the word?" she asked Lou.

"The guys pulled the plug like you said, so everyone is in the parking lot while the fire-house guys from up the street check things out."

"Get in the car," Cain said to Sabana.

"I know you wanted—"

"The best option you have right now is to shut up." Control was something she'd always enjoyed and the reason she could live how she wanted. She couldn't figure how she'd lost that now that the rest of her life was perfect. Did people suddenly see only that part of her that was in love and had settled down and think she'd lost her edge?

"Tell me what you want," she said to Sabana.

"I want you to hand over the man who gave the order to kill Rick."

A perimeter of police, fire, and federal agents circled her club, giving Lou no choice but to stop so they could walk the rest of the way. "Lou, see if they'll let you through."

"You want to go inside if they're done?" Lou asked her.

"See if that's an option." While they waited she thought about Sabana's answer and how to some it would probably sound foolish. "If I do that, what do you plan to do with him?"

"You have to ask?" Sabana stared at her as if she'd suddenly lost her reasoning.

"Rick worked for me from the time your father passed away, so you know how long that was. He did his job well, did as he was told, and never unholstered his gun in all that time." Lou was walking back, obviously ignoring the short police officer following him.

"That's all true, but if something had happened to me or my mother, what do you think Rick would've done?"

Lou opened the door, a clear sign that she could enter the building if she wanted to. "Get with Lou later and work out where and when you start. I'll okay it after I hear from your most important reference."

"You know you can trust me."

She looked at Sabana and saw the same eagerness in her

expression that she saw on Hayden's face, and remembered how she felt at Sabana's age. She had considered only the freedoms that would come by embracing the lifestyle she wanted, but never imagined some of its burdens. "If I didn't trust you, Sabana, you wouldn't have made it through the door. This isn't about that," she said as she got out of the car and didn't stop Sabana from following her. "When I hear your mother's okay, you have a place with me."

"And if she doesn't give it?"

"We already have an agreement in place, and you'll have to live with it if you want to get anywhere with me."

Sabana walked fast enough to keep up with her, and Cain could tell the anger that drove her was on a thin leash below the surface. "And what if I just go it alone?"

"This is a free country, little girl, but if you decide to work alone, you'll be cut off from me and everyone who works for me." She stopped and locked eyes with her so there'd be no misunderstandings later. "That means no more advice from Uncle Lou and no one to cover your back."

"I didn't mean—"

"Do we understand each other? The answer is yes or no, so I don't need any other explanation."

"I understand perfectly, and I'll have Mama call you."

This would be a problem, she felt it in her gut, but if Sabana blew, she would do her best to guide her or at least aim her in the right direction. *Now, though, let me deal with the other cluster brewing in my life*, she thought as she entered Emma's, having passed the large group of federal agents who stood close to the door appearing anxious to swarm back in.

"The gatekeeper's back, boys and girls, so I don't think so," she said softly to the empty room, and empty is how she planned to keep it.

❖

"They said they don't give out that kind of information," Deidi Morgan said to Johnny outside the studio offices. The young prostitute had been as willing to go with him to start his search for his daughters as she had been to spend her nights with him. Or at least she'd kept mostly quiet as he painted her body with bruises.

"Did you tell them what I told you to?"

She nodded. "The woman in here said Dallas Montgomery doesn't have any sisters, and she'd call security if I didn't leave."

"Get in the truck." Johnny knew the studio would never give up Katie Lynn's home address, but he didn't think they would consider the information of whether she was in town or not to be a big deal. It didn't matter, though, since he'd demanded that Bob tell him where Katie Lynn was staying.

Her asshole manager had stalled at first, but relented when he'd threatened to find his daughter and take her back to where she belonged. Bob wasn't about to lose the little money-making bitch, so he'd given him the address.

"Where we going?" Deidi pressed herself against the truck door when he slapped the side of her head so hard his fingers stung.

"You think you can ask questions now?" he asked as he pulled over. "You're here to do what I say and that's it—you got me?" Deidi wouldn't look at him but she was nodding as he screamed at her. "If that's not something you want to do, then I'll fuck you one more time and put you back on the street where I found you."

"I'm sorry, Johnny. I won't do it again."

She flinched when he reached over and opened the glove compartment, sure that she'd noticed the pistol he kept in there. In the top section was the scrap of paper where he'd written Katie Lynn's address. "Where's this?" he asked.

"Not far if you head back that way," she said, pointing behind her.

"If you want out this is your chance."

Deidi stared at the still-open compartment before she looked over at him. She seemed to be a smart girl if she was thinking he would use that pistol on her. "You gonna pay me?"

"Every dime I owe you as soon as we're done." It wouldn't be hard to get rid of this one once he had what he came for, since she was beat down by life already. It hadn't taken much effort on his part. "But right now you need to get busy," he said, and unzipped his pants, guiding her head to his lap.

It wasn't Katie Lynn, not that she'd ever done this for him, but once he chained her to the bed she'd learn to do it as well as Deidi. No way would he leave someone like Bob in charge again. His daughters, his late wife kept telling him, were a gift from God, and it was past time to enjoy them.

CHAPTER NINE

Tomas Blanco stood at the door of the suite his boss Hector Delarosa had reserved at the cusp of the French Quarter. They had returned from Jarvis Casey's funeral to find Miguel Gonzales waiting for them after his flight from Bogota. The late-arriving Miguel was Hector's business manager, and aside from Tomas, whose responsibility it was to keep Hector safe, Miguel was the only man Hector trusted.

Hector and Miguel had their heads close together and had been in deep discussion for over an hour. The main topic was the dead bodies left behind Cain's club and at Remi's. Hector was pouring money on the street for information.

"Tomas, did we hear from Rodolfo yet?" Hector asked. They'd been up for hours but Hector, in his starched shirt and charcoal suit pants, still appeared full of energy even though it was midnight.

"Carlos, his head man, took my call, but not yet. You want me to try again?"

Hector laughed and relaxed back into the sofa. "The old man has to have some idea of what's coming. If he doesn't he's as out of touch as his nephew Juan said when he called me to make a deal."

"I'm surprised you haven't heard from that little idiot," he said, and Miguel nodded.

"He's lurking, I'm sure, but I want to get to Rodolfo first," Hector said. "We need to expand in places where it's not obvious we're stepping on anyone's territory, at least until we're ready to take over and have the muscle to back us up."

"From what I found out, Rodolfo is still in control in Mexico, but the headway he made here with Nunzio and Junior Luca's help is unraveling faster than he can keep up with," Miguel said.

"He hasn't gone back to Cozumel because Cain's breathing down on him so close it's fogging up his glasses." Hector glanced up when the extra bedroom door opened.

Marisol Delarosa, Hector's oldest daughter, had demanded to learn his business even though he wasn't convinced it was a good idea. Trying to change a twenty-five-year-old's mind was like trying to dig a ditch with a teaspoon—not impossible but more trouble than it was worth, so he'd relented after his wife asked him to.

"Why are you so interested in this Cain woman, Papa?" Marisol entered and smoothed down the silk blouse she was wearing.

Her expensive education in Massachusetts had taught her more than business management, and her outfit was a good example of her fashion sense. So far, Hector had let her sit in on the discussions, but he knew she would try to capitalize on this opportunity to get more involved in his business and make her mark. She was beautiful, but so far he hadn't seemed to regret his decision because Marisol had a sharp coldness about her that would cement her place in a man-ruled world once he did turn the operation over to her.

"The American saying 'don't reinvent the wheel' applies here. She's worked hard to be well connected in every aspect of her business, so if we can partner with her we can tap into that network." He patted the cushion next to him so she'd sit. "Rodolfo is the competition here and in the surrounding states, but if we can get all that business and add it to what we already have in New York and LA, no one can touch us."

"You think that's enough to take the Kalinas down?" Marisol asked.

Tomas knew all three of Hector's children since he spent so much time with the family, but Marisol was the only one who was always ready with a question. Marisol's constant need to know drove Hector insane at times, but she was the daughter most like him.

"Cesar Kalina went for the big markets, leaving it to his middlemen to expand," Tomas said.

"I know that, Tomas." She flipped her long black braid as she smiled at him. "But he was able to lock everyone else out and it's kept him on top."

"New York, Los Angeles, and Miami are big markets but you can't think that narrowly," Hector said. "It's a pain in my ass every time I have to give up a percentage of my business for the luxury of bringing in our stuff, but we have to play by Cesar's rules for now. There's no way to eventually make those operations ours, though, unless we've got something going on there now."

"So this is our backup?"

"With Casey's help this place will be the point of origin for our entire operation in the States. With Cain on board, not only can we get our shipments in safely, but we'll be able to transport them without any problems."

Tomas listened to the conversation but kept his eyes on Marisol. It wasn't time yet but eventually he'd prove himself worthy of her and finally be able to share with her and the world how he felt. No matter what happened he would stay loyal to Hector, but Marisol was his and he'd kill to keep it that way.

"How can I help you?" Marisol asked her father.

"Right now I need to find a way to charm Cain into doing business with us."

"I can be charming," Marisol said, and Tomas and Miguel laughed.

"That's true, *mi amor*, but Cain won't be an easy sell. She transports illegal liquor and cigarettes into this country, and to her and her family, her business is cleaner and more legitimate than drugs."

"From what you said, though, the FBI has been hot after her for years. If her operation is that small, why would the government waste their time?"

Hector smiled. "You misunderstand me, Marisol. When I said liquor and not drugs, I meant on a scale that has made Cain not only very wealthy, but very powerful. She surrounds herself with a small number of people she trusts, but her operation is massive. The government is so interested because it's costing them millions in lost revenue and she's killed without reservation to protect her business and those she chooses to deal with."

"When we got here to research Rodolfo's setup everyone on the street was willing to talk," Tomas said, knowing Hector appreciated his input. "It's one of the reasons the old man is losing his grip on power, but what little information we have on Casey costs us more than we've ever had to pay. It's from people so far out on the fringes of her business that we can't totally trust it."

"No one has that much loyalty to anyone nowadays," Marisol said, acting as if what he said was absurd.

"Nonsense," Hector said. "We're lucky enough to enjoy that kind of friendship and loyalty from Tomas," Hector said as he looked him in the eye. "You start with one person and you build on that and you treat people with respect. It's easy to understand."

"I didn't mean to offend you, Tomas," Marisol told him, as if her father's not so subtle hint hadn't clued her in. "I just meant that you're devoted to him in a way that I doubt carries all the way down the chain."

"Fear is always a good motivator," Tomas said.

"But that's just it, Tomas," Hector said with a large smile. "Casey's appeal doesn't come from fear, and I want to tap into whatever it is. I believe she likes me…well, enough that she turned to me for a favor."

"Debt is also a good thing to rely on," Miguel said.

"The favor didn't have any strings attached."

"Then if we show her mutual respect we might soften her up, Papa. I can't wait to meet her, so promise that you'll take me."

"Compared to our business Cain is really a small fish but, like I said, she does have the gift of making those close to her loyal. She's reluctant to do business with us, but eventually she'll see that by joining us she'll gain the kind of power that makes her untouchable."

"And if she still turns you down?" Marisol asked.

"It won't be hard to take away the little control she's accumulated, but I don't want it to come to that," Hector said as he studied his nails.

"Why not?"

Hector placed his hand on Marisol's knee and smiled, making Tomas smile as well. "That loyalty she gets is what she gives in return. If she helps us establish what could be the lynchpin of our entire operation, she'll work to make us successful."

"Then we'll work to entice her to join us," Marisol said, making it sound easy.

"I believe that can happen simply because we're not Rodolfo Luis."

❖

"The meeting with the Jatibons is a bad idea," Carlos Santiago said to Rodolfo. "They're setting a trap for you, I can feel it."

"No trap, Carlos." Rodolfo tapped his cheek with the tips of his fingers. "They just want what I can't give them."

"We're still looking, but Juan hasn't been spotted here or back home. I hope he realizes how much time and effort we're wasting looking for him."

The mention of his nephew's name was like an arrow through the heart. Rodolfo had poured his time and affection into Juan only to have Gracelia completely betray him. And that's who had to be helping Juan, because he couldn't have disappeared so effectively on his own.

"Juan will be found when Gracelia wants him to be, and not any sooner," he said from the backseat of the limo Carlos had ordered for their short trip to Pescadors. "Her, I'll find in a few days when we get home."

"I hope you forgive my anger toward her, but I don't understand the disrespect she's shown you."

"My sister is a spoiled child who had her toy taken away, and she wants to punish me for it."

"She should be grateful you got rid of that scum Ortega for her, if that's what you're referring to. A life with him would've been one full of disrespect when he moved from woman to woman." Carlos adjusted his shoulder holster. When his hand dropped to his thighs Rodolfo placed his on Carlos's knee. Both of them looked down and, not for the first time, Rodolfo noticed that their hands were shaped the same, down to the fingernails. Rodolfo could see that Carlos was thinking along those lines as well.

"Tonight when we finish I want you to come back up to the suite," Rodolfo said before he took his hand off Carlos's knee. "I have a lot to tell you and I think it's time."

"You can tell me anything and I'll do it."

"I don't need anything done. I need to say something."

The car stopped at the club and the driver quickly opened the door. Simon was waiting outside for them and waved them past the line at the front door. The place was crowded but a spot at the back of the room had been cleared, with plenty of muscle standing to keep the stupidly curious away.

"Welcome, Rodolfo," Ramon said, with his hand out to him. "Patrón, right?" Ramon asked, pointing to the frozen shot glass full of tequila waiting for him.

"Yes, thank you." He shook Ramon's hand but locked eyes with Cain after he glanced at Remi. "My condolences on your loss, Cain, but I'm glad you're here. After our last talk I didn't think we parted as enemies, but were at least on the way to being cordial. My business here and in other parts is suffering, and I have no one but you to blame," he said, extending his hand to her next.

"You have a funny way of offering an olive branch," Cain said, not letting go of him and pulling him toward her. "And you aren't very bright, talking about your business under the watchful eyes and ears of our friends over there." She pointed to the agents sitting at the bar.

"My patience for insults is at an end, my friend."

"Ha," Cain said, loud enough for the agents to move closer, as if it would help them hear better. "We will never be friends, but one little bit of information will keep us from being enemies. You know that and yet you refuse."

"I can't give you what I don't have or know. That you can't understand that doesn't make you too bright either."

Even though his skin was dark, Rodolfo's face was red from the anger Cain could tell was building. "Sit down and let's see what you know or not."

Ramon laughed softly when Rodolfo chose the seat farthest away from Cain. "I thought this was a meeting between us," Rodolfo said, waving his hand between himself and Ramon. "That was my understanding."

"Rodolfo." Ramon said his name and sighed as if frustrated. "Cain and I are business partners in more than one venture, so your lack of cooperation, or at least that's how it appears, troubles both our families. You're a businessman, so surely you can relate to our dilemma."

"I'm looking," Rodolfo said, close to a shout, and his man Carlos seemed concerned. Rodolfo smoothed his jacket down and appeared upset with himself that he'd lost control. "My nephew seems to have found a crack in the earth and fallen into it, but that doesn't excuse the movement against my business—"

"Ramon," Cain said. "Maybe we should move upstairs before we have to make bail."

Joe and Lionel stood when they did, but sat back down when Ramon and Remi led the group up the wide stairs. Before Cain turned away from them she fought the urge to wave good-bye, deciding not to antagonize the vultures.

Upstairs Ramon showed them to an empty poker salon equipped, as was the rest of the floor, with measures to keep anyone from electronically listening in. Once everyone's drink was replaced, he closed the doors.

"When Juan took my pregnant wife and shot one of my people

I did make some adjustments to your business," Cain said, watching Carlos grip his thighs so hard she figured it'd leave an impression of his fingers on his skin. "And before you give me the indignant routine, ask yourself what you would've done in my place. If you'll be honest like I'm being with you, your actions would've been the same."

"Juan is no longer part of my family."

She considered his response and believed him. "I can see why, and because you told me, I'm sure you won't have a problem with how I handle Juan once I find him."

"You can do whatever you like, but one more move against my people on the street and there'll be no peace between us. I will come after you and yours even if I have to bring an army from Mexico to do it."

"My initial anger at you and your family is played out, Rodolfo. Call those days my incentive for you to find Juan."

"Our street people are deserting us everywhere because of the deaths," Carlos blurted out in Spanish, like he couldn't hold himself in check any longer. "The numbers increase every day." Cain looked to Ramon to translate for her.

"That I know," Cain said to Rodolfo, "but it's not my responsibility. My interest isn't with you or your business, but solely with Juan." She crossed her legs and barely blinked as she kept eye contact with him.

"You expect me to believe you?" Rodolfo said, and laughed. "You really must think me stupid."

"Your problem is," Cain said in the same calm tone of voice, "your perceived self-importance."

"What do you mean?"

"That you think you're important to me, or maybe that I find your business irresistible," she said, then took a sip of her neat whiskey. "Trust me, neither is the case. I'm telling you the truth because I have nothing to gain by lying. I don't want anything from you except the nephew you've disowned."

"But you said you knew about my problems."

"New Orleans is my home, not a place I'm visiting to make a buck then fly back to Mexico not caring what happens here. It's my home, my family's home, and where I make a living, so it's part of my job to know what happens on my streets." She waited to see if he'd give his usual hotheaded response. "You have a problem here and in Mississippi, that I know, but beyond that I don't because it doesn't affect me, my family, partners, or business."

"We monitor closer than most at the casino in Biloxi," Remi said, "since we don't want any more law enforcement on the property than necessary, but some of the other casinos are catching the heat from your one-sided war."

"I agreed to this meeting today to tell you this. One more act against me and I'll have no choice but to give you this war you speak of." Rodolfo spoke softly and spread his hands out in front of him like he was trying to calm a wild pack of dogs.

"That would be misguided as well as unwise," Remi said. "You have our word that we're not interested in your business unless it affects ours in a negative way. Remember that when we bought the casino we removed everyone who was working for you and Nunzio Luca, and no one died."

"If not you, then who?" Rodolfo asked.

"That I really don't know, but whoever it is does want your territory," Cain said.

"I thought you knew everything that happened here," Rodolfo shot back.

"Again with the self-importance," Cain said with a smile. "I know you've got a problem, but not who's giving you one. Give me some time and I might find an answer."

"Why would you help me?"

"Because I'm starting to have the same problem, and my solution might lie with what's happening to you."

Rodolfo nodded, then glanced at Carlos. "Do you plan to trust Hector Delarosa with this solution?"

"Touché, Rodolfo." Cain saluted him by tapping a couple of fingers against the side of her forehead. "I'm not the only one aware of what's going on around me."

"I know Hector and of your desire to do business with him, but I should caution you before you sell your soul to Satan."

Cain laughed softly. "I'm familiar with the devil, señor, and I've already struck my bargain, but it isn't with Mr. Delarosa. I'm as interested in doing business with him as I am with you."

"Then be careful. Hector's as ambitious as he is dangerous."

The sentiment seemed genuine, and for a second Cain felt sorry for this man who appeared to be an island with no family. "I appreciate the warning, and I'll be in touch if I find out anything about our mutual problem."

"What makes you think it's the same?"

"We've chosen different paths for our lives, but I do believe we have one thing in common," she said, and he shrugged. "If I wanted to destroy you I would go after you, Rodolfo, not those in the lowest positions." And that was true. When she'd sent him a message to cooperate, she'd gone after those much higher in the chain. "Just like I know you would come straight for me if we had a problem."

"This has happened to you?" Rodolfo asked, moving to the edge of his chair.

"Not to the extent that you've experienced, but there's always a start to everything, don't you think?" She finished her drink and shook her head when Ramon pointed to her empty glass. "All I can ask is that you keep me informed if you hear from or about Juan."

Rodolfo opened his mouth, then closed it as if he'd rethought saying what had come into his head.

"New Orleans isn't Los Angeles or New York, but it's big enough for all of us, Rodolfo, if we learn to stay in our own sandboxes," she said in an effort to relax him. "We may not agree on our business choices, but we'll never try to stop you from making a living unless you go against us or anyone in our families."

"You can trust us with whatever you want to say," Remi said.

"I realize Juan needs to be punished," Rodolfo said slowly. "But he isn't capable of carrying out attacks like these against us."

"Juan has no problem with violence, from what I can tell," Ramon said.

"That's not what I mean." Rodolfo reached for the bottle and poured himself another shot. "I tried to make Juan a man since his father would never be in his life, and I tried to bleed out any trace of the scum who fathered him."

"But blood is thicker than anything sometimes, isn't it?" Cain said.

"I gave him everything, but Juan mentally could never handle what I expected of him. If you aren't responsible for my setbacks, I promise you they're not Juan's doing either."

"His ally is Anthony Curtis, and I bet that's who's guiding him," Cain said.

"Not just that snake," Rodolfo said, almost spitting on the floor, to judge from the set of his mouth. "The real puppeteer is probably my sister, but I'll let you know."

When Rodolfo jumped up and waved his fingers in his guard's direction, Cain was certain he'd raced through that confession. Having to admit what he did was bad enough, she figured, but there was more, and he was too embarrassed to share it.

"We'll be in touch, then," she said, before he followed Carlos from the room.

"You think his sister is helping Juan because she knows Rodolfo's pissed?" Remi asked.

"Partly that and partly because of what Rodolfo did to Juan's father. The guy must've been a hell of a lover for her to still hold this much of a grudge."

"I bet Emma would if something happened to you," Remi said, and laughed. "If that's the case, why go after our people?"

"I can't prove it's these idiots, but if I wanted to carry out an agenda, what better way to do it than by granting whoever's helping me a part of theirs."

"The sister wants Rodolfo, and Juan wants Emma."

"That's about it," Cain said, and wanted nothing more than to go home to Emma. "Rodolfo is smart enough to realize that his mentoring slid off Juan like mud off a turtle's shell because no amount of tutelage can make up for stupidity. Juan thinks he has the *cojones* to run his own organization. He just doesn't have the brains to carry it out."

"What about this sister, Papi?" Remi asked Ramon.

"Rodolfo has come to drink and gamble here, but we aren't friendly enough to talk about our families."

"Cain, any insights here?" Remi asked.

"Only what Hector shared with me about Juan's father," she said, and let out a long breath of frustration. She was tired of being behind the proverbial eight ball of lacking information so she could navigate among the new sharks who'd invited themselves into her pool.

"Problem?" Ramon asked.

"If I want to know anything pertinent to someone or something here, I just have to make a few harmless, uncostly calls. Mexico and farther south is out of my range." She felt comfortable admitting her limitations as she stood.

"Do you think Hector Delarosa can shed some light?" Ramon asked.

"I'm sure he's expecting my call, and I'm equally sure he knows all about Ms. Luis, but picking up the phone this time will cost me. The only thing I'm really sure about is that I refuse to do anything that'll put me or anyone I care about in debt to Delarosa."

"We'll find some other avenue, then," Remi said. "And that can wait until tomorrow."

"Thank you both for your support today, and it'll be good to start fresh in the morning," Cain said, and hugged them both.

It would take plenty of tomorrows to put everything back that had gone askew in her life, but she wasn't stressed this time because Emma would be there through it all. Cain had learned that she couldn't be strong all the time. She could finally admit her weaknesses to Emma, no matter what the rest of the world saw.

❖

"Is Mom coming home soon?" Hayden asked Emma, who was enjoying the icing stuck to her fork.

"If something's up you can talk to me, you know," she said, cutting off another small corner piece of cake. He drained his glass of milk and stared at the ceiling to give himself time to respond, Emma guessed, since he swallowed like he was in some sort of competition all of a sudden. "Or you can wait and talk to Mom before you float away," she joked.

"Sorry," he said, his eyes dropping to the countertop. "It's not that I don't want to tell you, but it's guy stuff."

She had to smile thinking of Cain at this age and wondered if girls had made her eyes flit everywhere around the room except on the parent sitting across from her. When they'd met, Cain had been the ultimate player who very seldom struck out when she met a woman who interested her. And that had held true until they went out. Emma's approach had been different from what Cain had been used to, and it had thrown her off her game a bit. By the time Cain had regained that confidence, she'd fallen in love with Emma.

"It's okay, buddy. If it's a girl who's the problem, Mom's the one to talk to."

"She married you, so don't worry about her knowing too much about other girls," he said, making eye contact with her as if alleviating any worry on her part was more important than his embarrassment.

"I'm never worried about that. I just meant that, on the girl front, she's got a bit more experience." Emma licked her fork again and wiggled her eyebrows at him, smiling.

Those few dates were a wonderful time for her. She'd finally given in to all the cravings she'd ever had but had kept bottled because of her strictly religious mother. To Carol Verde, love between two people of the same sex was something depraved and wrong. All those long lectures her mom had given fell from her head the first time she saw Cain, and the hardest thing about accepting that first date was not ripping her clothes off at the end of the night and begging Cain to touch her.

"Why are you blushing?" Hayden asked, laughing when she felt her face get hotter and probably redder.

"Pregnancy does that to me," she said.

"Uh-huh," he said right away, apparently not buying it. "You're okay with me wanting to talk to Mom, right? I mean, I'll tell you if you really want."

She longed for one more day when she could hold him like she could when he was three and had done something to try to please her. What she'd been so sure of in those lonely nights in Wisconsin was right. He needed the balance of who she and Cain were together to make him happy. That he'd let her in again was a blessing she gave thanks for every day. By being willing to share a secret he'd meant only for Cain, he was trying not to hurt her feelings.

"How about we make a deal?"

"I'm only gone a couple of hours and he's got you blushing and making deals?" Cain asked as she stripped off her jacket and started rolling up her shirt sleeves. "This should be good."

"We were talking about girls," Hayden said, with a big smile that was such a carbon copy of Cain's it made Emma put her hand over her middle and wish for the same miracle Hayden was to her.

"Not exactly," she said, sinking back into Cain when she moved closer. "But kiddo here needs to talk to you, so I'll head up and change." She kissed Cain, then Hayden, and started for the door, thinking about how her life had changed for the better in such a short time.

"Mama," Hayden said, stopping her in the hall. "You really don't have to leave."

"It's okay. Go ahead and talk and I'll be upstairs if you stump her," she said with a wink.

"You're a good kid, Hayden," Cain said before starting on what was left of Emma's dessert. "What's up?"

"Mama's planning a party for me." His tone meant that Cain should know what he was talking about.

"That's what she told me, yeah."

"You don't think that's lame?" He glanced at the door and seemed relieved that Emma had excused herself.

"It doesn't matter what I think, bud, so let's have it," she said, happy that finally she was facing an easy problem.

"Mom, I'm pretty sure that thirteen-year-olds don't have birthday parties their mom planned, and if they do their friends will think it's way lame."

He had a point, but Cain knew that Emma was trying so hard because she needed to make up for all the birthdays she'd missed when they were separated. Their son had given her the gift of forgiveness soon after Emma and Hannah had moved in, since he needed his mother more than he needed to carry that anger with him. Guilt was a bitch, and unfortunately Emma insisted on carrying her own portion of it.

"It's your day, and while everything's that's been happening didn't let us really celebrate it, you should be the one to choose how we do it."

"But I don't want Mama to think I'm lame either."

She raised her hand to stop him. "Let me finish. Did she tell you what she's planned?"

"She wanted to surprise me." He said like it meant Emma wanted to take a picture of him wearing a tutu.

"Remember that you can do whatever you like and I'll back you up, but your mama had in mind a party with your friends and people of the opposite sex. Maybe a cookout, some music I probably won't like, and some computer-game tournaments for some cool gifts she ordered."

"Oh," he said, glancing at the doorway again, only this time looking almost disappointed that Emma wasn't standing there. "I didn't think that's what it was."

"What, you guessed pin the tail on the donkey and a cake in the shape of a race car or something?" She laughed when he shrugged. "For future reference, you should know that your mama is as cool as she is beautiful, and the most embarrassing thing she'll do to you is kiss you in front of your friends. Even though you can carry her around now, you're still her little boy. And that's the most important thing you should know, son, that you're her little boy. She feels like she's got a lot to atone for."

"She doesn't. What happened to us was weird, but I don't blame her, not anymore."

"She knows that, but between us, her head is way ahead but her heart is having trouble catching up." She spoke softly, thinking that he had most probably figured that out, but saying it out loud would only make his relationship with Emma that much stronger.

"Did she invite Julie?" he asked as a way of changing the subject, and Cain didn't worry because she knew he'd received the message.

"The cute brunette you talk about like she invented air?" She laughed when he blushed. "That was the first invitation sent out, and she's already responded she's coming."

"Thanks, Mom."

"No problem, and I hope you're okay with the fact that this is so late."

"Mama and my new sibling came first, and that's all I cared about."

"Anything else bothering you?"

"It sounds so bogus now that I was worried about it." He picked up the dishes and stuck his hands so far down his pockets she thought his pants would fall off. "You aren't going to tell Mama what I said, right?"

"Not a chance."

They climbed the stairs together and Hayden kept going toward the master suite while she checked on Hannah. It was still early. She wanted to go to bed and make love to her wife, but she still had to deal with Muriel since she'd left right after the fire alarm. Katlin had tried to call her, but Shelby had told her the day had finally worn Muriel down and she was sleeping. Cain's anger over the Emma's Club incident had died down enough for her to wait and talk to Muriel later. Cain owed her a meeting with a level head where they'd both be happy with the outcome.

When she looked through the door of their room, Emma was sitting in her favorite reading chair with Hayden sprawled on the floor at her feet, his head resting in her lap. Emma was combing his hair back and telling him something that was making him laugh. *Mum, I hope you and Da can see the family I've built*, she thought in as close to a prayer as she could conjure up. *They're a fine addition to what you and Da gave me*.

"Mom, you didn't tell me Mama hosed you down with alcohol the day you met."

"Day we met?" she asked and pointed her finger at Emma. "She spilled half the bar on me, *then* introduced herself."

"I got your attention, didn't I?" Emma asked, then blew her a kiss.

"I'm sure that's what it was."

"Let me go before you get too sappy," Hayden said, sitting up so he could kiss Emma. "Good night," he said, then kissed her before he left, closing the door behind him.

"Anything serious?" Emma asked after a few minutes passed.

"He's okay. All he needed was a pep talk about his cool factor, or lack of it."

"Your son thinks he's lacking cool?" Emma stood and tightened the belt on her robe. "He's delusional if that's what was on his mind."

"In my opinion he got all he needed and then some from both sides of his family tree, and that's what I told him. We'll have that talk more than once until he comes into his own. Nothing to worry about." She opened her arms and turned Emma around when she stepped into them.

"Why do you think that?" Emma kissed her biceps when she undid the robe tie.

"Experience, mostly." The dark blue silk nightgown was sheer enough for her to notice how hard Emma's nipples were. "The Caseys are sometimes the worst-kept secret in New Orleans, so depending on where you fall in the pecking order, it's a given almost as to what your future will be."

"And for him being second from the top of that totem pole is a problem?" Emma sucked in a deep breath when Cain brushed the flat palms of her hands over her nipples.

"Sometimes that position is like someone handing you a size twenty shoe when you're learning how to walk. You can do it, but not easily. He doesn't want to try a lot of stuff now that'll tarnish him getting that job he wants so badly in the future."

"Did you want it that bad, mobster?" Emma asked, pressing Cain's hands to her chest as if needing more stimulation.

"Why wouldn't I?" She lowered her head to suck on Emma's earlobe. "It's a stressful but cool job." She moved down Emma's neck. "Comes with good perks."

"Any I should know about?" Emma asked, stepping forward so Cain could remove her robe.

The nightgown's thin straps left most of Emma's shoulders bare, and Cain took advantage, slowly running the tips of her fingers along the smooth skin. "Good hours is what most people would say." She moved her hands down Emma's back so she could start lifting the garment off her.

"That's not what was important to you?" Emma asked, moving away from her and pressing her hands against her chest, which made her step back to sit on the bed. Emma made sure the door was locked before getting naked and standing before her.

"Getting the girl to notice me because I was the one in charge— that was and still is the greatest perk." She spread her legs so Emma could move closer. "You are so stunningly beautiful."

"I'm so happy you think so," Emma said, unbuttoning her shirt for her.

"Muriel will be here in a bit, lass, so why not let me take care of you?"

"No." Emma kept unbuttoning until she reached her belt buckle. "I want…no, I need to feel you," she ran her hands over her shoulders then up her neck to the base of her hair, "everywhere. Baby, please."

Cain stood and finished pulling her shirt out and unbuckled her pants. She exhaled so hard her nose flared when Emma stepped around her, lay down, and spread her legs and her sex open for her. The act was so sexy that Cain stood and stared, admiring how white Emma's fingers were next to the rosy pink lips. Emma was so wet she was dripping.

"Blessed was the day I was baptized in beer," Cain said softly before lowering her head between Emma's legs.

Pregnancy changed Emma's unique taste because of the different foods she craved, and with the first swipe of her tongue, Cain knew she would've guessed pineapple even if she hadn't watched Emma consume a large serving of the fruit at almost every meal. It gave Emma a sweet taste that Cain craved as much as Emma did pineapple.

Using a flat tongue was going too slow for Emma, who slapped her on the shoulder with her bare foot. "Baby, I love when you dawdle, as you say, but this isn't the time…please." Emma lifted her hips as if showing Cain where she needed her attention. She brought her hands down again and spread her sex so her clitoris was easy to see.

"You're so wet," Cain said, and almost laughed at the only thing her mind could come up with since Emma's actions were turning her head to mush.

"Put your fingers inside." Emma lifted her head off the pillow as much as she could and looked at her. "I need you to make me come."

Cain closed her lips around her clit as her fingers slid into the hot folds as far as they'd go. The way Emma bucked her hips and moaned made it difficult to keep pace, but she never let up the pressure of her mouth or the motion of her hand.

Emma lasted longer than she thought before the walls of her sex clamped down and she stopped moving while the orgasm she'd been so desperate for swept through her. Her body heaved one last time and Cain used just her tongue until Emma begged her to stop.

While Emma caught her breath, Cain moved up to her pillow and opened her arms so Emma could press against her.

"I love you," Emma said, wiping tears from her face. The overload of emotion happened often when they made love but was more frequent when she was pregnant. "I wish I could find the words to tell you how lucky I am that I found you, but whatever I say will fall short."

"That was a good way of putting it, love."

"Not really," Emma said, wiping away more tears. "My life would be so empty without you."

"Then your life will always be full, because I'm not going anywhere." Cain kissed Emma's fingers, then used the corner of the sheet to dry her face. "I'm not a fortuneteller, but fate has a lot planned for us. Some of it will be bad, most good, but the one certainty is longevity. You're mine, wife, but for a lifetime. One that I plan to fill with as much happiness as I can manage, and at its end, you'll know no one could've loved you more."

"Do you promise?" Emma placed her hand on her chest over her heart.

"I do." Cain wanted to stay and prove how she felt again, but the world would stop spinning for her only so long, then her time was up.

CHAPTER TEN

Cain took a shower while Emma slept and dressed in a pair of chinos Emma had bought for her to relax around the house in. Emma had argued that casual clothes were easier to play with the kids in, so she chose the new cable-knit sweater that was now part of her wardrobe.

Downstairs Muriel was waiting in the study looking out the window at the building rainstorm that lit the sky. For the first time in her life Muriel appeared defeated.

"Do you remember when your dad and mine let us share a drink in here with them?" Muriel asked, moving her glass in a small circle so the ice would clink against the side. "Up till then the study and their meetings had been off-limits to us."

"I thought Billy would drop a load of Irish crystal on the floor when Da asked him to pour," she said, sitting behind the desk where Muriel had placed her drink. "Mum would've had him shot in the yard. These glasses have been in her family for six generations, seven now that they're mine."

"Do you ever wish you could go back?"

Cain took a sip and replaced the heavy etched glass on the coaster. "No," she said, after weighing the options. "Life isn't always perfect, but my choices, and those circumstances I couldn't change, have led me here."

"And where's here for you, cousin?" Muriel asked as she poured herself another drink.

"Home," Cain said, placing her hand over her glass when Muriel started to refill it. "A place where a woman I love and I are raising the children who'll carry on for us and drinking out of glasses that some distant relative contemplated the same questions over, I'm sure."

"No regrets?"

"You know better than that, Muriel," Cain said, trying to bite back the anger building in her gut. "I don't think anyone alive knows exactly what all my regrets are better than you."

"I do, and now I've gotten my taste."

Cain wasn't looking forward to adding to hers, but it was better to say something now than after their relationship was destroyed. She wanted to protect their family by eliminating a threat, but still make Muriel feel a part of the Caseys.

"We'll miss Uncle Jarvis, that's a given, but you shouldn't add regret to the load you're already carrying. You didn't get to see him right before he died, but a lifetime isn't summed up in one moment." She moved next to Muriel. "Please believe me that his mind was on you and how proud you've made him."

"I should've been there, and our last conversation shouldn't have happened. The last thought on his mind was probably what a traitor to the family I am. You know how much pride he had in the name we carry."

"Sometimes it's as much a burden as a gift, though, isn't it?" Cain said softly, putting her hand on Muriel's shoulder. "Sometimes it means we have to put aside something we want because it simply won't fit into the lives we lead."

"I don't think I could give her up, if that's what you're talking about."

"Shelby is *who* I'm talking about, but I'm not about to tell you what your relationship with her should be. We've been over this already, and please don't think I'm trying to add to what you've been through, but it looks like Shelby is important to you."

"She is, and it won't interfere with my job here."

Cain shook her head and put her hand up for Muriel to keep her mouth shut. "It already has. Tell me what today was about. Sanders had done the job earlier today by keeping the Feds outside, but that changed after you got there." She kept her voice as even as she could and watched Muriel to see what kind of response she would get. "Give me an explanation so *I'll* understand."

"We don't have anything to hide in the office or in Emma's."

"That's your explanation? Are you kidding me?" She stopped and took a deep breath. "Since when do we invite anyone like the FBI team trailing us every day to enter anywhere they don't belong for any reason?"

Muriel raised her voice. "When we have nothing to hide."

"As of tomorrow I'm putting Sanders in charge of the office," Cain said, deciding that being blunt was the best way to deal with the situation. "You need to take some time off and decide what your role will be, but whatever that is, it has to be different from what it is now."

Muriel stood and clenched her fists, but Cain didn't move. "Are you forgetting something important?"

"What?"

"You can't take away my birthright." She hit her chest with her fist and moved closer to Cain. "I'm a Casey, and that's my office—my firm."

"I agree that what happened today was minor, but you stand there and tell me you were thinking clearly when you asked Shelby's team in for a guided tour? Tell me your relationship with her and her team didn't taint how you handled that."

"It didn't," Muriel said, too quickly for Cain.

"I love you, Muriel, and you're one of the few people in my life that I'd do anything for with little or no questions."

Muriel threw her hands up in obvious frustration. "Then why are we having this conversation?"

"Because this doesn't just affect me. My birthright gives me the responsibility to keep us all whole." She stood and placed her hands on Muriel's shoulders. "Shelby, like I've said, is not someone I'll try to push out of your life no matter how I feel, but choices have consequences. This is yours."

"That's it? You're cutting me off from the family?"

"Listen to what I'm saying. Your working role with our day-to-day operations will have to change. We're more than bootleggers and attorneys. That is what we do, but what we are is family."

Muriel turned away from her and took a deep breath. "Where does that leave me?"

"Free to live your life knowing that I love you and want you to be happy. I'll take care of you, Muriel."

"I don't need your charity."

The words stung and shocked her. She'd never questioned her relationship with Muriel because it was like what she'd shared with her brother Billy. They didn't always agree but at their core was a devotion forged through blood and time.

"In my position what would you do differently?" Cain asked evenly.

"I would trust you and know that betrayal wasn't in your makeup."

"Is that what you think, that I don't trust you? I've earned more respect than that." She stood and moved back behind her desk. "I trust you with my life and those of my family."

"But not enough to keep my position with you."

"I don't trust Shelby and I don't think this is the right choice for you, but I don't count in this decision," she said, her frustration growing.

"I love her."

"And I love you, but this is the end of this discussion. Enjoy your time off, and when you're ready we'll redefine your job." Cain sat with the desk between them, delineating the parts they played within the family as clearly as she could. "I'll be here for you no matter what you might think of me right now."

Her head fell back and she swiveled toward the window when Muriel left without responding. "Uncle Jarvis, if Emma's right and Shelby isn't with her for the right reasons, bend Muriel's path back to my door. If we're both wrong, then I'll keep my promises to you no matter if she moves away from me or not."

Jarvis's funeral popped into her head, and despite the many things she was upset about, one topped her list. Perhaps other people's cultures allowed them to act differently in certain situations; then again, her annoyance might contain the solution to this particular problem. She picked up the phone and called someone she thought could give her the answer.

❖

The French Quarter was full of tourists wearing name badges, though Remi couldn't make out what convention they were with as she walked down Bourbon Street with Simon slightly behind her. It was late, but she'd told Dallas she'd stop by.

"Mano's going to be at your father's by ten," Simon said, loud enough for her to hear over the music and people.

"After we get to Dallas's door you can take off, and I'll drive back later. Dallas took my car earlier when Emil drove them home."

"Do you remember what happened today?" Simon asked, coming shoulder to shoulder with her. "Someone out there has a problem with us, so I'm not leaving you alone."

"I love you, Simon, but you need to relax. Kristen just got here and I'd like to go more than a day before I freak her out."

"I love you too, so don't expect me to let up." They stopped close to the entrance of Pat O'Brien's across the street from Dallas's place. "Those girls," Simon pointed to the plain door that led to the patio Dallas loved so much, "are survivors. Don't forget that."

"They've been alone too long, though, and it's time for someone to take care of them. I want Dallas to believe that'll be me."

"She's a smart woman, so don't try so hard for something you already have." Simon cut her eyes toward the patio door. "Concentrate instead on getting the rest of what you want."

"Thanks, Simon," she said, hugging her. "And if it'll make you feel better, I'll call you in a couple of hours when I'm ready to go."

"I'll be waiting, but I've got odds on that you won't call until tomorrow morning," Simon said, waving over her shoulder.

Remi laughed as she pulled her key out of her front pocket. They might not be living together, but Dallas didn't want her to wait outside either. She scanned the street and no one really stood out as a threat, but something made her look once more.

Another glance behind her still didn't locate anyone who seemed dangerous in the crowd of tourists mixed with locals. The ones to watch out for were the people anxious to look you in the eye and those who couldn't. Here, though, everyone appeared to belong, so she stepped into Dallas's sanctuary and left the noise of the street behind when she relocked the door.

"I thought I'd been stood up."

Dallas was standing in the middle of the space, having changed into her favorite jeans. With her hair around her shoulders and no makeup, she didn't look like a budding star, but she was the most beautiful woman Remi had met. Though Dallas was still keeping secrets from her they were making progress, and from what little Dallas had hinted about her father, she understood why Dallas had trouble sharing the whole truth.

"My father says that only idiots keep beautiful women waiting." Remi closed the gap between them and kissed Dallas slowly as she wrapped her arms around her. "I may be an idiot, but I love you."

"I love you too and no one, especially me, would think you're an idiot, baby," Dallas said, wrapping a lock of her hair around her finger. She was wearing it a little longer because Dallas had asked her to. "Is everything all right?"

She looked at Dallas in the soft light and ran her fingertips along Dallas's brow. "Where's Kristen?"

"In her room unpacking. It's like all those years we were apart were the dream, now that she's upstairs. Do you know what I mean?"

"Considering what Mano means to me, you're a stronger person than I am for having the willpower to stay away from her. I don't know if I would've lasted."

Dallas took her hand and led her to the lawn furniture. "If it would've kept Mano safe you wouldn't have had a problem." When Remi sat back into the chair Dallas snuggled against her. It felt great to have her so close, but at times Dallas seemed to do it so she wouldn't have to look her in the eye while they were talking.

"Anything bothering you?" she asked, combing through Dallas's hair.

"Does it bother you that everything you know about me was mostly made up after I became Dallas Montgomery?" Dallas made air quotes.

"The only thing that would bother me, *querida*, is for you to hold back because you think I'd be disgusted or ashamed of you."

Dallas bunched the front of Remi's shirt in her fist, then went back to the rhythmic circles she'd been making with her palm, as if she craved touching her as much as Remi wanted to in return. "I don't think that."

"Good," she said, kissing the top of Dallas's head.

"I know it."

"Today while we were at the funeral someone delivered a box to my place with the body of one of our new bartenders from Pescadors inside. She died, I suspect, because of who she collected her paycheck from." She encouraged Dallas to look up at her, surprised to find tears in the blue eyes. "This girl didn't ask for what happened, but someone for their own selfish reasons decided to lash out at me."

"That's horrible, but you can't take the blame."

She kept her thumb under Dallas's chin. "It is, but you should think about it as a lesson. Whatever happened to you that wakes you up because of bad dreams wasn't your fault either. I've told you to take your time, but I'll be here no matter what it is."

"You're sweet, and I believe you won't leave me. I want more than anything for you to stay with me because you love me, not because you pity me."

"A story only has the power to hurt you when you keep it inside and let it eat at you, but I won't force it out of you." She never took her eyes from Dallas's but she heard the screen door open slowly.

"It's okay if you want to tell her, Dallas," Kristen said, obviously having overheard their conversation. "This is our chance."

From what little Dallas had told her and after researching the town Dallas and Kristen had run from, Remi had some theories of what had happened. She had declined when Cain offered to hire one of Muriel's friends who practiced law close to Sparta to investigate what the sisters were so afraid of.

The papers she'd gotten from Bob Bennett's house didn't refer to what he had on Dallas to control her for so long. But as an attorney Remi figured Dallas couldn't have broken too many laws simply because of the profession she'd chosen. The few movies she'd made had been shown all over the world. If Bob's blackmail had a legal component, someone would've taken advantage of it when they recognized Dallas onscreen.

No, the whole story had more to do with the monsters that children ran from, made more terrifying by a sick fuck like Bob. Eventually the only way to stop the nightmares was to open the doors and flip the lights on to expose the ghoulies to the light. All Remi wanted was to have the patience to move at Dallas's pace.

"Kristen, come over here." She put her hand on the empty space beside her. "You and Dallas already have your chance, and I won't be the one to take it from you. When Dallas is ready she'll share what she can, and if she can't, you both will be part of my family. You can move out on your own only when you're ready."

"I almost believe you," Kristen said.

"You can," Dallas said, reaching across Remi for Kristen's hand. "She's as honest as she is cute."

Remi's phone rang, and while she hated to break away from them because they were making progress, the screen showed her brother's name. He was still at his office in the casino, which was quiet compared to what was happening here, but she looked for that to change.

"Mano," she said, standing when Dallas moved over.

"Two casino directors have phoned me since this afternoon. Three small-time dealers were killed in the parking lot of one place, and two others were taken out on the grounds at the other place," Mano said.

"Anything coming from your contacts on the street?" She squeezed the back of her neck with her free hand.

"It surprised everyone I talked to. The changes we made caused problems because some of the clowns who worked for the Luca family tried to set up the same size operations in other locations. We can't keep out all the scum selling this shit, but we can ignore them for now."

"Sometimes you have to look the other way when a guest needs to self-medicate to forget their losses," she said, looking back at Dallas, who had her head pressed to Kristen's. "Nothing with anyone's staff?"

"No, but five murders in one afternoon has the local police running. All the law enforcement is making people in the casino nervous. You want me to call Cain and tell her?"

"Go ahead in case she has any questions, then tell her to call me if she wants to meet again tonight."

She was afraid a war was coming and they were going to be pulled in even though their business had nothing to do with drugs.

Emil was sitting at the kitchen counter and waved to her through the open door. He was eating a sandwich and pushed the plate away when she walked in.

"Everything been quiet around here?" she asked.

"The girls had a late lunch with your mom and Emma at the Casey place before we came back home."

"You planning to pull out tonight?"

Emil spent his days with Dallas, then once she was home and the alarm was activated, he left. She'd wanted to post someone else for the night shift, but Dallas had asked for privacy so she could get reacquainted with Kristen without anyone watching.

"Yeah, unless Dallas says otherwise. If she's spooked, I'll sleep on the sofa."

"Call one of the guys and tell them to watch the door from the street." She glanced outside to make sure Dallas wasn't coming in. "The manager at Pat O's will give them a place to sit."

"You're not going to tell her?" Emil swiveled around and put his feet on the floor. The black alligator boots looked like they were made from an entire large gator. "Don't be shocked if she gets pissed when she finds out. She's cute but she's got street smarts. If she goes out unexpectedly, she's gonna make them."

"She can get pissed with me in a little bit, then, when I tell her, and add that I'm not changing my mind."

"About what?" Dallas asked, having made it to the kitchen in the moment Remi looked away.

"I'm adding security—"

"No," Dallas said, not letting her finish. "I love Emil, but that's enough."

"Outside—they're going to stay outside, and until I know what's going on and who ordered all this, we're all going to have to live with an overabundance of caution." They'd never fought, and she didn't want to make a habit of it, but she refused to back down.

"I'd like to think I've got some say when it concerns me," Dallas said, obviously not backing down either.

The tone didn't sit well with Remi, but then she'd given Dallas wings and expected her to use them so she wasn't about to punish her. She opened the door and waved Dallas outside. "When it comes to security during times like this, I'll be honest about what's happening, but I *will not* waver from what works."

"Even if it's something I don't want?" Dallas asked, crossing her arms over her chest.

"Yes, but I'm not going to force you to accept something you can't live with."

The angry pose dropped and just as quickly Dallas smiled. "I'm glad you can see it from my view, baby. Sometimes I feel like a caged exotic pet that needs to be watched."

"If that's how you really feel, then I'm really sorry for putting you in harm's way to begin with." She was sure Dallas didn't see what the alternative was.

"Don't be so quick to take the blame," Dallas said, moving closer and resting her head on her chest. She peered up with a surprised expression when Remi's arms didn't automatically come around her. "What's wrong?"

"I love you, but you have to understand something." Remi found it almost painful but she stepped back. "If you don't feel comfortable with the security that's necessary at times, then I don't have any choice but to remove the threat some other way."

"What exactly does that mean?" Dallas asked, crossing her arms again, but she appeared to be trying to comfort herself rather than expressing any anger.

"In this case the threat is me, and I love you too much to let anything happen to you. But more important, I love you enough not to make you do something you're not comfortable with."

"You'd leave me?" Dallas asked incredulously.

"If it was the only way to keep you safe," she said, pointing to the street. "Sometimes my world isn't pretty, so what do you think it would do to me if, because of me, something happened to you?"

"Nothing's going to—"

"Happen," Remi said loudly. "Is that what you were going to say? What Juan did to Emma wasn't that long ago, Dallas, so don't make it sound like it would be easy for me to leave you. But I'll be damned if I'd let something like that happen to you."

"Do whatever you want, then," Dallas said, turning away from her.

"What I want is to keep you safe," she said softly. Dallas's answer meant she didn't understand the choice Emma Casey had accepted after she learned a very hard lesson. "But like I said, I won't force you because I'm not Bob and whoever came before him. When I said you were free to make your own choices, I meant it. The biggest one you have is to accept that being with me comes with a price, and I'd totally understand if you don't or can't pay it." She tipped her head back and stared at the dark violet sky as a way to keep her emotions in check.

"I'll place the man outside until everyone understands we're no longer together, so you'll be removed from my radar. After that you can choose someone from studio security if you're not happy with Emil." Dallas still hadn't turned around and was still silent, so that was answer enough.

It had been a while since Remi had cried, but her tears dropped as she headed for the gate. The noise of it unlatching evidently motivated Dallas toward her. Before she could swing it open, Dallas was there holding it closed.

"You promised me you'd stay," Dallas said from behind her.

"Loving you will never be something I could stop doing." Her voice cracked at the end. "But today was the first time I admitted to myself the cost of your feelings for me. You can find safer choices out there."

"You're right." Dallas melted into Remi's back and put her hands around to flatten them against her abdomen. "But none of them would be you."

"Most people would believe that's the best part of all this." Remi was so relieved that Dallas had stopped her she wanted to sit before her knees gave out. "That none of them were me, I mean."

"Do whatever you think is right, even if it means somebody hanging from every light fixture in the house," Dallas said.

"It's not that drastic, love," she said, turning around and giving in to the craving to hold Dallas.

"Don't scare me like that again," Dallas said, clinging to her and sobbing. "You're mine and I won't lose you."

"Keeping you whole is my job, but I don't want you to hate me for it."

"Aside from my sister, you're the only one who's ever loved me and isn't with me because of what's in it for them."

"Well, what's in it for me is that you're mine too, and I'm selfish enough to want to be happy because you are." She bent and picked Dallas up. "Come on, I'm exhausted after all that."

Dallas felt limp in her arms and Remi was glad to find the path all the way to the bedroom clear. What had happened to Cain and Emma was on her mind as she set Dallas down. No matter how many people Cain had lost in her life, the hardest had to have been losing Emma for those years. The loss had changed her, and the old Cain had resurfaced only since Emma's return. It had to have been a raw wound that healed when her heart found what it had been missing. Only a small glimpse of that kind of pain was enough to motivate Remi into not repeating her friend's mistakes.

CHAPTER ELEVEN

Two weeks after the surgery Anthony felt like he might wake up from the nightmare his life had become if he tried hard enough. Gracelia's company was the one thing that had kept his mind off the subjects that were too hard to think about. Through his drugged haze her voice was his only tether to reality.

Gracelia had a way of putting things that made his life come into focus. At least the purpose of his life was clear now. When she touched him and told him how underappreciated he'd been at the Bureau, and how he'd let people like Cain disrespect him because he didn't realize his strength, it all made sense. After his surgery Gracelia had stayed with him, sleeping next to him, always touching, always comforting. The attention she lavished made him crave her as much as Juan's teak box.

"Today you become the man who has the power to do what no other has done in years," Gracelia whispered through the gauze covering his ear. The exam room was dimly lit and they were alone waiting for the doctor to finish seeing his patients for the night. The surgeon had come to the house often to change the bandages, but Gracelia hadn't let Anthony see his face.

"The power to do what?" he asked, shivering as she slid her hand into his shirt and ran her fingers around his nipple. She'd kept him in an almost constant state of arousal and if she'd do something about it, he'd do whatever she asked.

"To be the man in my bed," she whispered again, only in the other ear. Her perfume seemed to envelop him even through the thin barrier of gauze that covered most of his nose.

His face really didn't need the bandages anymore, but Gracelia had insisted on using some vitamin E cream mixed with herbs she'd gotten from an old medicine man. According to both of them, the old ways of healing would cure the cuts faster.

"You've been in my bed for days, but," he thought of a way to finish without insulting the beautiful woman he'd started dreaming about, "you're only willing to go so far."

"You weren't ready when you got here." She pinched his nipple and he hissed out a short breath when his pants got tighter. "You still dreamed about your former life, Mr. FBI." Her hand moved outside his shirt and slowly made its way down. "That badge and the people you worked for can't and won't ever give you what I can." She grabbed his hard penis and pumped it a few times before she released the pressure but didn't move her hand. "I'll make you a man people respect, and I'll give you the life you've only watched up till now."

The blood in his body seemed to have pooled in his dick and he wanted to take Gracelia right there. "What do you want?" His voice sounded to him as tight as his pants felt. "You're confusing me."

"How can me telling you what I want confuse you?"

He turned so he could see her. "Because you're a refined woman who acts like she wants to get fucked."

"I want you, but," she lowered his zipper and put her hand on his hot pulsing shaft, "only if you're truly with me."

The tips of her fingernails bit into the sensitive flesh, but the slight pain only increased his desire when she squeezed him again. "What makes you think I don't want you?"

"If you aren't honest with me, we can never be real partners." Gracelia took her hand away and turned her back on him. She'd baited her hook weeks before and it was time to mount her catch where she could enjoy the sight of her cunning. She wanted what she wanted and was smart enough to know Juan wouldn't have what it took to get it.

"You can tell me the truth, you know." She tried to sound defeated. "If you don't think you can work with me, I'll let you go. I can't make you accept my plans for us, but I don't want to give myself to a man who only wants to use me for his own gain. I've done that already."

"There's nothing for me in my old life—you have to understand that."

She shook her head, still facing the door that Lorenzo was guarding since she needed to finish what needed to be done. "No one strives hard to become an agent to just let it go because of a woman. Don't insult me."

"I could turn you, Juan, and the whole operation in, and I'd still end up in federal and state jails for all the shit I've done." His feet hit the ground and she smiled. "You're the only one who's offering me a place and a purpose, Gracelia." She could feel how excited he still was when he pressed himself to her back. "I'll do whatever it takes to prove myself to you, but only if you meant what you said about partnership."

"When we get home, you have to prove only one thing to me." She turned in his arms and kissed the side of his neck. "The rest can wait until tomorrow." And she meant it. Juan or Gustavo—she was still getting used to the name change—was busy doing the small jobs she'd asked of him. Her warnings about any deviation from the plan had obviously worked, and so far she'd had no problems.

She guided him back to the exam chair and opened the door. The doctor was talking to Lorenzo, but moved when she indicated they were ready. "Let's see what we have," she said to both men, and for the first time since Armando, she felt almost giddy.

❖

"Why don't you meet me for lunch today?" Shelby asked, dressing for work. "You haven't left the house in days."

"What exactly would I leave for?"

Muriel spoke in a flat tone that summed up her outlook since the massive changes in her life had occurred.

When Shelby had thought up the undercover assignment, she figured she'd be further ahead than this. She knew only a little more about the Casey operation now that Muriel's sudden detachment had given her the run of the house. That alone wasn't getting her any closer to her goals since Cain had circled the wagons, leaving not only her but Muriel outside.

Muriel's loss of her longtime position as the family counselor had been Shelby's fault, and as Muriel's lover she felt horrible. It had been her job, though, to get inside to see some of Cain's security set-up when the bodies outside Emma's had been reported. The choice wasn't easy but she'd made the right one, and any guilt she felt lay buried under her convictions.

So far the only development in the case was the dead bodies of the guys caught on the security cameras at Emma's and at Remi's building.

The strange thing was that, according to Annabel Hicks, neither Cain nor the Jatibons were credited with the hits. The initial delivery of bodies was still a mystery to everyone because Cain and Remi had as many feelers on the street as they did.

"Honey." She put her arms around Muriel from behind, trying to tear her attention away from the newspaper. Muriel read it compulsively, as if trying to find information about her family since no one related to her would discuss anything to do with the business. "Cain just needs to get used to the idea of us together and realize I'm not out to get her."

"If you think she isn't coping with the idea, then you don't know her at all," Muriel said, not putting her paper down. "She's used to it and she acted accordingly."

"Call her and ask her to lunch."

"Sure, and afterward we can have a sing-along." The paper had obviously lost its appeal since Muriel crumpled it and threw it on the floor next to her chair. "Leave it alone, it's done."

She kissed Muriel's cheek and didn't say anything else until she said good-bye when she left for work. She would probably drive the wedge between the cousins deeper, but she had to try. Since Cain and Emma's home was so close, she pulled up to the gate and asked for an audience.

"Park over there and wait for someone to escort you," the guard said. The man was so muscular his neck appeared too short for the broad shoulders.

"I wonder where she finds these people," Shelby said to herself as she followed the guy's instructions.

She was about to get out of the car when the front door of the house opened. When she saw Cain escorting Hayden and Hannah out with the other big guy who was Hayden's shadow, she waited. She had a hard time reconciling this side of Cain with what they knew she'd done but weren't able to prove.

"They're crazy about her." She watched through her rearview mirror as Cain talked to her children and hugged them before she sent them to school. Cain's attention stayed on the car until it left the property.

"Agent Phillips," Cain said through the glass when she walked up.

"Thanks for seeing me." Shelby opened her door and stepped out, expecting to follow Cain inside, but Cain headed for the walk along the side of the house.

"It would seem that you're part of the family, so why wouldn't I see you?" Cain asked, slipping her hands in her pockets as she walked. Before the brick wall had been built, Shelby had watched her take this walk, usually with a cigar, as if trying to figure something out. "What do you need?"

Information about your whole operation so I can move on with my life, she wanted to say, knowing Cain would probably find it funny, but this was about Muriel. "You fired Muriel."

"I reassigned her, but I don't plan to waste my breath on something you won't understand."

"You took away something important to her because of me, and I'm asking you to reconsider." The group of gardeners putting in spring bedding plants all said good morning as Cain walked by. The view out the large expanse of windows when they started blooming would be nice, but because of whatever was on the glass she couldn't see which room it was. The coating was like Cain's life. Unless she opened up a sliver and let you see inside, you wouldn't.

"You make it sound like I'm being petty by punishing Muriel." Cain stopped at the side of the house and studied the higher wall with its walkway that surrounded the side and back. A guard could walk the perimeter and check for any threat trying to come over. "What I did was for Muriel's benefit."

"Don't patronize me, Cain." Shelby looked up at her, having to shield her eyes from the brightness because Cain had her back to the sun. "What you may not realize is how much Muriel's hurting."

"I talk to her every day, and I've stopped by numerous times, so I know exactly how she's doing. She's my family and I haven't forgotten that," Cain said, starting their walk again.

The property, even by old New Orleans money standards, was huge, with manicured gardens in various spots that made it seem like a park. This was the first time Shelby had seen the yard since Cain and her family had moved back in, because the front wall blocked their view. She tried to take it in as what Cain said computed. Muriel had never mentioned the calls or the visits.

"I'll always be in Muriel's life, Shelby, no matter what you think of me." The grass was still wet with dew but Cain stepped off the slate path toward the rose garden ahead of them. "You'll never understand our family because you'll never truly be a part of it, but Muriel does understand. Sometimes I'm sure she doesn't agree with me, or is pissed because of my decision, but she does understand."

"Aren't you worried that all she does is sit around all day?"

A pair of snippers was hanging from the wrought-iron fence that surrounded the garden, and Cain used them to cut a long-stemmed pink rosebud. "Her father just died, and she's doing better than I did when my father passed away. If you love her—"

"What do you mean, if I love her?" Shelby screamed at Cain, making the guard pacing a few feet above them stop. "You're an idiot if you think I don't."

"There are different types of love, and all I have to compare yours to is my own experience. Love is a partnership that shouldn't require sacrifice from only one side."

Shelby usually enjoyed talking to Cain, though she seldom got the chance, but no matter the situation Cain delivered her words in that same confident voice that wasn't exactly monotone, but revealed very little emotion. Her intelligence, combined with the cool tone, made you either admire her or want to take a swing at her. That she spoke that way about Muriel made Shelby favor hitting her.

"So you blame me?"

"Between you and me," Cain lowered her voice and smiled, "and your buddies outside," she pointed toward the front, "I know a few things for sure. Muriel and I are a lot alike because we were raised by parents who were a lot alike. She's strong, independent, and loyal."

"I know all that. It's why I'm with her."

"It's not often easy but someone like that can be broken, and when it happens it's easy to worm your way through the cracks. The allure of something new and unknown can be blinding, but I'll give you a warning."

Cain was smug but not really condescending, so Shelby held back her annoyance. "Don't you mean a threat?"

"What I'm talking about has nothing to do with me." Cain smiled, holding the rosebud to her nose. "Muriel's one of the smartest people I know, and if what you feel for her is genuine there won't be a problem."

"But if the great Cain Casey says there is, then what?"

"Sarcasm doesn't suit you, Shelby." Her smile vanished. "I won't have to say anything because Muriel will figure it out on her own. Up to now she's been the one making big changes, and you, I'm sure, are there encouraging her to fix what was never broken."

"You can't have forgotten everything I've done for you," Shelby said, trying to change tactics. Going head-on with Cain was always a losing proposition. "I was there for you and Emma when you needed me."

"You and your little band of thieves out there wasted time chasing me while you were breeding your own little Barney Kyle." Shelby was amazed that Cain could be so clear speaking through clenched teeth. "Only Barney was a man who went after me, though the same can't be said of Anthony."

"Things happen that we can't always control. You've lost enough family to have learned that lesson." Her answer hit a nerve because Cain pulverized the rosebud in her fist.

"Thank you," Cain said calmly.

"For what?" If she momentarily had the power it was gone, because Cain looked to have repaired the momentary crack in her façade.

"I was a bit conflicted as to how to proceed with Muriel, but now my direction can't be more crystal. Your input has been invaluable."

"Wait," she said, but Cain turned to cut another flower.

"I'd think you'd quit while you were behind, Agent Phillips," Emma said, standing behind her. "You've worn out your welcome, so be nice enough to follow Lou to your car."

Damage control was the first thing on Shelby's mind because she was sure Cain would be on the phone before she could make it to the street. She followed Lou but glanced back right before they turned the corner. Emma had accepted the second rose Cain had cut and was looking at her while she stood by Cain's side.

"Muriel, if she gets to you first, please give me a chance to explain," she said as she turned back toward Muriel's.

❖

"What was that about?" Emma asked.

"A lecture about how I'm ruining Muriel's life."

Emma laughed. "Doesn't she mean how she's ruining Muriel's life? But hoping she'd be that honest is wishful thinking, I guess."

"Feel better?" Their day had started with Emma's morning sickness.

"A few more weeks and I promise I'll stop throwing up on your shoes."

She kissed Emma and hugged her hard enough for her feet to leave the ground. "You can throw up on my head, lass, if it means we get another cute kid at the end of all this."

"And the Feds wonder why I fell for you."

Lou walked back alone and lifted his hand as if asking for permission to interrupt the intimate moment.

"Did Agent Phillips peel out of here to get back to Muriel and explain herself?" Cain asked.

"She did, but you've got another visitor."

They walked back to the house along the back so they could enter through the sunroom. New Orleans police detective Sept Savoie stood and kissed Emma's cheek before she excused herself. The tall white-haired officer had gone to school with Cain and they'd become friends despite the fact that their families had chosen opposite sides of the law. The Caseys were who they were, and the Savoies' family business was law enforcement, with generations of officers on their family tree.

When they were alone, Sept accepted Cain's brief hug. "You look good, Sept," Cain said, waving her into a chair. "How are your parents and siblings?"

"Mama's upset you haven't introduced her to your daughter yet," Sept said, crossing her legs and tapping her fingers on the heel of her shoe. "She hasn't taken Dad's warning about hanging out with the city's criminal element to heart."

"This criminal element got you plenty of dates in high school, Detective Savoie, so don't go knocking me right off," she said, and laughed.

"Is that an admission?"

One of the house staff brought in a tray with coffee so Cain smiled at Sept until the woman had finished serving. "I keep telling you I'm a simple barkeep, but you don't listen, so I like to play along every so often."

"The nuns would rap your knuckles with a two-by-four for telling lies like that, Casey." Sept put her cup down and reached into her jacket pocket. "I'd love to sit and reminisce, but unfortunately this is an official visit."

"Unfortunately after you accepted that badge they're all official visits, old friend."

Sept nodded and handed her some photos. "Recognize any of these guys?"

Six men, all Hispanic looking, all dead. She flipped through the pictures slowly before glancing up at Sept. "The last time I saw them they were taking boxes out of a truck behind Emma's that contained some people who didn't deserve what happened to them." She gave the stack back to Sept and sighed. "So you're here to ask me why I hit back?"

"Only two of these idiots are my cases, and no matter what you think, I don't believe you're responsible for this," Sept said, flicking her finger on the pages.

"Why are you here, then?"

"You've had people out asking a lot of questions, that I've gotten from some of my CIs, but you haven't seemed to get anywhere. I could be wrong, but I have a hunch whoever ordered the murders and deliveries was clamping down on any potential leaks."

"I have no idea who these people are, and I don't have a clue about the motivation behind all this either."

Sept put the pictures back in her pocket and picked up her coffee, then held the cup between her knees as she sat forward. "I believe you and I'm not here to accuse you of anything. Just hear me out before you get pissed and have Lou fling me out on my ass."

"You think I need Lou for that?" She laughed. This was an opportunity to see if the police had found something her people had missed. "Let's treat this talk like we did English and religion classes."

"It's an ongoing investigation, Cain. There's only so much I can tell you."

"Then you can do your English homework all on your own, good Catholic girl, and I'll find someone else to work on the religion help I need."

Sept shook her head and muttered something Cain took for a curse. "I'm only doing this because I know you're better at keeping secrets than the pope," Sept said, making Cain laugh harder. "Your buddies outside told me Hector Delarosa came to Jarvis's funeral. I'm sorry about that, by the way. He was a good man."

"Hector was a surprise to me, and I'm not sure what he's angling for since I told him I'd never do business with him."

"We were starting to make strides into Luis's operation, but now the city seems to be up for grabs. Six murders in one night scares the administration, so I want to know if we've got a turf war on our hands."

Because of their positions they'd never be totally honest with each other, but they could give enough to help the other get what they wanted. "Rodolfo Luis is losing his grip on the area. I don't have any proof, but that's the rumor on the street. Hector's in town but I think he's here buying real estate."

"Like this, you mean?" Sept tapped her jacket pocket where the pictures were.

"Understand that Hector and I are barely acquaintances, not friends, but that doesn't look like his style."

"He's a drug dealer, Cain."

"You want to hear this or not?" She waited until Sept nodded and sat back. "He's much more than a dealer, and I'm not telling you how to do your job, but I'd start putting a task force together if I were you."

"We already know he's at the top of the cartel's food chain, and we know how they stay in power."

"True, but I don't think he's doing this. Hector has a little more style, like I said, or he acts like he does. But pushed, I'm sure he can be as much of a butcher as any of these guys."

"So you're going with your gut here?" Sept asked, sounding like she was wasting her time.

"If you've got a ditch to dig and some guys show up with shovels and fight over the stretch that needs digging, what would you do? If you're smart you sit back and wait."

Sept blinked a few times as if considering what she'd said. "There's another player?"

"We've all got the worst situation here, then, because I was hoping you'd tell me who killed my people."

"Our guys were working the angle that it was Delarosa."

That answer wasn't completely off, but her instincts told her that Hector hadn't started applying pressure yet. "What happened is strange at best, and extremely stupid. I don't know who it is because it makes no sense."

"You've got no idea?"

"I'm not holding back on that, and I really don't have a clue. Actually, if Remi hadn't gotten her own delivery, the message would've been lost completely—whatever that message is. All this managed to do was piss me off, and I've got nowhere to take my anger."

"It's unbelievable you've got no clue."

"My crystal ball's in the shop. If I find out anything, though, I'll make you my first call."

"I'm sure," Sept said, smiling. "Just remember that a turf war doesn't help anyone."

"Noted, and keep your head down. When stuff like this goes down, no one's safe." Cain stood and offered Sept her hand. "When someone doesn't respect business, they won't fear the badge either."

"That's why I thought the Feds were wrong. Emptying a clip into a bunch of cars isn't *your* style." They talked while walking to the front door.

"Don't believe everything the gray suits tell you. You have to know there's a pecking order and they're not about to let you into their sandbox."

"I grew up with you, so I know when someone is blowing smoke up my ass," Sept said, laughing. "Congratulations on the new baby. Lou told me you've got other things on your mind besides plotting revenge on a pack of idiots."

"You know me, I play nice with everyone. It's the people who harm my family that change that."

"And a beautiful family it is, so you keep that head of yours in one piece." Sept hugged her and slapped her on the back. "I can help you this time, Cain, if you let me. These types of people don't deserve for you to do something stupid."

"I wasn't joking about calling you, and come back if you have any other questions." She was willing to help Sept as long as she stayed away from her business. Someone like Hector or Rodolfo, though, she'd serve up on a silver platter if it meant fewer headaches for her.

"Ms. Casey," Carmen, the housekeeper said, "Mr. Delarosa's on the phone."

"Maybe it's time to start polishing the silver," Cain thought as she closed the front door.

CHAPTER TWELVE

His face was still swollen, but that wasn't what he found strange. Staring at himself in the mirror was like looking at a stranger with his hair. A stranger named Jerome who now had the things he'd always envied as Anthony.

"Do you see something you don't like?" Gracelia asked, pressing her naked breasts into his back. They'd spent most of their time since getting back from the doctor's office in bed, where she'd fucked any reservations he'd had right out of him.

"You must've really not liked my face," he said, rubbing the jawline that was now much squarer and had a slight cleft in the chin. He hadn't been sure about that feature, but Gracelia had spent so much time running her tongue along it while she rode him that he'd come to appreciate it.

"What I like is that I get to keep you now," her hand went to his groin, "and I don't have to worry about everyone who's after you. To answer your question, I loved your face before and I like you. I'll get used to this one."

"You're going to kill me," he said, not removing her hand. The shower was running behind them and they had dinner reservations at the resort Ventanas, but his mind softened as he got harder. "It's time to return the favor, babe." He saw her smile as he faced her and she dropped to her knees, taking the length of him in her hand before she did with her mouth.

It didn't take long. He needed rest before he could hold an erection to give Gracelia what she wanted. As she had for the past couple of days, she scrubbed his body with a sea sponge and bath gel as soon as they got wet. Up to now she'd stirred his passion by talking to him like an experienced phone-sex operator, but it was time to go back to work.

"Did you think about what I said?" Gracelia asked, rubbing his stomach in small circles.

"First tell me where Juan is."

"He's doing something for me," Gracelia said, her circular motions going lower.

It was the first time he'd stopped any of her advances. "Where is he?" She looked up at him with her right eyebrow raised. "You want this to work, you let me in, or you can work alone."

She hesitated a few more moments but started talking when he let her hand go. "I sent him to New Orleans with orders to start putting pressure on Rodolfo's business."

"That's it?" Her response sounded incomplete. "Juan isn't known for his obedience."

"You'll have to get used to Gustavo, Jerome, and he knows better than to deviate from what I told him." He rinsed and shut the water off, leaving her standing in the large stall alone. "What? I told you what you asked."

"You're either lying or you left out a big part." Pissing her off was a gamble, but this wasn't going to be the kind of relationship he had with Annabel, who had no respect for him.

"From what you both told me, the city has its power players," she said, before he made it out with a towel wrapped around his waist.

"New Orleans is a perfect location for what you have in mind, Gracelia, because the cops are understaffed and overworked, but they're not totally incompetent. Add to that the eager agents Annabel's got working for her, and you have to be careful being too ambitious." He propped one hip against the counter and crossed his arms. "What exactly did you have *Gustavo* do?"

She described the checklist and what her son had done so far. He let his head drop back as she spoke, thinking that Juan hadn't inherited his stupidity only from his father. "I thought this would shake up the power structure and get them off their game."

"More like you galvanized two of the three families into hunting down whoever did this. Brilliant plan," he said, dropping the towel to search for clean clothes.

"Juan told me—"

"Get it through your head, Juan will never have the brains to run a pig farm, much less something as complicated as the operation you have in mind." He shoved his legs into a pair of jeans so savagely he thought they'd rip. "I realize he's your son, but face the truth before you get us all killed."

"He only needs a little guidance," she said, trying to put her hands on him. "My brother was a horrible influence, but the two of us can change that. With your help he can become the man I know his father was."

"Are you kidding me?" He grabbed the first shirt he found in the closet and left it unbuttoned as he looked for his shoes. "Juan isn't a leader. He's more like someone who needs to be kept on a very short leash."

"Did you forget you're a guest in my home? Keep talking like that and you won't forget the last seconds of your life when I have you flung off the back of the house to the beach." Her chest was red from anger and she showed no modesty as she stood naked in the middle of the room.

"How long do you think the men you've surrounded yourself with will stay when you tell them you plan to put Juan in charge? They'll fight over who gets to call Rodolfo and beg to go back, and I'm not telling you this to be cruel."

"Really? You have a strange way of being nice."

"You can have me killed, but then you'll have done away with the one person who can keep you intact." Pushing the rumpled sheets aside, he sat on the bed. "Dreams are one thing, but now we've got to deal with reality. What you did concerning Rodolfo was a good move, but giving Juan his way was not." When she sat next to him he took his shirt off and offered it to her. "We need to redirect everyone's thinking now."

"What does that mean?"

"You let Juan go after Casey by having five of her people killed, and Remi by taking out one. Did he tell you exactly what the theatrics were all about?"

"So Cain could picture herself in one of those boxes soon," Gracelia explained, like she was describing Juan's role in the school play.

"And Jatibon's delivery?"

"He said she's another freak of nature."

"Jesus Christ," he said disgustedly. He closed his eyes and took a few deep breaths so he could calm down enough not to take his anger out on Gracelia. When he was centered he got up and dipped the small golden spoon into the dish of coke Gracelia kept in the bedroom. One a day was all he allowed himself, sure he could keep from becoming an addict.

"We have a fucking disaster, and there's only one way to turn it to our advantage," he said, zeroing in on a plan of his own.

"Do you plan to tell me or do you need to insult Juan some more? He is, after all, in New Orleans making sure nothing can be traced back to us."

"Casey's like a bloodhound when threatened, and she won't stop until she's found and destroyed whoever went against her. The only way to redirect her is for her to become the hunted."

"That's Juan's plan."

"Juan's plan is to take Emma Casey, who said no, and who'll rip his balls off the first chance she gets if he's lucky enough to succeed. No, the pressure has to come from someone other than us."

The plan was different, and if everyone involved put it together it would make theirs much easier to bring to fruition. He was certain, though, that it would produce the results he was after.

"Are you sure about that?" Gracelia asked.

"Think about who'll be blamed, babe, and when that happens, Casey will have other problems to think about."

"I hope you're right, because if you aren't, you'll create the perfect storm against us."

❖

The sun bled through the teak slats of the plantation shutters covering Dallas's bedroom window. In the streaks they created she watched the little particles of dust that floated in the air, but it was hard to concentrate on the sight. She'd woken up with Remi's head between her legs, and the light touch of her tongue on her clit was driving her insane.

"God," she said, the only word she'd been capable of since she'd opened her eyes and her clit was so hard she was afraid it would pop. Remi had her ready and wet, and she lifted her bottom off the bed by pressing her feet into Remi's back, but Remi refused to give her what she wanted.

When chasing Remi's tongue didn't work she slapped the side of Remi's head with her foot. "Do you intend to finish what you started?"

she asked, looking down at Remi's unique eyes. The one blue and one green were full of that mischief she loved to see because it was such an important part of Remi's personality. In a way Remi embodied Dallas's permission to break all her own self-imposed rules.

Remi suddenly changed what she'd been doing and sucked her in—hard. When she let go Dallas heard a popping noise. "Are you sure you're awake?" Remi licked gently again. "I don't want you to sleep through what'll hopefully be an awesome orgasm."

"Do you think you're funny?" she asked, reaching down and encouraging Remi to come up and pin her to the bed.

"I'm trying to be romantic," Remi said, pressing her pelvis into hers, which made her want to be touched. "I woke up with my hand between your legs and you were wet."

She ran her fingers along Remi's jaw until she hooked them behind her neck. "See, even in my sleep I can't get enough of you."

"Right now I want you to get just enough of me." With her weight held up by one arm Remi slipped her fingers deep inside, touching Dallas in a way that made the walls of her sex clamp down. The sensation was so good that she pressed her feet to the bed to get as much of Remi's fingers inside as possible.

The way Remi held her hand made the side of the knuckle of her index finger rub the length of her clit on every down stroke. Dallas could hear her heartbeat in her ears, but the moaning she couldn't help muffled it. It'd been like this from the first time they were together. Remi touched her and the rest of the world was locked out so nothing could hurt her, not even her memories.

She held the tide back as long as she could, but her orgasm came when she pushed up against Remi so hard that she almost knocked her off.

When she begged Remi to stop, Remi reversed their positions and held her against her chest. In these moments Dallas knew with certain clarity that she'd share her life with Remi.

"Will I see you at the studio later?" she asked when she was able to speak again. "I don't think I can tell you enough how much I love you in the little time we have this morning."

"I really like it when you get sappy on me," Remi said, squeezing the cheeks of her butt and making her laugh. "Actually I've got a few meetings outside the studio today, but Dwayne and Steve will make sure everything turns out okay," Remi said, mentioning her law partners who helped her run the studio. "I should be finished by dinner if you and Kristen are interested."

"We'd love to."

They shared a shower and went down for coffee. Remi was wearing the suit she kept in her closet, but she'd put on a robe since it would be hours before she had to be anywhere. She smiled when they found Kristen talking to Emil and Simon. Everything seemed normal in an abnormal way, since not too many people found a couple of armed guards in their kitchen.

When Remi left, Emil excused himself to the coolness of the patio, leaving Dallas alone with Kristen, who didn't have her orientation tour of Tulane until ten that morning. Her sister was on her second piece of toasted French bread with strawberry preserves, and Dallas was reminded of one of the few happy memories from when her mother was alive. They would spend the morning picking wild berries and the afternoon making preserves.

"Why are you so quiet?" Kristen asked between bites.

"I was thinking about when Mama made preserves. I buy the strawberry kind all the time, but none of them taste the same as hers."

"Right before I go to sleep every night I spend time thinking about her. It was like she was there one morning making us breakfast, then when we got back from playing she was gone." Kristen took a sip of coffee and closed her eyes, her face suddenly a reflection of sadness. "After that I used to pray like she taught us that you wouldn't go away too and leave me alone."

Their mother had left when she was twelve and Kristen was seven. She'd been old enough to hear the nightly arguments and the sound of slaps that would mean her mama would have new bruises to add to the ones she always had everywhere. It hadn't taken long after she left for Johnny to start visiting her room. At first, shame, not bruises like her mama's, had marred her life. The bruises, though, had come not much later, since Johnny couldn't help himself.

"I hated her for a long time after she left us there," Dallas admitted softly, making Kristen push her plate away so she could hold her hands. "Her life with Johnny was hell, but I always wondered what kind of mother leaves her children with someone like him."

"Do you still hate her?"

She looked at Kristen and shook her head, her eyes blurry with tears, as they always were when she thought of their mother. "I did for so long, but one day I wondered why. The answer was the same one I'd give you if you asked why I'd leave you. The only way I'd do that was if I was dead."

"That's what I think too," Kristen said, squeezing her fingers. "And I think dear old dad killed her."

"That's the main reason I decided to run with you when you were eleven. I really thought we'd get caught," she said out loud for the first time. "That rat hole we lived in was all I knew, and I figured we'd only get so far and he'd find us and drag us back."

"Dallas," Kristen said, coming around the counter so she could hug her, "it's why I thank God every day that you found Remi. You discovered this place, and you have your career, and you've given me a life that's as far from where we started as you could've, but you're still running. Aren't you tired after all these years?"

"I'm not—"

"Yes, you are," Kristen said, still holding her. "You need to be fair to yourself and to Remi. She's the one last gift that fate has given you, and it's time you told her your remarkable story. And that's how I see you."

"I'm far from it."

"How many people start as a runaway and end up with your life?"

If she couldn't face the truth of what it had taken for them to have this moment, how could Remi? It hadn't come because she was remarkable, but simply because she'd used what Johnny had taught her against her will and made it work for her. The men she'd had sex with in those tapes had disgusted her to the point that she'd never felt fully clean again, but it was the one sure way for a seventeen-year-old to keep a studio apartment and feed and educate her little sister.

Cain might've found the tape she had a starring role in, but there were others. She doubted anyone would ever recognize the skinny girl with jet black hair as Dallas Montgomery, but that was no guarantee in an industry that loved to dig up dirt and expose it to the world.

"You need to start getting ready," she told Kristen. This was as far as she could go on this subject today, and Kristen must have understood when she kissed her temple and left her alone with her coffee.

Maybe she should stop running from all the things that in reality weren't her fault. Admitting who she really was and what she'd been capable of doing, though, seemed more of a gamble than running from Johnny. And if life had taught her anything, it was that fate had a way of catching up no matter how hard and fast you ran. But she couldn't build a future on a shaky foundation.

"Hey," she said into the phone. "Do you have time to talk today?" It was like throwing the dice Remi loved so much, but it would take a while before she knew if they landed on snake eyes and the game ended.

CHAPTER THIRTEEN

Y ou ever get tired of that?" Sabana asked, pointing behind them.

The surveillance had picked up considerably all of a sudden, and Cain felt like everyone was in on a secret no one had bothered to share with her. A bunch of dead delivery men who, after a couple of days of searching she still couldn't identify, didn't explain the two cars with tinted windows in front of the van she was used to. They were getting close to the office and her gut told her to keep going.

"Lou," she said, after glancing back through her own tinted windows, "keep driving. I feel like breakfast out today."

"Something wrong?" he asked.

"I feel a little hinky surrounded by so many Feds, so let's change our routine a bit." Next to her, Sabana couldn't seem to stop looking back. "This happens every so often," she said.

After Sabana's mother had come to talk to her she'd decided to be an active participant in Sabana's training. In Sabana's short time on the job, Lou had reported what a good shot she was and, despite her size, a good fighter.

It was apparent now that Rick had started his sister's training long before she'd asked for a job. Most encouraging, Sabana's anger toward the world had cooled considerably. Cain's intuition told her this wasn't the time for an overzealous hothead on her payroll.

"To answer your question," she told Sabana to make her stop staring at the pack of hunters behind them, "you learn to work around it."

"Unless you're good at shaking these idiots, I don't see how."

"That's why she has people like us," Lou said, "and don't ever think they're stupid. That's the fastest way to get caught. Where to, boss?"

When they passed the office the lead car behind them broke from the line and pulled alongside them as if trying to get a look inside. That was less likely to happen than for her to see through their dark windows.

"Lou, try to find a right turn somewhere," she said, putting her hand on the armrest. They were in the middle of the block and the car next to them sped up and passed them as the one behind them took its place at their side.

"They've got us boxed in," Sabana said in obvious panic, reaching for her shoulder holster.

This wasn't the movies, so if these weren't Feds, then there weren't any bulletproof barriers to stop the fire of whoever was on the other side of the glass. If they had fully automatic weapons, Cain and the others would look like the guys in Sept's stack of photos.

"Wait," she said as Sabana drew her gun. There was a grocery at the end of the street. "Lou, pull in there." She pointed to the parking entrance. The car in front stopped and blocked their path forward.

"What the hell is this?" Sabana said, almost screaming and fighting Cain's grip on her wrist.

"Calm down," Cain said, but was ready to let Sabana's hand go if this wasn't what looked now like an arrest. "Are you okay?" she asked, making Sabana look at her.

"Yeah." Sabana divided her attention between her and the cars now surrounding them.

"Put that away," Cain said, watching the doors of the car open and the two men in gray suits get out. "You too, Lou. I don't know what this is, but call Sanders and Muriel, and tell them to be on standby."

Two more agents walked up on the other side of them and knocked on the glass. The guy was as big as Lou and he didn't seem to care that he was about to break it with his fist.

"Open the door and show your hands." The two on Sabana's side drew their weapons, and while they held them with both hands in a defensive posture, they pointed them down at the street.

"Do what he says but stay inside," Cain said to both of them. "I doubt this has anything to do with you." She cracked her door a little, allowing the big man who'd been knocking to finish the job for her. "Can I see some ID?"

"Sure," he said, laughing as he produced his FBI credentials. His head took up much of the photo, but before she could read the name he grabbed her by her jacket lapels and practically lifted her out of the car.

His strength was impressive and she couldn't stop her face from slamming into the trunk when he spun her around and pushed her head down. When her bottom lip crashed into her teeth, splitting it enough for her to taste the blood, the pain was explosive. Her right eyebrow was the first point of impact when she did lift her head, obviously too far for his liking, and he slammed her head down again while his partner handcuffed her.

She felt woozy when she was stood back up and was herded to one of the cars. Her head was bleeding now so she had to close her right eye to keep it from stinging.

"What exactly is this about?" she asked the agent who'd cuffed her and was helping his partner guide her. Instead of answering, he read her her rights and asked if she understood. Before they managed to get her in the backseat she noticed that the regular surveillance team never got out of the van. When they started moving she could see the look of fury on Lou's face but she was grateful that he'd kept his head, as had Sabana.

The car made the trip to the federal building in short time, heading into a basement parking area. Her face was still bleeding from both places and the taste of blood was making her nauseous. This was new—new agents, new procedures, and a new set of rules, or disregard for them. Muriel had warned her about the changes after September 11 and law enforcement's newfound freedoms at the expense of the individual's, but that had to do with terrorists. She was many things, but no terrorist.

"You don't look so smug without backup," the big man said when he opened the back door.

"Tough talk for someone who had to handcuff me and who travels in a pack." He was rough pulling her out but she was glad to be away from the car and off her hands since the cuffs were too tight.

"You act tough, Casey, but you're no different than any other low-life scum out there on the street who thinks they can do whatever the hell they feel like. This time, though, you went too far and you're going to pay," he said right in her ear so the others couldn't hear. "What you should pray for is to make it to trial. Sometimes shit happens and trash gets taken out."

"Your threatening techniques sound a little clichéd." She tried to cock her head back and out of the way when he swung, but with the other agent so close his fist had no problem connecting with the cut already open over her eye. The instant darkness brought an end to the explosion of pain.

❖

"What the hell was that?" Sabana asked, sitting next to Lou as he followed the caravan that had taken Cain.

"Get on the phone and find Sanders."

Lou followed but had to break off when they entered the parking facility. He explained to Sanders what had happened and told him to find Muriel so they could get to Cain. "We have to get back to the house and tell Emma."

"Are you sure we should leave here?" Sabana asked.

He gazed down the entrance where the cars and van had gone and wanted to hit something. Cain was his boss, but families like his and Sabana's had been with the Caseys for a long time, so Cain was part of his family and heritage. His responsibility now was to tell Emma in person and pray the news didn't harm the baby.

"I don't want to, but Emma has to know and she has to have us there. This isn't something to spring on her over the phone." His cell phone rang and he answered as he headed back to the house.

"Muriel's not responding and the housekeeper said she's not available," Sanders said.

The day couldn't get any more bizarre. "Send an associate over there and tell them not to leave until they see her. These idiots did a number on Cain's face right in front of us, so I can't imagine what's going on with no one watching."

"I'm almost there, don't worry."

"Sabana, you did well today, and you need to keep your cool for the rest of this, okay?" He put his hand on her shoulder briefly while he kept his eyes forward. "Once this is over payback will come, and you can be a part of it."

"I know you think I'm a child compared to you."

"You and I have a lot in common when it comes to life, so I understand you better than anyone. That's why I pushed to get you what you wanted, but go at the pace you're comfortable with and do only those things you're comfortable with."

"I'm ready for whatever, Lou."

Emma was dressed and standing in the kitchen with Carmen when they arrived. She smiled at them but her eyes moved to the door. It was amazing how quickly her face lost color when Cain didn't appear.

"Lou?" she said, placing her hands flat on the counter. "Tell me."

His first instinct was to not share everything, but that wasn't fair to Emma.

When he finished, Emma asked calmly, "Did you tell Muriel?" He explained that situation and she lowered her head. "I see."

Her posture didn't improve when Sanders called and informed them that while they weren't denying they had Cain, he couldn't get any information on her whereabouts or why she'd been picked up.

Katlin and Merrick arrived from physical therapy and Sabana told them what was happening. Merrick rolled her wheelchair closer to Emma and took her hand. "You need to stay calm," Merrick said slowly. She worked every day until she was exhausted, and her strength was returning. "And you need to be strong like you did when she got shot. This family is yours too."

"Carmen, could you call and cancel my lunch date, with my apologies," Emma said, nodding to Merrick. They had resolved any ill feelings between them long before now. "Lou and Katlin, let's meet in the office."

"What about me?" Sabana asked.

"You sit with me," Merrick said, laughing at Sabana's frown. "It's time you learned a few things from someone else." Emma looked back before leaving and Merrick smiled. Emma had taken an active role in her recovery. "I'll be here if you need something," she said to Emma.

In the office Emma hesitated before she sat in Cain's chair, but they'd discussed this and she didn't have time to waver. "Tell me everything again, Lou, so Katlin can understand what happened."

Lou's voice sounded tight, as if he was sitting for her sake but really wanted to run out of the room. She put her hand over her abdomen, trying to calm her stomach as she listened, and sighed when he described how they jerked Cain out of the car. Her lover was hurt but, at the moment, beyond her reach.

"Sanders said they wouldn't give him any information on her?" Emma asked.

"They'll have to give us something eventually, but right now they can use the booking process as an excuse." Katlin adjusted the double shoulder holster she wore. "I know what Cain said about Muriel, but we need to call her and get her down there."

"Lou's tried a couple of times," Emma said, picking up the phone. She wasn't willing to accept "not available" as an excuse. "Rosa, good morning, it's Emma Casey. I need to speak to Muriel and I need you to tell her it's an emergency." She ran her fingers along the leather blotter that was the only new thing on the desk. She had given it to Cain when they'd moved back in and she'd redecorated.

"She apologize, Miss Emma, but she no can come to the telephone."

"Thank you," Emma said, ending the call, then asking Lou for Sanders's number. "Anything?"

"Something big has obviously happened," Sanders said, a lot of traffic noise in the background. "Whatever it is has made everyone in the building hostile, so my guess so far is that they're blaming Cain."

"I'm on my way down there, but call me if anything new comes up. I've got one stop to make, and I need to know anything you find out as soon as you do."

"You two have no idea what this is about?" Emma asked, gently putting the phone down and resting her fingers on the receiver.

"She asked, but the asshole was more interested in humiliating her than in answering any questions," Lou said.

"She left this morning for a meeting with the Jatibons to talk over what they had so far," Emma said, trying to figure out what she was missing. "Whatever it is, I can't believe it has anything to do with what she's dealing with out on the streets right now."

"Let's go," Lou said, standing as if he needed to move.

Emma wanted Muriel with her to navigate the complicated legal web the government had cast.

The house seemed quiet and Rosa had the door open before she could knock. "I told her you were here, Miss Emma, and she be down in a minute," Rosa said, leading them to the den.

Emma was the only one to sit, with Lou and Katlin flanking her chair. She glanced at her watch until four minutes went by and Muriel finally appeared. "Muriel, thank God," she said, standing and walking toward her.

"Sorry you had to make the trip, Emma," Muriel said, after briefly hugging her. "Whatever it is will have to wait, though."

"Why?" Emma could almost hear Cain's voice telling her that

here was where the trail began, whether she wanted to believe it or not.

"Muriel, come on," Katlin said, but stopped talking when Emma lifted her hand for silence.

"Why?" she repeated.

"Shelby's packing," Muriel said, looking back up the stairs. "Someone killed her parents last night. From the preliminary reports it was a hit, and not something random."

"And you think—" Katlin said, shutting up this time because Emma turned around and glared.

"Do I think what?" Muriel asked, looking at all three of them.

"You should go and finish up, then," she said, for the first time understanding why Cain always sounded so cool on the subject of Muriel.

"She's leaving alone, Emma, and it's because she thinks our family had something to do with this."

"She's not the only one."

"Listen, she told me about the visit she paid you guys yesterday, and how it ended. Last night someone walked into her parents' home and shot both of them in the head. It was hard to hear."

"My condolences to her," Emma said, starting for the door. She wouldn't be leaving with Muriel, but at least she had the answer to their mystery.

"If it's something important, call me later," Muriel said.

"It's nothing that concerns you after all."

❖

The Formica-topped table felt cold under her cheek when Cain came to, and when she slowly lifted her head she found two small pools of blood. She rarely let herself fantasize about killing anyone in law enforcement, but the big asshole who'd hit her while she was wearing cuffs rated her consideration.

"Here." Annabel Hicks placed a box of tissue in front of her and sat back again.

Her lip felt like it was still oozing, but she'd tear her jacket and use that before she accepted anything. Instead she spat the blood in her mouth on the floor, not caring how crude she might look. The handcuffs were still on but now only on one hand, keeping her tethered to the table.

"You should've used better sense than to resist Agent Cehan when you were stopped," Annabel said, picking lint from her skirt. "I only wanted to talk to you, but now I've got something to hold you on."

Cain ran her finger along the side of her face and her eye to try to get the dried blood off. The accumulation was making it uncomfortable to blink. She didn't know if Annabel had watched the tape of her arrest—if it existed. It didn't matter if she had and ignored it or hadn't, because the agents felt she was due a beat-down. Either way it'd be a waste to argue about it.

"That's not like you to give us an opening like that," Annabel said, as if she were holding up her end of the conversation. When she stayed quiet Annabel finally glanced up from her picking. "Nothing to say? Here I was looking forward to your unending stream of wit."

"Agent Hicks, would you like to explain why I'm here, or do we wait for my attorney to arrive?"

"From my understanding, your attorney's not coming," Annabel said with a large smug smile. "Perhaps there's no defense this time."

"Well, maybe you should tell me what I've done in case I've got some overwhelming desire to confess. I wouldn't want to get the details wrong."

Annabel peered over her shoulder to the mirrored glass she was sure was there, but only for a second. "Did you meet with Agent Shelby Phillips this week?"

"Don't insult me, Annabel. If anyone is familiar with my social calendar it's you. All those hours of watching and waiting for me to spit on the sidewalk so you can justify your existence should be good for something." She spat on the floor again for effect and tried to keep her breathing calm.

"I'll take that as a yes."

"Say it already before you choke on it."

They stared at each other until the agent who'd arrested her came in. Agent Cehan was the name Annabel had used and Cain stared at him, noticing what she could before he joined his boss on the other side of the table. His short hair, reasonable suit, and polished shoes didn't distinguish him from all the other male agents she'd dealt with. The difference was the too-large-to-be-professional, but distinctive belt buckle with a set of horns engraved on the silver.

"Haven't you tripped over your feet enough today?" Cehan asked. "Any more clumsiness on your part might leave a scar."

"What about that meeting set you off?" Annabel asked, ignoring the big man's threat. "I've known you to effectively deal with threats, but this was beyond cruel."

Something obviously had happened to Shelby after their meeting, and Muriel believed whatever it was. Nothing came to mind since she hadn't even called Muriel after Shelby had left the day before. Her head hurt, and no matter how she tried to come up with an answer, she couldn't.

"This was against one of our own, scumbag," Cehan said, stabbing his finger on the table.

"If you want, put me in a cell, Tex, because I'm not saying anything else. The Texas-lawman routine might intimidate others, but the twang's not working. You're new to this job and the area, but let me give you some advice. Whatever smoke they blew up your ass at the University of Texas about hookin' 'em is something you might want to relearn. Trade the white hat in and rope yourself a desk job because you'll be a joke in less than a month on the street."

Her assessment might be off but not by much. In the commotion of the morning she'd missed the accent. "And, Agent Hicks, you and I both know an attorney is here on my behalf. I'll wait however long it takes, but this interview is over. I'm not in the mood for games."

"This is your one opportunity—"

"To help myself, I know the drill. Either spell it out or book me, but I'm done. One session of having a big strong man beat on me while I've got cuffs on is enough for one day."

"You think not having them on would've made a difference?" Cehan asked, making her laugh when the question got more of a rise out of Annabel than her.

"So much for my bout of clumsiness, Agent," Cain said, and laughed harder when he stood up and loomed over her.

"Outside," Annabel said with a hand on his arm. They left her alone and Cain went over what little Annabel had said, but nothing registered. At the moment that wasn't what worried her. Her mind was on Emma and her reaction when Lou told her what had happened. Emma would handle it, but any stress she suffered affected the baby. If that happened, Agent Cehan would learn a new meaning to roping and branding.

❖

"Bring up the arrest surveillance," Annabel said to Lionel Jones, one of the team's agents she'd assigned to Cain.

"Our equipment was offline for maintenance, ma'am," he said.

"Claire, that's your story too?" she asked Claire Lansing, the team's other computer and surveillance expert.

"It's routine, ma'am, but you'll have our reports that it was a clean arrest."

"I'm sure everyone will have the same story, but you all better pray that nothing concrete contradicts you. Cain Casey loves nothing better than to make my office look like idiots, and I'm tired of it." Annabel addressed all of them, letting them know she understood their allegiance to Shelby and that what had happened was more important than procedure. "Brent, I realize you're new to the team, but careful about how zealous you are."

"If you looked at the crime-scene photos, he wasn't zealous enough," Joe Simmons, the new team leader, said. "Shelby's dad was retired, and her mom didn't have any law-enforcement experience. If Casey had anything to do with this, we should save the taxpayers the cost of a trial with a cheap bullet."

"We need evidence since you provided her alibi with surveillance, but that doesn't mean she didn't hire a gun. Find the link to whoever did this and tie it back to her," Annabel said, watching Cain through the glass. She hadn't really moved but she was cuffed to the table. Anyone else would've shown fear by now, but Cain was still showing as much of a relaxed posture as she could in the hard, uncomfortable chair. "Focus and work fast. We all owe that to Shelby."

"Ma'am," another agent said from the door. "Shelby's waiting in your office."

When they'd gotten the news she'd arranged for Shelby's travel and some agents to escort her to California. Her eyes were red and puffy, but Shelby wasn't crying as Annabel hugged her. The file that had arrived from the Los Angeles office was open at the edge of the desk with a sheet of notes next to it.

"Let us work this one, Shelby. You'll need all your strength to get through the next week."

"My father was a practical man who didn't want to burden me when the time came, so he's made all the arrangements. All my aunts and I have to do is show up." Shelby laughed but Annabel could hear her pain. "I won't interfere, but please don't shut me out."

"Is there any way Cain figured out your new assignment? Could she know you're working undercover and using Muriel as a way in?" The questions were difficult since they sounded like they laid blame, but it was a place to start. "It would go a long way in providing us with a motive."

"I don't see how. You're my only contact and I didn't push Muriel too hard. You and I both knew slow was the best way to make progress."

"What I don't understand is why, then. We know more than enough about her and this doesn't fit."

Shelby shuffled through the pictures until she found one she looked at closely before handing it to her. "I know Cain, and she prides herself on her subtlety. Big acts aren't her, which is what Kyle never really understood about her. He was always trying to find the big flaw, when the answers were in the minutiae."

The photo was one of many the responding agents had taken around the house. Next to the fireplace was a bar, and the wall above it was covered with pictures of Shelby's father's work highlights. He was smiling in every one, standing next to other people in uniforms, but nothing about the area looked out of the ordinary.

"Is something out of place?" Annabel asked.

"My parents were social drinkers and they entertained friends who liked to drink, so from the time I was little, that bar was well used." Annabel studied the photo again as she spoke. "Even though our house was always full of cops, they all were gin and vodka drinkers."

"Maybe they made some new friends."

Shelby picked up the image when Annabel put it down. "My father's run with the same guys since he graduated from the police academy, and my mom and their wives made up the other part of their circle. After all these years they opened their home to a Jameson whiskey drinker? The drink of choice of Cain Casey? Do you really believe that?"

"I can't build a case on a bottle of whiskey."

She sat back and crossed her arms over her chest. "It's the small things, ma'am, and I won't stop until I find the connection."

"She's downstairs right now. I had her picked up for questioning and she resisted, so Brent brought her in."

That made her sit up again. "She resisted?"

"I'm looking into that because her face bears the result of not cooperating, but everyone's telling the same story with no tape to back it up."

Biting down on her lip must have been making Shelby's lip hurt but she didn't stop. "Lionel didn't record it?"

"They were updating the equipment so it wasn't online," she said.

"I love them, but please tell them not to give her an opportunity to squirm out of this."

"Go take care of your family and I'll deal with this personally."

Shelby combed her hair back with her hands and stood. "I appreciate it, ma'am, and I'll be back as soon as the services are done."

"Take more time than that," Annabel said, moving around the desk to be closer to her.

"Unless you order me not to work this case, I want to see it through. This is the last mistake Cain's going to make as a free person."

CHAPTER FOURTEEN

"Do you have an appointment?" the receptionist asked Emma, but her eyes darted from the silent Lou to Katlin, who stood close behind Emma.

"No, but if you could tell Mr. Talbot all I need is five minutes of his time." When faced with what appeared to be an impossible situation, Cain had always said to think how to turn it to your advantage. The FBI had taken Cain, and that was a different game than Juan taking her. You couldn't exactly hit back without causing yourself a more serious problem.

"I'm Mr. Talbot's secretary," another woman that joined them said. "What can I do for you?"

"My name is Emma Casey. Cain Casey is my partner," Emma said, reaching for the woman's hand. "I believe Cain's in danger and I need Mr. Talbot's help."

George Talbot was the U.S. Attorney for the fifth district in New Orleans, and he had a history with Cain that had nothing to do with trying to prosecute her. Years earlier Cain had saved his daughter from a life of drug abuse after she fell victim to some loser she'd started dating.

The young girl had been holed up in an abandoned apartment in one of the worst neighborhoods in the city. Cain had shared the story with Emma only recently when she'd wondered why George had helped in the trap the government had set for Barney Kyle. It'd been the only time Cain had told anyone about it since she'd acted as one parent helping another, no matter what George's position was.

From what Cain had said, her people had found the girl naked and alone on a mattress surrounded by rotting trash. The guy she'd run with had hooked her on heroin and, from the look of it, had turned her out as a prostitute to feed their habit.

What Cain had done to scare the girl straight wasn't part of her story, but even through her drug stupor it had made enough of an impression to transform the addict into becoming a successful prosecutor in the district attorney's office and a mother of four.

But George and his daughter were the most thankful that no one would ever use her past against her since there was no police record. Only Cain knew what happened to the boy who later could've been a blackmail threat, and her only explanation was that he was keeping Big Gino Bracato company. That meant the only other threat had been buried so deep he wouldn't get the chance to drag the Talbot girl down again.

"Cain didn't exaggerate when she told me how beautiful you are," George said from the head of the hall lined with doors. "How about you folks relax out here and Ms. Casey and I'll have a talk," he said to the guards and his staff.

The credenza behind the large desk was lined with photos of little boys in an array of activities with George, and some with him and an attractive brunette. "You have a beautiful family," Emma said when he sat next to her instead of behind the desk.

"They are all a gift, as I'm sure you know. My daughter was one, but my grandsons are my joy and the reason I'm contemplating retirement."

"Cain was arrested today," Emma said, thinking she didn't have any time to waste.

"Agent Hicks did send a preliminary report over to that effect," George said, crossing his legs.

"Cain had nothing to do with Shelby Phillips's parents, Mr. Talbot. She's never left the state, didn't give any orders, and knows nothing about this."

He hiked his eyebrows and laughed. "You sure know a lot about this, young lady."

"More like I've learned how your system works, sir. If something goes wrong, then without considering anyone else you come after Cain, and I'm getting tired of it."

"If you live with someone like Cain, you have to figure it was only a matter of time before she got caught," Annabel said after walking in with a file under her arm.

"Agent Hicks, everyone is required to knock," George said, standing up and sounding peeved.

"I was in the neighborhood filing charges, George, not trying to insult you." Annabel smiled, staring at Emma. "But now that I'm here I can ask you in person for no bail on this one." She handed him the file in a way Emma could see Cain's name.

"Why not go ahead and say she's guilty, Mr. Talbot, and save the taxpayers money. It's Cain, so she must be guilty," Emma said, lifting her purse from the floor. "After all, your people," she said looking at Annabel as she spoke, "felt free to beat her, take her in, and deny her right to counsel."

"Your girlfriend resisted arrest, Ms. Casey, and she was being processed when Mr. Riggole arrived." The way Annabel laughed made it sound like her cause was hopeless. "This isn't a conspiracy against you and the supposed angel you live with."

"Since you tape every moment of our lives, can we see what happened? Because I seriously doubt Cain lost control and attacked one of your people," she said, turning in her chair so she could fully face Annabel. "You finally found a way in, Agent, and I bet you can't wait to gloat. Here's your chance."

"She's right, Annabel," George said when Annabel didn't respond. "You brought the report, so pull out the CD and I'll pop it in," he said, standing and walking to his computer. The CD tray slid out and he peered up at Annabel over the rim of his glasses. "Annabel?"

"The file has the reports of all the agents involved, but video wasn't possible this time," Annabel said, seeming to tighten her arms across her chest. "It doesn't make the arrest any less sound."

George fell back in his chair and looked at her. "She's right, Ms. Casey."

"Please, Mr. Talbot, call me Emma," she said, opening her purse, which made Annabel drop her arms as if she suddenly presented a threat. "Even though I wouldn't describe Agent Hicks's employees' behavior toward Cain as a conspiracy, it is harassment. When a group is this determined, shortcuts become the norm." She pulled a CD out of her purse and held it up for Annabel to see. "This is your chance to change your story."

"Please," Annabel said, and laughed as if she'd told her a funny joke. "You expect me to fall for this? What is that?"

She stood and handed George the disc. "This, Agent Hicks, is me correcting what you said. Two cars and a van couldn't provide a tape, but if your agents were really interested they should've asked the security guard at the grocery."

Sabana had paid a thousand dollars for it since the guy who patrolled the store for shoplifters said the cameras outside actually worked. The idea to ask had occurred to Emma as they left Muriel's house, and Sabana had come through.

Considering where they'd been pulled over, what had happened would be on the tape. It was a gamble because she hadn't had time to watch it, so it could prove what Annabel had said—but this was about how well she knew Cain, not what Annabel and the others speculated about her. The odds were in her favor.

"We can't verify what's on there," Annabel said.

"I don't really know what's on there, Mr. Talbot," she said pointing to the disc in his hand. "It could prove what the agent said, since everyone told the same story."

"George," Annabel said when he put it in the slot, "I could take it back and have our lab verify it."

"Sit," he said, prompting the computer player. The tape was date- and time-stamped, so George looked at the file and fast-forwarded to the time reported. Just enough of the street was showing so they could see two unmarked cars, the front of the surveillance van, and Cain's car.

Emma watched as the large man slammed Cain's head to the back of the car twice, and she gripped the edge of the desk when Cain was cuffed and lifted back up. A line of blood was visible down her face as she was shoved into the car. Emma was so angry she could hear her heartbeat in her ears, and the thought that she was right about Cain's control brought no comfort.

"You're right, Agent Hicks," she said, not caring if her voice was too loud. "Cain must've blinked too much or offered a sarcastic comment, which proves she was resisting."

"That doesn't tell the whole story," Annabel said, talking more to George than to her. "There was another altercation at intake downstairs."

George nodded as he picked up the phone. "Stan, this is George Talbot. I want the footage from the Casey booking today from the time the cars entered the garage." He hesitated a moment, obviously listening. "And, Stan, it wouldn't be a good career move to tell me that the equipment was down for maintenance. That's right, all of it," he said after pausing again.

"I have the right to hold her for seventy-two hours," Annabel said when he hung up. "This is more than resisting."

"Mr. Talbot, I'm sorry I wasted your time," Emma said, closing her purse. "You and Agent Hicks have a job to do, and I've got a responsibility to Cain." She stood and smiled at George. "I'm sure what she's referring to is the deaths of Shelby's parents in California. That was tragic, but it has nothing to do with Cain or anyone in our family."

"Nice speech, but how did you know about that?" Annabel asked.

"Agent Phillips is living with Muriel Casey, Cain's cousin, and Muriel's my partner's attorney. I stopped at her house first when I found out about Cain's arrest. She couldn't help me because she was tending to Shelby."

"We are building a case. That's why we stopped Cain this morning. We wanted to ask her to come in for questioning."

"And she helped you out by slamming her face into the trunk of her car twice so you could arrest her for resisting," Emma said sarcastically. "Your job is to hide in bushes disrupting people's lives, but I'm going to be up front with you, Agent Hicks. Cain deserves to be treated fairly, so if her attorney keeps getting denied the right to see her, I plan to take that tape and call every media outlet that wants the story."

"That's evidence now," Annabel said, making George laugh at the stupidity of what she'd said, Emma guessed.

"I'm sure she made copies, Annabel," he said, proving he was thinking along the same lines.

"Along with my copy of the tape, I'll dredge up the story of Barney Kyle, who was working for Gino Bracato while serving as an FBI agent. Once I'm done you'll be sorry you brought up the word 'conspiracy.'"

"Ms. Casey," George said before Annabel could say anything else. "Would you mind waiting outside a few minutes? You have my word it won't take long. And this is a gift, right?" He pointed to the CD drive and she nodded.

"Well?" Lou asked when she sat next to him in the outer office.

"He said to wait," Emma said, glancing at her watch then her cell phone. There was still no message from Sanders. "Mr. Talbot is either in there congratulating Annabel for pulling out all the stops, or he's chewing her out."

"Which one are you leaning toward?" Katlin asked.

"I'm never sure when it comes to dealing with these guys, so I'm not going to jinx myself."

"Ms. Casey," the secretary said. "Mr. Talbot said you can go back in."

"Emma, I spoke with the detention center, and Cain's attorney's on his way to see her," he said when she sat again. "I'd like your patience a bit longer while I review a few more things."

"Can I see her?"

He nodded. "After I study all the information, I'll make my decision about either bail or setting her free."

"As long as Cain is alive she'll never really be free of things like this, Mr. Talbot, no matter if they're fair or not."

"You may not trust me, but I'm here because I believe in the law, and I take my oath to uphold it seriously."

"Thank you, then."

"If you want, I'm sure Agent Hicks won't mind walking you next door so you can see Cain."

"I'd appreciate that." She shook his hand and started walking, figuring Annabel was in no hurry. All she wanted was Cain and an answer to who was doing this to them.

❖

"Are you here on business or pleasure?" the customs agent working the entry gate in New Orleans asked when Jerome handed over his Mexican passport. He was wearing an expensive suit that had been a gift from Gracelia and carried a briefcase full of files about silver jewelry. Just another businessman making calls on his contacts in the U.S.

"A little of both," he said, smiling.

The guy laughed as he stamped the documents after glancing at his computer screen for what Jerome knew was an instant background check. "Welcome to the United States, sir, and enjoy your stay."

"Thanks." He walked through, totally ignoring Gracelia. He'd talked her into that for security reasons, he'd told her. Actually, he didn't want any evidence of them together because some government agency would flag her before he ever got started.

He took a cab to the hotel and had a drink waiting for her when she arrived. The city felt different since he'd been gone, but that was okay as he looked out the large window. His return would change it even more, and he'd work until he owned it.

"You not going to say hello?" Gustavo said from the bedroom door. He picked up Gracelia's drink and downed it. Juan didn't resemble his old self in the least. Not even his mother would've recognized him if the change hadn't been her idea.

"You look happy with yourself," he said, moving to a chair. Gustavo, as usual, wasn't alone, and Jerome didn't see any sense in provoking him before his mother arrived.

"Unlike you, taking it easy in the sun," Gustavo pointed to Jerome's tan, which was fake since he hadn't had time to sunbathe, "I been working."

"Any more deliveries I should know about?" he asked between sips.

"What I did has changed the game, so don't tell me shit about it." Gustavo poured himself another drink and the three men with him turned the television to a soccer match.

"It's a simple question, Señor Katsura. You don't have to get pissed." Gracelia was forty minutes late, and Jerome was starting to worry. He needed her to stay in control long enough for him to take it away from her.

"I the man with the *cojones* now."

And the fact that you sound like a moronic caricature hasn't changed either, he thought, forcing himself not to roll his eyes. "Yes, your mother can't stop bragging, but I really want to know if you've checked anything else off your list."

"I don't have to. What I done has Rodolfo scared and your idiot friends pin it on Cain."

He whipped his eyes up at Gustavo, only to see the smug smile. If he wanted more he'd have to beg for it. "The team picked her up?" he asked, not caring about pride.

"The guy I got watching tell me it happen this morning. They stop and beat her like a dog before they take her." Now it was obviously more exciting for Gustavo to tell the story than to taunt him with it. He couldn't talk fast enough. "They drive away and drop her in a hole, the way her people are acting."

Juan or Gustavo could take all the credit he wanted, but his useless little escapades had nothing to do with Cain getting picked up. The news tempted Jerome to try his access number to log in and get all the details. Annabel had probably left that carrot untouched as a way to track him.

"A few more days of them running around like idiots and I take the rest of them down," Gustavo said, making him stop daydreaming.

The door opened and Gracelia's faithful Lorenzo led the bellhop in with all the bags, followed by her. She smiled and opened her arms to Gustavo, holding his face in her hands before she kissed him. When she embraced Gustavo she smiled at Jerome over his shoulder, and the sight was like a bomb blast destroying his old life. His mother would never be able to hug him like that again because Anthony Curtis was no more.

"You look good," Gracelia said, Juan's face again between her hands. "And you've done even better." She accepted the new drink he'd poured and sat next to him after she finished her preening over her little boy. "Did you find what I asked for?"

"We'll have to travel outside the city, but the guys found it."

Jerome looked from one to the other, realizing he was in the dark one more time. "Found what?"

"Retribution," Gracelia said, patting his hand gently like she was trying to calm a puppy. "Finally."

CHAPTER FIFTEEN

Deidi sat on the curb about a block from the address Johnny had given her and watched. That day only a tall woman left with an older woman, both wearing nice suits, but only the young tall one stayed the night. Deidi had spent days out there until her ass was numb, but she still hadn't seen no Dallas Montgomery.

Her cell phone started ringing again and she sent it to voicemail again. Her pimp called twenty times a day trying to find her, but she was working for Johnny now. The pay-off he'd promised was enough to find her own place and maybe start working for herself. She wasn't good in school but was smart enough to know that she didn't need some guy sucking three-fourths of what she made.

"Nothing still?" Johnny asked, suddenly beside her. This guy was seriously creepy, and she didn't know what he wanted with the chick behind that door, but it was real important to him. The only up side was the obsession had nothing to do with her.

"Just that woman and her friend I keep telling you about, but I haven't seen the one you showed me a picture of." She accepted the cup of coffee he brought, needing it to fight off the monotony of sitting for hours. "Maybe she moved," she said, not afraid he'd lose it since he tried not to attract attention in public.

"This the big bitch you been seeing?" he asked, shoving another picture in her face. The black-and-white photo wasn't great, but the smile was the same one she'd seen earlier.

"That's her," she said, reading the caption under it. *Remi Jatibon's making changes at Gemini Studios and it's paying off.*

"According to the rags around here she's sleeping with Dallas, so you still thinking she moved, stupid?" The way he balled his fist made her not want to bring up any more alternatives. "We should've seen her by now since that goddamn door is the only way in or out."

"Maybe she goes through the back."

The coffee spilled all over the front of her shirt when he seemed to forget himself and slapped her hard across the head. A few people on the street slowed, but no one looked like they wanted to get involved.

"Why the fuck didn't you say something sooner?" he hissed as he hauled her to her feet by her arm. "What the fuck do I keep you around for?"

"I'm sorry."

"I can make you sorry, girl, so shut up."

They walked a block over and started down a street that looked like an alley. The doors had business names until they reached one that had a small door alongside a garage door. It appeared more residential than the rest.

Johnny stopped and ran his hand over it. "You can't hide forever," he said, like he was talking to it. He tried the knob gently and Deidi screamed when it swung in suddenly and the biggest man she'd ever seen was standing there.

"Find someplace else to turn tricks," the guy said, putting his hand on Johnny's chest and pushing him back. He hadn't made a sound but he looked as shocked as she did since his hand was still up as if he had it on the knob. "You two deaf? Get lost."

The yell snapped Johnny out of his trance, and he grabbed her by the arm again. They started walking fast in the direction they'd come from, and when she glanced back, the man was still standing there. If the place belonged to the woman Johnny was looking for, he'd just announced their arrival, and she'd be the one paying for the mistake.

❖

Cain felt sick and her head hurt. Sanders sat across from her with his briefcase on his lap, staying quiet after she had requested silence.

"Are you all right?" he asked after a long stretch.

"I will be," she said, putting her hand on her stomach. Breakfast was long gone but she felt like she would throw up. The nausea was getting worse with every breath. This had happened to her only once before, when a kid in school had swung a bat without realizing she was standing right behind her. She didn't get the full brunt of the backward swing, but it'd been enough to cause a concussion.

They had talked only about who Emma was meeting with. Emma's clear thinking was the only bright spot in a crappy day. A loud knock made her close her eyes and take another deep breath, her headache flaring. The door opened and she was in Emma's arms before she could open her eyes. It pained her to push Emma away, but she had no choice.

After she bent away from Emma and threw up on the floor, she almost passed out again. The pain in her head made her see spots when her stomach clenched once more and she gagged until she got rid of what little she had. Behind her Emma held her head and pressed herself to Cain's back, the heat of her body making Cain focus on her breathing.

"Open your eyes, love," Emma said softly. One more deep breath and she struggled to open them as Emma wiped her mouth with a tissue, careful with the cut on her bottom lip. "You need a doctor," Emma said as she studied her eyes.

"One pupil bigger than the other?" she asked.

"Yes, and how did you get this?" Emma touched the side of her temple. "You have a huge bruise."

"Depends on who you ask, but according to these guys I tripped and fell into this guy's fist."

"You stupid bastards," Emma shouted toward the glass pane. "She has a concussion and you have her chained to the table? You've been chasing her so long you're willing to cut corners and kill her on a hunch?"

The door crashed open, making her shut her eyes again because of the noise. All the abuse of the day felt like it had coalesced to drag her down.

"Agent Hicks," Emma said, her arm around Cain's shoulder. "I will use every contact we have to make sure this costs you your job if something happens to her."

The threat made someone unlock the cuffs. After the pounding in Cain's head subsided, she opened her eyes and found Annabel back in the room with a guy who looked like a medic.

"Ms. Casey," the guy said, placing his bag on the table. "Could I take a look at you?"

"We have a doctor, thank you, and I want to know why we aren't free to go see him?" Emma asked.

"Ms. Casey, we should stabilize her before you move her anywhere," Annabel said.

"Your people caused this condition, so you're crazy if I believe you suddenly want to make it better. Either cut her loose or get us before a judge and give us bail." Emma was squeezing her shoulder as she spoke. "What's it going to be?"

"We have a legitimate case," Annabel said, her eyes were closed to slits and her lips white. "This office doesn't respond well to threats."

"You're full of shit," Emma said, making Cain put her arm around her hips and pat her side. "And you're an idiot for not taking my offer."

"You better quit before you join Cain as a guest of the government downstairs."

"Actually, the people won't be pressing any charges," Sanders said, looking at his phone. "Someone from our firm is in Mr. Talbot's office, so please check in with his staff."

Emma was still staring Annabel down as Sanders was talking when she felt the first twitches go through Cain's body. Before she could look down, Cain started to convulse.

"What's wrong?" Emma asked the medic, tasting bile in the back of her throat. "Cain?" She tried to hold on to Cain but her size and strength was too much and the medic helped Cain to the floor.

"Ma'am, call for an ambulance," he said to Annabel. "Now," he yelled, when she didn't move fast enough for him. "Ms. Casey," he said close to Cain's head, "don't fight it. Just try to relax. You'll be fine." He knelt next to her and made sure she didn't hit her head on anything else. When Cain stopped moving she was semiconscious and didn't fight him when he opened her eyelids to start his examination. "She needs to go to the emergency room. This is beyond my scope."

"What's wrong with her?" Emma asked, wiping away the tears that had started when Cain hit the floor.

"We'll know more after they run a few tests, but it's probably a severe concussion."

The room got crowded when the EMTs arrived with a stretcher being led by the huge man with the gaudy belt buckle, so Annabel and Sanders stepped out. Once Cain was loaded up, Emma walked beside the stretcher and held her hand. As they passed Annabel and the big man, she wanted to slap the smile off the man's face, but that was for another time. If she had to beg Cain, she would to see to it that this guy paid for what he'd done.

❖

"Are you sure you don't want me to go with you?" Muriel asked. She was driving Shelby to the airport alone, but a car full of agents was following them. "You were there for me when Dad died. I'd like to return the favor."

"Don't take this the wrong way, but I'd rather you didn't," Shelby said, her head turned away. "I need a few days alone to sort through this and make some sense of it."

"Shelby, you know in your heart Cain didn't order this." She reached for Shelby's hand, but Shelby lurched away from her.

"No, I don't know that. And you'd better be all right with me doing whatever needs to be done to put a needle in her arm for this one."

The departures section of the airport was crowded so she had to wait for the line of taxis ahead of her to unload their fares. "I'm not sure how to respond."

"Easy. For once in your life think for yourself and do the right thing," Shelby said, turning to face her for the first time since she'd gotten in the car. "You can do that by telling me what you know so we can hold her."

"You know that won't happen."

"Then this is really pointless, isn't it?" Shelby said, sighing.

Muriel kept her hands on the steering wheel to ground herself somehow. "Why are you with me?" Choosing Shelby had left her in a strange no-man's-land. "And tell me the truth, since you have set beliefs about my family that make you think you're right. If you don't open yourself to reexamine them, our being together is pointless."

"I'm with you because I care about you, and because I thought you were different."

Shelby seemed to say what she thought Muriel needed to hear, and truth seldom played a role in such an answer. "Do you mean I'm no butcher?"

"Let me tell you something," Shelby said, telling her the story Cain had already told her about the night she met Shelby and how it ended. "I don't think I've ever been more scared."

"But Cain protected you. That should prove something."

Shelby put her hand on the door handle and shook her head. "What stayed with me more than anything was how much she knew about me and my family. She threatened my father that night in her own indirect way, but I ignored her because I fell for her smooth style." She opened the door and looked back at her. "She really is someone who keeps her word, and she'll keep tearing families apart because people like you think she's a crusader."

"I'm not that idealistic."

"You can't have it both ways, Muriel. I won't give myself to someone who allows a murderer to keep on killing."

"Have a safe trip," Muriel said, cutting off the conversation. She started moving as soon as Shelby slammed the door since the agents in the car behind her had Shelby's bags.

On the way to Cain's she thought about her next step. Betrayal wasn't in her makeup, but this time that loyalty would cost her the possibility of happiness.

❖

"Baby, please," Emma said as she and Dr. Mark Summers walked alongside the gurney the EMTs were pushing into the emergency room. "Cain, I need you to open your eyes."

The seizure had frightened her so badly that Annabel had her sit down and drink some water as they loaded Cain up. Cain's vitals were fine but she was lethargic and she seemed to struggle to open her eyes. Emma's plea, though, made Cain look up and smile at her. "Try and keep them open, okay?"

"I'm fine," Can said, but she glanced around as if she was confused.

"Do you remember what happened?" Mark asked as he helped slide Cain to the bed in the trauma room.

Cain turned her head and winced. "Nothing that would land me here…Emma."

"I'm here, but try and stay still until he finishes your exam."

Mark did a thorough job then motioned Emma outside. "She definitely has a concussion, but I need to run a CT scan."

"Why?" This couldn't be happening again. Cain was always so careful. That, combined with Cain's strength, had erased the images of the night Kyle had pulled that trigger. "What's wrong?"

"I need to rule out any bleeding in her brain, Ms. Casey, but you have to think positively. She doesn't need to see you panic." He put his hand on her shoulder briefly. "We'll talk again after I get the results, but no matter what, I'm admitting her for a couple of days for observation. She doesn't have a history of seizures, right?"

"Cain has a history of never getting sick, Doctor."

"We need to be sure, so try not to think worst-case scenario. I want to be sure, though, because head injuries aren't something to ignore."

"Emma?" Dr. Sam Casey, Emma's OB/GYN, walked quickly to her side. "The office didn't mention you'd be here."

"It's Cain," she said, her vision blurring through fresh tears.

"What's going on, Mark?" Sam asked as he closed Cain's file. "Emma's my patient, and a lot of stress isn't good for her."

"Just tell her," Emma said, glad to see a friend.

"You don't need me to preach," Sam said when Mark finished, "but you need to make an appointment when you can. It's only to be sure, like Mark's doing with Cain." The door to Cain's room was open so Sam led her back in. "Hard head, don't you know it's not a good thing to worry your wife while she's pregnant?" Sam told Cain.

"It's too hard for any real damage, so you better be ready to run if you tell any jokes at my expense," Cain said, holding her hand up for Emma to take. She stayed quiet while Sam went through the same exam Mark had just finished. "I'll live, right?"

"Longer than the rest of us, but try and behave. You both have my numbers, so use them if you have to."

"I knew that last name of yours was good for something," Cain said, smiling. "Promise me you'll stay close and take care of my girl while I finish being poked."

"You two sit tight and let me call my backup, and I'll be happy to sit with the good-looking one in this group while you have your head examined." Sam lifted Cain's other hand and held it between hers. "God knows I've been recommending it for years."

The joke made Cain groan, but this was the first time in hours she'd felt like laughing. "You're a good friend, Sam."

"You both worry about relaxing and I'll be right back." Sam looked Cain in the eye and said, "Emma will be fine with me no matter how long it takes for you to finish your tests."

"Lass," Cain said when Sam left, "tell me what happened."

"Not now. The doctor said you have to rest."

"I heard the part about staying here, and I don't plan to fight it." Cain blinked a few times, trying to clear her vision. Whatever was wrong with her was draining her and making it hard to think. "I want to know why I woke up here."

Emma didn't appear comfortable telling her the story, but she did. "That big son of a bitch—"

"I know, and we'll deal with it," Cain said, not wanting Emma to talk about Cehan. "What I need is for you to sit."

The orderlies arrived to take her, and then Sam showed up. "Take it easy," Sam said. "Emma and I will be sitting right outside the test room having some orange juice and telling funny stories about you."

"I love you," Emma said before kissing her.

"I love you."

"No wonder you two get pregnant so fast," Sam said. She put her arm around Emma and mouthed to her that Emma would be fine.

On her way out Cain placed her hand on Emma's midsection. "Remember, I'll be fine, so don't lose sight of the things we want."

"The top of my wish list has always been you."

"That you already have," she said, and she meant it. The life they both wanted would come even if she had to kill to get it.

CHAPTER SIXTEEN

In the silence of the main section of the suite, Carlos sat looking out over a nice view of the city. The afternoon had been quiet so far, and Rodolfo had taken a nap after they finished meeting with Santos Esvillar, Rodolfo's manager in Mississippi. Now Carlos was waiting for Rodolfo to come out and have the talk he'd promised days before.

Whatever was on the old man's mind was something Carlos figured he'd never hear from Rodolfo himself. He was the son of a cook in Rodolfo's kitchen in Cozumel. Boys like him grew up poor and hungry, so it was easy to lead them into the first step of the drug business—harvesting coca leaves and making the drug so many craved. Though it was a way to survive, no one at the bottom ever got rich. He, however, had only seen that part of the business at Rodolfo's side the very few times he went to visit the fields to give a small bonus to his best producers.

His mother had worked in the kitchen, but he'd been sent to private school with Juan and started working with Rodolfo as soon as he graduated. He'd paid in blood for the chance he'd been given or, more accurately, the life he and his mother had been saved from. To keep Rodolfo in power he'd done things his mother would never find out about and that sometimes visited him in his dreams. But he'd killed as many times as ordered so he wouldn't lose Rodolfo's respect and affection. That was his greatest treasure, and he knew the one thing that had caused it.

"He's still sleeping?" Fausto Valdez, one of Rodolfo's men from Mexico, asked. He was there on Carlos's recommendation because he wanted people he trusted around Rodolfo. Until Juan, Gracelia, and the others who'd abandoned their jobs were found, he lived in a constant state of tension.

"Santos had nothing but bad news when he came today," Carlos said, looking at the closed bedroom door. "We lost another group of guys, so now the only place we're making money is from the production end. Until we find who's doing this, it'll be hard to get people to work for us here."

"Sounds like you want to go home."

"It's the safest place for him." He pointed to the bedroom. "People still remember what he's done for them and that they owe him their livelihood. We'd be begging tourists for pennies if he hadn't given us a chance."

"Sometimes people only see money, and obviously an asshole is shelling it out because even some of our most loyal old guys are gone, and I don't think it's because something happened to them."

"Nothing happened to people like Lorenzo Mendoza, Fausto," Rodolfo said. His hair was combed and he'd changed clothes, but he still appeared drained. "I'm sure Lorenzo, like the others, are stuck to my sister like maggots to a rotting corpse."

"That's why we're still looking for her and Juan. They have plenty to answer for," he said.

"Fausto, could you step out, but don't go far," Rodolfo said. When they were alone he sat across from Carlos. "I'm glad you sent for him. He's a good man."

"We need people we can trust until this is over."

"I appreciate your tenacity, Carlos," Rodolfo said, opening the drawer of the table next to him and taking out a stack of papers. "I'm an old man, and while I'm proud of the loyalty of you and a few others, I've made enemies during my life." The confession didn't seem easy for Rodolfo to make because he turned his head away when he spoke. "The ones who hate me most are my own sister and nephew."

"You shouldn't waste time mourning their loss, patrón. They don't deserve it after the way they've been so ungrateful for what you've done for them."

"They won't stop until they destroy me, so you need to know some things before anything happens."

"Don't say that." He forgot his position and placed his hand on Rodolfo's knee. His job didn't matter if he lost the only father figure in his life. "I'm here to make sure nothing happens to you."

"You are why I don't regret losing Juan." Rodolfo handed him the papers. "If something happens to me, I want my business and my possessions to go to my son, and this will has always been written with those wishes in mind." He stopped and sighed. "Maybe that's why Juan and I never grew close."

"You have a son?" he asked, hoping the man was nothing like Juan.

"Read the first page."

The words were familiar to him from what little he knew of legal documents. *I, Rodolfo Luis, bequeath my estate and bank accounts to my only son and heir, Carlos Santiago.* The sentence made his fingers so numb, he finally dropped the page on the third reading. "Me?"

"Don't think I've waited until now because I was ashamed of you."

He lifted the papers off his lap and put them aside before he looked up at Rodolfo. "Then why? Why wait, and why now?" It was the first time in his life he had spoken to Rodolfo in anger. He guessed the only reason Rodolfo had been so generous was payment for having his mother in his bed to do his bidding all these years. Carlos was shocked.

"I promised your mother. She got pregnant but knew what a target you'd become if she allowed me to acknowledge you."

He curled his hands into fists and ran his knuckles along his thighs. "You're blaming my mother?"

"You don't know what it was like back then," Rodolfo said, standing and beginning to pace. "I was starting to build this empire, so I couldn't put a wall of protection around us like I can now."

"So what? You acknowledged Juan."

"I didn't have a choice." Rodolfo raised his voice. "Gracelia pushed that bastard on me and disappeared for a few years to spite me, I'm sure. To honor what your mother wanted, I kept both of you close and gave you everything I could. When you came to work for me I wanted to tell you, but it seemed too late." He stopped behind his chair and looked him in the eye. "I can see my fear was valid and it's too late, but even if you choose to hate me you're entitled to what's mine."

"I could never hate you." As he spoke he was sure he could never change this fact. "You had to know I idolized you and thought of you as a father." He recalled all those trips Rodolfo took when he was a boy and the gifts he brought him. They had made him feel like Rodolfo cared for him, but it was still hard to fathom he had given them to him because he was his son.

"Maybe I don't deserve it but I ask your forgiveness," Rodolfo said.

"Knowing this," Carlos had to stop to find the right word, "doesn't change how I feel about you. But I need time to understand and come to terms with what you've told me." He stood and began to leave.

Stopping him, Rodolfo said, "There's one more thing before you go. Call Fausto and the others in."

The suite he and Rodolfo shared was a few floors above the rooms where the men were staying, so it took a few minutes for them to file in. They stood in an almost perfectly straight line and looked nervously between them.

"Don't worry," Rodolfo said. "I don't have more bad news, but I have news." He stood next to Carlos and placed his hand on his shoulder, which Carlos allowed. "If something happens to me, I want you to respect my wishes and follow Carlos's lead."

The proclamation made Carlos turn his eyes to Rodolfo, and he didn't move only because Rodolfo tightened his hold on him. Carlos seethed. Rodolfo couldn't acknowledge his bastard even now.

"I ask this because Carlos is my son—not only in name, but by blood."

"He's your son?" Fausto asked, seeming to be the only one with the guts to ask.

Rodolfo repeated that he had wanted to protect Carlos, but a small part of Carlos believed he had acknowledged him because his time was running out and because Juan had rejected him. He couldn't bring himself to smile as the men came to shake his hand in congratulations.

When they were alone, Rodolfo said, "Like I told you, I can't force you, but please consider forgiving me."

"Did you ever love my mother?"

"Your mother was as close as I came to taking a wife, but I wasn't ready," Rodolfo said, sitting again. "I always thought I would have time to settle down after I tasted what life could offer me, and without me realizing it, the years piled up."

"So your answer is no," he said, his anger growing.

"My answer is yes, but I was too stupid to realize how rare that is when it's genuine, not bought or forced. I love your mother still because she gave me something precious."

"What, a bastard who wasn't good enough to deserve your name?" he yelled at him.

"No, a son my father would've been proud of, and that's where Gracelia failed miserably." Rodolfo flipped through the papers he'd given him and handed him one of the sheets. "As for your name, this is the correction I made with the authorities in Mexico." The birth certificate now listed Rodolfo as his father. "You don't have to, but I've arranged for you to take the Luis name. The people who matter in my organization know, and I ordered them to tell everyone who works for me, down to the harvesters. You mother and I thought it was safe for you to claim what's yours."

"Like I said, I'll need time." He left, wanting to get some fresh air and find someplace to call his mother. It wasn't every day that the roadmap of your life was erased and redrawn. Rodolfo hadn't asked if Carlos would accept the name change. Perhaps the Luis name and what Rodolfo felt it stood for would die with him, no matter when that was, because the name Santiago had served Carlos well so far.

❖

"Is Remi back yet?" Dallas asked when they finished signing the contracts for her first starring role, scheduled to begin in a few months. She'd been interested in the part because she could relate to some of the character's problems, but more importantly it was due to shoot in New Orleans. A local movie meant she'd be home with Remi every night.

"Her meetings got postponed, but she still hasn't come in," said Steve Palma, one of Remi's partners, thumbing through the pages of what she'd just signed.

"She didn't say why?" The screen of Dallas's phone showed no messages.

Dwayne St. Germaine, Remi's other partner, shook his head as he straightened one of the copies. "She didn't leave a message."

"Anything else, guys?" asked Angus Christian, her new manager. Both men shook their heads and watched her fool with her phone as if by checking all the message options, she could conjure up one from Remi. Because of all her secretiveness, she was starting to get paranoid about Remi pulling away from her, and she had to watch herself not to take it out on her lover.

"Do you want us to see if we can find her?" Steve asked.

"No, I'm sure she's up to something with her father, and Mano was coming in for the day." She lifted her eyes from the useless device in her hand. "Thanks, guys, I'm looking forward to going back to work."

All of them stood before she did, and Emil stepped back in as Angus pulled out her chair for her. "Remi called," he said to her softly. "If you're finished here she said to call her back, but you can do it from the car so we can get going."

"Is something wrong?" She waved over her shoulder and followed Emil out. "Why didn't she call me?"

"She's all right, and she told me not to bother you until your meeting was over since there was nothing you could do." He opened the door and the car was parked a few feet away.

"Where is she?" The powerful engine of Emil's sedan turned over and he stared at the gate. "What's wrong?"

"Sorry, I thought I saw something," he said, shaking his head as he started them moving. "She's at the hospital with Cain, but it's Cain who was admitted." He told her what he knew and entered the medical center through the parking garage to avoid the reporters stationed by the main entrance.

The elevators opened to the third floor and Dallas turned in the direction all the people at the nurses' station were staring. She had to laugh at their obvious fascination with the bad girls who had landed on their ward. It never mattered to supposedly straitlaced, law-abiding men and women that Cain and Remi's reputation deserved a wide berth. The more salacious the rumors, the more they were interested. She didn't worry about the men, but the women were usually as beautiful as they were interested.

"Why does shit like this always turn into a circus?" Emil asked.

"Because people are always curious about what they don't know about," she said, picking up the pace when she saw Remi standing in the hall talking to Lou. Remi appeared to be engrossed in their conversation but looked her way before she could reach her. "How's Cain?"

"The test results showed no bleeding so they put her on steroids to bring down any swelling and she's confined to bed for the next three days," Remi said, opening her arms to her. "You finish at the studio before you heard about this?"

"I'm all yours." She was concerned about Cain but she wanted to enjoy the warmth of Remi's body a little before going in for a visit. "Did anyone offer to give you a sponge bath while you were here?"

Remi laughed and she loved the rumbling vibrations as she pressed her ear to her chest. "Not yet, but I might get lucky on that score later."

"Is it okay to go in?" Her ears got hot when Remi lowered her head and kissed her.

"Emma's waiting for you," Remi said, and kissed her again. "Let me finish up with Lou and I'll join you."

The room was large, and since it was the last one at the end of the ward it was fairly quiet. Cain had her eyes closed and her face was purple in places from bruises. Next to her Emma sat in a recliner and held Cain's hand, but her eyes were open and she was smiling. Emma was starting to show and Dallas wondered if Remi wanted kids. She'd never considered having any because she'd essentially raised Kristen, even though their ages weren't that far apart.

"Sit," Emma said, pointing to the small sofa next to her.

"Is she going to be okay?"

"She tells me that hard heads are a Casey family trait, but I'd rather have it proved to me during a healthy debate of whether she should take vitamins." Emma laughed but she kept her eyes on Cain's chest as if to assure herself she was still breathing. "I'm sorry I had to cancel lunch today, but this happened this morning."

"No need to apologize. I needed to talk to you about something," she said, looking at their linked hands.

"I've got nothing but time now, and Cain will be out for a while. After we got here and they said she was fine, and I had my own checkup, she went to sleep."

"The last thing you need now is to listen to all my problems. It can wait."

"It doesn't have to," Emma said, gently releasing Cain's hand so she could move closer. "I have an idea what's bothering you, and I'd like to help."

You can't possibly know what's bothering me, she thought, and suddenly felt she couldn't share her story with anyone. "Really, it wasn't that important."

"Dallas, I hope you'll be happy with Remi. You both deserve the joy that comes from finding the person who completes you." Emma glanced back when Cain let out a small snore. "So what's bothering you is either related to who Remi is—"

"It's not that."

"Let me finish," Emma said, wagging her finger at her. "Or it has to do with who you are. Either way, doubts will eat away at you until it messes with all the wonderful things yet to come."

Dallas folded her legs under her and stared at the floor. "Did you ever doubt?"

"I doubted Cain once, which led to me believing someone else instead of her." The pain was evident in Emma's voice even now. "It cost me years away from my son, which was painful, trust me, but my lack of faith almost lost me the love I couldn't replace." Emma put her hand on Dallas's knee, forcing her to look up. "Let me help you not repeat my mistakes."

Cain's breathing was deep and even, and she seemed to be sleeping. Dallas thought this would be hard, but she didn't feel like she could do it with Cain present. "The one thing I want is Remi," she said, wiping her eyes in frustration that the tears could start so quickly. "Let's wait for this, okay?"

"That night I saw the two of you walk into that restaurant to join us for dinner, I was thrilled for Remi," Emma said, making her nod. "But I was thrilled for me too because I saw a friend and a woman who I could be myself with. The partners we've chosen make us members of an exclusive club, and I want to give you what Marianna Jatibon has given me."

"I'm sure she was sorry Remi didn't find you first."

"Remi's all yours, honey, and the sooner you put that boulder you're carrying down, the sooner you can enjoy the peace that'll bring you."

She looked at Cain again before closing her eyes to clear her head. Her story started with what she remembered of her mother and the life they endured with Johnny. "She was only gone four days before he came to my room," she said, covering her mouth with both hands to try and stifle the sob.

"Take your time," Emma said, moving closer to her.

As she told the rest, she pretended it had happened to someone else. Her father had been a sadistic son of a bitch who hadn't denied himself anything, though his daughter was on the receiving end of his depravity.

"I hated him, but I took it so he'd leave Kristen alone. That motivation actually kept me sane. One of us deserved to come through this without nightmares."

Emma opened her arms and held Dallas as she cried. It was the first time she'd told anyone except Kristen, and she was overwhelmed that Emma didn't turn away in disgust.

"What you endured wasn't your fault, and if you share this story with Remi she'll tell you the same thing," Emma said, as she ran her hand in a circle on her back. "Is that what you're worried about?"

"I'm not who she thinks I am, and she deserves better."

"No, you should realize that your strength, because that's what it took to overcome what you did, is exactly what she needs in a partner." Emma released her to reach for a tissue to wipe her eyes. "How did you get out of there?"

Dallas tipped her head back and tried to blink away her tears. This was hard but she did feel lighter after sharing with Emma. "Johnny had a group of friends that were as cruel as he was, and when he started to get tired of me he decided it was okay to start sharing as long as there was something in it for him."

"He did that?" Emma looked horrified. "Oh, Dallas, I'm so glad you had the guts to run."

"When he told me what he had in mind, I was numb, but I also knew that if I wasn't enough anymore, he would start the cycle again with my little sister." She could still hear his tone of voice as he calmly explained how Timothy Pritchard would stop by and she should be nice to him if she knew what was good for her. "He has a still in the woods and it's how he makes money, so he left me to start what I guess was another business venture."

"You have nothing to be ashamed of," Emma said, since Dallas had whispered the last part so softly. "This bastard deserved to be shot even if he's your father."

"It was how he hugged Kristen and patted her bottom before he left that made me snap. That night he went to start the still for the season and told me to wait for Timothy. I decided to leave. When he started walking I packed what I could and took his can of money."

"How old were you?"

"A couple of months shy of seventeen. Way too young to be out with a little sister in tow."

"And you're embarrassed telling this story?" Emma placed her palm on her cheek. "It's amazing."

"It's more like white-trash-from-the-hills drama that'll turn Marianna against me. I'm sure the last thing she wants for Remi is some hillbilly who was her father's bed warmer."

"Marianna will respect Remi's choice, and you're Remi's choice."

"I killed someone," she blurted out.

"What...who?"

Sparta, Tennessee Eight Years Earlier

When she reached in the can for the money she was already shaking, and Kristen was crying behind her. Kristen didn't want to stay, but she was terrified they'd get caught and of what the consequences would be. Dallas planned to run to the highway that headed west, but it was twenty miles and she didn't drive. No matter—she had to try.

They made it to the edge of the yard that led to the woods and found Timothy standing there. "Where you two going?" he asked, smiling, which made him look even meaner because of his crooked, rotting teeth. "Couldn't wait to get to me, huh?" He laughed.

She looked at Kristen and motioned for her to stay put. "I'm just sending her away so we'll have time alone." She dropped her bag and walked slowly toward him. "Close your eyes. I got a surprise for you," she said to Timothy, with the most relaxed smile she could manage.

"Well, come on, girl. I can't wait to get going," he said, his eyes shut so tight he had deep lines next to them.

The rock was really too big for her hand but she wanted the first blow to count. She didn't hesitate as she swung and connected with the part of his head she could reach. Her strike produced a lot of blood and he bent over, putting his hands over the large cut the jagged part of the rock had made. With her sister's encouragement, she lifted it over her head with both hands and brought it down as Timothy turned his head and reached for her.

His knees buckled and he fell forward, the side of his head now bleeding from the huge gash she'd opened. It was dark, but in the moonlight she could see he wasn't breathing, and she couldn't go back. She stuffed the rock in the bottom of her bag and took Kristen's hand. The hike through the woods took five days, and the small amount of food had run out by the time they hitched their first ride.

The problem was, no matter how many miles and time she put between her and her old life, she couldn't completely erase what she'd done and who she was. Timothy Pritchard had been a bastard, but his death was on her head and she'd kept that rock all those years to remind herself how true that was. Getting caught would cost so much more than her time with Kristen now. She refused to burden Remi with having to wait for her to pay for her sins.

❖

"Johnny didn't catch us before we made it to the interstate, and what I did that night hasn't caught up with me yet," Dallas said, feeling drained.

"Did you want to be with that guy the night that happened?" Emma asked.

"No," she said, louder than she'd intended, and glanced over to make sure Cain was still sleeping.

"Then you were only protecting yourself from rape, and what happened was self-defense. As for Remi," Emma said, placing her hands over hers.

"I don't know how to tell her."

"That's not what you have to ask yourself. Do you trust her or not? And do you trust what you have together?"

"She's right," Remi said, walking into the room. "I love you for who you are. Who you were before you came into my life shaped the woman I know."

How much had Remi overheard? Dallas buried her face in her hands and thought of running from the room to keep from having to face her. "How can you love me? I'm nothing but used and broken."

Emma stood and moved to the bed, where she sat next to Cain. "I wish Cain and I could leave to give you the privacy you need, but we can't," she said, smiling.

"I don't have to hide what I have to say," Remi said. She moved and knelt before Dallas. "Emma's right. You didn't ask for what happened to you, and what happened because of it isn't indefensible. You fought for yourself and Kristen, and now you don't have to do it alone. I love you enough to carry the weight of that rock, but only if you let me. You have to decide to trust me not to hurt you."

"I trust you, but you deserve better than me."

"For me there is no one else, *querida*. I don't want to pretend what you went through didn't happen, but I want to help you accept that you don't have to go through this alone anymore." Remi reached out and it felt good to lean into her touch. "I love you with all I am, and I promise no one will ever hurt you like that again whether you stay with me or not."

"It's so hard." And it was. Her movie success didn't matter to the scared little girl inside her.

"Just think about what happens going forward. I can't change the past, but I'll be the one constant in your life. Nothing you've done willingly or had to endure unwillingly will drive me away," Remi said, her face wet with tears. "As for my mother, she loves you and she'll be fine with whatever you feel comfortable sharing with her."

"See, I told you," Emma said. "She's a keeper."

"Yes." She moved forward and pressed herself to Remi. "I may or may not deserve this, but I love you too, and I don't want a life away from you." She figured her face looked like hell from all the crying but she felt happy—truly happy, which was a foreign concept. The future would be easier with a partner and friends who now knew the truth and still found her worthy.

Timothy Pritchard, though, was a ghost that would continue to haunt her no matter how powerful Remi or Cain was.

CHAPTER SEVENTEEN

Their business meetings were going well, but Marisol Delarosa wasn't paying attention to her father's business manager, Miguel, as he rattled off figures. Her mind was on Cain Casey in the hospital and what had happened earlier in the day. The information had come from Rodolfo Luis, and she still hadn't figured why he'd told her father.

"Are we boring you?" Hector asked.

"Never, Papa, but we're still missing the piece that would finish what we need. I'm thinking about Cain, and why we heard it from Rodolfo," she said, glancing at Miguel. "I thought we'd made some connections here."

"We have," Miguel said, sounding defensive. "But Cain isn't vital to the connections we need to make. We have other priorities."

"I think she gets the point," Tomas Blanco said.

She smiled at her father's guard for coming to her defense, even if she didn't need his help to hold her own. "Funny, because these past weeks all I've heard is how much easier she'll make this."

"A mysterious group doing stupid things didn't cause Cain's condition," Hector said as he clipped the end of his cigar. "The FBI has an interest that borders on over-obsessive, probably because she's eluded them so successfully. She's become a frustration with no outlet to those agents."

"So they picked her up and put her in the hospital."

Her father studied the cigar he was rolling between his fingers to loosen the tobacco, as if he were trying to come up with an answer. "I don't know why or for what reason," he said, finally lifting his eyes to hers. "But neither did Rodolfo, so he's not that far ahead of us."

"Do you know who killed the dealers in Biloxi, and Cain and Remi's people?" she asked, not really pinpointing anyone.

"Like I've said, we've got other things going on," Miguel said.

"Papa, we'll finish later," she said, standing and waving Tomas off. She left, knocked on the door next to their suite, and picked one of her father's men. "Call down for a car," she said to the young guy, whose name she couldn't remember.

"Marisol," Tomas said, coming up behind her.

"Go back and finish with my father." The way he acted at times made her realize they needed to have a frank talk soon. Tomas had feelings for her that she'd never return, and he was having more difficulty hiding them.

"Where are you going?" His question made the guy she'd told to order a car freeze a few feet from the door.

"Tomas, you forget yourself," she said, pointing for the other guard to do what she'd asked. "I answer only to my father, so go back inside." She met his glare with her own. "I believe I told you to order a car," she told the man behind her since she didn't hear footsteps. "Now."

"Marisol, I'm only interested in your well-being," Tomas said, lifting his hand to touch her.

She grabbed it before he got the opportunity. "I know my father trusts you with his life, but your job doesn't give you any privileges with me."

"Your father trusts me with your care as well, and I can't do that if I don't know where you are."

"When I get back the three of us are going to talk and I'll explain what level of care I need." She followed the guard to the elevator, not giving Tomas another look. "What's your name?" she asked the man once the doors closed.

"Fidel Lopez, ma'am," he said, playing with a button on his jacket.

"Fidel, how would you like a promotion?" Her question made him stare at her as if she'd suddenly switched to English. "It seems I need a bodyguard, and I'm offering you the job."

"What would I have to do?"

"Keep my confidences and not tell anyone where we've been, even if that person is Tomas."

"Señor Tomas is the boss."

"Tomas's money doesn't pay your wages, Fidel, and if you want to make more, you'll remember that. The job with me is yours if you want it, but if you're loyal to Tomas I'll see to it that you're sent back to do day labor in Colombia." She laughed when he nodded so fast he almost knocked himself out on the back of the elevator wall. "Good, let's pay a visit to the one everyone says is our future."

"Who's that?"

"An Irish god, if I'm to believe all the hype."

❖

The drive after Muriel dropped Shelby off had helped cool her temper, so she decided it was time to talk to Cain to see what she knew about Shelby's parents. Turning into the driveway of Cain's house she was shocked not to see any surveillance outside except for the security walking the walls.

She felt strange ringing the bell, but this didn't feel like an extension of her home any longer. When Sabana answered the door she tried to keep her face neutral after seeing the shoulder holster that most of Cain's security preferred. The look on Sabana's face made it hard not to show emotion, considering this was the same person who was sweet enough to visit after her father's death.

"Can I help you?"

"I'm here to see Cain, so bring the attitude down a notch before I tell her you need a leash. She's not a fan of guards who are aggressive for no reason."

The electric whirl of Merrick's wheelchair broke the silence. "Come in, Muriel." Merrick touched Sabana's side and got her to move away from the door.

"Are you two the gatekeepers now, or are you under orders to keep me away?" She tried not to stare at the side of Merrick's head where the bullet had entered. The spot had left a scar, visible since her hair hadn't grown back to the usual length.

"I just asked you to come in so, no, we're not trying to bar you. We figured you'd be at the hospital, though."

The house was quiet for this time of day, and she glanced around the foyer, trying to see into the downstairs rooms. "Why would I be at the hospital?"

"Shelby had to have told you," Merrick said, backing away and steering toward the kitchen.

"Tell me already." She didn't want to think about the possibilities of more loss.

"Shelby's team picked up Cain today and blamed her for what happened to Shelby's parents, so I'm surprised she didn't mention the lead suspect," Merrick said slowly, seeming frustrated. "After they stopped her they beat her and didn't stop until she ended up in the hospital."

"What time was that?"

Merrick's answer meant that Shelby's lone visit to the office was while Cain was in custody.

"Thanks," she said, pulling her keys out. She had to get to the hospital, and thankfully the one Cain was in was only a few blocks away.

After showing her ID, she took the elevator up to find Emma talking to Remi and Dallas, surrounded by a few guards. When Emma's gaze fell on her, Emma's expression turned from a smile to something much angrier.

"I'm sorry I didn't get here sooner," she said, stopping when Emma put her hand up.

"Why are you here at all?" Emma asked, obviously not caring who overheard.

"Emma, be fair. Cain's my family."

"Your family?" Emma laughed. "If you mean that, you've got an interesting way of showing it. You couldn't even ask why I came to ask for your help. Instead of taking a few seconds, you had other priorities."

"All I'm asking is for you to be fair, and that's not," she said, looking at Emma and feeling a pain in her chest. It was hard to accept that she was a stranger to her family.

"No, Muriel, that's the truth, and I won't sugarcoat it for you like Cain's done so far." Emma pushed her toward the nurses' station with more strength than she thought Emma could muster. "Get out and go back to what you think is important, because I don't want you here."

"I'll go, but what's wrong?"

"They beat her until she was unconscious with a concussion because of Shelby's parents. Those assholes think she either did it or ordered it, and instead of doing something earlier, you didn't even bother to ask." Emma began to push her again and Muriel grabbed her by the wrists.

"Muriel, don't make this harder on yourself," Lou said, shaking his head. "Let her go."

"You don't have the right to keep me from seeing her."

"The hell I don't," Emma said, slapping her. "Go home and forget about what you care nothing about."

Emma was upset, but Muriel couldn't back down as she stood there feeling the heat of her cheek. "You can't believe that."

"You haven't bothered to see what this is doing to her, have you? You're screwing the woman who wants to put her away or on death row. You don't deserve the name you've been gifted with," Emma said, finally bringing her voice down. "Your cut was as close to fatal as you could have made it. You went from being her closest friend and confidante to sleeping with someone who can kill and hurt with impunity."

Lou had come up behind Emma as she said, "I don't want to believe you've forgotten what you were, but you don't leave me a choice. Get out."

❖

The short woman was out of control, and as much as Marisol wanted to watch the commotion, she couldn't pass up this opportunity. Three crisp twenties got her the room number she needed, and another one got her the best way to reach it.

"This is why you always have to pay attention, Fidel," she said as they entered Cain's room.

The woman who everyone talked about like little boys talk of superheroes didn't disappoint, despite the cuts and bruises that seemed to be concentrated on her face. Marisol took her time looking at Cain and felt the pull even though she was sleeping. She had to laugh at the foreignness of the attraction. Young men with rippling muscles were much more to her taste.

With a quick nod she sent Fidel to the door so she could get closer. She ran her fingers gently along the bruise on her temple and grimaced when she saw the cut at its center held together with very small, even black stitches. Her touch didn't wake Cain so she moved to her lips and, with only her fingernail, traced the edges, finally causing Cain's face to tense.

As Cain's eyes opened so did the door, and the noise the small blonde made caused her to move back from the bed. Before she could call Fidel back to her side he was pinned to the wall by the big guy they'd seen outside, and from the way Fidel was pawing at the long arm, the man was applying enough pressure to shut off his airway.

"You don't have a lot of time before your man can't hold his breath anymore," Cain said, sounding rather alert for having just woken up.

Marisol hesitated, keeping her eyes on Cain, but could hear Fidel grunting behind her. When she turned she saw the panic in his eyes since the ape hadn't shown any mercy. "I'm Marisol Delarosa," she said, watching as the big man now hesitated before letting up. With what looked like one last harder squeeze he did, and Fidel fell limp to the floor.

Cain laughed in a way that sounded like true enjoyment. "You see that, Lou," Cain said as the short blonde walked past her and sat on the bed. "No way I'll ever treat you like you're expendable."

"That might be good advice for you, Ms. Delarosa," the blonde said. "I highly doubt he'll put himself in harm's way for you."

"What can we do for you?" Cain asked, putting her hand in the blonde's lap.

"You both know who I am," she said, moving to the chair and sitting. "Who are you?" she asked, tilting her head slightly in the blonde's direction.

"Emma Casey. And the other lesson you should try to learn is to keep your hands off people who don't belong to you."

"You are the one with no manners. I only came to convey my family's concern for what happened to you," she said to Cain, deciding instantly she didn't like Emma. "My father speaks so highly of you and is thinking of possibilities for us to work together."

"Thank you," Cain said, and her eyes seemed to be dissecting her as if she could figure her out by something external. "Your father was helpful the one time I asked him for some information. If I can do the same for him one day, I'd be glad to return the kindness, but our businesses have nothing in common."

"You'll see how persuasive he can be. Both of us, actually."

"Ms. Delarosa," Cain said as she elevated the head of the bed.

"Marisol," she said, and smiled.

"Ms. Delarosa, I appreciate the visit," Cain said. "I'll be sure to thank your father for sending you, but this isn't the time to try to broker deals and build alliances."

"At least you seem open to the possibilities."

"No, that would be the last thing I would ever do now or in the future, so if you don't mind, I'd like to rest."

Marisol would prove to her father she was ready for her own territory by convincing Cain with incivility, since civility didn't seem to work. "It was wonderful meeting you, and I'll see you soon."

"One thing," Cain said, stopping her before she could move. "How did Hector know I was here?"

"How do you know my father told me?" She felt free to move closer to the bed. "I could be the one who found out."

"You could be, but you weren't." The way Cain smiled at her annoyed her because she felt she was being made fun of, and lying about how her father knew put her in a weak position. If she said her father was watching Cain, that implied she meant more to his operation than he'd ever admit. That was worse than telling her the information came from Rodolfo.

"You're right," she said, smiling. "Papa told me."

"That I know, Ms. Delarosa, but I don't know who told him."

"My father's always on top of things," she said, trying to keep her smile. "Like you said, you need your rest. Fidel," she said to her man, who was back on his feet but still rubbing his neck. One backward glance at Cain gave her the impression her visit had been damaging.

❖

Having no other option, Muriel sat in the floor's waiting room watching the elevator. She was in the type of shock she had experienced the night Cain told her of her father's death. Emma was a strong woman, but being on the receiving end of her protective streak had left her hurting.

She needed to see Cain, but she also wanted to talk to Shelby and ask what had prompted her old team to make the arrest. The twentieth call, like all the others, went to Shelby's voicemail for no reason, since her flight had arrived hours before. Muriel had called the airline to verify that.

The ding of the elevator made her put her phone away. Katlin emerged and hesitated, then walked toward her. "I'm glad you're here," Muriel said, opening her arms to her cousin.

"This is serious, Muriel," Katlin said, letting her go and stepping back. "I hope you brought some new information, because I can't explain why this happened."

"I came because Merrick told me what happened. Merrick, not you." She was angry, but the only real target she could zero in on was herself. Fate had thrown all she'd ever known and what she'd come to want in the air, and all of it seemed out of reach. "Have I really screwed up that bad that you don't include me?"

"I've done nothing but defend you," Katlin said, jabbing the space between them with her finger. "And you can choose to forget that you were one of the first people I called today. We needed you to do what you're good at, but you didn't come to the phone. Don't try to lay a guilt trip on me."

"I'm sorry, but Emma just tore a piece of my ass and you're giving me attitude."

Unlike Cain, who was slow to anger, Katlin grabbed her by the front of her shirt and dragged her into the one-person bathroom by the elevator. "You've been through your share lately, Muriel, but it's time to pull your head out of your ass. Don't you remember asking Cain for more to do?"

"I was tired of sitting on the sidelines."

"She gave in," Katlin said, throwing her hands up. "Probably not as much as you would've liked, but you fucking pay her back with Shelby? Do whatever the fuck you want, but remember that today Shelby's team picked her up and spat on the law they love to brag about."

"How the hell would I know that?" she asked, pushing Katlin away from her. "Emma told me I couldn't go in."

"Emma's protecting what's hers against what she doesn't know anymore."

"You all honestly think that I'd betray Cain because I care for Shelby?"

"I'm lucky," Katlin said, straightening her jacket. "Merrick and I both think and care about the same things. If that weren't the case and Merrick didn't support what I do and what my family means to me, I'd have to choose what was most important."

"And you think Shelby's my choice?"

Katlin laughed but Muriel knew it was pure sarcasm. "You shouldn't give a shit what I think. You should care what Cain thinks."

"Why's that?" she asked, even though she was in no mood for the answer.

"Cain will always love you, Muriel, but trusting you is another matter. You've given her no choice but to doubt you."

Katlin opened the door and walked out, and the silence she left behind was deafening.

CHAPTER EIGHTEEN

Anything you want to tell me?" Cain asked Emma. After Marisol left, Emma still appeared on edge, which was making Cain a little crazy since she was trapped on the bed for now.

"Why don't we make a deal not to talk about work until you get out of here?"

"Come here," she said, not wanting to watch Emma pace any longer. Having Emma lie next to her actually alleviated her headache some. "You should check all my decisions while my head's fuzzy, but I can't just stop working, considering what's going on."

"This isn't a complaint, but do you think it'll always be like this?" Emma asked, fooling with the tie on the hospital gown.

"I could be a nice quiet accountant, lass, and we'd experience some of this turmoil because it's human nature. People see something that looks better than what they have and they try their best to take it away from you." She kissed Emma's forehead and scratched the back of her neck. "Unlike the majority, though, I plan to dish out double what we've been through when the time is right."

"And that'll prevent it from happening again?" Emma asked, looking up at her.

"Maybe, and in some aspects, no."

"Then why do it?"

"Because it'll make us feel better," she said, and smiled even though it hurt. "At least it'll make me feel better to beat the crap out of someone who tried to mess up my good looks." The joke hit the mark and Emma laughed. "Want to tell me now what's bothering you?"

The more Emma relayed about how Muriel had handled her calls, the more tense her shoulders became. "She's here?" she asked when Emma finished.

"She wants to see you," Emma said, then hesitated. "I told her to go to hell."

"Don't worry about that, but could you have one of the guys go get her?"

"For what? Lame excuses are way late, and apologies won't erase the bruises and the concussion."

"It's time to give Muriel back something she's been missing."

Emma sat up and combed her hair back into place. "Family's important, but I'm not in a giving mood."

"She might not be in a receiving mood either, but I don't want to be the one to sever her ties to us," she said before kissing Emma's palm. "Before I talk to her I need one thing from the house." She'd thought long about what to do with the box she needed, but it was time. After today Muriel would either retake her place or be lost to her forever.

❖

The night view from the suite didn't appeal to Rodolfo. Instead he kept his eyes on the wide sidewalk and the stretch of street he could see from his window. Carlos had been gone all afternoon and Rodolfo was starting to worry, so he'd sent Fausto and a few others to look for him.

Finally admitting that Carlos was his son had liberated his imagination and he had been spinning scenarios of what the future would hold as he started to hand over his business. When Dolores, Carlos's mother, had told him she was pregnant, he'd come close to getting rid of her, but the beautiful peasant had touched something in him, and it enraged him to think of anyone else touching her.

He'd lied to Carlos by saying Dolores had wanted to keep his identity secret, but back then it had been an embarrassment to father a child with a woman who barely read. No, Dolores's hips and mouth had kept her in his bed for so long, and then he had Carlos in his life to do with as he pleased. But he hadn't lied about being an old man.

He had women whenever the mood struck him, but Dolores was the only one who'd given him a child. And whether he liked the idea completely, Carlos would be his only legacy.

"Anything?" he asked Fausto when the phone rang. "Keep looking."

He glanced at his watch and decided to try a few of the bars they'd visited when they came to the city before. Wearing only his shirt and suit pants, he figured he looked like every other tourist out that night, and he left through the back of the hotel for Ramon's club.

The street was fairly deserted and he whirled around when he heard footsteps close behind him. He really was getting old if a well-dressed young man could scare him for no reason. He returned the guy's smile and turned back in the direction he was headed. Something bothered him, though, and he sped up his pace when the guy came even with him.

"In a hurry, Rodolfo?"

The way his name rolled from the man's lips made him stop. His voice was familiar but his face wasn't. "Who are you?"

"I'm the past catching up with you," the man said, standing under a streetlight, his face totally visible.

The voice slammed into his head and he suddenly recognized it. This man had perfected Juan's voice, but Rodolfo couldn't identify him. "Aren't you too old for riddles?" he asked, fighting the urge to run when he heard more footsteps.

"If you think hard enough, I'm sure you'll understand why I'm here, you son of a bitch." The man's laugh was the same as Juan's. "Wasn't that what you called me when you thought I wasn't listening?"

"What are you talking about?"

"Or was it bastard?"

This guy didn't seem to need him for this bizarre conversation. While Rodolfo listened he looked around, trying to find a way out of what his gut was telling him was a deadly situation. The man with the familiar voice lifted his hand as if he were accepting something, which drew his total attention to the strange act.

"You always found me lacking."

"I don't know you, so why in the hell would I care?" A car driving down the street made him look, and in the headlights he saw either his chance to make it back to the safety of the hotel or his death. When it stopped even with his tormentor, he had the answer he didn't want, especially when he saw who got out and accepted the man's hand.

"Gracelia," he said, but his eyes were on the man with his nephew's voice. "And Juan, I assume."

"My name is Gustavo now, but for tonight you can still call me Juan."

"Is this why you've been hiding?"

"Hiding?" Gracelia asked, laughing. "It was more like preparing," she said, and he felt the warm metal of a gun pressed to the back of his neck. "Get in the car, Rodolfo, and if you're looking for a way out I've got some men on the corners convincing people they should detour."

"Where are you taking me?"

"Someplace you're familiar with."

Whoever was behind him pushed him hard, making him stumble, and Gracelia and Juan were in the backseat before he was thrown in the trunk. He wasn't a religious man but he prayed Carlos would forgive him enough to avenge him. Death was certain, but the last mystery he had to ponder was how it would come about. "Knowing Gracelia, it won't be quick, and pain will be my last companion."

❖

The hospital's visiting hours had ended, but no one stopped Emma as she arrived with her children and the box Cain had sent her for. On Cain's floor, Muriel was still sitting in the waiting area, and Emma walked by, wanting Cain to have some time with the kids before they had to go home again with Mook and Sabana.

Hayden glanced in Muriel's direction, but he took her hand and kept walking. It was as if he knew the reasons for her exile, even though Emma hadn't told him anything about that. She'd just told him what had happened to Cain and had felt good when he'd gotten Hannah ready to go.

"Don't be scared, okay?" Hayden said to Hannah. "Mom's hurt but she'll be home soon." Hannah held his other hand with both of hers and nodded.

Cain assured them she'd be fine, and Emma held Hannah while Cain and Hayden put their heads together for a quiet conversation. Whatever Cain told him made him nod before kissing her good night.

"Here," she said, handing Cain what she'd asked for. "I'll wait outside until you're done."

"I have to do everything possible to know what angle everyone who comes close to us is working," Cain said, opening the small box and showing her the tapes inside. "This time instead of proving we were right, I thought I'd lock these away because of what they meant."

"Keeping secrets from me, mobster?"

"I thought about it, but I want you to know what's on these before we call Muriel in," Cain explained. Emma wasn't surprised because she could see why Cain had put them in the safe. "When we pick love, we all want to believe our hearts."

"Sometimes we can," she said, sitting down and facing Cain. She intended for her kiss to heat up Cain's passion just enough for her to know how she felt. "You're my choice and I know it's right."

"And you're mine." She hissed when Cain pinched her nipple hard enough to wake up her clit. "But save any more kisses like that until we're done."

"I don't mind waiting outside, baby. Muriel should hear this without me being here to embarrass her." She kissed Cain briefly but held the roving hands. "I love you, and I want you to take your time. Muriel deserves it, even if she's not my favorite person today."

Cain closed her eyes when Emma left, trying to calm the pounding in her head and lip. She didn't want to take anything to dull her senses any more, even if the doctor had allowed it.

The intake of breath meant that her face shocked Muriel. "Are you coming in or don't you recognize me?"

"What happened?" Muriel asked, her feet glued in place.

"Come in and sit." She opened her eyes. Muriel was like a stranger. Something seemed to have come between them that was so much more than Shelby, and it was time to talk about it. "I'm sure Katlin or someone told you what happened, so let's not waste time."

"I know you're pissed I wasn't there today."

"One of the things they taunted me with while they had me cuffed to the table in that small room is that you weren't coming. Annabel and her minions made it sound like they already knew your choices when it came to me."

"You believe that?"

She took a deep breath and folded the blankets over her lap to give her some time to answer. "I believe something's changed between us and I'm tired of reacting to try and keep up. We have a problem and I want to know what it is."

"You don't have to know anything, Cain, because you have the final say on everything and it's non-negotiable. That means I'm out, Sanders is in, and there's nothing more to talk about."

The defensiveness appeared sooner than she expected, and Muriel's anger was almost predictable. "Drop the bullshit self-pity routine and be honest. Up till a few months ago we lived fine with those parameters, so what's changed?"

"I'm sure your ready answer is Shelby."

"Today and this," she said, pointing to her face, "was about Shelby. Her parents are dead and I'm to blame."

"That doesn't sound like the team Shelby worked with."

"Are you telling me you know them better than you know me?" she asked. If she felt better she'd get up and hit Muriel for the first time as an adult. "When have you ever known me to lie to you?"

"Calm down."

"Shut up," she said, talking over Muriel. "And sit the fuck down or I swear I'll have somebody tie you to that goddamn chair." It was time to stop coddling her. "You're going to sit and listen to what I have to tell you, and then you can do whatever the hell you want. I'm damn tired of watching you turn into some whiny, sniveling idiot who can't remember what and who's important."

"I'm not ten anymore."

"I said shut up," she said, pressing her hand to her temple when yelling blurred her vision, it hurt so bad. "You think you're the only one who's lost a parent and that I'm stealing your birthright?"

"You had no right to remove me from my office," Muriel said, crossing her arms over her chest. "It hurts that you don't think I can separate Shelby from my responsibilities."

Muriel watched as she opened the box and placed the tape numbered 5 into the small recorder and pressed Play. When Shelby's voice began, she leaned forward.

"Hey, Granddad," Shelby said, a television playing in the background. "Go ahead and watch, baby, this won't take long."

"Anything new?" a woman asked.

"I found the address of two warehouses, but she doesn't keep many files in the house. I'm trying to find a way to get into the office without an escort. Jarvis's death has distracted her, but the building is never empty and I haven't found the security codes in case I do get an opportunity."

"What do you think the warehouses are used for?"

"I'm having the information run now, so I'm not sure. This could be how Cain moves product, and if we can find out if the buildings don't have an elaborate security system we can set up our equipment to monitor any movement."

"One last thing. You're sure no one, especially Cain, suspects you?"

"Want anything?" Muriel asked.

"No, Granddad. I'm fine and don't need anything. I'm glad you're feeling better, and I'll call you soon."

She shut the tape off and handed the box to Muriel. "I'm curious," she said, pressing against her temple again. "Did she want something?"

"How did you know?"

"We'll get to that," she said, glad to see Muriel had lost her fight for now. "Because of this we lost the wine warehouse and the overflow space in the east. On top of that I had to waste manpower to sit on every property until I know which ones we eventually need to take off our list. Instead of finding who killed our people, I had to plug the security holes your girlfriend caused us."

"I didn't know."

"No, you didn't, because you believed a lie instead of what I was telling you. In the future remember that I may not say what you want to hear, but I'll never lie to you."

"How long have you been aware?" Muriel asked, running her finger over the six other tapes in the box. "I'd think you would've loved rubbing it in that you were right."

"My head hurts, Muriel, so don't push me into throwing you out." She meant it. "I got to wondering," she said, when Muriel lowered her eyes, "who answers a call in the middle of a funeral, and that's what Shelby did as we were burying your father. Tapping into someone's phone isn't rocket science."

"If today hadn't happened, would you have told me?"

"Lately you've had a lot going on, and I didn't want to pile on top of that, especially since you'd think I was being petty."

"I'm sorry, but it really hurt that you cut me off." Muriel moved to the end of her seat and put her hands on the bed. "I wanted something you have, and I guess it never occurred to me that I was jealous. Today, though, wasn't about that. Shelby was upset and I wanted to be there for her."

"You don't have to apologize," she said, having to close her eyes again to keep the room from spinning. "I really do think Shelby cares about you, only her commitment isn't as deep as yours. I'm sorry, because you deserve someone in your life you can count on."

"Are you kidding?" Muriel said, laughing. "Shelby's with me because I'm a fucking moron too absorbed in self-pity to notice she went through my office. Do you realize how stupid that makes me?"

"Don't get carried away knocking yourself."

"She didn't even want me at her parents' funeral, Cain. Does that sound like someone in a relationship?" The bed moved a little when Muriel slammed her hands down on the mattress. "She can fuck herself for what she was doing."

"Not so fast," she said, the nausea building again. "You aren't there because they really do think I ordered the deaths, for whatever reason, but you tell her why you want her out of your life…" she said, stopping to breathe.

"And it makes them believe it's true," Muriel said, finishing her thought.

Muriel put the basin under her mouth in time so the bile that came up didn't soil her or the bed. "You need to keep this from her when she comes back, and I want you to go back to work," she said after she rinsed her mouth.

"This can wait. Let me go get someone."

"I want to finish because I need to know Emma won't be alone through this. But, Muriel, I can only be forgiving up to a point if you decide to work on your own. I've trusted you all my life, but I'll have to cut you off completely if we have to have this conversation again. And you can't know how hard and painful that is for me to say."

"Don't worry about anything. I'll do whatever I need to make this up to you and Emma." When she closed her eyes again Muriel sounded like she'd come closer. "Are you sure you're okay?"

"My head feels like it's about to pop. Take Emma home and we'll talk again in the morning." She heard Muriel's steps as she moved even nearer, then the strangest sensation came over her. Her last thought before the room went black was that she'd never enjoyed being cruel, but she intended to skin Agent Cehan alive right after she shoved that belt buckle up his ass.

❖

The car stopped and Rodolfo strained to listen for any clues to where they'd taken him. Aside from the slamming of car doors all he heard was Gracelia's muffled voice giving what sounded like orders. Whatever sick idea his sister had come up with was about to shatter any illusion of dying an old man in his bed.

"You aren't sleeping, are you?" she asked when Lorenzo opened the trunk and helped him out. "Juan went to a lot of trouble to find this place."

They'd stopped in a clump of trees and the only light was from the headlights of the two vehicles. When he saw the base of the largest one, he knew what she had in mind. "You blamed me all these years for Armando's death, but at least give up the dream he was coming back to you."

"He loved me, and you stole the possibility of him knowing his son."

"Your bastard was one of many, you stupid bitch. When we found him he'd already found your replacement and laughed that he got someone of your standing to spread your legs so quickly." His death was certain but he'd get the satisfaction of speaking his mind before the ants finished their job.

"Lying now is pathetic, Rodolfo," Juan said.

"You can change your name," he said, wincing as his arms were tied behind him. "What you can't change is that your father was scum and your mother's a whore who's slept with every man she could interest. Hate me, but I've paid to keep everyone from talking, since she's never associated with anyone with class."

"You're jealous because none of them were you," Gracelia screamed. "You don't think I saw how you looked at me and what you wanted. You're the sick one. Your desire for me sealed Armando's death, and I'm going to make you pay for it."

"I see Lorenzo's doing your bidding now," he said, trying to hide the shame of having his pants and shirt cut away by the man he was talking about. "He was starting out with me back then, but I'm sure he remembers when we found the virtuous Armando fucking one of the maids who worked for the rancher we bought meat from. She begged for his life because of the two sons he'd left her with."

"Liar," Juan yelled.

"You're going to kill me no matter what, so you might as well know the truth. If he'd lived, your father would've come by for only two things—money and your mother's ass." He laughed as Lorenzo smeared honey on his groin and chest, then jumped back when he relieved himself on Lorenzo's shoes.

"One day when you get pushed aside for whoever is sharing your mother's bed, remember what I'm saying. And if this shit tells you the truth," he said, jutting his jaw out in Lorenzo's direction, "you'll know you killed the one man who tried to make you live up to the name I gave you."

The ants had covered his legs, and as they started to feed on the honey coating his genitals the pain blossomed into agony, but he didn't scream. "After you were born, she left you with me for two years while she fucked whoever ended up in her bed for the night. She came home and pretended to be the caring mother only after she'd gotten her fill of more assholes like your father."

He strained against the restraints, wanting nothing more than to knock away the persistent insects that now covered his body. They weren't like the large black ants he'd fed Armando to, but the small red ones seemed to be determined to finish him in record time.

"Now you can be Gustavo, whose mother whores herself to farm hands and gardeners." He laughed hard when the first bullet ripped through his gut. "You'll be the perfect example of the term 'son of a bitch.'"

He couldn't stop his death, but his last thought was that he wouldn't suffer. He just hoped Fausto would watch over Carlos like he'd asked.

CHAPTER NINETEEN

A re you sure?" Dallas asked as they rode the elevator to Remi's penthouse condo after dropping Simon off at her place. She'd called Kristen to tell her not to wait up and that Emil was staying on the sofa.

"I'm sorry you had to go through all that, but I'm not sorry it led you to me." Remi guided her to the bedroom, not turning on many lights, then took her time undressing her. "You're mine, and I'll kill to keep you whole."

"All you need to do is love me," Dallas said, lying back and spreading her legs. After the emotional wringer of the afternoon, she wanted Remi to touch her until she forgot the past. "I'm yours and I'll give you everything you need to keep you happy."

"I already have that," Remi said, putting her hand over her sex and sucking in an already hard nipple.

Dallas was wet, had been from the time they'd gotten in the car, and she tried to ignore Simon, who was driving, as Remi touched her over her clothes. "Put your fingers in, baby. I need you." She felt ravenous for an orgasm as Remi's skin pressed against hers. When she put her heels on the small of Remi's back and met her thrust by pumping her hips up into her, for the first time she didn't think of herself as a woman who had only her body to offer.

"Tell me again," she said to Remi, grabbing the hair at the sides of her head.

"You're mine," Remi said, the tendon in her neck standing out as she kept moving her hand. "This is mine," she said, stopping for a moment and pressing her thumb hard against her clit. "Forget about what you think you did wrong, because no one but me is going to touch you like this again if you stay with me."

"No one but you." Remi's thumb was still stroking even though her hand was still, and Dallas clenched the walls of her sex around Remi's fingers to try to postpone the end. Tonight she wanted that feeling only Remi had brought into her life to last, but once Remi started moving her hand again the orgasm washed through her and she came hard, pressing her body close to Remi's, wanting her weight on her.

"You're really good at that." She kissed the side of Remi's head. "That sounds so canned but it's true."

"Good to hear because I feel honored to be able to touch you like this." She smiled at how the confidence Remi had displayed during their lovemaking gave way to the sweetness reserved only for her.

"I meant what I said, baby." Dallas locked her feet in place to keep Remi where she was. "I still have issues about why I'm worthy of you, but I'm all yours."

The ringing phone made Remi lose her smile, so Dallas reached for it and pressed it to Remi's ear. It had to be something important because it was the intercom line that came from Simon and Juno's place under them. She could hear Simon's muffled voice through the receiver and went with Remi when she rolled over.

"What's he want?" Remi asked, still lying down as she listened to Simon's answer. "It has to be tonight?" Dallas let go when Remi sat up. "Tell him if he wants that he'll have to wait." There was a long pause as Remi listened. "Shit," she said, to end the call.

"You have to go now?" Dallas asked, taking Remi's hand.

"Rodolfo's man Carlos is at the club and he's hysterical. Told the manager he wants to talk to me and Cain tonight. He hasn't threatened anyone, but I'm not in the mood to draw any heat right now. Leaving, though, isn't on my agenda."

"Has anything else happened aside from what you already shared with me?"

"Something's always going on, but right now it revolves around the deaths I told you about. It's like finding the pieces of a puzzle, only this time they aren't coming easily."

Dallas rubbed her cheek against Remi's shoulder. They didn't have any secrets between them now, and while that gave her a new beginning, it brought more fear. These puzzles Remi spoke of meant someone out there was targeting her.

"It's okay if you have to go, just be careful." Remi stood up after kissing her and Dallas enjoyed her naked body outlined by the city lights. The house in the Quarter was great, but she enjoyed making love with Remi in this room with its three walls of uncovered glass.

"I won't be long, so stay and take a nap."

"Can I do anything for you before you go?" she asked, following Remi into the bathroom.

"That's why I want you to take a nap, beautiful lady."

Sleep wouldn't come easy after what they'd just shared, but she loved Remi's playful mood.

"I want to thank you again for sharing your story with me. I love you, and you can trust me."

"That goes for me too, baby. I'll keep your secrets as well as your heart safe."

❖

Bugs flew around Gustavo's head as he stood in the beam of the headlights with his chest heaving and his gun at his side. This was one of the only times he'd been the one pulling the trigger, and he was staring at Rodolfo's slumped, lifeless body hanging from the tree they'd tied him to. The ants didn't seem to care he was dead as they crawled higher up his chest, making it look like living red lines were drawing new designs as they worked their way to the bone.

"I've waited over twenty years for this and you let him escape with no pain," Gracelia said, her hands on her hips. "He got his way even on this."

"You wanted to listen to what he was saying about you and my papa all night?" he asked, Rodolfo's voice ringing through his mind. Rodolfo's version didn't resemble anything his mother had always told him. Gustavo bounced his gun on his leg as he considered his family history. "Was any of what he said true?"

"Rodolfo knew we'd finally won, and you're going to believe the fantasies of his desperation?"

His mother seldom screamed at him, but he wasn't interested in her reaction. Supposedly Lorenzo had been there when they'd found his father, and if what Rodolfo said was true, he wasn't an only child. Instead of the golden son his mother spun tales about, he was one of the bastards Armando Ortega left behind like dirty laundry as he moved from conquest to conquest.

Lorenzo was loyal to his mother, one of the first men to leave

Rodolfo for her, and not for her promise of a larger take. He stood behind her now and wouldn't meet Gustavo's gaze. Gustavo knew it was because what Rodolfo had said was true, but Lorenzo loved his mother too much to expose what he knew. The old bastard didn't realize his mother would string him along but never be interested in anything but him doing his job.

"I have brothers and sisters?" he asked, wanting to find out at least some of what had been kept from him.

"You are the only son your father had who mattered," Gracelia said, leading him to the car and pushing him inside. "You know who you are, Gustavo, even if the name still sounds foreign to you. Rodolfo was a dried-up old man who took pleasure in hurting both of us all his life, and that was true tonight as well. All that talk just showed he had no character."

"He might've been an ass, Mama, but he never lied to me."

"That you know of. Rodolfo told you and everyone around him what he wanted them to know. He took the whole truth about his life with him."

He watched Lorenzo walk the area, making sure they left nothing behind before he got into the front passenger seat. "What now?"

"Tomorrow we call Santos for a meeting and ask him if he'd like to help run the Biloxi part of the business like he did for Rodolfo. If he refuses, we kill him and go to the next guy in line. Once we establish ourselves here, I'll return to Cozumel with Jerome to take control of the production end."

"You're planning to leave me here?" If she allowed him to stay in New Orleans, he could concentrate on taking down Casey.

"Do you want me to leave Jerome?" she asked, reapplying her lipstick. "I trust you, and you don't need to be told what to do."

"No, I want to stay." He didn't want anyone supervising him. "Are you sure you can trust Jerome? He has a different name too, but he's still a fucking cop under the new face."

"You leave him to me," she said, running her tongue along her lips after she finished with the makeup. "He's going to be a great asset to me…to both of us."

The way she said it and the way they interacted in the hotel made Gustavo guess his mother hadn't settled for a gardener or day worker in her bed this time. Since she'd taken Jerome as a lover, eventually she wouldn't need or have any room for him. He hadn't gone through all this not to take the control Rodolfo had never shared with him.

He would do that even at the expense of teaching his mother a lesson. She would eventually forgive him, but Jerome could screw himself—if he lived to think about it.

❖

It was late but people were still drinking and having a good time in Pescadors when Remi arrived. Her father was upstairs and had sent a few men down to keep an eye on Carlos and the man who'd come with him. The two were sitting where they'd met with Rodolfo before, and as she walked close with a neutral expression, not happy considering what she'd just left, he didn't see her because he had his head down. When she cleared her throat Carlos must've heard her even over the music, because he stood and combed his hair back.

She didn't know him well but, like Simon, who stood behind her, Carlos seemed to be the stoic watcher who was seldom heard. His youth told her that he was deadly enough to be the one who had earned his spot behind Rodolfo. Considering their business and the choices Rodolfo had to make, this young man made her curious enough to put her aggravation aside.

"Don't you think it would be better to wait for Rodolfo?" Simon asked her softly. "These assholes don't scare me, but we don't need the pain in the ass we'll get if his boss thinks we're going behind his back."

"That's this guy's problem," she said, stopping a few feet from Carlos.

"Does Rodolfo know you're here?" she asked him in Spanish.

"I'm not here to play games, so cut the shit and tell me what you and Casey did with him," he yelled back. "If he's hurt I won't stop until I kill all of you."

His threat made her father's men move in and put their hands in their jackets. "Unless you explain, you're the one playing games. You were here when we met, and unless you were sleeping, you heard that Cain and our family want nothing to do with you. Why the hell would we move against Rodolfo?"

"Then Casey did it without you."

"You call me for this?" she asked, dropping into one of the leather chairs that were replicas of the ones her father had in his clubs in Cuba. "Sit down and spit it out." He stayed on his feet and combed his thick jet hair back again, and she saw that it was disordered. Carlos was panicked and that was driving his anger.

"He's gone," Carlos said, sitting, "and if not you, then Casey."

"He's gone?" This was a new angle for these guys. "If he is, it wasn't us or Cain." She didn't want to share what had happened to Cain, but it would explain to Carlos why Rodolfo wasn't on their minds at the moment. "If that's true, how did anyone get past you?"

"That's not a story I have time to waste on," he said, not meeting her eyes.

"You don't have a choice because you don't get to come in here and accuse me of something, then only tell me bits and pieces. That's what Rodolfo did, and it sounds like it didn't work out for him." She stood and faced the door to let Simon know she was ready.

"Wait," he said, springing to his feet. "I need you to get me in to see Cain, then. I'm sure they won't let me into her house."

"Carlos, I wasn't lying about where she is," she said, shaking her head and losing her patience. "She's in the hospital with a head injury, and it's late."

"If I wait until tomorrow, it'll be too late for Rodolfo." The attitude was gone and what was left made her think of a small child who needed someone to tell them what to do. "This isn't my home, so I need your help. If you say no, I'll never get him back." He glanced back at the one man he'd brought with him. After a deep breath, he apparently decided to tell her something to help persuade her to give him what he needed. "Rodolfo is more than just my boss, he's my father."

If that was true, it made no sense to Remi why Rodolfo had given Juan so much of his time and presented him as his heir. He stared at her as she considered what he'd said, and it was like he'd guessed where her thoughts were. "I'm sure you don't believe me, but he told me today."

That was all he had to say to make her believe him. The short explanation also answered how whoever had taken Rodolfo had gotten past him. Carlos wasn't there protecting him because he was off licking the wounds Rodolfo had ripped open in his pride. "If we go see Cain, your man will have to stay downstairs with Simon," she said, pointing to her guard.

"Would you do that if you were me?" he asked, his attitude getting a lifeline.

"If I asked someone for help, I must've trusted them a little," she said, offering him her hand. "You have my word that nothing will happen to you because, like I said before, my friend Cain and I have no interest in you or your father." He took her hand and seemed relieved. "Up to now your family has given Cain the problems."

"If you're talking about Juan, if I find him before she does I'll give her the bullet I'll personally dig out of his head. He's nothing but a piece of shit."

"Come on, then." She waved her arm toward the door and led him out. "I'm not making any promises, but hopefully we'll find what you're looking for."

"Whatever it is, your help means that I won't come near you when I take revenge if something has happened to him."

Of all the newcomers to town trying to stake their piece of the drug trade, this seemingly simple man was the best of the lot she'd met. And a war was coming, because if Rodolfo was gone and out of Carlos's reach, he was dead. But perhaps that held the answer to the questions they'd been asking.

❖

"Why aren't you sleeping?" Emma asked from her side. They'd argued about Emma staying home when she took the kids back, but only Emma had the energy to win that fight. After Cain's visit with Muriel she'd had another seizure that left her drained and a little confused.

"That's all I've been doing all day," she said, conscious that she should admit what had happened. "And I'm enjoying feeling you so much that I'm not sleepy."

"You can be honest and say you're pissed that I forced myself on you."

"I'm not mad at you, lass." She wasn't, but in all their time together fear had never overwhelmed her like this. Feeling like she'd lost control of her body made her crazy. "Being here is a waste of time, and you know how I am when I don't feel good."

"After all the sleep you don't feel better?" Emma put her hand against Cain's cheek, knowing her well enough to have picked up on something.

This was the opening she needed, and neglecting her promise to be open and truthful with Emma was making her headache worse, so she opened her mouth at the same time the door did. She was surprised to see Remi there so late.

"I'm sorry, guys," Remi said, coming in and obviously feeling comfortable enough to sit. "I didn't want to bother you now, but this is important."

Emma sat up and straightened her clothes, not appearing too happy. "Are you sure it couldn't wait?"

She lay back and listened, not minding if Emma acted as her protector and only opening her eyes when Remi said Rodolfo was missing and mentioned who was waiting outside. She thought about her meeting with Rodolfo in her office after Juan and Anthony had taken Emma and how he'd backed down when she threatened Carlos.

"He's Rodolfo's son?" Emma asked.

"That's the first thing I've heard from all these guys that I believe," Cain said. "I should've seen it before now."

"According to Carlos, Rodolfo only admitted it today. The shock of hearing it probably drove him out and let someone in long enough to take Rodolfo." Remi crossed her legs and covered her mouth to hide her yawn. "He's upset he can't find him."

"No clue as to who, if this is something other than Rodolfo taking a walk?" Emma asked, saving Cain the trouble.

"I know this isn't the best time, but I think that's why he asked to see you."

"Why me?" Cain asked, finally tired after staring at the dark for hours. "You're a good contact if he's looking for help."

"He laid the blame on both of us, but you have more against Rodolfo than I do," Remi said, spreading her hands out. "If we help Carlos, we might find answers to what's a dead subject on the street."

"Send him in, but give us a minute," she said, holding Emma in place by wrapping her fingers around her wrist. "Stay," she said to Emma when Remi left. "I need you to listen in case I miss something."

"You don't usually miss anything," Emma said, concern in her eyes. "If you didn't already have a concussion, I'd pop you in the head because I know you're keeping something back. This isn't the time, Derby Cain Casey, to get stoic on me."

"I promise you can scream at me later, but I won't look very outlaw-like if this ass comes in here and you've got me over your knee."

Emma sighed but didn't move. "At least tell me if I'm right."

"You're right, but I don't feel good enough to fight about it."

"I'm not mad. I just love you enough to want to know when you're hurting. That means physically and emotionally."

"I love you too, and I didn't want to worry you." The ache in her head eased and the strange, unconnected feeling she'd experienced before the seizures disappeared, to her relief. "Every so often I get tired of all this crap," she admitted.

"You thinking of retiring, mobster?" Emma asked, rubbing the center of her chest.

"Nah, but I do fight the urge to take out everyone who annoys the hell out of me," she said, and smiled. "I don't want to look even more psychotic than the FBI gives me credit for."

"That's because they don't realize what a softie you are."

The arrival of Remi and Carlos broke their lips apart, and she dropped her smile when Carlos came in with an expression of disapproval. "You can turn around if you don't lose the face," she said, and he looked confused until Remi translated.

"I'm not here to be lectured to," he said, and Remi again translated.

"Then turn around and get out."

Carlos seemed hesitant, almost defiant, after Remi spoke.

Cain glared at Carlos. "I've been tied up all day, so I'm not the one seeking you out. You're the visitor here."

"Today I got what I've always wanted," Carlos said after Remi stopped translating. "And now, before I could accept my gift, somebody took it away."

Cain figured she felt sorry for this guy because of what she'd experienced today. "I know Rodolfo," she said. "Not well, but he seems like he'd still be handing out cigars to celebrate the gift of a son."

"I'm sure he expected something more in a son, but those hopes weren't enough. I won't know anything for sure until I find him and talk to him." His honesty conveyed through Remi made Cain want to help him. "If I'd come to that conclusion earlier, we'd probably still be having that conversation."

"If you got mad after he told you, you can't blame yourself for what happened to him, *if* anything happened." She pointed to the sofa under the window. "We aren't friends, but I'm not your enemy."

"That's not what you've said in the past."

"Rodolfo isn't my enemy, but because he didn't turn Juan over or help me find him after what happened to my partner, we were never going to do business together. And we aren't going to share a drink like old friends." She was careful to use the present tense and hoped Remi did the same. "Why are you here?"

"You probably will take pleasure in turning me down, but I need your help." He laced his fingers together, appearing mortified. "In

Cozumel and the surrounding countryside, Senor Rodolfo," he said, and pressed his fingers together harder, "I mean my father, is a god. Here, though, he was building on what he already had. The ability to get things done quickly aren't within his power yet."

"Carlos," she said, waiting to see if he objected to her using his name. "The last time we met I understood two things. Rodolfo finally realized what he had under his roof all those years, and—"

"If you mean Juan, he's dead once we find him. Don't doubt either of us on that."

"I said I got two things," she said, reminding him not to interrupt. "Also, he was holding something back."

"That wasn't anything against you," Carlos said hesitantly. "It was family business, and none of that is yours."

"Don't you mean he was protecting his own, and to hell with us?" Emma asked, her obvious fury making Carlos lean back. "That animal Juan deserved to die, but Rodolfo did everything he could to let that bastard go."

"What does he know that he didn't want to share with us? Tell me or you can go to the police and report him missing," Cain said, taking a deep breath. "I'm sure they'll call the DEA and hop right on it."

"You won't help me?"

"Why should I? You aren't willing to help me, and you know why I'm asking. Five of my people and one of Remi's are dead, and Rodolfo knows or at least suspects why that is and who had a motive to do it."

"He told you about his sister," Carlos said, waving his hands as if he wanted Remi to talk faster. "That should prove he had nothing to hide."

"His telling me about her was like someone telling me the FBI is after me," she said, and laughed. "It's not a lie but it gives you an overview that isn't very helpful. There's a story buried in there somewhere and I want to know what it is."

Carlos beat his fists on his lap and mumbled something that made Remi shake her head, meaning she couldn't understand what he was saying. When he looked up he apparently had come to a decision. "When my father killed Gracelia's lover, she changed from a harmless flirt to someone who went off the deep end trying to embarrass him."

Cain could tell he was having a hard time talking about this.

"The only time she tried to make peace with him was when Juan was about five and she'd just come back from one of her adventures that kept her away for months. Gracelia asked to be made part of the business since Rodolfo had fought his way to the top of it in Mexico."

"I take it he turned her down," she said, figuring Rodolfo was dead and his sister had taken his life.

"He said the only part of her that would be close to the business was her son. Since she'd left Juan with him for over two years after his birth, Rodolfo had no choice but to care for him. All that time, and nothing made an impression on Juan." He beat his fists down again and she believed he hated Juan as much as she did. "That bastard believed all the stories Gracelia told him, and that's what he latched on to."

"And you have no idea where Gracelia is? I believe that you don't know where Juan is."

"Rodolfo talked with her a few months back, then my mother told him that she'd packed and left. We haven't been able to find out where she headed, and believe me, I've got every man I can spare out looking."

"What's her full name?" she asked, feeling like she could sleep for days.

"Gracelia Vivian Luis is what I remember him saying one time." He looked at her like she could give him the answers he desperately wanted. "Why do you ask?"

"Carlos, thank you for being so honest, and I promise to be so with you," she said, and smiled. "If something has happened to Rodolfo, we have a few possibilities." She stopped when he pressed his fingers to the bridge of his nose. "Law enforcement's first choice will be Hector Delarosa, since he's here after the same things you and your father are."

"But you don't think so?"

"Hector is after me more than he is Rodolfo. Eventually he'll get around to you, but for now his interests lie elsewhere."

"Then who else?"

The logical answer to his question would also give him the answer he most likely didn't want to hear. "I give you my word on the grave of my father that neither Remi nor I had anything to do with harming Rodolfo," she said, and he nodded. "That leaves only one person who would've wanted to try something like this, so we have to know for sure if Gracelia is in New Orleans."

"I would know if she's here."

"Like you said, this isn't your home, and you have limited contacts to get real, pertinent information. Go back to your hotel room and leave this to me and Remi."

"He's my father, so I'd like to be a part of whatever you're planning."

"You seem like a reasonable man, Carlos," she said, and he relaxed his hands somewhat. "I'll keep you informed as to what I'm doing, and if it turns out to be Gracelia, I'll hand her over with a bow in her hair. But believe it or not, our best shot at finding out something quick is to call the cops."

When Remi told him what she'd said, he stood up and laughed. "You think this is a joke? I want your help, not to get arrested, but you've laid there and listened to my problem only to make fun of me."

"Do you want me to help you or not?" She waited until he decided to sit again. "I'm not trying to get anyone arrested and I'm not joking about the police. And I'm not talking about the FBI, but the New Orleans Police Department."

"What can they do?"

"If something's happened to him, they can tell me if they've found him, but do you think Gracelia hated him enough to kill him?"

"In a heartbeat and with no remorse."

"Okay, then," she said, holding her hand out to him. "I know it'll be hard, but go back to the room and wait for my call in the morning. Keep your men on the street but don't call too much attention to yourselves."

"If you help me, you do know I'll be forever in your debt."

"I appreciate your saying so, but trust me that this won't cost you much." She glanced over at Emma and was relieved to see her face wasn't tight. "Lass, write out my number for him and get his, please." She shook hands with him and saw the bit of hope in his eyes. "Carlos, you might not have known that he was your father until tonight, but I can tell Rodolfo is proud of the man you are."

"Why do you say so?" he asked, still holding her hand.

"Because only a good son would care enough to search for his father to either bring him back or avenge him if someone has stolen him from you."

"If Gracelia has done this, I'll hunt her down and drive a machete through her forehead."

He left after slightly bowing over her hand, with Remi following him out. "I feel sorry for this Gracelia if she did do something to

Rodolfo, but then she might deserve what he's got in mind for bringing Juan into the world," Emma said.

"A machete through the head is what her son will pray for when I find him."

"You're such a romantic," Emma teased her, "but it's time for bed for mobsters." She turned off the lights and lay down next to her again. "Do you need anything?"

"I need you to make a call for me, then I promise I'll follow all your orders to the letter," she said softly, giving Emma the name.

"You'll make the FBI jealous, baby."

"I only want to show them what they're missing out on by not being nice to me," she said, wanting nothing more than to go to sleep and hoping the morning would bring some clarity.

CHAPTER TWENTY

Dallas rolled over and reached across the bed, waking up when her hand hit the mattress. The sun was starting to rise and Remi wasn't back yet, so she got up to make sure she wasn't in the condo somewhere. Whatever had happened with this Carlos guy she'd told her about before she left had kept her out longer than she'd anticipated.

When she got back to the bedroom she knew she wouldn't be able to sleep. She felt great about there being no secrets between them, and her scripts were arriving from the studio today. It was time to take Emma's advice to be happy, and the only way to burn off her energy was a long run. Since it was so early she figured not too many people would be out when she jogged home.

She got dressed and stretched in the bedroom close to the window so she could watch the boat traffic on the river. Then she wrote a short note so Remi wouldn't worry if she got home before she made it to the Quarter. After she left it on Remi's nightstand she took the extra elevator key from the kitchen.

The morning was cool and a slight mist was falling through the morning fog, but not enough to make her turn back. Since she was at Remi's she'd have only her breathing to listen to on the way home, but feeling the burn in her legs made up for not having her iPod with her. She was right that there weren't many people out this early so she ran down from Remi's past Café Du Monde to the French Market, then cut over to Bourbon.

Sweat was starting to run down her back when she saw her house through the fog and she pulled out her cell phone to tell Kristen to come unlock the door. The shorts she was wearing didn't have pockets so she hadn't wanted to carry more than just the phone. Nothing seemed out of the ordinary until the man rushed from the doorway where a girl had been sitting and grabbed her hand and pulled her to his chest.

Any thoughts of screaming died in her throat, not because of the gun he had pressed to her abdomen but because of the shock of seeing him. It had been years but Johnny's face was burned in her memory despite the fact that he hadn't aged well. All her hard work and he'd still caught up with her, but mainly she thought what a fool she'd been not to listen to Remi and her constant lectures about security. The only way she could've made it any easier on him was if she'd driven to Sparta and walked through his front door unarmed.

"Miss me, little girl?" he asked, bringing his other arm around her waist and pulling her closer. His face had that stubble she hated and it scratched her face when he got close to whisper in her ear. "You done run off without saying good-bye, so I had to come a looking for you."

"Let me go, Johnny, and you won't get hurt."

He laughed as if what she was saying was the most ridiculous thing he'd ever heard. "I don't think you understand how hard I've worked for this little reunion," he said, prying her phone from her fingers. "You stole from me, and I'm not just talking about that can of money you're going to work hard to replace." He scrolled through the numbers in her memory and she was close enough to see where he stopped. "Oh, no, you stole something that was my right."

"Take me and I won't fight you, but leave her alone," she said, staring at Kristen's name highlighted and his finger on the Call button. "She doesn't deserve this."

"What you need to do, you dirty whore, is shut up before I lose my temper and shoot you dead on this street. I've known where you were the whole time, but the money stopped and I haven't been able to get in touch with Bob."

It seemed surreal that he was carrying on this conversation with her while he held a gun on her and no one was coming out to help her. She was less than a block from her home on one of the most famous streets in the country, and Johnny was going to win. "Bob is no longer in my life."

"Good for you," he said, pressing the button and holding the phone to his ear. "That boy was nothing but a greedy son of a bitch."

"If it's money you're after, I'll get you whatever you want. Just leave us alone."

"Hello, you," Kristen said, and Dallas heard the groggy voice since Johnny was holding the phone so close.

"I want you to listen to me," Johnny said, his eyes on the front of her house the whole time. "I have Katie Lynn with me, Sue Lee, so don't do anything stupid like waking that nice big man taking care of the two of you."

"Kristen, don't listen to him. Go get Emil," she yelled, making him press the gun to her forehead.

"If you want, I'll call you Kristen, but no matter what names you two want to go by, believe me when I say that I'll kill her right here, right now, if you don't do everything I say. You do that and you can hide behind that animal, but Dallas will be out of your reach whether I'm dead or not."

"Don't hurt her."

"That's not my plan. I'm your father, after all, and all I want is my family back. Now get your ass dressed and get out of that house without company, or like your mama, you ain't ever going to see Dallas again," he said, and hung up. "She'll be out here and then we'll go."

"Johnny, this is your one chance to leave and never look back," she said, finding the courage to stand up to him from somewhere inside her that had been nurtured by Remi. "You don't know the extent my lover will go to get me back."

"If you're talking about that bitch that's been spending an awful lot of nights with you, forget it. She'll get over you soon enough, just like you will her once you get a taste of what you've been missing."

This could not be happening to her again, and as soon as she got the chance she was going to smash his head in like Timothy Pritchard's, with no lifetime of regret. Johnny Moores deserved killing, but she'd have to be patient as she watched the gate open and Kristen step out, looking around. Any curiosity as to how he would get her over to where they were was answered when the girl she'd seen sitting on the steps walked over and held her small purse to Kristen's side.

"Nothing fancy, girls," he said, once the four of them were close together, "or I'll kill the both of you. I done lived without you all these years."

They walked two streets over where Johnny had parked his truck. She felt afraid for the first time when she saw the wooden box in the back with holes drilled in the side. This would be the way they made it back to Sparta, Tennessee, to pay for all her sins.

"We're going home."

Suddenly Kristen dropped like a rock beside her. Before she could comprehend what was happening, she felt the sudden pain as the butt of Johnny's gun or something as hard smashed against the back of her neck. She had been happy and anticipated the future only hours ago, and now there was only darkness.

❖

"I'm telling you, Shelby, we dusted, and all the surfaces are like someone meticulously cleaned and vacuumed before they left. Even the vacuum bag is gone," the lead agent in charge of the investigation told her.

She'd landed and gone directly to the funeral home where she'd met her father's sister, now her only living relative. From that moment until they'd buried her parents with most of the police force present, she'd allowed herself to grieve, but now she had to put that luxury aside. That morning she'd left her hotel with the two agents Annabel had sent with her and driven to the house she'd grown up in. All those happy memories and laughter she'd shared with her folks were hard to conjure up as she walked the crime scene and saw the massive amount of blood.

"The blood-spatter guy said, from what he sees, your father got to the door first," he said, pointing to a spot on the wall, then the floor. "Did they often leave the door open?"

"They must've been expecting company, and Mom didn't believe friends should be kept waiting." The large dark stain on her grandmother's rug made her eyes well up with tears. This was her father's blood and all she had left of him in the physical sense.

"We found your dad here on his back, which led us to believe he heard the door open and went to see who it was. Our best guess is sawed-off shotgun to the center of his chest," he said, and she nodded. She hadn't wanted to see the wounds, but from the reports the hole in his chest had been massive enough that no other weapon could've been responsible.

He walked her to the next room and she saw the fine mist of blood that had stained her mother's favorite couch. It had been re-covered numerous times throughout her life and she could almost hear her mom's voice as she read to her while she rested her head in her lap.

This had been her life, and now she couldn't even enjoy the pieces that held so much sentiment because the evil that had come in and taken it all away had tainted them.

"She must've heard the shot and started running in this direction," he said, pointing to a path that led either to the kitchen or her father's study.

He relinquished the lead and followed her to the study, where she opened the top drawer of her father's desk and pulled out a nine-millimeter pistol, checking the clip that was still full. "She was running in here for something more substantial than a pot," she said, holding up the gun.

The bar she'd mentioned to Annabel was close to where her mother had been shot in the back and left to die facedown, and the bottle she'd seen sat right behind the labels she'd seen on the bar all her life. When she stooped to take a better look, it gave her a bit of hope.

"She couldn't have been this stupid," she said to herself.

"What was that?" the agent asked, looking like he was trying to figure out what had captured her attention. "None of them except the gin and vodka bottles have prints."

"Bag the Jameson and try for any DNA along the neck. I'm sure our suspect wasn't stupid enough to drink directly from the bottle, but you never know," she said, not able to take her eyes off the open bottle with about a fourth of it missing. It was worth a shot, even if the bottle had the stamps on it that proved it was legal.

"That won't be necessary," a newcomer behind them said.

The statement made her purse her lips and flare a shot of air through her nose.

"You don't know what you're talking about." She turned around and came close to following what she'd said with a slap to the woman's head that was topped with the reddest hair she'd ever seen.

"I do know what I'm talking about, and I don't believe in wasting time," she said, and the second thing she noticed about the woman was that even her lips had freckles. The badge hanging from her jacket pocket displayed a local detective's credentials, so she'd probably been the one assigned to the case before the FBI moved in, considering whose parents had been killed.

"I'm sure the person responsible for this left it behind to taunt me," she said, crossing her arms over her chest and standing as tall as she could make herself.

"Fiona O'Brannigan, ma'am, and I'm terribly sorry for your

loss. Your father was one of my closest friends and he was constantly bragging on you," Fiona said, holding out her hand.

"How do you know him?"

"A new program through the department had us matched for the last year. I couldn't believe my luck when I got the best of the retired guys as a sort of mentor to help me hone my detective skills. For the last year I've closed forty percent more of my cases because I've used what he taught me instead of waiting for the forensic guys to do the work for me."

"He would've mentioned that to me if it's true," she said, turning and looking at the bottle. Her theory of the crime dissolved in the woman's last name since what she'd told Annabel was true. To make their friends feel welcomed, her parents always had their favorite drink on hand. It wasn't a long shot to think that anyone with the last name of O'Brannigan would drink Jameson.

"I'm not surprised he didn't. When he told me about your calls and the cases you're working, he said he didn't want to waste time talking about what he was doing since it would cut into the time he had with you," she said, moving closer to the bar and tapping the top of the whiskey bottle with her pen. "I'm not saying Cain Casey didn't do this, but this bottle is here because of me, not a sick gift to torture you. After a few months of meeting your father at the coffee shop downtown, your mother started inviting me over for dinner. We had a standing date every Wednesday night after I got off shift."

"You were here more often than me, then," she said, cursing inside because of what she'd said. "Do you see anything else out of place?"

"I've walked through here a hundred times already." Fiona stood in place but turned in a circle. "Whoever did this took nothing and left nothing of themselves behind. Even a somewhat newbie like me can tell you that's the first sign of a professional hit, but it's almost too perfect."

"That was our first impression too," the lead agent said. "The only thing the killer left behind was the bodies and buckshot he used," he said, grimacing when it seemed he realized he was talking about her parents.

"Either whoever did this was good enough to know what we'd be looking for and cleaned all that away," Fiona said.

"Or it was second nature to him because it was a cop trained in crime-scene investigation," she finished for her. Could that be possible?

"That's my first impression," Fiona said. "Your dad told me once that most times your first impression is the one that turns out to be true."

"He taught me that as well. It's why I thought I had the suspect right when I saw that bottle," she said, looking from her mother's blood to the bar. The suddenness of the crime didn't fit with the meticulous time the killer took afterward. "Do you know who they were expecting?"

"They had a pretty active social calendar, but I can tell you that it was their off night. It was the only night of the week they watched television and ordered out."

"That's right," she said, suddenly remembering it was the night she usually called as well, but she hadn't had the chance.

"It still fits, though," the agent said. "The door wasn't locked and the killer walked in. Your father unlocked it thinking it was their order."

Shelby dropped into one of the dining room chairs and rested her head in her hands. Everything she'd thought as an initial reaction was wrong, and she could hear Muriel's voice telling her how Cain didn't have anything to do with this. It wasn't a stretch to think she did, because Cain was just as meticulous as whoever did this, but it could also be someone in law enforcement. If that was true, it made no sense.

"Do you have any other thoughts after your initial assumption?" she asked Fiona, who'd sat next to her.

"We all have enemies," she said, glancing back at the still-visible signs of carnage. "But this doesn't feel like someone who got out and blamed your dad for a long stretch, or the family member of someone who did time."

"How about someone who blames me for turning a family member against her?" she asked softly.

"That depends if you think they're capable of this," she said, pointing to the spot where her mother had died. "Your dad told me a little about Cain Casey, if that's who you're thinking about."

"And you think you know her well enough to render a judgment on her guilt or innocence?" she asked, and almost laughed at what she saw was Fiona's inexperience on display.

"I only know her from what your father said, and his opinion was that we all have our Captain Ahab moments chasing a monster that eludes us no matter how hard we try," Fiona said, not meeting her eyes, but Shelby believed her. "Cain is that monster you chase but never seem to get the kill shot on, Agent Phillips, but don't let your prejudice against her blind you enough to not get whoever is responsible for this."

"So you know Cain well enough to know she didn't do this?"

"Your father's stories made me curious enough to read about her, but I'm sure you know her better than anyone, so don't take what I'm about to say the wrong way."

What had her father always said about a fresh pair of eyes? Fiona with her shiny new gold badge didn't care about Cain one way or another, but if she'd been the one to order this, Fiona would surely shoot her on sight as payback for what Cain had taken from her. Sitting beside her was a blue-line kind of cop, and the bastard who'd done this had crossed it.

"Please go on."

"Your agency doesn't release everything, but from what I read she isn't the butcher type. She's a killer, I'm not naïve enough to think otherwise, but she supposedly only kills in response to something or if someone has wronged her."

"Wronged her?" she asked, not believing this woman interested her father. "Cain kills almost as a hobby."

"Who's on your list that you believe she's responsible for but haven't been able to prove yet?" Fiona asked, sounding a little peeved.

"The Bracato family, a bunch of drug dealers, her own cousin, and God knows who else," she said, ticking them off on her fingers.

"Your dad said she believed the Bracatos killed her father, mother, and brother, am I right?" Fiona asked, and she nodded. "Look at every confirmed kill and see the motivation behind it. She's a killer but not a butcher who does it for sport."

"You make her sound like an avenging angel."

Fiona's short red hair bounced out of place when she shook her head and stood up, apparently realizing she was wasting her breath. "I believe Casey has very few angelic qualities, Agent, but I look at what happened here and I don't see her hand in it. Because of that I'm afraid the real killer will go free while you chase what you all see as the most logical choice."

She turned and walked away from Shelby, stopping at the large stain where her mother died. "And they deserve better than that. I want whoever goes down for this to know why they're getting the needle or whatever kills them. Remember that, because the case has been reassigned to you guys, and I'm sure sharing information with me is the last thing that'll happen."

"Wait," Shelby said, standing up. "You've spouted off about who you think didn't do this, but let's hear who you think did."

"I don't know yet," Fiona said, and smiled. "Believe me, I'd bug the hell out of you to send your bloodhounds in that direction."

"You didn't come here just to preach to me everything my dad taught you without a theory, Detective. I'm not that stupid."

"It was someone who either has or has had a badge. They left enough behind to tell you it was a professional hit, but the trail ends there. Find the motivation of why that is and you'll be on the right track."

Fiona seemed earnest enough, but there was no reason for her to be right. No one involved in law enforcement would do this. Unless... she sat again because her legs felt like the rest of her, drained of strength at the worst-case possibility.

"Are you all right?" Fiona asked.

She stared unseeing at the floor as what Fiona said made her look in another direction. "Did you interview all the neighbors?" she asked, talking fast.

"Both organizations did," the agent said. "No one saw anything out of the ordinary."

"Define ordinary," she said, looking up at Fiona.

"It was late afternoon, not many people out," she said, sitting next to her again. "This is mostly a retirement neighborhood, so there weren't any children on the street at the time, and the few people who heard the two shots figured it was someone's television. The neighbor on the left side said she looked out her kitchen window as she did the dishes, but all she saw was the lawn-service truck parked outside."

"Lawn-service truck?" Shelby asked, her pulse picking up.

"I know where you're going. We interviewed every one of the guys who work around here, and all of them checked out with backups from their clients. The only two people we couldn't talk to were the ones who obviously couldn't tell us anything," she said, putting her hand on her shoulder. "I'm still looking to see who your dad used so we can talk to them and check if they saw anything."

"My dad told you about Cain but didn't tell you how obsessive he is about his lawn?" she asked, not believing no one was following up on this line.

"Fuck," Fiona said, pulling out her phone and calling for backup to come and canvass again.

"Did the neighbor say if she saw the lawn guy?"

"She saw one man by the truck and another come around the back with trash bags and a rake. She didn't think anything of it because they both looked the part and it's something most people around here see on a daily basis."

"You mean they were Hispanic and carrying lawn equipment around the shotgun they used to kill my parents?" she asked, and Fiona nodded. "They used what everyone considers negative profiling to fit right in."

"And it worked," Fiona said, the house coming to life around her as the agents started filing out to talk to the neighbors. "What's your first impression of that?"

"That the government trained the mastermind behind this and he told our grass cutters what to do," she said, walking to her father's study. "What I don't know is why," she said, opening the drawer where her father's gun lay. "Thanks, Fiona, you were right. I was blinded by my first impressions but now I'm on the right path, and I need you to do me a favor."

"Name it."

"I need you to mail me this here," she said, writing her home address.

"Can I ask why?"

"Sure. I need it because when I catch who did this I intend to use it to explain *why* I emptied the clip in his head. There won't be a trial on this one."

"If that's the case, you'll need help," Fiona said, reaching for the gun and the address. Both items dropped into her jacket pocket. "I'm sure your boss can arrange that."

"I'll have all the help I need after I talk to the master of hitting back when something like this happens," she said, hoping Cain would be willing to see her when she got home.

"That's true, but it helps to have someone other than Cain Casey backing you up."

"Get packed and meet me at the airport. If we're lucky we won't find a better teacher in the art of revenge."

CHAPTER TWENTY-ONE

"Just when I think I understand you, you manage to shock the shit out of me," Sept said. "No offense, Emma."

"You think cursing offends me?" Emma asked and laughed, accepting Sept's hug as she came into the room. The call Cain had her make the night before had sent Sept out looking for something unusual, and she'd called that morning to tell them she might have found it. "Cain doesn't do it often, but every once in a while this one can curl your hair with some of the stuff she comes up with," Emma said, pointing her thumb over her shoulder in Cain's direction.

"Come over here by me, funny girl, and let the decorated officer sit down."

"Wow," Sept said, placing her hand on her forehead. "Those guys did a number on you, huh?"

"It's their new system of upholding the law," she said, smiling even though she still felt bad. "Instead of protect and defend, it's more like assault and beat down."

"Sorry I wasn't around," Sept said, sitting in the chair Emma had moved closer to the bed. "Stuff like that gives us all a bad name."

"It had to happen sooner or later, and I'm not putting you in the same category as the people responsible for this." She sat up straighter in the bed, trying to motivate herself to feel better. "Did you find anything like I asked last night?"

"I convinced the sheriff's office over in Plaquemines Parish to send me the crime-scene photos early this morning, and I walked the scene myself last night. New Orleans has its share of bizarre murders, but so far from what I've seen, this one takes the prize. Those guys over in Chalmette don't know what the hell to make of it."

Sept handed Cain the pictures, and she kept them at an angle so Emma wouldn't be able to see them unless she asked.

"I don't have to tell you that I'm not supposed to be sharing these with you, but I figure it's part of your religion homework, and now I need help with my English," Sept said, giving her time to look at what she'd brought.

"By the time the son of the man who owned the land came home from his date, the victim had been dead, by the coroner's estimate, an hour or two. In that time the kid almost missed the dead guy strapped to a tree at the edge of their estate because he was completely covered in ants. Forensically it was a nightmare because they couldn't remove them without wiping away potential evidence."

Lying on the gurney in a body bag, Rodolfo appeared swollen and disfigured, but it was definitely him. "You know the guy?" Sept asked, taking the pictures back and putting them away.

"About as well as you do," she answered, already making a list of what had to be done. "Rodolfo Luis was retired last night, by the looks of that, and you're right, it's bizarre, but I can tell you exactly why he was killed by insects."

Sept nodded and scratched the side of her neck. "And what'll it cost me to hear that story?"

"Your credit is good with me, so I'll throw it in for free. Should you feel the need to toss me a bone in the future, though, I won't turn you down."

"You get older but you never change," Sept said, laughing and tapping the mattress without touching her. "I'll tell my mother to say a prayer for you, Emma. Your partner is always perfecting the art of the deal."

"I can use all the ones I can get," Emma said.

"You want to hear this or not?" Cain asked, cocking her head and slightly thrilled that it didn't make her nauseous. She told her the story she'd heard from Hector months before and why the prime suspect in this case had to be Gracelia Luis. She didn't leave out any aspect, figuring it was better to have a little help from an organization that had even more employees than she did. Sept would put the word out, and between the two of them someone would find Gracelia. And when that happened, Cain would find Juan.

"So you're sure the sister killed him?" Sept asked, shivering. "That's cold."

"Not cold, Sept, revenge. This crazy bitch has held a torch for some scumbag, from what I've heard, for too many years, so it makes sense she took out Rodolfo the same way he took out her lover." She grasped Emma's hand and lifted her knees to support Emma's back when she rested on her. "That means Rodolfo is gone but now you have the worst-case scenario. I'm sure she killed him so she could take over and put her son in charge."

"You're talking about Juan Luis?" Sept asked.

"Yes, and if that comes to pass, you'll long for the days the old man was running things." She looked up at Emma. It wasn't time to be totally honest about Carlos. She'd never willingly help anyone, aside from Vinny Carlotti, get established in drugs, but this was an important opportunity.

With Carlos as the new boss of Rodolfo's crew, she'd have less trouble than she would if Gracelia won this battle. Carlos owed her, and she intended to point him in the right direction.

"You really think she's got a chance?" Sept said, taking notes as they talked. "Most of the idiots I pop for drug-related murders aren't exactly up on taking orders from a woman."

"Depends on the woman," she said, making Sept laugh. "If she was gunning for him, some of the issues you've been seeing on the street make sense, don't they?"

"The higher-ups have been reporting that this is the beginning of a drug war, and they've got double shifts trying to turn it around."

That was true, but they were up against people who killed with no thought as to who they directed their hail of bullets at. "If you want my opinion," she said, making Sept put her notepad down, "you can tell your bosses that last night one of the sides won a battle, but the war is coming."

"So far we have Delarosa on one side and this Gracelia on the other. You think that's it?"

"No." She wanted to warn Sept about Carlos without actually giving him up. "You have to take Rodolfo's crew into account. Some of them, I believe, have already picked sides against him, but others will be loyal to him until it kills them."

"Thanks, Cain, you almost sound like a CI," Sept said, clearly joking as she put her notepad away. "But don't worry. I won't ruin your reputation by letting anyone downtown know that you're not all bad."

"Okay, smart-ass, but remember how much help I gave you today and share the wealth if you find something."

"I promise you'll be hearing from me."

"You want me to call Carlos?" Emma asked when the door closed.

Nodding, she said, "Tell him to come alone, dress casual, and take the stairs. When we're done, we need to meet with the doctor and ask if I can go home."

"No," Emma said adamantly. "You've got two more days to go, and you don't have a good enough excuse to convince me you don't need to be here."

"I need to go back to work, lass, and that's not really easy from here."

"You tell me what you need, who you need to talk to, and I'll do it. Even if it takes me killing someone to make whatever you have planned work, but you're not leaving until he gives you a clean bill of health."

"It won't come to that," she said, encouraging Emma to come closer. "If it makes you feel better, we'll get it done from here." The last thing she wanted was to upset Emma, but she didn't want to give the FBI a head start. They could keep track of her visitors too easily when she was in here. "We begin with Carlos."

"And who do we end with?"

"Whoever stands between us and restoring order."

❖

"I'm almost home, but I'll turn around and be there as soon as I check in on Dallas," Remi said to Cain after answering her phone. She'd followed Carlos back to the Piquant and gone up with him for something Cain had asked for. It was hard to track someone when you had no idea what they looked like.

After a few hours, a couple of pictures came up from the front desk after Carlos's mother faxed the most current pictures she could find of Gracelia. Remi had groaned when she glanced down at her watch, so she'd stopped by the French Market and bought a dozen roses for Dallas. It didn't hurt to try and make her feel better for not only leaving but for having to turn around and go out again after she changed clothes.

"He's dead?"

"A big ant buffet, from what I could tell," Cain said, making her laugh. Leave it to her friend to be funny in this situation.

"Did Emma get Carlos?"

"He's on his way, and I need you here to let him know what happened to Rodolfo."

She took the elevator up after Simon parked and checked the area, making sure that whatever was going on hadn't followed them home. "Give me about forty minutes. If you want I'll bring Dallas and she can take Emma out for breakfast."

"I'm sure she'll be grateful for a break."

She put her keys on the small table next to the elevator and walked to the bedroom with the flowers, dropping them on the bed when she found it empty. No water was running in the bathroom and the kitchen had been dark, but that's where she headed because Dallas couldn't have gotten out without the extra key.

The phone at Dallas's rang five times before Emil answered. "Did you come by here and pick Dallas up?"

"I was waiting for her call, why?" Emil said, sounding groggy.

"Could you get Kristen up and ask if she's heard from her?" she said, heading back to the bedroom. Juno hadn't said anything and Simon hadn't let Remi know that Dallas was down there visiting them, so Dallas hadn't told Juno that she was leaving.

In the bedroom she opened the closet and found the clothes Dallas had worn the day before hanging neatly and her running shoes missing. While she was waiting for Kristen to come to the phone she picked up her land line to call Dallas's cell phone. The note was sitting there, and something Remi had harped on when it came to security had finally sank in with Dallas. She'd put the time in the upper right-hand corner.

Two hours! Remi's stomach hurt. Dallas had been gone two hours, and unless she'd run through the next town over to get home she should've arrived an hour ago. Even if she wasn't in love with Dallas, she wished she'd learn not to make herself such an easy target. It was clear that's what she'd done by going out alone, probably thinking the early hour would protect her.

"Remi." Emil's voice made her jump slightly since she was expecting Kristen's. "She's not here, but she left a note." Remi sat in relief, thinking maybe the sisters had met at the gym. "Oh Christ."

"What? God damn it, tell me."

"She put the time and wrote *Johnny Moores has Dallas*."

Hadn't Remi promised Dallas the night before that no one would ever hurt her again? It wasn't right that the very next day Dallas would end up with the one person she had tried the hardest to get away from. "Get dressed and get over here," she told Emil, and hung up.

If what Kristen had written was true, then Johnny had an hour on her. Should she look for them in town or start toward Tennessee? "Think," she said to herself as she tapped her fingers against her head.

While she considered her options she called her father and brother. Ramon would be here in less than twenty minutes, but Mano would take a little longer to make the thirty-minute flight from Biloxi. She picked up the bouquet and threw it against the glass.

"Did you call Cain?" Simon asked, walking in from downstairs. She picked up the flowers and handed them to Juno—her partner and Remi's assistant.

"I'm not worried about that right now," Remi said, louder than she usually talked to Simon. "The last thing that concerns me is the crap going on with Rodolfo's family. If he'd taken care of his business when he had the chance, we wouldn't have to clean up after him." She could give herself the same lecture. If she'd gone on what she assumed wasn't a long flight or taken Cain's offer to visit Johnny after they'd dealt with Bob, she could have spent the rest of her day reminding Dallas how dangerous it was to go out alone. But she hadn't. Johnny Moores was buried so deep in Dallas's past that she'd ignored the threat like a kid on her first day on the job.

Simon sat next to her. "Unless you need me here, I'm sending Juno with one of the guys to help Cain translate her business with Carlos. You need to stop blaming yourself long enough to put your brain to work. Once we get them back and they're fine, we need to give Kristen a lesson on what to do when someone like Emil's on the sofa and this happens. It'll involve not walking out the door into a trap."

"You're a good friend, Simon, but if I go after him and miss, I won't get her back, because he'll take her somewhere I can't find her."

"Think like that and he's already won," Simon said, pulling her to her feet. "You need to concentrate on how you'll kill this asshole so Dallas and Kristen can stop looking over their shoulder."

"He had to have been watching her because how would he have guessed she was out alone today," she said, dialing Dallas's cell phone. She didn't think she'd get an answer but wanted to see if it was still on. It rang ten times before going to voicemail. As she hung up Emil walked in and stood in front of her, looking like he was waiting for his dressing down.

"I'm sorry, Remi, and if you don't want me here, I'll go."

She peered up at him and could see the pain in his face. "This isn't anyone's fault but Johnny Moores's, and that's who we'll make answer for this." She moved them to the den when her father arrived and started the meeting, not waiting for Mano.

They all had their eyes on her as she dropped the file Cain had gathered about Dallas's past. Up to now it had been locked in her safe. She'd planned to destroy the bundle of information after she showed it to Dallas, but Johnny had beat her by a day.

"He lives in Sparta and, from what Dallas told me yesterday, runs a still to make money. I looked before cleaning out Bob Bennett's house but never found any connection to Johnny. There had to have been one since he's laid low all these years and only shows up now," she told them, flipping through the pages until she found the address she was looking for. Johnny's mailing address was a post-office box. Nothing in what Cain and Muriel found in that initial investigation gave a physical address.

"What do you want us to do?" Ramon asked. The elevator opened and Remi's mother came in and hugged her. "You're in charge."

"Call everyone you know and find him if he's still in the city," she told Ramon. "I'm not sure what he looks like, but you know all I do when it comes to this guy." Ramon was the only person she'd confided everything to.

Ramon stood and started making calls, and by the time Mano showed up an hour later Ramon had discovered where Johnny had been staying and that he'd checked out. The phone rang and the doorman announced a guest. When the elevator came up, Merrick rolled in with a young woman.

Merrick said, "I can't come with you and neither can Cain, but she wants you to have your share of people watching your back so you can do what needs to be done." The young woman with the intense expression who stood beside Merrick resembled a younger version of her. "Sabana's young but I believe she'll be an asset."

"Would you send someone on a training mission if this was Katlin?" she asked, not needing the baggage Cain wanted to saddle her with. "I'm leaving for Tennessee with Mano and Simon, but thank her anyway."

"When you get there and have to start questioning the locals to get a lay of the land, who do you think will get a better response, you, Simon or Sabana?" Merrick asked. She moved closer and signaled for Remi to bend down. "She's innocent looking but she's ready to prove herself. If she'd hold you back I'd still be at home trying to lift weights and doing my best to get out of this chair."

"Tell Cain thanks, then, and I'll call when I get back."

"Emma wanted me to give you a message," Merrick said, giving her as good a smile as she could manage from the trouble she appeared to have moving her lips. Remi took Merrick's hand and bent down farther. "She said you need to have Dallas back soon since she owes her a breakfast."

"Thanks, Merrick." She patted her hand and returned to the den, turning her head for Sabana to follow her. "We need to get there before he does and find the house," she told the group that had gathered. Her biggest fear now was that Johnny wouldn't be able to control himself before he reached what he thought was his safety zone. Not that it would turn her away from Dallas if he did something to her, but she wanted to spare Dallas any more pain. "But we also need to get out of here without our chaperones."

"That's easy," Ramon said, putting his hand over his phone's receiver. "I already took care of it, so get ready to move."

"I don't need much," Remi said, moving quickly to her bedroom and pulling out her guns. As she changed her shirt she looked down at the half of the cobra head tattooed on her right arm. The other side of the deadly snake's head was tattooed on Mano's arm and had fueled the rumors of what some on the street called Snake Eyes.

So many nights Dallas had run her fingers along the design, ending at the eye that was a die in the one position. It was time to strap on that persona again. "Hang on, baby, I'm coming," she said to the picture on her nightstand. "You know in your heart that I'll be there, so keep the faith."

❖

The bed had become torturous so Cain was sitting in a recliner one of the nurses had brought in. News of what had happened to Dallas had opened more wounds than the beating she'd had. Of all the times she had to be laid up and not able to help Remi. Even if she could crush Hector and Juan with what she was planning, she'd trade it to get Dallas back to Remi and put a smile back on Emma's face.

Emma had been so many things to her and had brought so much into her life but, most important, she had infused Cain's heart with an infinite supply of hopeless romanticism. Because she had found it in her own life, she wanted everyone she cared for to experience it too. Emma had changed Cain's mind about Merrick and Katlin, and had worked on Cain for weeks about persuading Muriel not to stay with Shelby. She wanted someone who would give Muriel the kind of love she deserved.

"Cain," Juno said, making her turn away from the window. Remi's petite assistant was the only person she'd ever seen make the serious Simon smile. "How are you?"

"I feel like a useless relic right now, old friend. How's Remi holding up?"

"When she was young I always knew that when she gave away her heart, only death would end the connection," Juno said, sitting close to her. "I hope fate won't do it so soon."

"Men like Johnny Moores don't intend to commit murder, but death might be less cruel than what he'll leave behind if he gets his way," she said, not to hurt Juno but to prepare for what could happen. "He'll go somewhere like Juan did with Emma so he can take his time, but there's something he's not counting on."

"What?" Juno asked, not seeming shocked at what she was saying, probably because of her experiences in Cuba before Ramon got them all out.

"That Remi wants to make Dallas happy more than that asshole wants to hurt her. Up to now no one in his life has stood up to him, but that's about to change and he won't survive it."

"Baby," Emma said from the door. "Carlos is here."

"Send him in," she said, glancing at the black clouds building outside. "Not a good day, is it?" she asked Juno, and felt her small hands on her shoulders as Juno came to stand behind her.

"Remember, for every rainy day, many are full of light and warmth. It's the cycle of life, so we must do our best to bear these with as much strength as possible."

"Good morning," Carlos said, following Emma in.

"I'm looking forward to one of those long warm days," she said to Juno before she had to tell Carlos the news he didn't want to hear. "Carlos, please come in and sit."

"Did you find him?" he asked, looking like he hadn't slept much. "We've been searching but so far nothing."

"I found out what happened to him, and I'm sorry," she said, giving Juno a chance to catch up. "He's dead," she said, going on to tell him how Rodolfo was killed. "From the way they found him and what I've heard about Armando Ortega, Gracelia and most probably Juan are in town and responsible."

"I would know if they were here," he said loudly. "We have a majority of our men on the streets and in places she would have to go. Do you know something about her being here?"

"No, but I haven't been looking for her. My efforts have been concentrated on Juan and Anthony Curtis. That's why I told you last night that the only reference Rodolfo made to her wasn't enough. When Juan came into the country under his father's name I figured she hated him, but I had no idea she planned to kill him."

"You did admit that this business wasn't that important to you, but to me nothing is more important. I thank you for the information and I give you my word that if you ever have need of my help I'll be more than happy to provide it, but I won't need you anymore."

"Are you sure?" She asked only to be nice, but if he refused her offer, she was done. She had other things to keep her busy. "You have my number, so don't think you can't call if you need something."

He stood and shook her hand with both of his. "My father," he said, pausing as if he still wasn't used to that title in reference to Rodolfo, "was wrong about you."

"Thanks for the compliment, and good luck." She watched him go as she gently scratched the stitches along her temple.

"You seem to be the most popular patient on the floor," Mark said, walking in and followed by the fellows on his rotation for the year. "Any more seizures or symptoms I haven't heard about?" he asked, coming over to her and starting his examination without caring that Juno and Emma were still in the room.

"My head still hurts a little but no more seizures and not much nausea," she said honestly. Emma was staring her down, ready to jump in, she was sure, if she didn't tell the whole truth. "I'm resting like you told me and I feel a lot better."

"You look like hell but your vitals are good, and from what your partner tells me you're on your best behavior," Mark said, writing something in her chart. "At this point I don't see why you can't keep doing what you are here at home."

"You're discharging me?" She was excited about putting on clothes since being in a hospital gown for more than two days made her feel like she would break out in hives.

"On one condition," he said, looking over at Emma. "If you

continue to rest for at least one more day, listen to whatever Emma tells you, and come back at the first sign of any symptoms."

"You passed medical school counting like that?" Cain asked, trying not to sound sarcastic. "That's three by my count."

"Call it a field sobriety test," he said, laughing as he wrote out a few prescriptions. "Take these as directed and I expect to see you in my office in two days. You have a lovely brain, Cain, so try to keep being good so it stays that way."

"These seizures I'm having," she said, not sure if she really wanted an answer. "Those are permanent?"

"The first blow to your head, from what you told me, was bad enough," he said, softly touching along her brow and temple where the bruising was especially dark, from what she'd noticed in the bathroom mirror. "That one most probably gave you a concussion, but the second blow concentrated in the same area really opened that cut and made that concussion more serious. Right now your brain is trying to right itself, as it were, and it's a wait-and-see."

"Wait and see? That's the best you got?"

"I'm not a witch doctor, if that's what you mean, but the brain is a complicated machine, Cain. It's important for you to pamper yours until the steroids and medication have a chance to do their thing. If you want my opinion, and realize that only time will tell, I believe that the seizures are in your past, but that's not a guarantee. Go home and lounge around with this beautiful woman and try not to excite yourself too much," he said with a wink.

"Thanks, Mark, and we'll see you in a couple of days," she told him, and stayed quiet when Emma followed him outside. "I believe the conspiracy against me is being plotted out there."

"You remind me so much of Simon," Juno said, coming around so she could see her. "You're both strong, but your lives would be so different without the soft influence women like me and Emma bring into them."

"Soft isn't the right word," she said, standing and accepting Juno's hand to steady herself. "My mother always told me that to carry the weight of family and marriage requires strength disguised as softness, but in reality it's the indestructible fiber that holds us together. Women like you and Emma are the foundations that keep us whole."

"I take it back. You're a lot smarter than my Simon. It took her years to come to that conclusion. You have a lot less gray hair than she did before she became so wise."

She laughed at Juno's words and accepted her hug. "You can go keep Marianna company, but please call me as soon as you hear anything."

"That's a promise, and remember what the doctor said. Let Emma be in charge for a change and take care of yourself."

"Don't worry about that," Emma said, opening the door wider so the orderly with the wheelchair could make it in. "The doctor supplied me with a blow gun with medicated darts in case she gets unruly."

Getting into the chair and letting one of her people pack up the room filled Cain with relief. At the moment she was helpless to do anything for Remi and Dallas, but she could start searching for Gracelia Luis, certain that her trail would lead her to the prize she wanted most. Juan was still out there, and she seriously doubted that Gracelia had killed Rodolfo all on her own. That kind of stunt required a crew and, if she had to guess, Gracelia's son.

If they were both in town, it was easier to explain the five boxes she'd received as a sick gift, even if she didn't have proof. Her gut told her their deaths were on Gracelia and Juan's heads, but why? Did they kill six people to introduce Gracelia to the game and show what she was capable of, or did Juan act on his own? Gracelia might be his mother, but she might not be able to control him any more than Rodolfo could.

"You okay, baby?" Emma asked when they got into the car.

"I'm fine," she lifted her arm so Emma could come closer, "just planning a little hunting excursion."

"Big game?" Emma asked as they drove by the surveillance van.

"No, more like I'm planning to take a page out of one of our least favorite people's book," she said, making Emma lean away so she could look up at her. "I intend to start small and work my way up."

CHAPTER TWENTY-TWO

"Busy night?" Jerome poured himself a cup of coffee and tried to keep his annoyance down since Gracelia hadn't come home and he hadn't seen her since they'd arrived.

"We have lived without each other all these years, so don't think that all of a sudden I won't be able to exist without you," she said, not looking up from the local paper in front of her. She was scanning the pages, apparently searching for something important. "I had things to do and it took longer than I thought."

"Tell me that means you didn't go out and kill someone," he said, opening the plantation shutters and staring outside for anything out of the ordinary.

"Rodolfo is no longer our problem, and starting today we have to move so we don't lose any of what he was able to capture here," she said, still not making eye contact.

These people were unbelievable. The only thing she and Juan didn't do was call the press before they did something to make sure everyone with a law interest didn't miss what they were up to.

But he'd give her the benefit of the doubt before he lit into her. "I see," he said, and it must have been his tone that made her head rise. "I know that was important to you, but I'm sure you did it in a way that he won't be found soon."

"I tied him to a tree and did the same thing to him that he did to my Armando."

"You left him tied to a tree covered in ants?" He laughed. "You can't be serious."

"It's what he deserved and it's done," she said, her expression resembling Juan's when he got angry. "What is your problem? You act like a scared old woman most of the time."

"Then I'll be a scared old woman living to a ripe old age, not surrounded by concrete and bars," he said, squeezing the cup in his hand so hard that it shattered. "Do you honestly think they won't know exactly who did this when they find him?"

"He won't be found, and if they do they'll never be able to identify the body from a pile of bone with no teeth. I know for a fact that Rodolfo's DNA was never in anyone's system." She threw a rattling bag on the table, and he didn't need to open it to know it was Rodolfo's teeth. "We both agreed that he had to die in order for us to get what we want. No one will care how it was done, only that he's dead. That goes for your precious FBI."

"Get a few things through your head or I'll walk away from you, and in this city, you'll never find me again. If that happens, I predict that between your theatrics and Gustavo's brilliant ideas, you'll both be serving a life sentence before the month is out. You can change Juan's face and his name, but you need me to pick up his slack."

"What about my son do you hate so much?"

"Stupidity annoys me, and when it comes to joining forces with him I'm annoyed with myself."

"You're saying you're stupid?" she asked, smiling at him in what he perceived to be total condescension. "I'll take care of you, don't worry."

"I'm stupid because I didn't realize sooner what a total moron your son is, Gracelia. As a former FBI agent I'm familiar with the jail system in this country, and it's my goal in life not to end up in one," he said, wiping the hot liquid off his pants. "The two of you act like you can't wait to start a prison sentence."

"If Rodolfo was news, it would be on the front page," she said, throwing the paper at him. "I went through the whole thing, not a mention."

A knock on their door made him decide to table their discussion for now, but it was far from over. When he opened it a small Hispanic man stood nervously fidgeting between Lorenzo and Gustavo.

"Santos, come in," Gracelia said, acting as if they'd been making love from the way she stood next to Jerome and looped her hand around his elbow. "I've been looking forward to seeing you."

"Rodolfo is dead, Gracelia, don't you care?" Santos said, stumbling when Gustavo pushed him through the door.

"Did Lorenzo tell you?" she asked, sitting on the sofa and pulling him down next to her. "Tragic, isn't it?"

"It was all over the local news this morning, and before Lorenzo and your other man showed up, the cops were already picking up some of the boys for questioning." As Santos talked, Jerome understood the word "news" in Spanish so he picked up the remote and turned on the TV. It took a few minutes before the news cycled back to the lead story featuring their action reporter standing near a clump of trees with police tape around it. Joe and Lionel were milling around the local police, and Claire was taking pictures.

Gracelia told Santos, "We'll be working hard to make sure whoever did this pays for killing my brother, but I'm here to make sure you understand I'm in charge of holding this operation together." The performance she was giving as the grieving sister could have won her awards on the stage, as she shook her head and sighed. "You'll report to my men—Gustavo Katsura," she said, pointing to Juan, and Santos showed no sign of recognition, "and Jerome."

"I thought Rodolfo put Carlos in charge in case anything happened to him. That's the word we all got yesterday," Santos said, looking nervous again as his eyes flitted from one person to the next.

"Why would he put Carlos in charge?" Gustavo asked, clearly annoyed. The way Santos suddenly widened his eyes showed that he recognized the voice. "He's nothing but a peasant."

"I might be wrong," Santos said, as if backtracking was his best defense. "I'll do whatever you want."

"Gustavo's right." Gracelia was still trying to sound soothing. "Why would my brother put Carlos in charge and not inform me?"

"I think you'd better call him," Santos said, putting his hands together. "That's all I was told."

"Santos, really." Gracelia stood and locked eyes with Lorenzo, who immediately pulled out his gun and started screwing his silencer to it. "Rodolfo never did anything without laying out all the facts. He was annoyingly consistent, so you can either tell me his reasons and go back to work, or I'll have Lorenzo shoot you and I'll find out anyway."

"He acknowledged Carlos as his son, and because he is, he left him everything, including the business." Santos spoke quickly, making it hard for Jerome to understand the rapid Spanish.

"Before he pisses on himself, you want to tell me what's going on," Jerome said to Gracelia. She gave him the short version and he wanted to gloat. "Does this guy know how Rodolfo died?" he asked, since the news hadn't exactly given all the details. His Spanish was limited but he had understood the phrase "like Armando" perfectly.

"If he knows that, then he either heard from the police or his new boss. Either way, he's a liability now," he told her, making Gustavo smile before unholstering his gun and fitting a silencer to the barrel. "Before you pull the trigger, though," he said as Gustavo's finger tensed white, "you might want to find out how he knows Rodolfo met his maker after you unleashed a pack of ants on him."

Santos rambled on for a few minutes, tears rolling down his face. "Carlos put out the word this morning, and before you ask," Gracelia said quickly, "Carlos found out from Cain Casey." As soon as the name left her lips Lorenzo jumped back, but not in time to avoid Santos's brain splattering all over his jacket and pants.

"You keep killing people before we finish talking to them and it'll make this process that much harder," Jerome said, not to Gracelia or Gustavo in particular. "So much for no one finding him until DNA testing could be done," he added, not being able to hold back.

"Anything else insightful to add?" Gracelia asked through her teeth.

"Only one point," he said, pointing at Gustavo. "Granted, Santos has been around you a lot. He didn't recognize your face, but he made you by your voice, so you might want to be careful in the future. It would be a shame to let all your mother's hard work go to waste."

"Any suggestions on how to fix this?" Gracelia said.

"All a sudden he your answer man," Gustavo said in his accented English so he'd get the message as well as his mother.

Come on, Gracelia, this is your chance to let me think you're building confidence in me, he thought as she stayed silent.

"You're right," she said, moving Gustavo's hand toward his gun holster. "Take care of it, since Jerome and I have more things to discuss."

"Like what, the weather?" Jerome asked. "You two are doing great on your own, so have at it."

He made it through the door before Gracelia or Gustavo could stop him. It was time for him to take a walk and weigh his options before his life expectancy became shorter than a fruit fly's.

"I wonder if Carlos is hiring," Jerome muttered.

❖

The late-afternoon sun filtered through the thick glass of Cain's study and she couldn't think of anything except how disgusted she was that she was still tired. When they got home Emma had allowed her only a few hours in the office, and she'd used the time making phone calls.

So far Remi dominated her thoughts but hadn't answered her call. That didn't concern her yet. Ramon had supposedly flown to Miami for a day trip, and the larger *Snake Eyes* jet took off for Biloxi. Surveillance on them didn't seem too concerned since the chatter concentrated on Ramon.

Remi was either still in the air or had her phone off so she wouldn't leave an electronic trail. After they took care of Bob, Cain had honestly thought Dallas would be free to live her life, and Remi had asked her to drop the subject. She'd taken the hint, thinking Remi would take care of any loose ends.

"I promise it won't ruin your reputation if you take a nap," Emma said, sneaking in.

"I'm tired," she said, her admission making Emma smile and sit in her lap. "But I'm more tired of sleeping, if that makes sense."

"It does," Emma said, bending down for a kiss. "When I walked in, your eyes were droopy and I glimpsed the future when we're old and gray. Hopefully all we'll worry about then is our dozen grandchildren."

"Considering I'll be retired, you're right, but when I don't have anything but time on my hands, you'll have to worry about me chasing you through this house." She moved her hand gently over Emma's breasts, ending on her middle. "I hope you know, my love, how much I enjoy my life with you."

Romantic declarations always made Emma tear up, and this was no exception. "Likewise," she said, and this time their kiss lasted so much longer. "Do you think Dallas will be okay?" Emma asked, fitting herself closer into her chest. "And I changed the subject because if I hadn't, I'd drag you upstairs, and I'd feel wrong doing that while she's in danger."

"Remi will find her, and depending on when, Dallas will have plenty of people ready to help her heal." There wasn't a hole deep enough for someone like Dallas's father, because what he'd put her through was even worse than what Juan had tried with Emma. "It'll be easier for her to get better if she knows the sick bastard is dead, and Remi will take care of that."

"I hope you're right," Marianna Jatibon said, entering with Ramon. "I'm sorry to intrude, but Katlin said it was all right."

"Any word?" Cain asked Ramon.

"They landed and Sabana rented a car, so they're on their way to Sparta. Remi said it's about a five-hour drive from the airport they picked in Kentucky. It'll take the Feds a while to come and check out such a small place, if they're that curious."

"If you talk to her again, tell her to drive somewhere else afterward and meet the plane there, because our friends are always that curious," she said, regretting the loss of Emma's warmth when she got up. "How are you holding up, Marianna?"

"The world fears them," she said, spreading her hands out. "To most, 'snake eyes' is a myth, but they're my children. My heart hurts that they have to deal with things like this."

Because Emma was so sensitive about Hayden being in that position one day, Cain was surprised when she answered. "But aren't you glad you raised them with the honor to take care of things like these? When Hayden's in this position and doesn't have another option, my heart will bleed for my boy, but knowing that the threat against him and the family is gone will ease anything I feel."

"You know this girl better than we do," Marianna said, looking at Emma. "Is she in love with Remi?"

"You don't approve?" Emma asked, giving Cain some insight into some of their talks over lunch.

"I didn't say that, but it's hard to form an opinion when someone acts like a frightened rabbit all the time."

"Maybe she thinks you're the big bad wolf protecting her child," Ramon said jokingly, making Marianna slap his arm.

"She's very much in love with Remi, and at the risk of getting hit too, I think Ramon's right. You've wanted love for Remi for a long time, but you never thought you'd question it when it finally came along." Emma sat on the edge of her desk and smiled at her old friend. "Remi's taking this chance because Dallas is the one you've been waiting for."

"Then I'll believe you and try to put my fangs away when she gets back," Marianna said, smiling in return.

"Dallas's story isn't mine to tell," Emma said, glancing at Cain for what she assumed was reassurance, so she nodded. "But your approval will be crucial if this man does something to her."

"And the Feds have the nerve to call families like ours barbaric," Marianna said.

"Cain," Katlin said from the door. "Sorry to interrupt, but we have a situation."

"Go ahead and tell us," she said, waving her hand around. "We're among friends."

"We put up the surveillance you asked for at Emma's and the pub, and we got something."

"Not another box?" she said, thinking someone was totally crazy if she was right.

"Yep, and our men grabbed one of the delivery guys before he could make it back into the car."

"Who was in the box?" she asked, Ramon looking just as interested.

"They haven't opened it yet, but a note on the outside was addressed to you and your new partner Carlos Santiago."

"That son of a bitch," she said, slamming her hand on the desk, her tiredness disappearing as the mystery of the first five suddenly and resolutely solved itself, with the help of the idiot who was stupid enough to try this shit again. Juan was back, so she was right that Gracelia wasn't in town alone. "Any of the guys recognize who was left behind?"

"No, but I got a picture on one of the throw-away phones."

"Show it to Carlos. I need a name before we have a chat with the guy they caught. And tell me they got plate numbers of whatever vehicle they used."

"That was my next thing. They used a van like the others, but rented, and the picture we got from the ID he used was of the guy we're holding. Though I highly doubt his name is John Wayne."

"Lass, I promise I won't strain anything, but I've got to go." Cain stood and cinched the belt of her robe. Sometimes things came hard and sometimes they came easy, and this seemed too good to be true. She tried not to think about it as she went upstairs to change, not wanting to jinx herself.

"Juan, I hope you're hungry," she said to the clothes in the closet. "You've got a reservation for tonight and your dick is on the menu."

CHAPTER TWENTY-THREE

A re you sure this is the way?" Remi asked from the front seat. She was so hyped to get to where they were going, she could peel her skin off. "That damn thing is wrong sometimes, you know." She pointed to the GPS Simon had brought with her.

"No way he beats us there, and your father hasn't found anything to suggest he stayed in New Orleans. If he drives all night he won't be here until at least early tomorrow morning."

"It's the possibility of him stopping that worries me," Remi said, not being able to let her mind accept that scenario. She took the prepaid cell phone out and called her father again, but they hadn't found an exact physical address for Johnny. "We have to stop and ask someone," she said after she hung up. They had crossed the state line an hour ago and the back roads didn't have a lot of signs. The last one they'd seen put them at less than a hundred miles from Sparta.

"Remi," Muriel said, as soon as Remi answered the phone. "Your dad lent me his phone."

"I'd love to talk, but can it wait until I get back?"

"I'd love to have lunch with you, but that's not why I'm calling. My client told me where you are and what you're after. I hired an old school chum to do some title searches in that area. Looking through some tax records, I think he found the vacation place you're interested in."

"Thanks," she said, writing down the address Muriel gave her. Hopefully Johnny owned only one property. They drove until the GPS put them within two miles of the house and she had Mano pull over.

The road was narrow. If someone was at the house they'd be on the phone to Johnny, and Dallas and Kristen would be lost to her forever. Their father, and she had a real problem using that term, was the type of guy who would probably kill both of them rather than give them up again. When she got out and Mano turned the engine off, she was surprised how dark and quiet the area was.

Thick woods were never her thing, and that's what lined both sides of the road. This was paradise for the outdoors type, but at the moment all she could imagine was a million hiding places if she didn't find a position that would keep them on top of anything Johnny had in mind.

"Anything wrong beside the obvious?" Mano asked, getting out and standing beside her.

"When Dallas told that story, she said he made money as a moonshiner. Cain told me that generations ago her family did the same thing in Ireland."

"Hard to compare her to this guy, even if we're talking about what they do for a living," he said, combing his goatee downward.

"That's not why I said that. Cain would rip her own heart out before she would ever think of doing this to her family, especially her children." She peered into the woods as she spoke, trying to spot what she was positive was there. "A good bootlegger doesn't live too far from where he works. You have to watch the still once you get it going."

"I'd think you could have something like that and work it when you want."

"Not if you want to make money. She also said that Johnny had a few friends as sadistic as he is, and I'm guessing they're out here somewhere. You go up to the house with the others and I'll take a look."

"No way we split up," he said, grabbing her wrist. "That's not how we work and you know it."

"I can't have one of these assholes warn him. You know that. I have to find them before they make us."

"Simon," Mano said, making her and Sabana open the back doors. "Drive up to the house and look around. If anyone's inside and they come out, Sabana, you be the one to ask for..." He took the GPS and punched in a few things, coming up with the name of the closest restaurant, showing Sabana the name. "Ask where this place is," he told her, making sure she saw it again.

"What exactly do the two of you plan to be doing?" Simon asked.

"Looking for Johnny's most prized possession, aside from his girls," Remi said. "Trust us, Simon. We don't have time to argue. Look at this place," she said in a harsh whisper. "Do you honestly think he'll stop anywhere for a taste when he can enjoy it to his heart's content here with no house or business for miles?"

"Be careful," Simon said, getting into the driver's seat.

Remi and Mano studied the GPS one more time to see what side of the road the house was on, thinking the still and any backup would be nearby. Remi shook her head, smiling when Mano stepped into the darkness first. Technically she was the oldest, thus the head of the family, a job Mano really didn't want, but he still tried to take care of her when he could.

Not that far into the ancient-appearing trees, the sparse moonlight disappeared, which made any light for what seemed like miles jump out as guides. It was easy to spot the fire burning a distance farther into the trees, and the quiet helped amplify the conversation taking place between what sounded like two men.

"Boone, you heard that?"

"Yeah, maybe Johnny comin' home."

"Or could be somebody who don't belong here."

They weren't talking loud but Remi made out the words, wishing Dallas had mentioned more names than Timothy Pritchard. Not that it would make a difference, but considering various options helped keep her mind sharp as she tried to move closer, keeping her steps as quiet as possible.

"Johnny?" the smaller man said when she was about a hundred yards away. Perhaps noise did carry more out here than she imagined, and she tried to make out Mano's profile in the darkness but couldn't. Not that she was scared, because she wanted to open fire on these guys who were wasting their time watching liquid drip out of a copper tube. She wasn't familiar with a still, but this thing looked bigger than she had pictured.

Better to stop and let them get engrossed in what they were doing again, just watch and wait for an opening so she and Mano could take these guys down without too much effort. The men walked the perimeter of where the firelight was strongest, but obviously grew tired quickly because they sat back down and passed a jar between them. They didn't talk much after they started drinking, and less than an hour later the small guy got up and fooled with the fire but didn't make it bigger.

"That's another four gallons for tonight, so let's get going," the larger man said, standing and stretching. After the other one had done what he'd asked, he picked up a kerosene lantern and started walking in the direction Simon and Sabana had headed. Once the fire started to burn down, the light died fast and the lantern the guy was using resembled a firefly on a black canvas.

When they were far away enough she heard Mano whisper her name. She opened the simple cell phone she'd had Juno buy her before they'd left. "I think we have the right place," he said. The glow of the screen helped him find her and they decided to walk back to the road instead of trying to follow the fools who probably could make the trip blindfolded. When someone knew the terrain that much better than you, it was easy for them to lead you into a trap.

"You think there's more than these two?" Mano asked as they jogged slowly down the road, not wanting to get too far behind them but not pass them. "I'd call Simon and the others but there's no signal out here."

"That'll be good because it means they can't call anybody either, and Simon could've done this alone."

He laughed and put his hand on her arm again. Someone was talking again to their left. "Who's the kid?" Mano asked as they slowed down. The men talking far to their left in the woods weren't making the only noise in the area, and what or whoever it wasn't coming from the house since that wasn't visible yet. Whatever it was moved fast toward them and they stopped in a defensive posture, straining to decipher what it was.

The large dog seemed to explode out of the woods and was on Remi before she had a chance to really set her feet. It was snarling and snapped a few inches from her face, though she held his neck with both hands. She couldn't make out the breed but the damn thing was big. One minute he was trying to take her head off, and the next he yelped and ran for the woods on the other side of the road.

"What the hell?" she said, wringing her hands out.

"No guy likes to have his balls lit up," Mano said, holding out his cigar lighter. "A little hint of heat and he was off to the races."

"And when Sylvia hears about that, you'll be making a huge donation to the pound," she said, talking about Mano's wife.

"Why do you think I didn't kill him, even though he was about to chew your face off? All I did was maybe singe a couple of hairs."

"Yogi," one of the men yelled, his voice sounding like he was standing right next to them. "Damn dog. Yogi," he yelled again.

"Leave that mutt and come on, I'm hungry."

"I feel like a spy or something with all this cloak-and-dagger crap," Remi said, getting up and brushing off her pants. Usually when they did something like this, she and Mano went in the front door and did what was necessary to turn a problem into an opportunity. That was the extent of their creativity when it came to the darker side of their work.

"Let's go see what we're up against so we can sit and wait," Mano said, stepping back into the woods when a large but poorly maintained house came into view. A porch ran along the length of the front and three lights were pointed at the yard. They watched as the two men stepped into the clearing and immediately raised their rifles and pointed at Simon and Sabana until the young woman got out of the car.

"Cain's hiring them young, don't you think?" Mano asked. In the dim light of the weak spotlights Sabana appeared to be maybe sixteen. "You never did answer my question as to who she is."

"Remember Rick? That's his little sister, and from what Cain said she's got a few pent-up anger issues."

Sabana walked toward the men, speaking so softly none of them could make out what she was saying. They lowered their rifles enough that she appeared less apprehensive about approaching them.

"What you looking for?" the big one asked. "Girl, you know what time it is?"

"Hey, if you're hungry you can come inside," the other cut in, elbowing his partner. "We was fixing to heat something up."

"That's a good idea, Boone."

They were all walking up the stairs to the porch together, the men so fixated on Sabana's backside that they forgot about Simon. That was their first mistake because she sliced through the bigger man's Achilles tendon, bringing him down, and the other turned with a shocked expression, giving Sabana the chance to drive her knife into his shoulder. It wasn't fatal, but it made him drop his weapon.

"I hope we have the right place," Remi said, and laughed, betting a month's take that Simon had already been inside checking the layout and knew it was safe to attack.

"Good work, Sabana," Simon told her as she kicked the rifles into the yard and out of their reach.

"You're going to pay for that, you old bitch," the big man yelled, holding the back of his leg like it would come off if he let go. "Come over here and let me show you some pain."

"This guy is either an idiot or the loss of blood had weakened his brain," Sabana said, doing as he asked.

When she was close he grabbed her, making Remi and Mano run

across the yard. Before they could pry his hand off Sabana's forearm, she stuck two fingers from her other hand up his nose and pulled so hard Remi figured she'd rip the damn thing off his face. "We came in here and cut you for no reason, so do we give you the impression that all of a sudden we'll forget that and lay down and grovel?" she asked the guy, who was sobbing now.

He said something that sounded so nasal Remi didn't understand him, but it sounded like, "Let me go." He'd released Sabana, so she seemed to pull her knife back out of thin air and pressed the tip to the soft tissue right under his eye. "Stop moving or I'll rip this one out and show it to the only good eye you'll have left." Her threat made both of them stop moving.

"So much for on-the-job training," Mano whispered as he picked up the two rifles, admiring them in the light. One of them made him whistle. "A Winchester repeating-arms rifle. Papi said he had one of these in Cuba."

"Put it down, mister, it belonged to our daddy," the small guy said.

"What's your name?" Mano cocked the old rifle he and Remi had seen in so many Western movies. "I'd rather not shoot you right here because I'd have to carry your big ass inside, so let's have it."

"Boone Pritchard," he said, trying to reach around to put pressure on his wound.

"And you?" Sabana asked, pressing the knife deeper.

"Timothy."

"You're Timothy Pritchard?" Remi asked, coming closer to look at the guy. Down the side of his face was the souvenir Dallas had left him years before.

"How'd you know my name?" he asked.

"I'm psychic," she said, motioning them all inside. That he was alive made her hurt for Dallas, who'd not only carried the guilt of thinking she'd killed him, but had suffered the humiliation Bob poured on her because she thought he had evidence she had. "After we get comfortable I'll tell your fortune."

❖

"Did you get a look at the boss's face?" Lionel asked Claire, just the two of them in the van. Joe was meeting with Annabel and a few other agents since U.S. Attorney Talbot had opened an inquiry into

Cain's arrest after he saw the surveillance tape from the parking garage. At this point they weren't afraid of losing their jobs but could possibly be reassigned.

"If I get somewhere it snows about a hundred feet a year, I'll seriously kick Brent Cehan's ass. How in the hell do you get that frustrated after being here like ten minutes? We've been at this for how long, and no one's given in to the temptation of pulling Cain over and knocking her head in."

They weren't watching the monitors since there'd been zero movement out of the house since Cain arrived from the hospital. "And if she's smart enough to elude arrest up to now, how do you think she'll handle the gift that big dumbass handed her?"

"If you're talking about Brent, he should be sent back to wherever he came from." He glanced at the monitor, watching Muriel's car stop at the gate briefly before it opened. "You notice something?"

"What, that the evil cousins have made up?" Claire took her headphones off.

Lionel shook his head. Claire had lasted longer than he had listening to all the "Oompa Loompa" lyrics from *Willy Wonka and the Chocolate Factory*. They were catchy at first but then made you want to run screaming down the street. Cain's special gift for picking such listening material revealed her wicked sense of humor.

"Did you find anything off about Shelby's reassignment?" he asked, thinking Claire wouldn't betray his confidences.

"If your guess is her sudden seriousness with Muriel has gotten her a shiny new undercover assignment, then we're of like minds," she said to him, putting her finger up. "But if that's not what you think, then forget everything I just said."

"This is between us," he reassured her. "But I doubt she went with Muriel only for that reason."

"She's not a prostitute for the Bureau, Lionel, but I do admire her for taking advantage of the situation. I was hoping she'd have found something by now so we could get her back."

His phone rang. "Nothing yet," he said, mouthing Joe's name to her. "She met with Detective Sept Savoie this morning, then Remi's assistant Juno before she got discharged. We stopped Savoie on the way out, but she said Cain was an old family friend and her visit had nothing to do with our case. Of course she didn't technically lie since we found out about the Luis murder site after she left."

"So no movement at all?" Joe asked.

"Her face makes ground meat look good, Joe, and she needed help getting out of the car, so I'm fairly sure she's in for the day." He shrugged at Claire and put his hand up when she kept whispering, *"What?"* "I don't keep a record of that kind of thing, but I'll try and come up with something."

"You don't have to lie, Lionel," Joe said, his voice a whisper. "I can take care of myself."

"I'm sure you can, but regardless of what equipment you're using, it eventually has to be taken offline for maintenance."

"I'm sure Mr. Talbot will understand why you chose to do that on my order precisely when Cain was getting her head bashed against the trunk of her car."

"You're not in here with me every minute, so you have no idea how many times we have to turn stuff off. Like I said, I won't lie, but in my report I don't have to include when my supervisor told me to take the equipment offline."

Claire was staring at him when he hung up. "I'm not willing to lie."

"No one's asking you to, and I realize you're new to the team, but this situation isn't worth Joe's job."

"Let me finish. I won't lie to cover Brent Cehan because he threw himself under George Talbot's wheels all by himself, but how can I back up whatever you come up with for Joe? I want to catch Cain too, but not using Brent's methods. You saw how Savoie looked at us when we stopped her to talk. Cops from cop families don't tolerate too many shortcuts, and what happened to Cain was a major shortcut."

"If you want, I can turn in the report without your name on it."

"Like you said, Lionel, I may be the new kid on the team, but I'm on the team. Did Joe say it was all right to come in?"

"He's arranging to have NOPD patrol, but we can go in and fill out some paperwork so we can get back in the field when Cain's ready to rock again. Want to lay bets that we nail her for killing Brent?" he said, and laughed. "I shouldn't say that because even if he's a macho idiot, he's one of us."

Claire laughed too, as if knowing he wasn't serious. "Do you think we need to give Shelby fair warning that Muriel seems in the fold again?"

"I'm not sure when she'll be back or if she plans to work any time soon, but why don't we pay her a visit and bring it up? Like you said, if she's undercover, that's not the only reason she's with Muriel, but

I'd rather have all the facts. I'm sure Muriel cares for her and won't do anything stupid—"

"But her family loyalty hasn't been truly tested."

"Right, and I don't want her caught in a battle between Cain and Muriel, especially if Muriel has closer ties to Cain no matter what."

"Agent Hicks mentioned that the California office in charge of the Phillips murders considers Cain a possible suspect for the hits. What's your take on that?"

"If Cain is our killer, all the time I've spent watching her has been a waste and I don't know her at all. She's capable, sure, but I don't see her being responsible for that, though I'm sure Shelby won't want to hear it." Lionel shut down the equipment and opened the door that led to the driving compartment, letting Claire go first. "We'll have to worry about that soon enough if they're right, but we need to keep our team together so we can finish this."

"I'm so glad you're so optimistic."

"Nah, I'm just too young to be completely jaded." He started the engine and took one last peek at the house, but the damn song he'd listened to for hours popped into his head again. "We'll catch her eventually, but after it happens I'll miss her."

"You're right. Cain Casey's one of a kind."

"Of course, that's what the agents following Dalton Casey said," he told her, coming close to waving to the guard on the wall. "Cain already has two and another one on the way."

CHAPTER TWENTY-FOUR

D o you promise you won't do any of the heavy lifting?" Emma asked Cain from the circle of her arms. Ramon was waiting for her downstairs, and the security crew outside had called and reported that her babysitters from across the street had pulled out. "Remember what the doctor said. You have a beautiful brain that matches the rest of you, and I'm in love with the whole package."

"My brain is fine," she said, kissing Emma and enjoying the way Emma's lips parted and let her in. "My groin, though, is another story, Mrs. Casey."

"You can stay home and let me take care of you while Katlin tends to whatever you think you need to go out for."

"Temptation, thy name is Emma," she said, kissing her again. "This won't take long, lass, so keep the bed warm and don't bother with pajamas."

"I know you're a multitasker, so think about something while you're out," Emma said, pressing her breasts into her with enough force that she could feel the hard nipples despite their clothing.

"What's that?" she asked, unable to take her eyes off Emma's cleavage.

"I'm at that point in the pregnancy where I crave sex," Emma said, putting her hand between Cain's legs and cupping her groin in her palm. "I've craved your touch from the first day you put your hands on me, but sometimes like now I need you to lay me down and fuck me until I can't take any more."

Cain was sure Emma's hand got hot after she finished talking because the little speech made her so wet and hard she was actually contemplating letting Katlin go without her. "Are you enjoying yourself?"

"I can't help it. It's not like I'm lying." Emma rubbed against her, which pushed the right button. "And you seem to feel better, so…" Emma stopped and pulled her shirt down, exposing her slightly larger breasts to the cool air of the bedroom.

"I do feel better and I do need to go out for a while, but nothing says I can't have a taste before I do." The dresser was the closest piece of furniture so she lifted Emma up, taking her skirt with her. She moved back momentarily only to let Emma unbutton her pants so they'd pool at her ankles. "Are you sure? A little while ago you were more worried about Dallas, and that threat's not over."

"You think she'd deny me this?" The question came as Emma put her hand between Cain's legs again and immediately took her clitoris between her fingers and squeezed. Cain moaned louder than was prudent with Hannah and Hayden a few doors away doing their homework. "I know Dallas will be okay. She'll come back a little bruised and her heart will take time to relax again from the emotional battering, but we'll all help her fight back to happiness."

"You know it," Cain said, thinking that if Emma pumped and squeezed any harder she'd have to stop talking or the beautiful brain everyone kept talking about would short-circuit. "Tell me what you want."

"I want slow," Emma said, slowing her hand to prove her point. "And I want to be filled," she said, spreading her legs and lying back. "But I'll settle for fast because you're not leaving without putting your fingers in me."

"God," she said as she slid her fingers in with no problem because Emma was so wet and open. "You feel so good." The walls of Emma's sex clamped down on her fingers and she wanted to press her lips to her sex, but it was important to Emma that they come together. She knew it from the moment Emma had undressed her and touched her. As much as they both enjoyed spending time giving the other their full attention, making love like this face-to-face, feeling the orgasms build simultaneously was important so they could see what they felt in this most intimate of acts.

Cain kept her eyes open as she moved her fingers, feeling how hard Emma was every time her thumb hit her clit on the way in. Emma hooked her feet behind her knees and opened her mouth as if encouraging Cain to put her tongue back inside and making Cain enjoy the carnal sound of her hand slapping against Emma's skin as she gave her what she wanted.

"Right there, baby," Emma said, pulling her mouth away and speeding up her hand. "Don't stop," Emma said, her voice wavering as she bit her lip. "Don't stop," she repeated, and her feet gripped Cain harder.

Since Emma was still moving her fingers, Cain had to come or step away from Emma's touch, but Emma was breathing like she was right there with her. They would reach the peak together, so she bent nearer and Emma put her free arm around her neck, biting her shoulder to keep from screaming. After feeling like crap for the good part of two days, it was liberating to stand there and pump her hips into her wife—rhythmically, at first, then with spastic jerks because her body had lost control to Emma's fingers.

The strength left Cain's legs, but Emma pulled her in and held her up as she panted in her ear. "You do give the most wonderful going-away presents, and the best part is you won't be gone that long."

"Why's that the best part?" Cain asked as soon as she got her breathing back under control.

"Because your homecoming gifts are even better. When you come back you can deliver that delicious ending, but you can take your time," Emma said, kissing her earlobe. "Go out and do what needs to be done, but when you finish, be prepared for me to be demanding."

"I can live with those kinds of threats, love," she said, standing up and laughing when she tripped over her pants and almost fell down on her backside. "I'll have to take care of this asshole who keeps dropping dead people at my door fast, so I can cater to your demands."

"I'd feel sorry for him, but anyone who makes you go out when you look like this," Emma said, helping her with her clothes, then running her finger along the gash that Mark had stitched with small neat sutures, "deserves whatever he's about to get. It's not like he didn't ask for it by killing people and stuffing them into boxes. You can't ignore stuff like that forever."

Cain stopped halfway through putting her coat on and stared at Emma, thinking her mother had come back from the grave and taken over her wife's soul. "You don't sound like yourself, lass."

"Do you remember the day we walked up to the small lake by Dad's place?"

"That day will never leave me no matter how many times I get hit," Cain said, tapping the unbruised side of her head.

"When I left for New Orleans with my heart in my hand, hoping you'd see me again, Daddy told me you would." Cain opened her arms and Emma almost collapsed into them. "I never thought he was right, and I went because I couldn't live another day without you. That might sound corny, but I was dying there in all that empty land wishing for what I had thrown away."

"I've already told you plenty of times that you need to stop beating yourself up over that. I might have these on the outside," she said, pointing to the bruises on her face, "but you carry them on the inside, my love, and it's past time to let them heal." She put her hand flat over Emma's heart. "And your father's a wise man because he knew. I could've kept you out, but my heart would have been as empty as all that land you left behind."

"That day I took you up there," Emma said, putting her hand over hers, "I saw it in your eyes, these beautiful eyes." Emma outlined the tops of her cheek with her fingers. "You let me back in from the cold, and even though the weather was frigid, I felt warm for the first time since I'd left. It was a miracle that you let me back in and gave me all I'd wanted, and I never took that acceptance lightly. I understood what I needed to give you in return to earn the right to be with you."

"Ah, lassie, you have no debts with me," she said, her heart hurting that Emma felt she had something to prove.

"It's not something I owe you," Emma said, taking Cain's hand and putting it over her abdomen. "It's something I owe myself because I knew you from the first day. You never lied to me, never tried to pass yourself off as someone you weren't, and it was my fault I stood on the sidelines and stupidly judged what I didn't think was right."

"Why are you telling me this now?" Cain asked. When Emma started to lament over things she couldn't change, she usually worked herself into tears Cain couldn't walk away from even if the house was on fire. "I love you with all that I am, and what happened isn't all your fault."

"I'm telling you because I want you to go out there and take off the shackles I've put on you," Emma said, her eyes clear. "Sometimes I realize that you know the most expedient way and you take another course because of what I might think. It's like that night I saw you with Danny's blood on your hands and I thought the worst. Your first instinct was to kill him, and you were right. Now the best thing for us, for our future, and for our family is for you to shed blood, and you're afraid I'll see and run."

"I've taken care of plenty of problems and you're still here, love."

"You've got a lot more waiting for you, and it's time for some of that old Cain to quit hibernating. These people are proving that they can hit you over and over, and the consequence isn't enough to keep them from doing it again. This is our future," she pressed their hands harder against her middle, "and when it's our children's turn, I want them to inherit a clan that only has to roar a little to send the assholes running."

"My mum would have a statue built in your honor for that little pep talk," Cain said, kissing Emma. "The world is changing since I took over from my da, and I don't mind getting my hands bloody if it's necessary. But this killing has become senseless. People back then didn't fill five boxes with innocents who no more deserved that than a pack of nuns, but scum like Juan changed that. They kill because they like it and because they don't have anything that makes life precious."

"That's what scares me the most, and it terrifies me to lose you."

"Don't be scared, but I don't think I could kill for no reason, like Juan."

Emma shook her head and pressed her nose to the side of Cain's neck. "I shouldn't be laying all this on you right before you go out."

"I don't want to leave and you don't have to ever fear saying what's on your mind. The future might be bloodier than I'd like, but it'll still belong to us because I plan to do what has to be done until I solve all our problems." She rubbed her hands along Emma's back. "You understand what I'm saying?"

"I do, and do you understand that I'll be here with the soap when you get home?"

"Soap isn't the best thing to wash away the blood," she said, smiling when Emma raised her eyebrow as if in question. "Loving me like you just did, that's what washes it away and keeps my soul light."

"You'll be careful, right?"

"No heavy lifting for me, and I don't have too much time to get creative, so we should be back soon."

"Creative?"

"It's like playing Russian roulette, only I load all the chambers and I don't take a turn," she said as Emma helped her put on her jacket. "If you're the one playing, it's a great motivator to talk."

"That's my devil."

"A little beat up, but good to go."

❖

"Katlin called and said she'd meet us there," Ramon said as they drove out the front gate behind the heavily tinted windows of one of the Suburbans she kept in the garage. "Carlos recognized the guy as Lorenzo Mendoza, one of Rodolfo's men who's recently gone missing."

Cain was glad Muriel was back in her life, but right now she was still aggravated that they had to take ridiculous measures to talk to someone. They'd left the house forty minutes earlier but were still driving, making sure they didn't see any surveillance because of Shelby's midnight raid of Muriel's office.

Once Lou was convinced they hadn't been tailed, he headed to the warehouse deep in the east side of New Orleans. The area was devoid of traffic and any movement, so Lou turned into the large entrance and Katlin was waiting to close the door behind them. When she got out she heard only the ticking noise of the engine as it cooled. This place would replace their wine-storage warehouse.

As they walked behind Katlin she saw Ramon glance at his watch, his lips pulling into a grim line, obviously because his phone was as silent as a stone. "You know her and Mano, so you know they're fine."

"Remi's capable, I'm not worried about that, but she isn't as focused as usual because of Dallas. This man is dead, or soon will be, but I hope she doesn't leave anything behind that'll be a problem because her rage has made her sloppy."

"That's why Simon, Sabana, and Mano are there. Sometimes we have to give in to our fears and anger when it comes to the ones we love, but that's how it is when you give your heart," she said, noticing the small office at the back and the large box at its center.

"Do you think this is the last ghost left to haunt Dallas?"

"Life can't always give us guarantees, but if it isn't, we have some work left to do," she said, feeling the slight chill through her jacket. "I do believe Johnny is the worst as far as Dallas is concerned. The rest are just opportunists we'll deal with if they decide to be stupid. But I'm willing to bet they don't haunt her dreams like her father does."

"Good, because I like Dallas and she's good for Remi. This is what she needed, and Dallas will make her happy since she seems as devoted to her as Marianna and Emma are to us," he said, and she nodded, her attention more now on the man strapped to the office chair.

Lorenzo was what Katlin said his name was, and Cain figured it was the white hair along his temple that made him appear relaxed. Experience counted for a lot when it came to courage, more sometimes than heart and guts, but she doubted it would last because the age that had given him the gray hair hadn't put him on the receiving end of this kind of meeting. When he noticed her he lifted his chin and glared at her as if daring her to do something.

"Do you speak English?" she asked, and his expression remained unchanged. "The silent type, huh?"

"A Benjamin he does," Ramon said, making her laugh at his willingness to bet on anything.

"Guys like Lorenzo here need motivation to shed some of that machismo they do so well when they're standing in front of their posse. Alone, they're like frightened little boys ready to piss themselves and ready to spill their guts so fast you can't get the information quick enough." When Ramon laughed at her insult, Lorenzo's spittle landed close to her shoe, a hint that he'd understood her.

"I usually go with the seven-bullet rule," she explained, removing her gun from its holster. "But I'm willing to make an exception in your case. Who's in the box?" she asked, but Lorenzo stayed defiantly quiet. "Katlin, any clues?"

"We opened it, but it's hard to tell with the big hole in his head. From what we could make out it looks like Santos Esvillar, the head guy Rodolfo put in Biloxi. We met with him a couple of times to talk about his moving on from the casino."

"It took more than once?"

Katlin nodded, her legs swinging as she perched on the edge of the desk. "These guys have the learning curve of a retarded slug, so it takes us having to get bitchy, and you know how much I hate bitchy."

"Why kill him?" she asked Lorenzo, who sucked his breath in hard through his nose, gathering the phlegm at the back of his throat, she was sure to spit again. Since he was strapped down, she rested the muzzle of her pistol on the top of his right hand and pulled the trigger before he could spit.

It was amazing how quickly he went from arrogance to hysteria when she opened a hole in his palm. "When I mentioned varying from the seven-bullet rule, that didn't mean using fewer bullets, genius."

She was sure the pain was still there, but he bit his lip and tried his best to breathe. "You kill me if you want, but I don't tell you nothing."

"I owe you, Ramon," she said, peeling a hundred-dollar bill out of her money clip and handing it to him before she shot the other hand. "You're going to die tonight. That isn't a question or something to bargain over, Lorenzo, so bravery will cost you a fast path to it," she said over his yelling.

"Kill me now, I don't tell no matter what," he got out through his tears.

"Do you remember Jesus?" she asked, referring to one of Juan's men who'd met a similar end.

"Yes," he said, rocking as much as he could as if it'd help with the pain.

"He was bright enough not to make it to seven," she said, putting the next one in his wrist. His scream died when he passed out, and she looked through the names in his phone while Katlin cracked a vial of smelling salts under his nose. Gracelia's number was listed first, but the chances that it was still a working number were nil, since one of the guys in the van had gotten away. "No sleep tonight, Lorenzo, because while I'm sure these hurt like a mother," the other wrist splintered with the next shot, "they're not life threatening."

She didn't know the other names in the phone, but they were a good starting point. When Lorenzo jerked his head away from Katlin, Cain pulled up a chair to sit across from him. "I think you missed that last part. I'm going to take it a few inches at a time before I put one right here," she said, putting her finger to the middle of her forehead. "Hands, wrists, elbows, and so on will bend your mind from the pain, but that shit won't kill you."

"You kill me now," he said, shaking his head violently enough to make tears and saliva fly off his face. "I no talk."

"I want you to listen to me," she said, standing again. "Every time you repeat that line, it'll cost you another bullet." To prove her threat she picked his lower forearm and shot regardless of his protests.

"Unless you have a weak heart, amigo, this is going to be a long night," she said, watching him as he mumbled and cried.

"Why kill Santos?"

"Santos loyal to Rodolfo and Carlos," he said, crying harder as he wet his pants.

"See, that wasn't hard," she said, signaling Katlin to hit him again to perk him up. "You had me confused for a long time wondering why Gracelia Luis had you kill five of my people, and even though I know who did it now, I still don't know why. Why five of mine and one of Ramon's?"

Lorenzo laughed like the pain had made him crazy. "You stupid or something?"

She gladly handed her gun over when Ramon held out his hand. Lorenzo widened his eyes when Ramon put the gun in the bend of his arm so the bullet would exit through his elbow. It took two vials to bring him around after that one.

"That 'stupid' comment will cost you every time, so try and control yourself," she told him, the gun back in her possession. His sobs were loud and she doubted he'd cried like that since he was a baby. "Why kill my people and Ramon's?"

"To show you how easy we could," he said loudly, as if he couldn't control his volume either. "No one want to work for Rodolfo no more, and it going to be like that for you. Work for Casey or Jatibon and you die."

She glanced back at Ramon. "That almost makes sense in a bizarre way."

"Sure, until we figure out the 'who' and wipe you and everyone down to the janitor working for you out," Ramon said.

"You never catch Gracelia," Lorenzo said.

"Well, right now we won't because we don't know where she is," she said, smiling. "But that's about to change. Where is she, Lorenzo? I don't take out the other elbow if you tell me, so it's up to you to stop the pain."

"Don't make me tell," he said. "I can't tell…please."

"You had to know that by hitting me first, I would hit back with help from the Jatibons. Those people you killed and defiled by stuffing into boxes and throwing out like the trash had nothing to do with our businesses except for one, and that young man was special to me. He worked for me in security but never carried a gun, never presented a threat to you, and didn't deserve what you did to him before he died. Knowing anything about our businesses won't help you, since once the breach is found, we plug the holes so fast you'll hit the wall we have around us hard. Tell me where she is and I promise we're almost done."

"She where Rodolfo stay," he blurted. "Now kill me."

"What name is she staying under?"

"Gracelia Luis," he said, just as fast.

"Katlin, could you call the Piquant and ask."

He looked panicked. "I tell you, so kill me."

"No one by that name, Cain, and we ran the other aliases, no luck."

Lorenzo's head shook back and forth as he rapidly repeated the word "no," but she shot through the other elbow. "I told you it was up to you, and lying isn't the way to make this stop. Obviously your hands and arms aren't all that important to you, but I bet I know what is," she said, and Lou cut through his belt and pants, leaving him naked from the waist down. Next he untied one leg and pulled it away from the other one.

"Please, no," he said, looking down at his groin.

"Where is she?"

"We staying at the Royal Sonesta in the French Quarter. The room in Jerome Rhodes's name," he said quickly when she pressed the tip of his penis to the chair with the muzzle. "I swear it."

"Katlin," she said, not having to repeat the order.

"Jerome had six suites booked but had to cut his visit short. He and his party checked out an hour ago."

"Who is Jerome Rhodes?"

"He Gracelia's man," he said, and she heard his jealousy in his voice.

"Her butler, guard, mule, lover, what do you mean?" she asked, leaving the role she suspected for last.

"He her lover and he work for her," he said, as if he'd forgotten the pain and that his manhood was on the line.

"What else do you know about him?" She racked her brain trying to place the name.

"He Americano and she trusts him."

"Where's Juan?"

"I don't know."

"Ooh, do you think that was the right answer?" she asked, taking her gun away. "Lou." He took out a switchblade that he worked through his fingers so fast he could have had an act in Vegas. "Since Mr. Lorenzo doesn't have a good view of the family jewels, you want to show him?"

When Lou pressed the blade to his testicles the muscles in Lorenzo's legs stood out in vivid relief as he tried to slam them shut. "No," he yelled. "Wait, I tell you."

"Where is he?" she asked, putting her hand up to stop Lou. "And remember there's a big penalty for lying."

"He with his mother, but I don't know where they go. Jerome make all those plans."

"I actually believe that," she told him, and Lou stepped back. "One more thing, Lorenzo, does Gracelia know Carlos is Rodolfo's son?"

"Santos tell her and Juan kill him."

"Good journey, then," she said as she stood and put her gun away.

"Lou, I can drive us back if you want to help Katlin finish up," she told him as Lorenzo's eyes moved from Lou to her.

"You got it, boss," he said, following her out a short distance.

"You still have plenty of territory, so see if our little friend has anything else to say, and I'll meet you back at the house."

"So Gracelia is as stupid as her son," Ramon said as she backed out. "From what he said the war will rage all right, but for now it'll be between her and Carlos until one of them kills the other."

"My money's on Carlos, but Gracelia sounds like the kind of idiot who thinks she can fight a war on two fronts. She'll still come after us to keep Juan happy. We need some more information," she said, getting on the interstate and heading for the Quarter. "How about taking a side trip to the Royal Sonesta?"

"Sure, the night desk clerk is an old friend of Remi's."

"Don't let Dallas know that, but befriending someone with access to great hotel rooms is admirable," she said, wiggling her eyebrows and making Ramon laugh.

"We were all young once," Ramon said.

"But beautiful women come with age too."

CHAPTER TWENTY-FIVE

W ho are you people?" Timothy Pritchard asked, trying to roll himself onto his back. Sabana had hogtied both of them, leaving them ungagged when they promised to be quiet.

"We're from the government and we're here to collect taxes on all that booze you got in those jars in the kitchen," Remi said from her seat at the kitchen table.

"That ain't ours," Boone said.

"My partner and I saw you working out there, so don't think you're getting out of paying," she said, smiling at Mano at how stupid these guys were.

"We just work here," Timothy said, "but the still belongs to Johnny Moores. He ain't here, but it's him you need to talk to."

She looked out toward the back, and if she wasn't in this situation she could actually enjoy the sun rising over the mountains in the distance. The sky was taking on a pink hue and marked almost twenty-four hours since Dallas had been taken, more than enough time for Johnny to make it home if he'd been smart enough to go the speed limit and stop only for fuel.

Gripping the side of the old Formica table rimmed in chrome, she tried not to think about the alternative. If he'd stopped somewhere, they'd be sitting here for a while. "Do you have any idea where Johnny went?"

"I work for him, so he don't tell me nothin'," Timothy said.

"I asked if you had any idea," she said, glancing down at him and disgusted at the sight. "You do have those, don't you?"

"You really work for the government?" Boone asked.

"How about I ask my brother to kill your brother?" she asked, looking at the back of his head. "That might jog your memory as to where Johnny could be. If you can't come up with something I can have him shoot you next, since he's dying to use that rifle of yours like an old-time cowboy. Does that sound like a good plan to you?"

"Who the hell are you?" Timothy asked. Mano cranked the rifle, chambering a round. "Wait, wait, come on, wait," Timothy yelled. "He left days ago and said if we'd keep our eye on the still, he'd give us a bigger share. If you know him, that don't happen often, so it had to be important."

"What's the only thing that would make him forget money?" she asked, knowing how she would answer that question. Dallas would supersede money, freedom, and everything else.

"Nothing but looking for his kids," Boone said, obviously taking her threats seriously. "They was taken a long time ago and it done broke his heart."

"Taken?" she asked, standing and using her foot to roll him over to his back and making him scream when he landed on his hands. "Who would've taken his kids?"

"He never told us that," Boone said. "But he never stopped lookin'."

She squatted next to Timothy then and ran her finger down the jagged scar along the side of his face. When she got home she would have that rock of Dallas's bronzed and release her from her nightmares of thinking she'd killed him, because she intended to do that soon.

"Sabana," she said as the room got lighter from the rising sun, "could you sit on the front porch and keep an eye out for Johnny?"

"Timothy," Remi said his name slowly, "how did you get this?" She ran her finger down his scar again.

He tried to pull away from her touch. "Bar fight, and you better git before Johnny gets back. He's mean as a bear, and I don't care if he owes you money or whatever you're doing here, you'd better be gone."

"A bar fight?" she asked, touching the thin-feeling skin again. "Are you sure about that? Did you tell him it was because you tried to rape his daughter and she knocked you stupid with a rock? Though she probably didn't have to hit very hard for that. Or did you keep your mouth shut since he's mean as a bear?"

"Who told you that?" He tried to pull himself into a sitting position, but the rope job Sabana had done pulled taut and he had to go back down. "No little slut's going to get close enough to me to do that."

"You're a lying piece of shit, Timothy." She studied him from his head down. Thinking of him touching Dallas made her want to start cutting off little pieces of him. "She hit you twice, so was it the first or the second that opened this little souvenir?"

"She tell you that?" he asked, looking away from her. "There's no way you know that used-up little slit."

She stood up so fast she almost fell over. "Remi," Mano said. "Not yet."

"I'll give you one more chance," she said, and put the tip of her knife in his ear. "You tell me the truth or I'll pin you to the floor with this. Did she hit you that night?"

"I had my rights," he said, stopping his squirming when she pushed the tip in farther, cutting his skin. "Johnny had taken my money, so it wasn't like I was doing nothing wrong."

"Was Boone in line to take a turn?" she asked, and he tried to twist around to look in Boone's direction. "Not the time to shut your mouth, so don't make me loosen your tongue."

"Boone was gonna have to save his money to take his turn, and he ain't too good doing that, so I had the whole night." When the knife came out he let out a high-pitched squeal. "I don't know why you're so worried. Johnny took so many turns that girl must've been kinda worn out."

"Do you want me to take care of it?" Mano said when she raised her hand and was about to plunge the knife into wherever it hit first.

"I want him to suffer," she said, relaxing her hand and giving Mano his answer.

"Give me a minute and I'll find what you're looking for," he told her, heading for the back door.

"Remi," Sabana said, coming through the front. "You might want to take a look at this."

The road to the house was about four miles from the main route out of Sparta, and it wasn't paved. The cloud of dust being kicked up by whatever vehicle was driving up the road was like a doorbell to tell you there were visitors. She wouldn't be able to determine who it was until they got out of the trees.

"Mano, gag the two morons," she called back to him. "Good job, Sabana, but it's time to go inside and get ready for our surprise party."

"Who's our guest of honor?"

She looked at a stump in the middle of the clearing in front of the house and figured out what to do with the three problems that stood between her and her family, because that's what Dallas and Kristen were.

"Johnny Moores and his band of misfits."

❖

"Did you find out anything?" Emma asked her. Cain had gotten home and changed, throwing the clothes she'd been wearing down to her underwear into the fire Emma had started in the fireplace in their room. After a shower with Emma she'd had breakfast with the kids before they left for school.

"We need to find this guy," she said, taking the copy of the picture the night desk clerk at the hotel had given them after Ramon had donated to her college fund. Jerome Rhodes looked American and had an English name, but he had a Mexican address in Cabo San Lucas, along with a Mexican passport, and he'd told the clerk when he checked in that he was in the jewelry business. "Find him and we find Gracelia. Find Gracelia and we find—"

"Juan, but that won't be easy if he realizes you're on to him. No one stands still if he knows someone's chasing him."

"At least we've got some idea where to start looking since I don't think Gracelia and Juan are done with New Orleans. But if they are and try to stay low for a while, I have a clue where to start in Mexico. Carlos and his men might be interested in a trip to the tip of the Baja."

"Who was in the box?" Emma asked, shivering as she slathered her toast with grape jelly and peanut butter. "And what did you do with it?"

"I plan to put it where they found the other five. No sense not letting the Feds take out our trash since it's really not ours. The guy in there was Rodolfo's manager in Biloxi." She watched, smiling at what seemed to be an inch of toppings on Emma's bread.

"Annabel Hicks will want to see the security tapes, and I doubt you want her to see you taking the former manager for a ride."

"I don't see that as a problem," she said, scratching the stitches again. The cut along her temple was starting to heal, she guessed, and it was driving her crazy. "I have Katlin and her team looking for this Jerome guy."

"It's hard to believe that Juan's back and we haven't heard from him," Emma said, drinking tomato juice and making Cain shiver now. The combination was a dead give-away to Emma's condition, if anyone didn't already know. "He's like a deranged Chihuahua that thinks he's a Doberman pinscher with a side of bloodhound."

"He's headed for the pound. It's only a matter of time, and I've already made arrangements to have him put down."

"Try and keep your weekend clean since I was able to reschedule Hayden's party."

"I'll make sure to keep to your calendar, baby." She stood, laughing and wanting to get back to the office so she could set a meeting of the families and a few others who could put out the kind of net that would eventually catch something. "Make me happy and stay inside today, please."

Emma smiled as she put down her empty glass. "What's in it for me?"

"What do you want?" she asked, loving Emma's revved-up sexuality.

"I'll think of something that involves little clothing and heavy whipping cream," Emma said, laughing as she put her hands in Cain's shirt. "Last night wasn't enough time for us."

"My date last night wasn't that concerned about your calendar," she said, laughing harder when Emma hit a ticklish spot.

"Cain," Carmen said, lowering her eyes as Emma rebuttoned Cain's shirt. "Mr. Delarosa is here and would like to see you."

"Did he bring the succubus with him?" Emma asked sweetly.

"He is with a man."

"Could you let him into the sunroom, Carmen? Thank you."

"I'll leave you to it if you promise you'll mention the touchy-feely Marisol Delarosa," Emma said, pulling her lapels together.

"I promise, but I have a feeling he'll bring her up before I do since little Marisol came without permission and got in over her head. She told him about it, but a man like Hector gets to be the big cheese in his business only because of his heightened sense of paranoia. She told him, but he didn't believe her." She walked Emma to the stairs and pressed their foreheads together when Emma went up two steps. "Today's about damage control."

"As long as it's not daddy trying to get his little girl what she wants, and from the way she was touching you, I think I know what she wants."

"You're sexy when you're jealous," she said, kissing the tip of Emma's nose. "You hold the papers on me, lass, not to worry."

"I'm not worried about you, sweet pea, but I won't vouch for the Delarosas, since they all seem to have a crush on you," Emma said before she started up the stairs again, blowing her a kiss from the landing.

"Cain," Hector said when she stepped in, holding up his demitasse cup in salute. "Your housekeeper is a wonder at the espresso machine."

"I'm sure plenty of places in town make good coffee, Hector, so what can I do for you?"

"You make it sound like we're not friends, and that hurts me." He put his cup down and stared at a spot behind her that she assumed was now filled with Lou's large, quiet presence. "And you act like we're not friends."

"I'm sure your man there," she pointed to the guy sitting in the corner staring out the window but knew better than to think he wasn't paying attention, "has at least two guns on him. The fact that I didn't strip-search him at the door means we're acquaintances, but friendship is still questionable, and should your companion decide to be unfriendly and move his hand anywhere near his jacket, I don't have time to explain the consequences."

"Tomas is harmless, or I imagine no less harmless than the mountain standing behind you, but that isn't what I came to talk about." He drained his cup with his pinkie finger in the air and set his cup down, leaving his hands hanging between his legs. "Marisol told me she went to see you in the hospital."

"Interesting child, your daughter," she said, leaving it at that to see how he'd interpret what she meant.

He shrugged and laughed. "What can I tell you? My wife and I have children, but only one isn't interested in sitting by the pool tanning for a living and celebrating a hard day's work in the clubs at night. Marisol wants to be my successor, so she's constantly trying to learn the business."

"And do you think I'm your business?" she asked, her phone buzzing in a message from Muriel.

"More like I'm interested in *doing* business with you, Cain, but to think you would be my business would be foolish on my part." He moved closer and made a show at grimacing at the condition of her face. "Work with me and I don't believe the Feds will have the *cojones* to do this."

"Why, so it'll be the DEA picking me up and beating the shit out of me? No thanks," she said, losing patience with his refusal to take no for an answer. "Our businesses have nothing in common, so there's no reason for us to be an obstacle to one another, but I'm running out of ways to tell you there's no reason I'll cross the street because I'm interested in doing business with you."

"Money is always the best reason, and I can make plenty for you."

"I make enough, and I'm not stupid enough to think I'm pure, but I find drugs distasteful and they're becoming the main reason the streets are smeared in blood. That's because no one seems to ever win the battle of who's the biggest dog in the kennel. So the police make it difficult for anyone to do business, whether it has to do with drugs or not. What's the big interest in the Big Easy, anyway?"

"Florida and California have more weapons in what your government calls the war on drugs," he said, pulling out a cigar and rolling it between his fingers.

"Not inside, if you don't mind."

"I didn't take you for that much of a prude."

She stretched her fingers out so she wouldn't seem threatening before she curled it into a fist and smashed his face. "My children don't need to be exposed to that and my wife is expecting. If you have that big a jones to light the damn thing, then you're free to leave."

He put his cigar away and dusted his hands as if to say, "You win." "Here, though, the DEA and the local police haven't caught up to the level of men and surveillance equipment. Combine that with the miles of waterways to move it in and the back roads to get it out, and more than me will come here trying to set up a big operation."

"New Orleans isn't that backwoods, Hector."

He laughed stopping when she didn't join in. "I'm not bringing my shipments down Canal Street downtown, if that's what you mean, but you've driven through the small communities within a hundred miles of here. You can find ways to float it in and plenty of volunteers to move it."

"Then I wish you the best of luck, because you have it all figured out."

"I'm offering you an opportunity to make good money and not

get your hands dirty if you find my field so offensive. I need only your contacts in city hall and the police department."

She glanced back at Lou and laughed. "That's all? Would you like me to throw in the mayor's number and my lucky penny?"

"Don't disrespect Mr. Delarosa in front of me," Tomas said, keeping his hands on his lap.

"Thin skin will get you burned in this climate," she said, her humor gone. "I called you once for information I needed."

"And I gave it to you gladly, expecting only a little in return," he said, contradicting what he'd said up to now that his help had been free. "I merely wanted you to take my offer serious enough to think about it."

"I'm going to repay it right now," she said, telling them what had happened to Rodolfo and who'd done it. "We've never met, but Gracelia sounds insane and she's likely to put that crazy son of hers in power. If that happens, I hope you realize it won't be in only my best interest that Juan and the rest of his family are eliminated."

"Gracelia is in town?"

"She is with Juan and a man named Jerome Rhodes. Ring any bells?" she asked, and heard Lou talking softly with someone behind him, probably Muriel, though she couldn't make out what they were saying.

"Who is this Jerome Rhodes?" Hector asked, but acted more interested in what was happening behind her. "I've never heard of him."

"Then perhaps there's something we can work on together after all. I want Gracelia because then I can find Juan Luis. Get that for me and I'll consider introducing you to some friends downtown who might make your job easier."

"You say you find our business distasteful, but I heard that you and Remi Jatibon are partnered with Vinny Carlotti already." He sat back as if he had suddenly decided to spend the afternoon. "And that's who you're willing to share your contacts and connections with."

"Vincent Carlotti and my father worked mutual endeavors together for years, so I've known his son Vinny all my life. Ramon and Remi Jatibon and I have a few things together because while they're newer to the city and first-generation Americans, I've known them all my life too." She stood and buttoned her jacket. "In my world you arrived today, Hector, that's how much I know about you and your motives.

Since we know so little about each other I should tell you that I don't respond well to threats, and I'm set in my ways."

"Does that mean there is no room in your old network of friends?"

"It means you should learn to pace yourself and ease yourself in. Learn the city and its players and you'll have more success."

He laughed but stayed seated. "I'm a man of action."

"Then you will find very little success here," she said, glancing back at Lou, who quickly moved closer. "When my family came from Ireland years ago they did like most did at the time in the same situation and stayed up north, but eventually the entire family found themselves here."

"Who cares about your history?" Tomas asked sarcastically, but stopped short when Hector glared at him.

"We have thrived here because this ancient place is as fond of tradition as we are," she said, continuing as if Tomas wasn't there. "Your people have done a good research job if they've told you the lay of the land, but don't forget to learn the people as well. You might find a lot of volunteers, as you say, willing to make money if you throw it out fast enough, but for every one of them there are ten along those bayous who'll gut you before you know you're cut. Cram yourself in by force and you might last a year, but then you'll find yourself at the bottom of one of those bayous being used for alligator bait."

"Moving speech, Cain, but force is what got me here."

"That's because you come from a place where you had all the guns and all the power. Like I said, this isn't backwoods and we don't all need your money to get us through the hard times. Push here and don't be surprised if you get pushed back."

"Is that a threat?" Hector asked, now rising to his feet.

"I believe I've already said that I won't get in your way if you leave me and mine alone. We can live in peace, if you understand that. I was just giving you some advice. I'm not the only one making my way here."

Hector snapped his fingers at Tomas and the man jumped up from his seat. "You may not think so, but we *will* be friends, Cain, because we are a lot alike, and because you will not allow me to become too powerful if my way is right."

"I'm a barkeep and I'm happy doing that, but I wish you the best of luck."

He held his hand out and she took it. "If I hear or find Jerome Rhodes I'll let you know. If it's tradition you believe in, then I'll bring you a token of my friendship."

"I'd appreciate that."

"As soon as we're settled, you and your partner will have to join us for dinner," he said, walking next to her to the front of the house.

"Settled?"

"I bought a house not far from here," he said, handing over a card with an address printed on it. "If I must become a native to get ahead, then I'm making my first step."

"I'm sure the neighbors will be thrilled," she said, putting the card in her pocket and imagining the look on Emma's face when she told her Marisol and Hector were going to be their neighbors. "Congratulations. I'm sure the house-warming gifts will come pouring in."

"My home is in Colombia, but for now I'll be here full-time until I can get this going and leave Marisol in charge."

"Good to know," she said, smiling, "and thank you for dropping by, but I've got a few things to take care of."

"Don't forget to think about my offer."

"And don't forget to think about my response," she said before turning and walking back to her office, patting herself on the back for not adding "butthead" to the end of her farewell.

CHAPTER TWENTY-SIX

They'd been sweating for what seemed hours at first, and now Dallas was holding on to Kristen trying to share body heat. She didn't need to be sitting in the front seat to figure Johnny's relentless driving was taking them farther north. They were going home, and when they got there he'd take and take until neither Remi nor anyone else would want what was left.

The box smelled of vomit and gasoline since Kristen had thrown up when she came to from the pain in her head and Johnny was, she was guessing, filling gas cans to keep from having to pull into a gas station and chance someone overhearing two women screaming for help. From the time they'd left New Orleans, he'd stopped for long periods of time only twice, and then they'd heard the box creak and a strange tapping noise as he talked to them. It was like he was sitting on the top and patting the wood in some weird celebration that he'd finally succeeded.

"What are we going to do?" Kristen asked, barely audible over the hum of the tires chewing up miles beneath them.

She pulled her arms tighter around Kristen and kissed the top of her head. It had been hours and he'd never opened the box, and if Kristen was as thirsty as she was, they wouldn't be able to put up much of a fight when he did let them out. But that was probably why he'd done it. "You have to believe we escaped once, so we can do it again. We'll be fine, but you have to stick with me no matter what, okay?"

"I'm scared," Kristen said before she groaned when the truck felt like it left the road and the sudden jolt made them bounce completely off the bottom of the box. "What's happening?"

In her mind's eye she could see the road that led to the hellhole

Johnny had built on the land he loved to brag had belonged to his father and had been, according to him, a major site for a battle during the Civil War. He talked about it when he was drunk on the shit he made, but like everything he said, it was a lie. The Moores like her father and the ones who came before him had deserved to die out before now, and if she got out of here she planned to beg Remi to do it for her even if Remi didn't want her anymore.

"He's headed to the house, so when we get there be sure to stick with me. Whatever happens, stay with me and close your eyes if you don't want to watch, but don't try to antagonize him," she said in a loud voice so Kristen would hear her over the rumble that made it sound like they were on a roller coaster. "Do you understand me?"

"I want to help you if I can."

"Kristen, you don't remember what he's like, but I do. *Do not* get in his way." Her last word seemed to echo when the engine shut off.

"Katie Lynn," Johnny said, knocking on the top of the box. "You're home now, so if you want to see the sunset you need to be a good girl when I open this up. Since you're nothing but a little bitch, though, I'm going to give you a warning." She heard the key ramming into the lock. "You try something and I'll put a bullet in Sue Lee's head, and then I'll make you dig the hole I throw her in." He slapped the top again. "We understand each other?"

"Kristen, please promise me that you'll stay behind me."

"Okay," Kristen said, tightening her grip on her.

"Tell me you understand me or I might just drop this goddamn thing in the lake," he said.

"Yes," she said in a loud voice, thinking that she'd keep her answers short to conserve her energy.

The sun was blinding at first, but when he straightened up, his body blocked it and she could see the gun in his hand. "I can hardly believe you're back," he said, grabbing her by the top of her hair and yanking her to her knees, the pain excruciating when her weight bore down on them. "If you want me to be nice, don't give me a reason not to."

"Who's that?" she asked, noticing the girl she'd seen briefly when he took her.

"Deidi, come closer and introduce yourself since your part in all this is almost over," Johnny said, waving her over with the hand not holding the gun. "You could learn things like how to listen from Deidi, because I couldn't have done it without her."

"If you have her, what do you need with us?" she asked, lifting her hand to shield her eyes from the glare when he jumped down.

"No one can replace you, Katie Lynn," he said, cocking his gun and lifting the muzzle a little in her direction. "But I'm a lonely man and Deidi here, she kept me company. She helped me out but she couldn't replace you." He lifted the gun and aimed it at her but at the last moment changed his target and shot Deidi, and Kristen started screaming.

Inside the house watching the girl hit the ground made Remi think they needed a distraction that would draw the weapon away from Dallas and the distressed Kristen. "Pick him up," she said to Mano and Sabana, talking about Boone.

"You want to throw him out?" Sabana asked.

"Send him out like this and it won't make much of an impression," she said, stepping back when Sabana slit the man's throat without her having asked. "That should do it."

Deidi was gasping for breath on the ground and Dallas was holding Kristen's head against her shoulder, trying to shield her face from the blood. When the screen door opened with a loud squeak, Johnny spun around and shot again as if it had scared him enough to pull the trigger. The bullet missed Boone as he flew off the porch from the momentum of his weight, but the blood made Johnny turn fully around and step closer.

"What in the hell?" Johnny said, walking toward the porch and stopping about halfway there. "Timothy, you in there?" A few steps closer was all he was willing to move since he stopped and tried to peer through the door as if something would come out and attack him. "You hear me, boy? Come out here and tell me what the hell happened."

"That should do it," Remi said to Mano, stepping away from the window. "Timothy, you ready to welcome Johnny home?" she asked as they pulled him to his feet. His head had been turned away when Sabana sliced Boone, so he seemed to be looking for him when he got up. She cut the rope tying his feet and pushed him through the door, waiting a beat behind him for him to see his brother.

At the sound of his anguished cry, she stepped out, glad to see Johnny looking at Boone's body and making his reaction time too slow. She didn't miss when she fired, hitting him in the hand he was using to hold up the gun. After he raised the stump that started at his wrist, he dropped and shoved it between his legs.

"Remi," Dallas said, looking right at her but acting like she didn't believe she was there. "Remi," she said, and from her expression she appeared as if she was trying to get her legs to work without letting go of Kristen.

Remi moved so fast that, like Timothy, she almost tripped as her feet hit the ground and she ran in the direction of the truck. Since she had the others with her, she didn't worry about anything but getting to Dallas and proving to herself she was fine. "You're okay," she said when she was able to jump up onto the truck bed and put her arms around her and Kristen.

"You came," Dallas said, sobbing. "You came."

"You only had to think about what I told you night before last. You belong to me, and you do because I love you."

"Katie Lynn, help me, girl," Johnny yelled at Dallas between grunts of pain.

"Come on, we're going," Remi said, helping the girls out of the box only to have them both pull away from her.

"We're disgusting," Dallas said, her tears starting again, though silently this time.

The smell of urine and vomit hit Remi only after Dallas said something, and her heart broke at how much this idiot had broken the children he'd been blessed with. "It'll wash off, *querida*, so don't worry about it. Come on." She coaxed them back to her side and smiled at Mano when he was there to help them down.

"I know you don't want to go inside, so if you want, take off and we'll be right behind you," he said to Remi after he'd hugged both Dallas and Kristen. "We have to clean up a little."

"Give me a minute," Remi said, walking them to the car that Sabana had parked in the back of the house. "Stay here," she told Dallas, kissing her hand when she grabbed her shirt front, not acting like she wanted to let go. "I'll be right back, and nothing will happen to you."

"Don't be long," Dallas said, then put her head on her shoulder. "And I want you to…I don't know how to ask you."

"I'll be right back, and when I do we'll never have this issue resurface again. I intend to do what I need to because of what he did to you, and because the bastard deserves it."

"Thank you."

"I love you, Dallas, and that's what someone who loves you is supposed to do. I plan to take my job of protecting you and Kristen very seriously, so you don't have to thank me."

"You're the only one who ever cared this much, so I do."

When she made it to the front the area was empty. Boone's body was gone, as were Johnny and Timothy, but judging from the yelling they were in the house. She stepped inside and found both men sitting at the kitchen table. Sabana was bringing gallon bottles of moonshine in from the other room and putting them in front of them. Despite his injury Johnny had a pile of broken glass by his chair as if he'd pushed a few to the ground and they'd broken, explaining the strong alcohol odor.

"You think you're going to get away with this?" Johnny asked, pushing another two gallons aside and breaking them as well. "You don't know who you're messing with."

"I do know that," she said, unscrewing a gallon and pouring it around the rest of the kitchen. Then she took another one and made a trail to Johnny's storeroom. "Your mistake was not realizing who *you* were messing with, Johnny."

"Bob told me about you. He said you were going to ruin Katie Lynn's career and life with what you wanted from her."

"What's that? To love her and give her the freedom to work without looking for my share, like Bob? To love her and give her the freedom to choose to love me back, not force myself on her like you and your sick friends?" She stood a few feet from the table and unholstered her weapon. "If that ruins her life it'll still be better than what she's had up to now."

"I brought that little bitch into this world and it was my right to do whatever I wanted."

"Those days are over," she said, and Simon yanked his chair back. "Timothy, you want to stand up or do we need to do it for you?" He was crying but did what she'd asked. The whole time she'd been talking his gaze was fixed on the body near the table, where Mano had dragged Boone. "If I didn't have Dallas waiting for me outside I'd take my time, but you need to understand the consequences of what you did. Where I'm from we deal with child molesters in a unique way."

"What, talking people to death?" Johnny laughed at his own joke.

He jumped back and ran into Mano when she opened fire, emptying her clip into Timothy's crotch. Every one of her bullets hit, even though he tried to shield his body from her until he went down screaming so loud that a neighbor two miles away would've heard him.

"Wait," Johnny said, seeming like he wanted to run, but Mano was holding him in place. "Let's talk about this," he said as she popped the empty clip out and replaced it. "I'm Katie Lynn's father," he said as she chambered the first round, getting the Glock ready again. "I just wanted to see her again. It's been years and I'm getting older, so all I wanted was to see my girls. You walk out of here and you have my word I ain't gonna bother them again."

Near the front door the girl who'd been riding in the front with him gurgled through the blood in her mouth. The hole in her chest was fatal, but for some reason she was hanging on, though Remi could see from her glazed look that it was a matter of time before her heart gave out.

"What happened to Dallas's mother?" Remi asked, swiveling her head from side to side and popping the bones in her neck.

"That bitch left and I ain't seen her again."

Mano pushed him back in the chair and moved away from him. "I believe we've established that you're a liar, Johnny, but if you want me to consider your offer of me leaving, that'll have to change. The girls wonder about the loss of their mother, and we both know you know what happened to her. A simple country girl disappears without a trace only because she's dead."

"Katie Lynn done it."

"Dallas was never a simple country girl, and she didn't really disappear without a bit of a trail. That's how Bob came into her life, but I took care of that problem," she said, walking behind him and resting the gun at the base of his neck. "No, a woman with no education, two children, and an abusive asshole for a husband goes away only because she's in the ground."

One more bullet from Mano's gun took care of Timothy so she didn't have to keep talking loud to be heard. "You swear you'll let me go," he said, his breathing rapid and his attention on Timothy's still body.

"I sure do," she said sincerely.

"She was gonna leave me, so I helped her out. She's buried out by the still."

"Where by the still?" she asked, making a mental note of the markers he rattled off. "Get up," she said, still standing behind him and twisting the gun to shoot at an odd angle. When the shot entered his backside and traveled up to somewhere in his chest, he seemed stunned for a moment before he dropped to his knees, hitting his head on the table on the way down.

"You said you'd let me go," he said, his voice barely audible.

"I am, and maybe you'll find forgiveness wherever you're going because you won't find any from me," she said, moving so he could see her. "Today is the last day you'll haunt their dreams," she told him, pressing her gun to his chest over his heart and pulling the trigger. "Light it up," she told Simon, throwing all the jugs Sabana had brought in to the floor.

Simon put a rag in one jug and lit it, throwing it against the wall close to the now-motionless girl whose eyes were still open, staring off into nothingness, and the dingy curtains in the front window caught like someone had doused them in gasoline. They stepped out and Remi stood alone in the yard at a safe distance, waiting for the evidence of what had happened to burn away.

After the back storeroom exploded, sending a ball of fire shooting up out of the back of the house, Dallas came and stood next to Remi, maneuvering herself under her arm. "Later we'll come back and get your mom and give her the burial he stole from her," she said, making Dallas start crying again. "Look, though, *querida*, and remember," she said.

"All I want to do is forget, but he never let me."

"I can't erase all the bad memories, but those flames mean it's over. Johnny can't hurt either of you anymore, and as long as I'm alive nothing or no one will have that kind of power over you again."

"That'll be hard to do," Dallas said, walking with Remi to the car as the all-consuming flames emitted an intense heat that was uncomfortable even from where they stood.

"At first maybe, but every time you wake up with me those fears will fade, and when we get home, I'll sell the condo if you want me to, but we're waking up together every day."

CHAPTER TWENTY-SEVEN

"So Eliot Ness is back in town?" Cain asked Muriel after Hector's car had left their property. "Now that she's seen what happened, will they use bullets this time instead of their fists?"

"I did what you said and acted concerned, but I don't know if I can continue this charade." Muriel sat in her usual chair in Cain's office and appeared like her old self for the first time in months. Her uncertainty had disappeared, and Cain was happy that all it had taken was time. "Something changed, though, because she wants to talk to you."

"She talks to me all the time, and she hasn't come up with a good enough argument to make me confess yet. I feel bad for what happened to her parents since no one should have to go through that," she said, knowing full well what it was like to lose them like that instead of to natural causes, "but that won't change my mind. I give to charity by writing a check to different organizations for the tax breaks as well as to help out. The tax break, though, does give me a warm fuzzy feeling since that's the government's main beef with me."

"I don't think she has your confession or strange sense of humor in mind," Muriel said, pouring herself a cup of coffee from the service on the credenza.

"Cain," Lou said from the door, holding his phone to his ear. "The Feds are at Emma's and they're demanding the surveillance tapes."

"Is Annabel there supervising?"

Lou nodded.

"Great, hand me the phone." Cain told the manager, "Find that bitch for me and put her on the line."

"This is Agent Hicks, who is this?"

"Cain Casey, Annabel," she said, and smiled at Muriel, who smiled back and shook her head.

"Try not to antagonize her too much. We have enough going on," Muriel said softly, then sipped her coffee again.

"Tell your people to hand over the tapes and save us the trouble of going to court," Annabel said over what sounded like chaos around her.

"I would, but our system was down for maintenance," she said, making Muriel groan. "And I expect a full report as to who the new body is and who dropped it off. This latest travesty should prove to you that someone's committed crimes in New Orleans and I'm not the one doing it," she said, ending the call.

"That's why you dropped the damn box over there, isn't it?" Muriel asked.

"Come on, I have to get my jollies somehow when it comes to these people. Besides, what better disposal service than Annabel and her merry band of misfits. As a bonus they'll have to concentrate most of their efforts back on Rodolfo and his demise."

"True, which frees us up to look for Gracelia and figure out which side Rodolfo's crew will choose."

"Carlos called this morning before my visit from Hector and said he's heading back to Cozumel and sending a crew to Cabo to see what he can find out." She picked up the new shipment papers for the month's deliveries and smiled when the numbers showed an increase.

"It sounds like you almost like this guy," Muriel said, making her look up.

"Carlos is a little better than Rodolfo, and a lot better than Juan, but I'm still not interested in changing who we are and what we do."

"I can understand that, and agree," Muriel said, something outside making her turn her head.

Cain twisted in her chair and saw Hannah running around the play area they'd set up for her outside. The courtyard close to the sunroom was being set up for Hayden's birthday party that would take place later that afternoon. Things like this kept her days grounded in normalcy and balanced the problems that often threatened her life.

"How's your head?" Muriel asked.

"It's getting there," she said, running her fingers along the stitches. "I still get those disconnected feelings but no more seizures. It scared me that they wouldn't stop."

"You forgive me, right? That I wasn't there when this happened."

"Muriel, I don't need to forgive you because nothing will ever cut away the part of me that shares a bond with you. You're so important to me that I'm always willing to give you the space you need to find yourself and what part you want to play here." She smiled and waved at Hannah when she reached the top of the slide. "You have to discover that place in your heart where you're happy, not with the person you're with, but with yourself, with no influence from me or anyone else. Until you do, don't be afraid that you'll drive me away."

"I'm still looking because Shelby, while I do care for her against common sense, isn't the person who will give me that," she said, standing and pointing out the window. "And that brings us back to Shelby."

"What does she want to talk about?"

"All she said was that it was important and she wanted the opportunity as soon as possible."

"Call her and tell her to come over."

"Are you sure? If they blamed you for whatever reason before she left, this could be a trap now that she's walked the crime scene."

"As long as you know I didn't do this, and Emma knows, I don't have anything to hide or worry about. Shelby needs someone to blame like I did when Big Gino took Da, then waited awhile before taking Mum and Billy. I finally could do something about it, but the pain of the loss doesn't go in the ground with the assholes that did it," she said, putting her hand over Muriel's when Muriel placed hers on her shoulder. "I could've killed that bastard a thousand times over and it still wouldn't make me feel better."

"The problem, though, is that she wants to put *you* in the ground for this."

"She can try, but like the fat bastard that did this to me," she said, touching the stitches again, "she'll find that actions have consequences when you do something without thinking and without proof. They can think whatever they like about me, but I never act without considering those two things. Without proof and intellect, you're only a thug with the ability to pull the trigger."

Muriel squeezed her shoulder before taking her seat. "I'm not disagreeing with you, but you might want to wait. Annabel's bosses are investigating the problems in her office, so she'll hang on to anything you throw at her to turn things around for her."

"Hicks needs to be brought down a few, and I won't be the one who helps her climb out of the hole she's dug for herself," she said, standing. "Get Shelby over here and I'll be right back." Muriel hugged her when she stepped from behind the desk. She returned the gesture, not needing to ask what it was for. That Cain would trust her alone in this room meant their relationship was mended.

Hayden was standing with Emma as the tables were brought out for the barbeque Emma had planned for late that afternoon. Inside, Carmen and the staff were making the sides to go with the thick steaks their butcher had delivered the day before. The new huge television was set up for the video-game tournament Emma had put together with prizes that would make whoever hadn't been invited sorry, and the cake was hidden in a box in their room, since it was her way of teasing him for worrying so about what his friends would think about his party. Barney the Dinosaur would embarrass him a little, but not enough to make him mad.

"Anything I can do?" Cain asked.

"Have you been looking out the window long enough to know it's safe to ask that question?" Emma asked, pinching her cheek.

"Guilty as charged," Cain said, kissing her.

"To think the FBI lives to hear you say that, but I could spank you every time you do," Emma said, making Hayden laugh. "I'm beginning to think that's why you say it," Emma whispered in her ear when she lowered her head to kiss her again.

"Guilty as charged," she whispered back. "Well, Hayden Dalton Casey, you ready for this?"

"Thanks for all this, Mama," he said to Emma, hugging her. "Everything you have planned should score me some dates."

"That's what I'm here for, but I doubt you'll need much help in that area."

"Before your friends get here, your mama and I wanted to give you our gift," Cain said, putting her arm around Emma since she'd gone out to get it the day Juan and Anthony attacked her. Cain had wanted to destroy the gift but Emma refused, saying it wasn't to blame for what happened. Mook came out with the box and handed it to her. "It's a two-part present, so go ahead and open this one first."

He lifted the top and placed his hands on the Purdey and Sons side-by-side game gun that she'd ordered for him months before. The shotgun was new, but it was the same model as the one she'd inherited from her father and the only gun she legally owned. Like her father's she'd had the barrel engraved with a long vine of Irish roses, and the leather case it came with had Hayden's name embossed on the side. He looked awed when he raised his head, and instead of lifting it to his shoulder to check the fit, he threw his arms around Cain.

"Thank you."

"The other part of your gift is a hunting trip later this fall. We'll try this out close to your grandfather's place that's supposed to be great for geese."

"Can Mama and Hannah come?" he asked, the question making her smile at Emma.

"They can wait by the fire until we're done," she said, feeling so good she thought her chest would pop the buttons on her shirt. "You can lock it in the gun safe in my office and we'll try it out on the skeet range next week."

"You made his day, mobster," Emma said, taking his place in her arms when Hayden felt free to check out his present, with Mook following him inside.

"We both did, so don't give me all the credit." Hannah had spotted her again and was climbing down from the fort part of the structure so Cain had a few minutes alone with Emma. "Shelby's back and wants to talk to me."

"I'm sure she does," Emma said, wincing when Hannah took the rope ladder a little too fast from what Cain could tell from Emma's expression of worry. "She'll ask for your help and tell you it's because of what happened and your form of justice is the only one that'll give her satisfaction."

"I haven't figured out if it's a trap or not."

"What does your heart tell you? Because I know what mine says," Emma said, looking up at her. "She's going to play your sympathies for a trust she doesn't deserve."

"Having this happen changes a person. I remember being carefree like that." She pointed to Hannah running full throttle across the yard toward them. "Then it happens and the intense grief makes you lose a bit of yourself you can't get back, and you're not so carefree anymore."

"Things never changed, did they?"

Cain caught Hannah when she jumped higher than she expected. "You lose in life, that you can't change, but Mum used to quote Father Andy all the time about how God doesn't give us more than we can handle. So I miss them, but God gave me something in return for that loss, whether I deserved it or not. It was the answer to the prayers I didn't know how to articulate."

Emma came back to her after she kissed Hannah and put her down to follow Carmen inside for lunch. "I think about them all the time, but now my conversations with them don't center around loss and sadness, but hope. You, my love, gave me a gift greater than what I lost. No matter what you believe in the form of a higher being, mine tested me by taking away my family but rewarded my survival by giving me one that cured the pain."

"I've always thought you were my salvation."

"And you mine," Cain said, starting them moving toward the kitchen.

The heart of their house was large and filled with noise as their family gathered for a meal to celebrate Hayden's day before his friends arrived. Merrick received applause when she made it to the table with a walker, having shed her wheelchair, but Katlin hovered close behind. At the door Shelby stood with Muriel, looking stunned, as if the shock of her ordeal had only recently set in.

The group might have been missing her parents and her siblings, but she felt them there nonetheless. "We still have so much left to do, but it shouldn't take away from days like today," she said softly to Emma, who stood in front of her with her hands on the baby growing inside.

"We have so much."

"And so much more to look forward to," she said, kissing Emma's cheek and feeling a swell of emotion. They separated and went to their places at the ends of the table, and Cain raised her glass. "To Hayden, our family's happiness, and to the things yet to come…"

"Clan," those that belonged answered together, affirming that family was the most important thing. It was the reason Cain was strong and those who were lined up against her would never have a chance. Though the Feds had tried to break Cain through legal means and force, her lost sheep who had a set of keys to the empire was back in the fold, closing the door on the outsiders who meant them harm.

Yes, the toast "clan" that her family had uttered for generations rang true again because everyone there belonged and believed in family as much as she did.

"Clan," she said in return, rested enough to enter the battle that was coming.

About the Author

Originally from Cuba, Ali Vali has retained much of her family's traditions and language and uses them frequently in her stories. Having her father read her stories and poetry before bed every night as a child infused her with a love of reading, which carries till today. In 2000, Ali decided to embark on a new path and started writing.

She has discovered that living in Louisiana and running a nonprofit provides plenty of material to draw from in creating her novels and short stories. Mixing imagination with different life experiences, she creates characters that are engaging to the reader on many levels.

Books Available From Bold Strokes Books

The Devil be Damned by Ali Vali. The fourth book in the best-selling Cain Casey Devil series. (978-1-60282-159-0)

Descent by Julie Cannon. Shannon Roberts and Caroline Davis compete in the world of world-class bike racing and pretend that the fire between them is just professional rivalry, not desire. (978-1-60282-160-6)

Kiss of Noir by Clara Nipper. Nora Delany is a hard-living, sweet-talking woman who can't say no to a beautiful babe or a friend in danger—a darkly humorous homage to a bygone era of tough broads and murder in steamy New Orleans. (978-1-60282-161-3)

Under Her Skin by Lea Santos. Supermodel Lilly Lujan hasn't a care in the world, except life is lonely in the spotlight—until Mexican gardener Torien Pacias sees through Lilly's facade and offers gentle understanding and friendship when Lilly most needs it. (978-1-60282-162-0)

Fierce Overture by Gun Brooke. Helena Forsythe is a hard-hitting CEO who gets what she wants by taking no prisoners when negotiating—until she meets a woman who convinces her that charm may be the way to win a battle, and a heart. (978-1-60282-156-9)

Trauma Alert by Radclyffe. Dr. Ali Torveau has no trouble saying no to romance until the day firefighter Beau Cross shows up in her ER and sets her carefully ordered world aflame. (978-1-60282-157-6)

Wolfsbane Winter by Jane Fletcher. Iron Wolf mercenary Deryn faces down demon magic and otherworldly foes with a smile, but she's defenseless when healer Alana wages war on her heart. (978-1-60282-158-3)

Little White Lie by Lea Santos. Emie Jaramillo knows relationships are for other people, and beautiful women like Gia Mendez don't belong anywhere near her boring world of academia—until Gia sets out to convince Emie she has not only brains, but beauty…and that she's the only woman Gia wants in her life. (978-1-60282-163-7)

Witch Wolf by Winter Pennington. In a world where vampires have charmed their way into modern society, where werewolves walk the streets with their beasts disguised by human skin, Investigator Kassandra Lyall has a secret of her own to protect. She's one of them. (978-1-60282-177-4)

Do Not Disturb by Carsen Taite. Ainsley Faraday, a high-powered executive, and rock music celebrity Greer Davis couldn't be less well suited for one another, and yet they soon discover passion has a way of designing its own future. (978-1-60282-153-8)

From This Moment On by PJ Trebelhorn. Devon Conway and Katherine Hunter both lost love and neither believes they will ever find it again—until the moment they meet and everything changes. (978-1-60282-154-5)

Vapor by Larkin Rose. When erotic romance writer Ashley Vaughn decides to take her research into the bedroom for a night of passion with Victoria Hadley, she discovers that fact is hotter than fiction. (978-1-60282-155-2)

Wind and Bones by Kristin Marra. Jill O'Hara, award-winning journalist, just wants to settle her deceased father's affairs and leave Prairie View, Montana, far, far behind—but an old girlfriend, a sexy sheriff, and a dangerous secret keep her down on the ranch. (978-1-60282-150-7)

Nightshade by Shea Godfrey. The story of a princess, betrothed as a political pawn, who falls for her intended husband's soldier sister, is a modern-day fairy tale to capture the heart. (978-1-60282-151-4)

Vieux Carré Voodoo by Greg Herren. Popular New Orleans detective Scotty Bradley just can't stay out of trouble—especially when an old flame turns up asking for help. (978-1-60282-152-1)

The Pleasure Set by Lisa Girolami. Laney DeGraff, a successful president of a family-owned bank on Rodeo Drive, finds her comfortable life taking a turn toward danger when Theresa Aguilar, a sleek, sexy lawyer, invites her to join an exclusive, secret group of powerful, alluring women. (978-1-60282-144-6)

A Perfect Match by Erin Dutton. The exciting world of pro golf forms the backdrop for a fast-paced, sexy romance. (978-1-60282-145-3)

Father Knows Best by Lynda Sandoval. High school juniors and best friends Lila Moreno, Meryl Morganstern, and Caressa Thibodoux plan to make the most of the summer before senior year. What they discover that amazing summer about girl power, growing up, and trusting friends and family more than prepares them to tackle that all-important senior year! (978-1-60282-147-7)

The Midnight Hunt by L.L. Raand. Medic Drake McKennan takes a chance and loses, and her life will never be the same—because when she wakes up after surviving a life-threatening illness, she is no longer human. (978-1-60282-140-8)

Long Shot by D. Jackson Leigh. Love isn't safe, which is exactly why equine veterinarian Tory Greyson wants no part of it—until Leah Montgomery and a horse that won't give up convince her otherwise. (978-1-60282-141-5)

In Medias Res by Yolanda Wallace. Sydney has forgotten her entire life, and the one woman who holds the key to her memory, and her heart, doesn't want to be found. (978-1-60282-142-2)

Awakening to Sunlight by Lindsey Stone. Neither Judith or Lizzy is looking for companionship, and certainly not love—but when their lives become entangled, they discover both. (978-1-60282-143-9)

Fever by VK Powell. Hired gun Zakaria Chambers is hired to provide a simple escort service to philanthropist Sara Ambrosini, but nothing is as simple as it seems, especially love. (978-1-60282-135-4)

Truths by Rebecca S. Buck. Two women separated by two hundred years are connected by fate and love. (978-1-60282-146-0)

High Risk by JLee Meyer. Can actress Kate Hoffman really risk all she's worked for to take a chance on love? Or is it already too late? (978-1-60282-136-1)

Spanking New by Clifford Henderson. A poignant, hilarious, unforgettable look at life, love, gender, and the essence of what makes us who we are. (978-1-60282-138-5)

Missing Lynx by Kim Baldwin and Xenia Alexiou. On the trail of a notorious serial killer, Elite Operative Lynx's growing attraction to a mysterious mercenary could be her path to love—or to death. (978-1-60282-137-8)

Magic of the Heart by C.J. Harte. CEO Susan Hettinger and wild, impulsive rock star M.J. Carson couldn't be more different if they tried—but opposites attract in ways neither woman can resist. (978-1-60282-131-6)

Ambereye by Gill McKnight. Jolie Garoul is falling in love with her assistant. The big problem is, Jolie is a werewolf. (978-1-60282-132-3)

Collision Course by C.P. Rowlands. Tragedy leaves Brie O'Malley and Jordan Carter fearful and alone. Can they find the courage to take a second chance on love? (978-1-60282-133-0)

Mephisto Aria by Justine Saracen. Opera singer Katherina Marov's destiny may be to repeat the mistakes of her father when she becomes involved in a dangerous love affair. (978-1-60282-134-7)

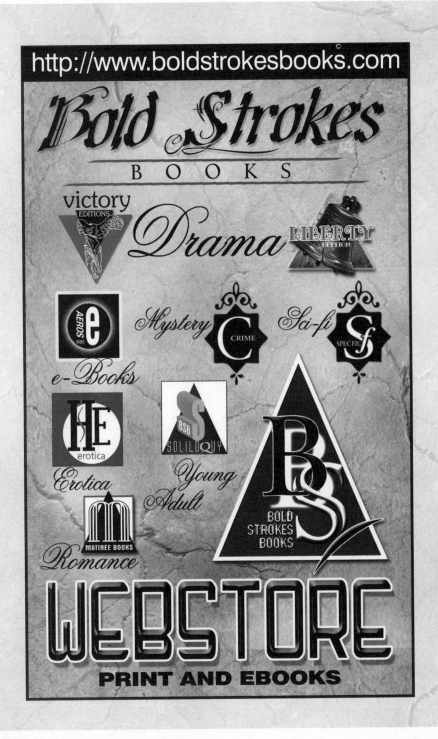